Petticoat Ranch

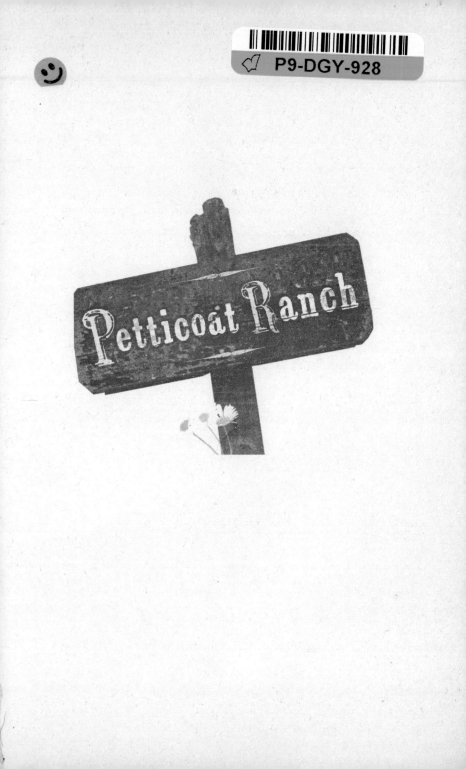

MARY CONNEALY

BARBOUR
PUBLISHING

ISBN 978-1-59789-647-4

All scripture quotations are taken from the King James Version of the Bible.

This book is a work of fiction. Names, characters, places, and incidents are either products of the author's imagination or used fictitiously. Any similarity to actual people, organizations, and/or events is purely coincidental.

Cover design by Lookout Design, Inc.

Published by Barbour Publishing, Inc., P.O. Box 719, Uhrichsville, Ohio 44683
www.barbourbooks.com

Our mission is to publish and distribute inspirational products offering exceptional value and biblical encouragement to the masses.

ecpa Member of the Evangelical Christian Publishers Association

Printed in the United States of America.
5 4 3 2

Dedication:

To Joslyn, Wendy, Shelly, and Katy.
Any resemblance to Mandy, Beth, Sally, and Lauren
is strictly coincidental. . .mostly.
And to Ivan who has been a really good sport
about me writing all these years.

One

Mosqueros, Texas, 1867

Sophie heard God in every explosion of thunder as she listened to the awesome power of the approaching storm. But there was more. There was something coming—something more than rain.

Over the distant rumble, Sophie Edwards heard pounding hoofbeats. Her heart sped up, matching the pace. The horse came fast. Something about the way it ran echoed the desperation in the pulsing of Sophie's heart.

Sophie whirled to race inside the cabin. Exhausted after another day of grinding work, she prayed for strength and courage. God would have to provide it; she had none left. She scrambled into her disguise and waited until the last minute to wake the children, hoping the rider would pass on. She stood near the can that held the vile-smelling Hector scarf, hoping she wouldn't need it.

Was this the night someone would come for her and the girls? The night she couldn't talk fast enough or hide well enough to survive this rugged, lonely life?

The back of Sophie's neck prickled in horror as the horse veered from the main trail and came toward her cabin. For a second, she thought the rider meant to come to her place, but there was no letup of the running hooves. Sophie's fear changed. No one could safely ride the narrow, rocky trail down the slopes of the creek bank behind her cabin at that speed.

The horse charged on. Sophie could hear it blowing hard, its wind broken, the saddle leather creaking. She hated the rider for abusing his mount, but inside Sophie knew it wasn't the rider's fault. This pace—this reckless, dark ride—could only mean one thing.

Pursuit!

And pursuit might mean a fleeing criminal with a posse on his trail. But not all pursued men were justly accused. No one knew that better than Sophie.

She almost ran out to wave the rider down. She let fear freeze her for a second. Then, ashamed, she grabbed at the door latch on her ramshackle cabin, praying, "Help me, Lord. Help me, help me, help me." Her prayers, like her life, had been stripped to bare bones.

The horse stormed past the heavy brush that concealed the house.

"No! Stop!" Sophie dashed out the door and down the stoop. "Stop! The cliff!"

She was too late. The rider was past. Within seconds she heard the dreadful screams of the falling animal, the coarse shouts of terror ripped from the throat of the rider.

Rocks dislodged along the top of the bank as Sophie ran in the direction of the accident. There was the rumble of falling rocks and the softer sound of the horse's big body striking stone as it plunged thirty feet to the creek below, neighing its fear and pain into the night. She heard the splash as the avalanche, and its unwilling cause, hit the moving water below.

She skidded to a halt and her long, white nightgown billowed around her. A gust whipped her blond hair across her eyes. Blinded for a moment, a cold, logical part of her mind told her that the best way to handle this was simply to ignore it and go back to bed.

But God asked more of her than cold logic. He even asked more of her than her own survival. It was a relief to admit it, because her strongest survival instincts couldn't stop her from going to someone in need, and she was glad to have God's support in the matter. She whirled away from the embankment and ran back to the house.

"Girls!" Her voice lashed like a whip in the darkness. The girls would be so frightened to be awakened this way, but there was no choice. If ever a family had learned to do what needed to be done, it was the Edwardses. "Girls, someone's fallen on the creek path."

Sophie tore at her disguise, putting everything in its place with lightning speed. She couldn't ever afford to be unprepared. "I need help. I'm going down. Mandy, bring the rope and the lantern and follow me. Beth, catch Hector and bring him. Don't take time to get dressed: just pull on your shoes. Sally, stay with Laura. Get blankets out and heat water. If he's alive he'll need doctoring."

Sophie heard the girls jump out of bed as she headed outside in her nightgown with untied boots on her feet.

She saw where he'd gone over and her stomach lurched. He couldn't have picked a worse drop. She stumbled and skidded toward the bottom of the creek, risking her own neck on the treacherous path.

Hearing Amanda call out from overhead, Sophie yelled, "Down here, Mandy. Quickly." Sophie picked her way over the jumble of dirt and stones edging the swollen waters of the creek. In the starless night, she couldn't make out anything. She glanced behind her and saw, with relief, ten-year-old Mandy coming with a brightly lit kerosene lantern.

Sophie continued to scramble over the debris. She stepped in mud and sank until water overflowed her boot. The thunder came more steadily now, until it was a constant collision of sound. The approaching lightning gained enough strength to light up even the depths of the creek.

Feeling her way, on her hands and knees now, she tried to pierce the utter darkness with her vision. *Where is he, Lord?*

A wailing wind cried at them that it was bringing disaster in its wake. Suddenly, the thunder and lightning held a worse threat than savage rain. The storm was coming from the north. It was probably already raining upstream. The creek might flood without a single drop of water falling here. And she now stood in the path of that flash flood. Worse still, she'd just ordered her children to come after her.

Sophie listened intently for the roar of oncoming water. She heard nothing. They still had time.

Mandy caught up with her. "Here's the lantern and rope."

Sophie took the lantern. "A rider and horse went over that drop-off. Help me find him, and hurry! It's raining up north!"

Her girls had lived in their little thicket hideaway long enough to know what it meant when rain came in from the north. Sophie saw Mandy glance fearfully over her shoulder into the darkness of the creek. Then, practical girl that Mandy was, she started searching for the rider.

"Oh, Ma. Can he have lived?" Mandy went ahead of Sophie to the very edge of the dimly illuminated area.

"I don't know, honey," Sophie said grimly as she surveyed the area, looking for a glimpse of fabric or a bit of horsehide. "I don't hear him. He might be buried under these rocks. He might have been swept away by the creek. We only have a few minutes to search."

"Here, Ma. I think I found him!" Mandy's voice was sharp with excitement. A bolt of lightning lit up Mandy's frightened face. Sophie saw Mandy's blue eyes, so like her own, glow in the jagged glare. Her blond hair, identical to Sophie's and the other girls', hung bedraggled and muddy to her waist.

Sophie rushed to her daughter's side and saw a single hand, coated with dirt, extending from a pile of mud and rocks. The two of them fell to the ground and began digging away the soil. They ignored the tear of jagged stones on their hands and the damage to their nightgowns, the only ones they owned. Sophie heard soft trudging steps as Hector came down the creek path. She dug faster, knowing that with the mule's help they could move the man as soon as they freed him.

Another rumble of thunder sounded closer. The lightning lanced the sky just as Sophie uncovered the stranger's face and pushed away the mud. The man was utterly still. As limp as in death. She didn't stop to check his condition. If there was life left in him after the fall, the suffocating dirt would snatch it away. She and Mandy uncovered his shoulders as eight-year-old Elizabeth came up.

"Get this rope around his shoulders, Mandy. Beth, hitch it around Hector's neck. We've got to get out of this creek before the water comes!" Even as she said it, Sophie heard the first distant crash of waves against the sides of the creek. Once the sound was audible, there were only minutes before the wall of water would sweep by their cabin.

She kept digging as she shouted commands. She reached deep into the muck to make sure there were no heavy rocks pinning him. Her girls worked silently beside her, following her orders. Sophie felt a surge of pride in them so great, she knew it to be almost sinful.

"Ready, Ma." Mandy turned her attention from fastening the rope under the man's arms and went back to digging.

"Hector's ready anytime, Ma," Beth shouted over the raging wind. A bolt of lightning flashed brightly enough for Sophie to see the man. His legs were still well buried, but there were no rocks on him.

He was so coated in mud that Sophie couldn't have told anyone what he looked like. She remembered the desperate speed at which he'd ridden and thought again the word: *pursuit*. Yet no one had come along behind him.

The thunder sounded again. The water roared ever nearer. Sophie shouted to be heard over the sound, "Once you start pulling, just take him all the way up! The floodwater is coming!"

Sophie knew Elizabeth, her second born, would handle the stubborn, rawboned old mule better than she could. Hector was a cantankerous beast on the best of days, but he had a soft spot for Beth, as did most animals.

Beth's gentle cajoling urged Hector forward to take up the slack in the rope. Mandy knelt at the man's head, and in the few remaining seconds, pushed more dirt off his arms and chest. Sophie braced herself to support his head and neck as he began to inch free. A bolt of lightning lit up their strange little group, this time with blinding brightness. The thunder sounded almost at the same instant. Sophie prayed for the man and asked God if the floodwater could just hold off another few minutes.

In answer, God sent the first icy drip of rain down the back of her neck. Sophie took it as a heavenly warning to hurry.

The man emerged slowly from the slide. As soon as he was free, with another lightning bolt to assist the lantern, Sophie yelled, "Keep going. All the way to the top of the bank. Mandy, you run ahead with the lantern." Anything to get her girls to safety, even if she didn't make it herself.

She looked at the man, now being battered even further by his ride up the hill. His body was coated in mud. The slime helped him slide along the rough ground. One particularly nasty jolt over the rutted path almost woke him. He took a deep breath and turned his head sideways. He vomited up filthy, muddy water and gasped deeply for breath as he was dragged along. It was the first sign he was alive. Sophie kept to his side to make sure his head didn't encounter a rock.

The rugged upward trail twisted and turned. Just as it faced the north along one of its steeper sections, a bolt of lightning split the sky. Sophie saw a wall of water raging toward her like the wrath of God. "Faster, Beth! The floodwater's coming! Get to the top!"

Elizabeth kicked Hector and yelled. Sophie knew her mule well, and whatever unfortunate qualities Hector had, stupidity wasn't one of them. She knew he headed for the top of that creek to save his own mangy mule hide, and if he saved the lot of them along with himself, well, that had nothing to do with him.

The path snaked back to the south. A few more feet. Twenty at the most. Sophie knew the water would come along right to the top of the bank. It had been cut to its current depth by these raging torrents over thousands of years. Sophie glanced over her shoulder and saw it coming. They weren't going to make it. Lightning lit up the sky just as Hector crested the top of the path. The roaring water changed to a scream. The thunder had become a constant jarring drumroll that only added to the fierce growl of the approaching flood. The rope dragged against the ground, and knowing she was out of time, Sophie reached down and twisted her arms through the rope that bound the man to the only anchor there was for them in the world.

The water hit like a crashing fist. Sophie heard her own cry of fear as she was swept sideways. Her arms wrenched nearly from their sockets as the rope tightened. Her body, literally tied to the man, lifted with the angry waters. The flood caught them as if it were a greedy child not wanting to let go of its toy. Sophie had a second to despair of Hector's strength and prayed Beth wouldn't be swept away with the mule. Flood water filled her mouth. The life her precious babies had to face without her was the image she'd die with.

Then they were up. They landed on the top of the creek bank like a couple of battle-weary trout. Sophie was too battered to move. She lay there, choking on muddy water as the world began to right itself. She tried to catch her breath and was having precious little luck, when Mandy got to her side, followed by Beth. Only when they rolled her off the man did she realize she'd been stretched out fully on top of him.

"Ma! Are you all right?" Mandy's anxious voice reached into her sluggish mind.

Her girls. She felt the scrambling fingers on the ropes that bound her to this stranger, and she heard their fear. She had to be strong for them. She forced the panic from her water-logged head. "Yes, I'm fine. Just got a good soaking. Let's see if our friend here survived it."

Sophie almost staggered when she got to her knees, but she didn't. The girls were watching. She turned her attention to the man and pressed her hand firmly against his chest. Beneath her palm was a strong heartbeat, even though, after his one spell of coughing, the man hadn't stirred again. She felt his chest rise and fall with a steady breath.

Sophie heaved a heartfelt sigh of relief. "He's still alive."

The spitting rain grew steadier, and Sophie wondered what a chest full of dirty water did to a man. A deep chill now might well be the last straw. With a renewed surge of strength, Sophie decided that, after all she'd been through, this man could just think twice before he up and died on her. Thinking aloud, she said, "There's no way we can carry him to the house, and we're not strong enough to get him up on Hector's back."

"If Hector goes slow, maybe we can just drag him," Mandy suggested. "Reckon it'll kill him, though."

Elizabeth said lightly from where she knelt beside her mother, "I don't know how he could get much worse. He appears to be mostly kilt already."

Sophie prayed in her heart, as she had been nonstop since she'd heard the first hoofbeats. But no better suggestions were forthcoming from the Almighty.

"Okay, we drag him. Take it real slow, Beth. Stay by his side, Mandy and. . .and. . ." Sophie was out of ideas. A sudden gust of wind and a prolonged glare of lightning, with thunder rumbling constantly now, prodded her. "Let's get on with it then."

They hauled him the same way they hauled logs to split for their fire. Hector pulled the unconscious man right up to the front door. When Elizabeth stopped Hector, Mandy asked, with the practicality her life had forced onto her, "Reckon Hector can drag him into the house?"

The house was small—one room, with a loft, no back door, and two front steps that passed for a stoop. Sophie tried to envision the big mule climbing the stairs, ducking through the narrow door, and then turning around in the cramped space. Hector was large and not given to cooperation at the best of times, even with Beth's gentle urging.

"How about we put him in the barn," Mandy suggested.

Barn was a highfalutin word for the Edwards's one and only outbuilding. The building remained standing more out of pure ornery stubbornness than sturdy construction. It was a three-sided shed that stood upright, thanks to the bramble that had wound itself around every inch of the building and practically reclaimed it as part of the vast thicket that hid the Edwards's home. Hector seemed inclined to head for it, though he usually disdained to go under the rickety roof.

The wind began driving the steadily increasing sprinkles straight sideways. The lightning and thunder continued, and the icy drops of rain grew fatter, soaking into their thin, mud-soaked nightclothes. This was all the man needed to finish the work of his fall. Sophie finally said, "The barn it is. Let's go."

They hauled the injured man down a nearly invisible trail that wound away from the cabin. Another small clearing, one of hundreds that appeared inside the twisting maze of the thicket, opened up at the decrepit *barn*. Mercifully, the rain was coming from the north and the shed opened to the east. The inside was dry except for the multiple leaks in the roof. A stack of the first spring prairie grass Sophie and the girls had cut took up the driest corner. With some quick pitch-forking, they got the man situated on a soft bed of fresh-scented hay. It was a better bed than the one Sophie had.

Hector was released. As if in a huff at the uninvited company, he went to the far corner of the tiny shed. That put about ten feet between him and the intruders in his domain.

Sophie knelt in the hay beside the still-unconscious man. "Bring the lantern up close, Mandy. Be mindful of fire."

"I'll fetch blankets and check on the little 'uns, Ma." Beth darted out into the storm.

As the lantern light fell on the man, and with a sudden extended flash of lightning, Sophie saw bright red soaked through the coating of dirt on his face and across the front of his shirt. The stranger was drenched in his own blood.

With a dart of aggravation, Sophie thought the man was determined to die one way or another. She felt stubbornness well up inside of her that would have humbled Hector. After all she'd been through, he'd live if she had to grab his worthless life and hold him on this side of the pearly gates with her bare hands!

Two

Where'd he get to, Harley?" Judd Mason roared into the storm.

Judd wheeled his horse around in a circle and looked along both sides of the forked path ahead of them. The rain slashed and their quarry's trail washed away like dirt in a Chinese laundry.

Judd pulled back hard on his mustang. The horse reared and fought the brutal hand on the bit. Judd whipped his mount hard with the long reins and swore at the unruly horse he'd caught wild and never really mastered.

He'd seen the horse that thieving trash rode. If Judd could have gotten his hands on that magnificent thoroughbred, he'd have put a bullet in the brain of this ornery cuss and kept the beautiful bay for himself. After all, a man catching horse thieves deserved some payment.

That was why Judd had sent the bulk of the gang after the rest of those no-account varmints when they'd split up, while he, Harley, and Eli had kept after this one.

He'd have made a deal with Harley and Eli somehow. Let them keep whatever was in the man's pockets or given them a bigger cut of the next windfall. He wanted that horse! It would have made a sound start for breeding on the ranch he'd be buying on Monday.

He thought of the Mead ranch and the twisting, turning path he'd followed so the Mead brothers' disappearance wouldn't be noticed. Now, the Meads' ranch would be his. But it wasn't enough. He wanted that thoroughbred bay!

"I'm sick of this weather, Judd. We're not going to track him in this." Eli wiped an arm across his face, but it did no good. Even with foul-weather gear, they were all soaked to the skin.

It was all Judd could do to not knock Eli out of his saddle. The day would come when he quit putting up with the constant carping. But for now, Eli had his uses.

Instead of knocking Eli down, he turned his temper on Harley. "Where'd ya lose him, Harley?"

"We ain't a-gonna catch 'im tonight, Mason." Harley, calm as usual, hunched his shoulders against the driving rain and tugged his hat low over his brow.

Judd jammed his spurs into his horse's scarred sides. The horse reared up, fighting the heavy hand. "He can't have gone much farther in this rain. I want that horse! No two-bit horse thief is gonna ride a horse like that while I'm stuck on this nag!"

Judd hated the black mustang. He'd done his best, but he couldn't beat the fighting spirit out of him. The animal was so vicious, he couldn't turn his back on it.

Harley didn't argue. "I might have seen a trail into the thicket back a piece."

"You think he left the trail?" Judd hollered. "Well, why didn'cha say so earlier?"

Harley said coolly, "Let's go back and see if he went down that way. He might have ducked into that thicket and found a hidey-hole we can flush him out of. If he's ahead of us, he's gone. We won't catch him tonight."

Judd turned back, determined to sniff out their prey like a wolf would sniff out a three-legged elk.

"Elizabeth, wait," Sophie shouted after her rapidly disappearing daughter. "He's bleeding."

Beth skidded to a stop and looked back.

"Bring rags and the water Sally was warming."

"Got it, Ma!" Beth ran on.

Sophie had lived on the frontier for a long while. She'd given birth to Mandy beside a jumbled shelter of fallen logs on her way west with her husband, Cliff. She'd fed two babies at her breast at the same time, because there was no other milk for growing girls. She'd buried a tiny boy, born too soon after she'd fallen from a horse while bull-dogging cattle, and watched Cliff withdraw from her. He'd wanted a son so badly. She'd run the ranch herself, with two old men her only help, while Cliff went off to war. Then she'd cut her husband down from a tree and dug his grave with her own hands.

All of this she had endured. In truth, she'd flourished under the hard life. The West did that to people. It changed them. They either grew bigger, stronger, reveling in the freedom that could be wrested from the wilderness with two strong hands. Or it broke them and revealed them as small, unfit for the bounty that could be wrested from the land. Cliff had been such a man.

And now, in the rickety barn, with no tools but warm water and rags, she set out to save a man's life. She began unbuttoning his tattered shirt. "We have to see if he's injured anywhere, Mandy. Now this is doctoring, so it's not improper to remove his clothes, like it'd be otherwise."

Mandy nodded easily and started coaxing the shirt off one broad shoulder.

It was hard to tell where the mud ended and the bruises began. His chest and arms were bleeding from a dozen cuts and scrapes. Sophie pressed against his ribs, checking to see if any bones gave where they shouldn't. The man groaned softly once, when she pressed high on his right side. The bone held firm, and Sophie was encouraged by the sign of life.

Something stirred in Sophie as she worked over his bared chest. It was almost—for want of a better word—recognition. She hadn't given much thought to the man's identity, assuming him to be a stranger. But now, she looked closer. His face was so filthy she couldn't make out features, even in the occasional burst of lightning. But his chest, the light covering of coarse hair across the top and the long, ever narrower line of hair down his stomach, struck a familiar chord. Sophie knew she couldn't identify a man from his chest, unless maybe she'd doctored him before, and she had only used her skills on Cliff and the girls.

She shook off the feeling. It didn't matter. Whoever he was, she'd help him. And if he turned out to be one of the town storekeepers, who were so cruel to her, she'd still get him on his feet and send him on his way—she just wouldn't be polite while she was about it.

She hesitated about his pants. It really was too bold to remove them. She looked up at Mandy, who seemed to feel the same way, and shrugged her misgivings at her mother. After a long struggle with her own sense of propriety, Sophie said, "We'll have to get them off later or he'll catch a chill, but let's leave him dressed for now."

She settled for running her hands down the man's muddy pant legs, firmly enough to satisfy herself that he had no broken bones. She came away with her hands caked with mud but satisfied that his lower half was intact.

The black sky opened up while she examined him, and the rain, whipped with the fury of the thunder and lightning, poured down. Sophie wiped her hands clean as best she could on the hay, just as Beth returned to the shed with a sloshing bucket of water and a bundle of rags.

"Thanks, honey. How were the little 'uns?"

"Good. Laura's asleep. Sally had everything ready for me. Is he dead yet?"

Sophie took a rag from her pessimistic daughter, wet it, wrung it out, and dabbed at the blood on the man's forehead.

"Nope," Mandy said placidly. "Pretty soon I s'pect, but not yet."

"Get that lantern closer, Mandy."

Beth began spreading the blanket over the man's filthy, inert body.

Sophie searched for the source of the bleeding on his head and found a nasty gash just under his hairline. The bleeding had already slowed to an ooze. "He should have stitches." Sophie cleaned the cut carefully.

"He should have a doctor," Beth said quietly.

Sophie didn't answer. It was one thing to do all she could; it was another to bring in someone from town. Once the townspeople knew she was here, the menfolk, with their dishonorable propositions and their anger at her refusal, would be back. Those men had driven them into this thicket.

A doctor to save this man's life might cost her daughters theirs. Of course, when this man woke up, their secret would be out anyway. Still, Sophie could do no less than her best to save him.

After she was satisfied his head wound was clean, Sophie explored his skull further and found another lump on the back. Between the two blows, it was no wonder the man was unconscious. Sophie was just ready to turn her attention to wiping the grime from his face when she heard, in the far distance, the sound of more hoofbeats. The pursuers? After all this time?

She knew she didn't have a moment to spare. "Riders coming. Elizabeth, stay with him. Put the lantern out. If he starts to wake up, do whatever you must to keep him quiet, including gagging him. Mandy, get to the house and cover things, then get up in the loft with Sally and Laura. Don't let them see you!"

They ran to get ready for intruders as if their lives depended on it. They had done it before many times.

The hoofbeats turned onto her path just as she darted into the door a step behind Mandy. Mandy tossed several large cloths over Laura's crib and high chair to disguise the presence of others in the cabin. Then she flew up the ladder behind Sally, who had heard the sound of someone coming and had gone into action without being told. Sally had the sleeping Laura in her arms and Sophie's disguise laid out.

Sophie grabbed her bulky housecoat for the second time that night. She pulled it on over her slender form. She dove for the fire and scraped a bit of ash out from the glowing coals with a knife.

She took the little bits of carved wood down from the shelf over the front door and slipped them between her front teeth and lips. A pillow came hurtling down from overhead, and she stuffed it up under her housecoat, into the special pouch sewn just for it. She tucked two pieces of clean, white cotton between her bottom teeth and her cheeks.

She twisted her rain-bedraggled blond hair into a bun, then grabbed for the nightcap, to which she had attached a heavy tress of Hector's tail, liberally greased, and pulled it on, so it looked like her hair was dark brown and stringy with oil. She checked the ash and found it cool enough. With a light, experienced hand, she dabbed it under her eyes just enough to look naturally hollow-eyed.

As her last act of self-preservation, she did something she hated above all—she popped the top off the tin milk can and pulled out the scarf. It was her masterstroke. It was what happened when you let a mule wear a wool scarf for a month. She heard Sally gag.

Mandy hissed, "Just hold your nose and keep quiet!"

Laura slept through it all.

The horses thundered to a stop outside. Sophie heard the creak of saddle leather and the treading of heavy footsteps. She rolled the long sapling from the side of the room so it would wedge against the door once it was open about three inches. Just as the pole was in place, a fist pounded on the front door.

Sophie took her time, letting them think they'd woken her, but judging by the battering force of the fist, she didn't dare wait long or the door might be knocked in.

She cracked open the door and looked into the red-veined eyes of the man who had killed her husband.

She couldn't go into her routine as the slovenly, crazy woman who lived in the thicket. She was too shocked to do more than stare. She'd never seen the man before that terrible night when he'd killed Cliff, but his face was burned into her memory.

In the seconds she stood frozen, the man tried to force the door, but it wouldn't give. Then, after a bit, he reeled back with a sickened grunt and pulled the kerchief, tied around his neck, over his mouth and nose.

Seeing him—this brute, this murderer, reacting with revulsion because she smelled bad—jerked Sophie out of her shocked silence. He wouldn't recognize her from that night. He wouldn't see through her disguise even if he did notice her the night he hanged Cliff.

"Whadaya want?" She spoke over the wooden mouthpiece that made her appear grossly buck-toothed. The teeth and the wadded cotton altered her speech, slurring it and giving it the thickness of someone who wasn't mentally quite right.

"A man!" The vicious, bloodshot eyes of the beast on her porch began to water from the acrid stench. Sophie's eyes watered, too, but that just gave her a rheumy look that was all the more repellent. He took another step away, which took him down the two steps.

From a safe distance he snarled, "We're chasing a horse thief! We lost him on the main trail and think he may have come this way."

"Hain't no one be comin' this way, this foul night." Her voice cracked, and she cackled with laughter. "No one stupid 'nough ta do it cept'n y'all. The path goes across the crick, and it's flooded right up to the rim. Has been for a while now."

The man, away from the meager shelter of her stoop, was battered by the wind and rain. Sophie could see the battle going on inside him. He was torn between the desire to run roughshod over anyone who turned him aside from his plans and his aversion to the squalid, stinking woman in front of him.

A voice from the darkness behind him said, "He's gone, Judd. Give it up, and let's go have a drink. This rain'll wreck his trail. So what if this one gets away? What say we just hang the next one twice." A burst of crude laughter followed that suggestion.

Judd.

Now, for the first time, she had a name. She had no way to use it—had no way to gain justice for her husband. But it was more than she'd had before.

The man whirled around at his grumbling companion. "I want that horse, Eli! He must have come this way!"

The other man, the one who hadn't spoken before, spoke up. "There are a dozen trails into this thicket. We can't explore 'em all."

The rain hit Judd full in the face and sent a visible chill through him. Then, with a dismissive grunt, as if his killing rage had only been some fun he'd missed out on, he gave a rough laugh. "All right. Let's go. Let's get out of this weather."

He turned again and stared at Sophie, who let her mouth sag and her eyes cross just a bit. With a shudder of obvious disgust, he turned away.

Hatred ate like acid at Sophie's soul. For that moment, when he stood with his back to her, it was as if there was a target painted on the man. She had a loaded shotgun hung over the door. She could kill him.

She'd die for it. The man's friends would see to it. Her girls would die, too. And maybe, before they died, they might face horrors so great it would destroy them, all the way to their souls.

But she was tempted. God forgive her, she was tempted to kill him where he stood. She knew she harbored hatred. She had carried the burden of that hate for two years. But she had never been so nearly overwhelmed by it—to the point that she was almost beyond control of herself. She shuddered under the weight of that temptation—to sacrifice everything for revenge.

The two men behind Judd rode off into the storm, their identities cloaked by darkness. Judd, just a few steps behind, swung himself up onto his horse's back. The animal fought against its rider and danced toward Sophie enough that she saw a brand.

J Bar M.

Judd and Eli. J Bar M. She had two names, a brand, and a face burned forever in her mind. At last, she had somewhere solid to pin her hate.

Sophie now called up another of her standard prayers. *It's evil to hate the way I do, Lord.* She gathered the shreds of her self-control and let the men ride away. It was the only thing she *could* do. She shoved her hatred down deep inside her, and if she couldn't bring herself to forget it, she would lock it away and ignore it, which was almost the same thing.

She closed the door and whipped the foul-smelling scarf off her neck. She shoved it into the covered pail and slammed the lid shut tight. It seemed to ripen in that pail, getting more hideous with every passing day.

"Ma, it takes a week to air the house out after you've done that," Sally groused from overhead.

Mandy started down the ladder.

"Sorry," Sophie answered. There was no point discussing it because it had to be done. Her disguise had evolved over the course of time. She had come to fear the attention of the men around Mosqueros, so she'd decided to play down her appearance. The trouble was, her main appeal was her ranch, and no disguise could conceal that.

Then the ranch loan had come due, and Sophie had been forced into choosing between the banker, Royce Badje, and eviction. It hadn't taken her a second to decide on the latter.

"I want to see the hurt man before he dies, Ma." The ladder creaked under Sally's feet as she brought the sleeping baby down to her crib. "I don't want to stay with Laura."

Sophie sighed at her insistent daughter. Her children's safety had been the reason she'd ended up here. She had no family anywhere, and nowhere to go. She had discovered this cabin during one of a hundred picnics with her girls. It had been like a little playhouse to them, deep in the thicket. When it became apparent that she was losing the ranch, she'd shifted what possessions would fit into it before the ranch was sold.

"You'll see him in the morning, Sally. I know you're curious, but someone has to stay with Laura, and I need Mandy. We might have to lift him, and she's stronger." Sophie removed her costume quickly, while Mandy threw open the two little windows so the smell would get out. Sophie removed the rest of her disguise and ran a quick hand to tidy her bun before giving it up as a hopeless cause.

"Can't I just take a peek?" Sally persisted. "If I have to wait till morning, he'll most likely be dead. I want to see him afore he croaks." It occurred to Sophie that her children were remarkably calm in an emergency, and just the littlest bit bloodthirsty. Part of being Texans, she supposed. They'd adopted Texas ways along with the drawl.

Sophie had to smile at Sally's wheedling. Really, the child didn't ask for much, and this was the most excitement they'd had in a long time. It had long ago become clear to Sophie that excitement was usually a bad thing, and she never quit being thankful to God for a boring life. "Is Laura fast asleep?"

Sally laid her little sister down and gently patted the baby's back to keep her asleep, but there was really no need. Once the toddler dropped off for the night, she could take a ride on a cyclone without waking.

"Just like always, Ma. I'll only stay out a minute. I promise." Sally acted like it was Christmas. Then Sophie remembered their scanty Christmas and knew this was easily bigger.

"All right, just for a minute. You girls can run on out while I get changed out of my nightgown."

The girls dashed off, and Sophie quickly discarded her cold, muddy flannel and pulled on a dry calico. She rushed after the girls, not wanting them alone for a second longer than necessary, even with an unconscious stranger. Beth knelt beside him, holding a damp cloth on the cut on his forehead. Her second born, who had an unusual love for all living creatures, was caring for the injured man as well as anyone could.

"Has he shown any signs of waking?" Sophie asked.

"Nope. He's been knocked witless. Out cold as a carp."

Sophie knelt on the other side of him and let Sally get in close to have her look. It took Sally about ten seconds to figure out nothing was going on.

"We may as well clean him up a bit." Sophie took a clean cloth from the stack Beth had brought and soaked it in the now-cool water. "It's chilly out here, but there's nothing for it but to bundle him up. We can't risk a fire in the shed with this dry prairie grass, and until he can walk, we can't get him in the house."

She wished she'd thought to put more water on to heat. She began bathing his face, the mud now almost dry and beginning to cake and fall off. It only took her a few seconds to clean away the grime. While she turned to rinse out the cloth, first one, then another, then the third of her girls gasped out loud.

Sophie became instantly more alert. Had the night riders doubled back on foot? She looked into the darkness for trouble, but the trouble wasn't out there. It was right here under the dirt.

Mandy said incredulously, "It. . .it can't be."

"What can't be?" Sophie turned her attention sharply to Mandy, still trying to find the danger.

"But it is!" Beth cried out. "It is, isn't it, Ma?"

Sophie realized both girls were staring in stunned fascination at the wounded man. Sophie turned to follow their gaze, but before she could look, Sally started to cry.

Sophie put her arm around her daughter but saw where she was staring. She turned to see what her girls were seeing.

"It can't be." Beth's voice broke. "But it is."

It was.

"It's Pa," Sally spoke through shuddering tears.

The husband Sophie had personally cut down out of a tree. Had personally released from the noose around his broken neck. Had personally buried on a rise overlooking the ranch they'd worked on so hard.

The husband whose death had etched her heart with hate and made her long, only moments ago, to commit cold-blooded murder. He was lying here unconscious, as men sought him to kill him all over again.

After what seemed like hours of stunned silence, Sophie leaned closer to the man.

Cliff.

"It isn't possible." She scrubbed more quickly at his face as if, when enough dirt was removed, the truth would be revealed.

"But it is, Ma. This is Pa," Sally said firmly.

Sophie considered herself to be broad-shouldered and levelheaded. She took what life handed to her, and with fervent prayers to her Maker for help, she made do with what she had. She wasn't a woman given to fancy. She stared at the man in front of her and knew it was Cliff. She thought back to that awful night two years ago and knew she'd buried Cliff. Those two absolutes clashed inside her brain and nothing that made any sense emerged. She stared and she washed and she tried to make the impossible fit into her sensible head.

Beth started crying next. She lifted the hand of the man who lay before her. "Pa?" She spoke so softly, it had the reverence of a prayer.

Mandy added her tears in next. "I c–can see it's him, but I saw you bury him. We all helped wr–wrap him"—Mandy's face crumpled—"in the quilt. How can this be, Ma?"

Sophie noticed several things about the man. He was more muscular than Cliff. He had an ugly round scar high up on one shoulder that could be nothing else but an old bullet wound. He had three slashing cuts on his right arm that were scarred but looked pink and fairly new. Cliff had none of these things. But that proved nothing. A man could build a lot of muscle in two years. And he could get himself shot and stabbed. Sophie remembered that sense of familiarity when she'd been bathing and doctoring his chest. The reason it had seemed familiar was, despite the bigger muscles, the man had hair on his chest the exact color, texture, and thickness of Cliff Edwards's.

With a sudden start, she thought of Cliff's birthmark on his right shoulder blade. "Help me roll him over. Your pa had a mole." All three girls added their strength, and they lifted the heavily muscled man a bit.

What they saw was an exit wound from the bullet. In the exact spot where Cliff had a large black mole, nearly an inch across. Or was it the exact spot? The wound was close enough that she couldn't be sure.

"Let him lie back, girls." Sophie sank from her knees to sit fully on the shed floor. Feeling boneless from the shock, she almost sank all the way down. The girls were all crying softly, and with a start, she realized she was, too.

She shook her head to clear away the fog, and then she gathered her senses. "I know one thing." The girls tore their eyes away from where they drank in the sight of their father and looked at her. "Your father is dead."

Sally shook her head. Sally had always been Daddy's girl, more than the rest of them. He'd left when Sally was too young to remember him, but in his absence, he'd grown into a heroic figure in her mind. And he'd only been back a few short months when he'd died—just long enough to get that longed-for son to growing in Sophie's belly, the one that turned out to be another girl.

Sophie had tried to help Sally see Cliff as he was, without harming her little girl's love for her father. But Sally had never been able to protect her heart from Cliff's small cruelties. She'd believed her pa's criticisms were just and tried harder than ever to win his love. She had been the one to be the tomboy. To be the son they'd never had. She'd carved out a special place in her pa's heart by tagging along with him everywhere for the little time they'd had together after the war. And it was no small trick to carve out a place in Cliff's heart. He wasn't a demonstrative man. He was a decent, honest man, but he was given to dark moods and sarcasm. Now, Sally had her pa back. She wasn't giving him up easily.

"It's him, Ma. We know our own pa!"

"It's. . .it's. . ." Sophie struggled to let go of the wild surge of hope that was building in her. Although their marriage hadn't been perfect, she'd loved her husband, at least to the extent he would allow it. But she couldn't build her life on a fantasy. "I've heard it said that for each of us, somewhere in the world, there is a double. Now, I've never put much stock in that myself, just because I've never seen any evidence of it. I've never seen two people who looked exactly like each other, except sometimes brothers or sisters come close, or a parent and child. But maybe it's true. Maybe—no, definitely—your pa has a double. Because here he is."

"Did Pa have a brother?" Mandy, the analyzer, asked.

"No. He was an only child and his pa died when he was little. His ma had passed on several months before I met him. He told me there was no one. Not even cousins. No, this man can't be a relative. At least not a close one. That's one of the reasons we ended up here after Pa died. With my folks gone, we have no family on either side to help us."

"So you think this man looks like Pa, even down to that birthmark?" Sally began chewing on her bottom lip.

"Now, Sally, honey, we don't know if there's a birthmark under that scar."

"It was right there, Ma, I remember," Sally insisted.

"Do you really think it's possible two men could look this much alike?" Beth asked skeptically.

Sophie was skeptical herself. But she also knew who she'd cut down out of that tree. "There can be no other explanation, girls." Sophie said quietly to her weeping daughters, "Look at me."

One by one they tore their hungry eyes away from a dream that all children who have lost a parent carry with them. They looked at her and waited.

"I don't know who this man is," Sophie said. "But I know who he is not. He's not your pa. Your pa is dead."

Mandy and Beth nodded. They knew it, too. They'd seen it with their own eyes. Only Sally wouldn't give up the dream.

They all turned back to look at him again. As they did, his eyes fluttered open.

Sally began sobbing and leaned over him. "He's alive!"

THREE

He was dead.

That was the only possibility. He was dead, and he must have been good, because he was in heaven being ministered to by angels. They floated around his head. They cried for him as if his death were a sad thing, which made him feel like his life must have been one worth living. They touched him, held his hand, leaned against his legs, and knelt and bowed over him. And every one of them had her blue eyes riveted on his face, as if he held the answers to all the world's problems.

He'd never known there could be such love for him. He'd never seen so many blue, blue eyes. The closest one caressed his head with a gentleness that almost broke his heart, it was so sweet. He sighed under the loveliness of heaven.

The angel who touched him spoke, but he was having trouble making sense of what she said. His mind seemed to be groggy, not working much at all. He thought a man should listen carefully when an angel spoke, so he tried his best to pay strict attention. Finally, after she'd repeated it several times and stroked his cheek as if to coax an answer out of him, it made sense.

She said, "Who are you?"

Shouldn't an angel know the answer to that?

The nearest angel was also the biggest. He looked from one angel to the others. They seemed to come in all sizes. One of them was crying hard, broken sobs that stabbed into his heart, as he wondered if he was the cause of her unhappiness. He couldn't remember the angel's question, and instead of answering her, he said to the one who wept so, the littlest one, "Don't cry, little angel."

He reached a hand up to comfort her. A spasm of pain cut across his chest. He cringed, as his head spun and his stomach lurched with nausea. He thought he might bc sick all over his glorious angels.

Funny, he wouldn't have expected there to be pain in heaven.

Even with the agony, he reached for that one brokenhearted angel, to try and make amends with her. Then he saw his muddy hands and knew he didn't dare touch her.

Funny, he wouldn't have expected there to be dirt in heaven.

He dropped his hand, but the little one grabbed it. "Pa? It's you, isn't it? Tell them it's you. No one believes it, but I know it's you."

Pa? He didn't understand. He knew she was talking to him. She was clasping his filthy hand to her chest, as if it were the greatest of treasures. He looked at that one little blond angel and wished he could be her pa.

Maybe that was it. Maybe this was his lot for eternity. That sounded very good to him. Tears of gratitude for God's goodness cut across his eyes. He held that little hand firmly, until darkness caught hold of his mind and pulled him under.

Sally almost flung herself down on top of him. Sophie grabbed her.

"It's him! Did you see the way he recognized me? Oh, Ma! Ma, he called me a little angel!" Sally looked up at Sophie. Sally's joy was so precious, Sophie wanted to say whatever Sally wanted to hear.

Suddenly, Sally gasped aloud. "If there *is* a double, then why not the other one, Ma? Why couldn't we have cut the double down out of the tree?"

Sophie ran her hand gently down Sally's uncombed white curls.

"They took him from right in front of me, Sally sweetheart. I was there. He was in the yard, just walking away from the house after supper. You remember how it was. You were there. I was standing in the door, watching him go."

They'd come charging in and surrounded Cliff. One of them, Judd she now knew, shouted that they'd tracked a horse thief to this property—right to this yard. Then they dragged him away before Sophie could so much as speak a word in his defense and tell them Cliff had been with her all day.

They'd galloped off, and Sophie had run after them, screaming. They hadn't even acknowledged her existence. When they'd left her hopelessly behind, she'd dashed back to the corral and caught a horse. She was good at it, having done largely for herself during the war years. She'd been riding after them within minutes. And she'd caught them just as they rode away laughing and sharing a whiskey bottle—leaving Cliff swaying in the wind.

She'd raced to the tree, thinking she might be in time to save him. But Cliff's face was a horrible, lifeless gray. His blue eyes gaped open, staring straight ahead at nothing. His neck was bent at an unnatural angle. All that had been left to do was cut him down and carry him home.

Sophie had gone for the sheriff, but he'd begun questioning her about the horses on the Edwards's property, as if he suspected the vigilantes might have been within their rights to hang Cliff. The sheriff had gone back to town without offering to so much as chase after Cliff's killers.

Sophie, beyond grief, with the fight battered out of her body, simply dug a hole next to the grave they'd dug for their baby boy. Late in the evening Parson Roscoe showed up with several townsfolk. The parson tried to comfort her, but Sophie couldn't even respond to his Christian faith. She was afraid if she accepted even a moment of comfort, she'd begin crying and never stop.

Others came out to pay their respects, but except for the parson, none of them were really friends. On top of Mosqueros's aversion to the Edwards's Yankee affiliation, Cliff had a knack for alienating people. There'd been a short ceremony, and Sophie had bitterly refused all help filling in the hole.

She'd also turned down four marriage proposals. Sophie was mortified her girls had witnessed the crude men trying to convince her to marry them over the fresh-turned earth of her husband's grave. The parson had ordered them off her land. The next day, Royce Badje, the banker, had ridden out to the ranch to notify her that when the next loan payment came due, he'd expect the full amount left on the loan.

Sophie had cattle to sell and a large part of the principal of the loan paid down. Mr. Badje said once the man of the household was dead, the woman was a poor risk. She'd either have to pay her loan in full or sell.

Sophie countered by pointing out she'd kept things going while Cliff was away fighting the war.

"Cliff was at Gettysburg, wasn't he?" Mr. Badje asked coldly. The banker's sons had died at Gettysburg, fighting for the Confederacy.

Sophie didn't answer. They both knew. Mr. Badje had given her thirty days to pay up or vacate the property.

While she was still shaking with anger, the banker proposed marriage. He offered to let her keep the ranch for their home, if she said yes. She'd said no. Then Mr. Badje asked how many years until Mandy was of marrying age.

Sophie's skin was crawling by the time he left.

The man stirred beside her and brought her thoughts back to the present, but he remained unconscious.

All three of the girls leaned forward, as if they were hanging on every breath that passed through his lips. Sophie studied his relaxed features, willing his eyes to open again, so he could answer some questions. A sudden fierce gust of wind rattled the shed, reminding Sophie of where they were and how late it was. She needed to get the girls away from him anyway, before they could fall more completely into the dream of getting their father back.

She studied her daughters, grim and mourning in a dark night split by lightning and shaken by thunder. She saw them as she hadn't seen them in a long while. They were tough as shoe leather, she knew that, but tonight, for the first time, she saw they were gaunt. She had waged a battle to survive on wild game and sparse greens.

Tonight, for the first time, she saw that she was losing that battle. Her girls were being hurt by this lean, hard life. She had to do something. She couldn't go on hiding, afraid of the hostile, hungry-eyed townspeople. Something had to change. But change took thought and planning. She didn't have time for either right now. She never had time for either.

"Girls, we have to get some sleep. And we can't leave Laura alone any longer."

Her girls each had a look of Hectorish stubbornness. Sophie understood, but they still had to put one foot in front of the other. And that started with sleep. She judged the situation and decided now wasn't the time for patience and kindness. She started issuing orders. "Amanda and Elizabeth, you go back to the house for now."

"No, Ma, we want to stay," Mandy protested.

Beth stormed, "It's not fair that Sally gets to help first."

Sophie hardened her heart to their pleading. They had to get through the next day without being exhausted. "Sally didn't go down into the creek. She's not soaking wet and shivering." That was true, but it wasn't the real reason. Sophie knew she would never pry Sally from this man's side.

She didn't waste her time trying to be reasonable. "Do as you're told. Get some sleep. Sally and I will sit up with him and keep him warm as best we can. You'll have to spell us later, so try and rest. Laura will wake up just as usual at dawn, and someone's going to need to have the gumption to take care of her. I'll send Sally in later to wake you, Mandy. Then Beth will have a turn."

In the intermittent lightning, Mandy and Beth looked stubborn-still, but the chance at keeping vigil later placated them somewhat. Sophie saw the dark circles under their eyes from the strain of this night, and she knew they'd sleep if they'd only lay their heads down. She didn't think Sally would. She'd just lie in the house and spin pipe dreams and hope.

In a slightly more gentle voice, Sophie said, "Go on now, girls. If he wakes up and can walk, we'll bring him in the house where it's warmer."

They grumbled, but Sophie had been in charge of this family for a long time. At last they moved away from their patient's side, and after hesitating in the opening of the little barn, they dashed out into the slashing rain and disappeared into the narrow pathway of the thicket.

Sophie exchanged a long look with Sally, who could barely tear her eyes away from the man. "It's not your pa, Sally. I'm sorry, and I know you don't believe me. We all want it to be him so badly. But it's not."

"But Ma, he's. . ."

"Don't you think I want it to be him?" Sophie interrupted. "Don't you think I've been fishing around inside my head for some way I'm wrong about who I buried that night? It was two years ago. You were only five. It's possible for you to convince yourself that things were different than they were. But I can't fool myself."

"But, Ma," Sally wailed. "All you have to do is look at. . ."

"I don't know what's going on," Sophie cut her off. "Maybe we'll find out your pa had a. . .a distant cousin or something. I think, with the way he looks, there has to be some connection between this man and your pa, but it's not him." Sophie softened her voice. "I'm sorry, sweetie, but it's just not him."

Sally's eyes wavered between the man and her ma. She finally whispered, "Okay."

And while Sophie knew her daughter believed her, she also knew the hope wouldn't die. The man stirred. The heavy woolen blanket that covered him slipped down, and goose bumps covered his arms and bare chest.

Moving slowly, as if in a trance, Sally stretched out beside the man and rested her little body along side of him. Just above a whisper, she said, "I'll keep you warm."

It was as if Sophie saw her daughter falling in love with this stranger right before her eyes. She didn't know what to do or say to stop it. In the end, when the man shivered again more violently, Sophie decided to leave it until morning. She rubbed the man's arms and pulled the blanket a bit higher. When that didn't make the goose bumps go down, she decided Sally had the right idea. She stretched out beside the man and huddled up close to him to share her warmth. She reached her hand across him to touch Sally's pale, worried face.

"Would it be so bad to pretend—just for tonight?" Sally asked.

Sophie smoothed her little girl's bedraggled hair back off her forehead. Then she felt a sudden easing of her heart. Sophie knew it came from a loving God who had proclaimed worry a waste of time.

"You're going to pretend anyway, aren't you, sweetie?"

Sally looked a little sheepish. With a shrug of her tiny shoulders that had already borne a lifetime of sadness, she said, "I reckon."

"So just enjoy it. It wouldn't be so bad to pretend we've got Pa back—just for tonight."

Sophie saw Sally unbend inside. Sophie knew Sally was pretending and feeling guilty over it, and that had lent strength to the fantasy of her father returning from the dead. But talking about it turned it into something less weighty. Almost a game.

He shivered again. Sally hugged him a little tighter. "Just for tonight."

The man's chills lessened as they held him. Sophie looked across that broad chest and noticed that Sally had fallen asleep with her head cradled on the man's shoulder.

Sophie lay awake and felt him begin to make more natural movements, as a person might do in his sleep. The tension that had been riding her since she'd heard his horse's pounding footsteps so long ago eased.

And that's when she remembered her children's hollow cheekbones and Judd's cruel, bloodshot eyes. Judd's viciousness had driven them to this life. The taste of hate burned her tongue.

It grew in her, like mold in that damp, musty shed, until it filled her and threatened to explode. She shook as she lay there beside the man Judd now wanted to kill. Her eyes stared into the black, drizzling night and saw nothing but hate. Satan gripped her heart, and she gave full sway to her thirst for vengeance. Hate roiled in her heart, guilt ate at her soul, and tears burned in her eyes. Then she forced her burning eyes to close. It was evil to feel like this about one of God's children.

With typical brutal honesty, Sophie admitted to God that she didn't want to let go of her fury. It was a betrayal of Cliff to forgive. It was ludicrous to love enemies such as these. She forced herself to pray, "Dear Lord, remove this sin from me. Soften my heart. Help me not to hate the way I do."

For Sophie it was a flowery prayer. Usually, she had neither the time nor the strength to be eloquent. She was too busy living through whatever life crushed down on her next. So exhausted, cold, and afraid, much the same as any other day, she spoke to God in words that summed up everything, "Help me, Lord. Help me, help me, help me."

That plea to God, that futile cry for something she didn't even want, was on her lips as she fell asleep. "Help me."

Help me.

Adam looked away from the horror before his eyes and glanced into the darkness behind him. He heard someone calling to him.

"Help me, help me, help me."

But there was no one here who needed him. The only ones left were beyond help.

His friends dangled from a tree. A noose around each neck. All dead. All but him.

Adam had crawled into the underbrush when the drunk, who was lashing his back with the bullwhip, had stumbled and fallen to his knees and passed out. Adam had tried to regain his feet, but the loss of blood from the gunshot low on his side and the ripped up skin on his back were too much. He got as far as one knee, thinking to go back and save Dinky and the other men he'd been ranching with, when he lost consciousness.

He awakened to the sound of fading hoofbeats and the triumphant laughter of cowards.

And his friends, lined up three in a row, each swinging slightly from a tree branch. In the chaos, they must have lost count and thought they had everybody. All black men looked alike to them, Adam thought bitterly. They hadn't noticed one was missing.

Adam watched his friends and tried to swallow his terror and his hate. And then he heard the voice.

Adam looked in the opposite direction of the hanging men. A woman. Adam gained his feet and took a few staggering steps toward the voice. Then he heard it again.

"Help me, help me, help me." So familiar. So precious to him. When he'd worked for her daddy, she'd tagged along after him, begging for a turn riding the horses or feeding the cattle, until he'd begun to love her like the child it seemed certain he'd never have. He'd know Sophie's voice anywhere.

It wasn't in any direction he could walk. It was inside his head. A message from her to him sent on the wings of the wind, blown to him by the breath of God. She called to him from Mosqueros, Adam knew that—somehow. Mosqueros, where he'd left her with that fool she'd married. Cliff had made it impossible for him to stay.

With one last heartrending look at his friends, Adam started out. He didn't take time to bury them. He couldn't save the dead, but maybe he could help the living.

The horses. The herd. Ten years' work. Gone. All of it gone. Right now that didn't matter, and it was a good thing it didn't. If he'd let it matter, he'd have hunted down those men and torn them apart with his bare hands. Sophie's call, "*Help me, help me, help me,*" turned him aside from that path—but only for now.

He took the handkerchief from around his neck, pressed it solidly against the bullet wound in his side, and walked. It was three hundred miles, but what difference did distance make? Sophie needed him. He'd go.

"Ma, you said you'd wake me!" Mandy's quiet, scolding voice hissed her awake.

Sophie moved, then groaned from aching muscles. She tried again to sit up and found she was anchored to a man by one strong arm.

In the full light of dawn, Sophie tried to take stock of where she was and why she was sleeping with a man.

Sleeping with a man! With a sudden squeak of surprise, she pulled against the man's grip—the man she'd just noticed lying beside her. He grunted when she pushed against him, and she remembered everything. Including that he might have some broken ribs. The ribs she was right now being rough with. She subsided immediately and looked sideways at Mandy, standing over her in a snit, with almost two-year-old Laura kicking and wriggling in her arms.

Sophie tried to get control of herself. She firmly reached for the arm that had found its way around her in the night. Just when she would have unwound it from around her neck, she saw him looking at her.

He said, "You're no angel."

Sophie opened her mouth to tell him he wasn't so great himself, but because of his condition, she controlled herself.

Then Beth came into the shed to announce that breakfast would be ready in five minutes. She looked down at the man. "You're not our pa."

Sally, barely awake and very content to be held close against the man's side, said, "Yes, he is."

"He is?" Beth asked in wonder.

"I am?" The man pulled his arm out from under Sophie, and her head dropped with a *thud* on the hard, packed hay.

Sally spoke securely from her little nest of warmth and comfort. "He's our pa. I've thought it over and decided God sent him back to us. Why not? He rosed Lazarus from the dead. Jesus can do anything, and God knows we need a pa."

Sophie sat up and looked from Sally to the man to see what he'd have to say about being declared resurrected and gifted with four children and a wife.

He was no help at all.

"I've been raised from the dead?" He spoke as if he had trouble accepting it but was willing to take Sally at her word.

"He's not raised from the dead, Sally."

"Why not?"

"It just doesn't happen, honey. Pa's gone, and that's that."

"It does too happen." Sally's voice rose. "What about Lazarus? God can do anything!"

"Yes," Sophie said. "God can do anything. But He just—He just—doesn't. . .do things like this. . .very often."

Mandy said smugly to Sally, "Why do you think it was a big deal to raise Lazarus up? It's 'cuz it doesn't get done very much."

"So that means I'm dead?" He rubbed his forehead. "Or I was at one time?"

Sophie felt kind of sorry for the poor, injured man. "No, you've never been dead." Then she thought of a way to solve the whole problem. "Who are you?"

All of them froze.

Sophie waited patiently.

Sally held her breath, hoped etched on her face.

Beth and Mandy exchanged wondering glances.

Laura. . .well, Laura tried to put her foot in her mouth and look at Hector at the same time.

"Didn't you just say my name was Lazarus?"

Sally patted his chest. "No, that's someone else who was raised from the dead, like you."

The man said uncertainly, "I—I don't know. I can't seem to remember anything. Except. . .except last night I woke up in heaven."

The minute he said that, he knew it was the wrong thing to say, because these females were who he'd seen there. So he must not have been in heaven at all. He must have been right here.

Another reason it was the wrong thing to say was it made the lady mad.

"You're not helping a bit." She crossed her arms and glared.

He shifted his weight and groaned from the pain, and the lady looked satisfied. No, she was definitely *not* an angel.

The girl who'd announced breakfast said, "Let's go eat. We'll talk this out in the house where it's warm."

The lady stood slowly. He heard her knees cracking. The little girl in his arms seemed content to stay where she was. The lady rounded him, reached down, snagged the little girl, and pulled her gently but firmly to her feet. Then she bent over him and put her arm under his shoulders. "You took quite a fall last night. Let's see if we can get you up."

He leaned on her as he tried to get to his feet. His chest was in agony. His head felt like it was full of angry gold miners, trying to chisel their way out. His knees seemed to have the consistency of apple jelly. He wobbled once, and the lady put her arm around his waist and helped him balance. All three of the girls reached for him. He was surrounded by swirling skirts and gentle hands and the sweet sounds of someone worrying about him. He reveled in it, until he thought his heart might break from the pleasure. Maybe he *was* in heaven. Or maybe the angels had been allowed to come back to earth with him.

The oldest girl, the one with the baby in her arms, caught him around the waist on the side the lady wasn't on. The little one—he remembered she'd wept over him in the night, and he wanted to hug her close and thank her for caring so much—she wrapped her arms around his middle and clung to him, as if she'd bear every ounce of his weight if he needed her to. Her head hit him right at his belly. She turned her worried face up and looked at him with pure love in her eyes.

The other one, the cook, rested her hands on his shoulders from behind and said with a voice that instilled confidence, "Steady there, mister. You'll be all right in a minute. Let us help you."

They all smelled wonderful. Sweet and pretty, except—he hated to find a sour note in what was one of the sweetest moments of his life—the lady was really rank. He tuned out that unpleasant discovery when she started fussing at the girls to be gentle with his ribs and the cuts and bruises. He looked down at his body and was stunned at the wreckage. He looked like he'd. . .he'd. . .

The lady said, "You fell over a creek bank."

He looked at his battered chest. "That sounds about right."

"You don't remember?" the lady asked.

The wiggling little worm of worry in his brain was growing into a coiled, sixteen-foot prairie rattler of panic in his gut. The truth was, he couldn't remember anything. Not how he came to be in this place. Not where he'd come from or where he was going to. Not even his name!

He looked between all these pretty women, in their gingham and calico, with their soft kindness, and said, "I don't remember anything, ma'am."

"Sophie," she supplied.

"Sophie." Suddenly, that name was the only solid thing that existed in a wildly out-of-control world, and he was determined to hold on to it. "I—I don't know why. . ." He faltered from admitting anything more. It seemed like a weakness to admit he had no memory, and it went against some instinct within him to admit to any weakness.

"So you're not Clifton Edwards?" the lady—Sophie—asked. There was a strange tone to her voice when she asked it, and he looked hard at her. He could tell from her tone that "no" was the right answer. But Clifton Edwards? Something about the name touched a chord inside of him.

"Clifton Edwards." He whispered the name aloud and tried to focus on what exactly bothered him about the name. The image of a face, a little boy's face, flashed in his mind. He didn't know who the boy was. He saw an older man, stooped with age. He saw a naked man—or nearly naked—leap up from the grass and raise a tomahawk in the air. An Indian. Blackfoot. He knew that. Then the parade of pictures faded. He absently reached his hand up to rub his aching head. He flinched from the stabbing agony of his ribs when he moved his arm. His stomach twisted and surged, and then the fact that he seemed to have no memories made the world spin.

"You fell a long way," Sophie said. "You took two hard blows to the head. Hard enough to leave big bumps and knock you senseless for hours. I reckon you'll be okay when you've had some rest."

"Don't any of you know who I am?" His voice sounded like it came from outside of himself. He saw a dead man lying on the ground in front of him. The vision widened. Ten dead men. A hundred. Blood everywhere. Bodies dressed in blue and gray. Severed limbs and the screams of the wounded. The smell. War. Sickening. Brutal. He wished he could forget it all. Forever.

From a great distance the lady answered his question, "No."

The littlest one said, "You're our pa."

The cook said, "You're not our pa."

The baby-sitter said, "You just look like our pa."

The toddler kicked her feet and landed one on his ribs and said, "Papa."

His knees went from apple jelly to apple cider, and all the girls' strength didn't keep him from sagging back to the ground. Through a roaring in his ears, he thought he heard someone, the cook maybe, say matter of-factly, "We shoulda got him to the house whilst we had the chance."

He also thought the lady, who smelled so bad, grew a second head that looked like a mule's head. Now that he thought of it, a mule was what she smelled like. A really filthy, old mule. Maybe one that'd been dead for a while. His last impression was that the mule kicked him in the ribs as he hit the ground, and maybe, just maybe, the mule said vehemently, "You are too our pa! You've been raised from the dead and that's that!"

Then everything went black.

FOUR

Mandy knelt beside the unconscious man. "Drat, he's out cold again. He really took hisself a whack."

Sophie shoved Hector's head off her shoulder. "Beth, can you get this ornery beast out of here?"

Elizabeth came around and soothed Hector, who had wandered outside after the storm but now wanted to see what the fuss was about in his house.

Sally fell to her knees beside the man. "He said he doesn't remember nothin'. Does that mean when you come back to life you don't bring your memories with you? Your whole life starts over at that moment? Does that mean he don't remember he's our pa?"

Sophie sighed at Sally and her resurrection theory. When you came right down to it, it made about as much sense as anything else. "It's much warmer this morning. The only danger he's in out here is from Hector stepping on him."

Beth came back without Hector. "I wouldn't put it past him, Ma. Unless you want to keep Hector tied up all day, someone's gonna hafta stay out here."

"I'm staying," Sally shouted.

Sophie took charge. "We'll eat in shifts. You girls go and eat now."

"I'm not leaving him, Ma!" Sally said adamantly, clearly planning to hold her ground until she died.

"You'll do as you're told, young lady!" Sophie gave Sally a stern look and continued, "I'll sit out here and nurse Laura while you girls eat. Then I'll eat while Beth watches him. Sally, it's your turn to wash the dishes, and there'll be no shirking. Whoever is with him gets Laura, too, so your hands won't be idle. We'll take turns sitting and doing the chores. If he wakes up, come running."

With a raised eyebrow at her third daughter, she added, "We're all just as curious as you are Sally, so don't ask for special treatment."

"The only trouble with that, Ma," Mandy said sensibly, "is that you smell so bad, I don't think Laura will eat. Plus, you'll stink her up."

"Yeah, and I already gave her a bath this morning," Beth added. "I've got water hot on the stove for you, Ma, and the washtub set up. Let Mandy and Sally stay here with Laura. I'll finish breakfast while you bathe. It's just biscuits. I can bring Mandy and Sally some out here."

"I promise I'll do my chores, Ma," Sally pleaded, "I'll go as soon as you're done washing up. I know we all want to spend time with Pa. I won't hog him."

When the girls ganged up on her, especially armed with common sense like this, she marveled at them. It was only then, as she thought of the logic of their reasoning, that she realized how much *she* didn't want to leave. Was it possible that she was harboring resurrection theories of her own? She looked at the unconscious form of her husband who wasn't her husband, and a sudden twist of longing made her breathing falter. That's when she knew she had to be the one who went to the house. She needed to get away from him and clear her head. And she took pity on Laura, who was already clean and sweet smelling.

"All right. Sally and Mandy take first shift watching out for him. Holler if he wakes up." Before she left, she took one last hard look at the man who kept falling back to sleep in her shed. As she turned away from him, she thought of all that lay ahead of her today. There was enough flour left for one more baking of biscuits. They needed food, and she would have to go into the thicket and search for it. She'd hope for a nest of pheasant eggs. If there weren't any, she'd have to set her snares and hunt for early-spring greens.

The girls could do a lot, but in the end it all fell on her shoulders, shoulders made strong by hard work and faith. There was Laura to tend and laundry to do after last night's muddy soaking. That meant hauling water and heating it. And on top of the regular struggle to survive, she now had an injured man to look after. All this came on top of a poor night's sleep. Her shoulders sagged as she made her way to the house.

Her morning prayers were the same as her night prayers and most of the prayers in between. Tears she would never let fall burned her eyes as she prayed, "Lord, give me the strength to get through another day. I can't do it on my own. Help me, Lord. Help me, help me, help me."

Luther awoke with a start and slid into the brush, away from the glowing embers of the fire. He glanced behind him and saw Buff roll out of sight into the woods. The two of them lay silently for a long time. They knew how it worked in the West. Get stupid, get dead. Simple.

What had made him move? The more Luther thought about it, the more he was sure it wasn't a sound that had awakened him. It was a—a nightmare. But that didn't quite cover it. Finally, into the darkness, Luther said quietly, "Buff, I've a hankerin' to see the kid."

There was an extended silence. "That what sent you runnin' for cover? Ya missed the boy?"

Buff didn't sound sarcastic, which Luther appreciated. Sheepishly he admitted into the night, "As I lay here, I reckon that's exactly what woke me."

Buff came to the fire matter-of-factly. "Movin' first an' askin' questions later keeps body and soul together."

Buff looked to be settling back in, but Luther knew he could not ignore that call for help. " 'Twas one o' them consarned dreams where a fella is fallin' and lands afore he wakes up."

"Had 'em," Buff said.

"Only 'tweren't me fallin'. It was Clay. An' it was almighty real. And a call for help. I think the boy's in trouble."

"Best check it out."

Buff put on the coffee while Luther led the horses to the creek for water. Without more than ten words between them, they ate breakfast and broke camp.

As the sun rose to the middle of the sky, Luther spoke for the first time since they'd set out. "Texas is a big state."

"Clay's a big man," Buff said. "He'll leave tracks."

Luther nodded. "Blackfeet're feisty in the spring anyhow. Might'uz well find a differ'nt spot."

"Yup," Buff said grimly as he swung his horse into a ground-eating lope aimed at Texas, most likely a thousand miles away or more. "Let's see if Apaches're friendlier."

Sophie bathed the Hector stink off herself and ate her biscuits and jelly, while Beth stood behind her and braided her still-wet hair. She was just getting up from the table when Mandy came tearing into the house.

"He's awake again!" Mandy dashed away.

Sophie and Beth were hard on her heels.

Sally was kneeling beside the man, talking earnestly to him, when Sophie got to the shed. Sophie heard her say, "And I'm your third daughter, Sally."

Sophie skidded to a stop and tried to walk sedately into the shed. Her patient turned his eyes toward her and tried to sit up. Sophie forgot to be sedate and dropped to the ground beside him. "Don't try yet. We shouldn't have let you get up earlier. It was too soon."

As if he appreciated being given permission to lie still, he sank flat on the ground.

"Now," Sophie said calmly, "can you tell us who you are?"

He rubbed his head and didn't answer for a long moment. Sophie saw her daughters lean ever closer. Even the practical Mandy seemed to be hoping this man would be their father.

When he didn't respond, Sophie added, "You rode your horse over a creek bank last night. We heard you fall and got you back up here. This is going to sound strange to you, but once we got you to where we could see you. . ."

Sophie really didn't know how to say it. "The thing is. . .you look exactly like my husband. And he's been. . .he's been. . ." She thought it best to break it to him gently. "The thing is. . .my husband—the girls' father—is. . . He's. . ." Sophie could find no gentle way. "He's dead."

The man was watching her like a hawk, hanging on every word. What little color he had faded from his poorly washed face. Sophie hated to go on, but there was no solution to this in silence. "I buried him myself two years ago. There can be no mistake. So you can see why the girls and I are. . ." Sophie faltered then went for a Texas-sized understatement, ". . .interested in who you are."

The man quit rubbing his head. He was staring at her and listening so intently, it was as if every word she spoke was coming straight from the mouth of God. "Earlier you asked me about a name?"

"Clifton Edwards."

His eyes narrowed, and Sophie leaned closer along with the girls.

"Clifton Edwards. Cliff," he muttered. "It means something to me."

He felt himself withdraw from the women as he searched inside himself. Visions flashed one after the other. A towering mountain. A battlefield. A half-naked Blackfoot charging him with blood in his eyes. A star. A silver star pinned on his shirt. When he saw the star, the floodgates opened. He sat upright so quickly Sally almost landed in his lap. "Clifton Edwards. I remember. No, I'm not Clifton Edwards. I'm Clayton McClellen. I'm Cliff's brother. His twin brother."

Sophie gasped at the same time she reached her hand out to support the man's unsteady shoulders. "Cliff didn't have a brother. He didn't have any family."

"Yes, he did. We'd been separated for years. My ma couldn't stand life in the West and went back to her family in Boston. We were young, three or four, but even then I knew I wanted the life we were living in Montana. Pa said Cliff hated it, so Ma took him and left me."

Sophie shook her head. "But. . .Cliff never said a word about you. Or about a father."

"Pa died while I was away fighting the war." Clay tried to make sense of what she said. Could Cliff have been so indifferent to Clay that he wouldn't even mention his twin brother's existence? "I guess when he picked my mother over Pa and me, he decided we were dead to him."

Sophie's blue eyes were kind and warm. Even though Cliff was long dead, Clay envied his brother. Sophie said, "No, I don't think that's true. Cliff used to talk about having a son. He wanted one so much. He said often enough that he was the last of his family line, and he wanted someone to carry on the name."

"The child would have been carrying on my mother's family name if Cliff called himself Edwards," Clay said bitterly.

"Yes, but his name wouldn't be his doing if he didn't know you and your pa existed. Three's awfully young. Maybe. . . Did you ever see your mother and brother again? Is it possible he forgot he had a brother?"

"Forgot? How could he? I never forgot him. Never!"

"But did your pa talk about him? Did he keep the memories alive for you?"

Clay nodded as he thought of the stories his pa had always told about the mischief he and Cliff had gotten into as toddlers. He thought of the sympathetic way his pa had talked about how unhappy Clay's mother had been during the brutal Montana winters. Clay had seen the sadness in Pa and he knew, even then, that Thomas McClellen had missed his wife and had loved her until the day he died. His pa had kept the memories alive, and he'd made those memories good ones. So he was never angry at his mother and brother. Only lonely for them—terribly, endlessly lonely—especially for the twin brother that he knew was out there somewhere. And then he'd heard that Cliff had died.

"Maybe your ma didn't do that for Cliff," Sophie said gently. "I know he would have wanted to have a brother. There was a loneliness in Cliff. I think in some way he knew you existed and he missed you."

Clay suspected Sophie said it mainly to offer comfort to an unhappy man, but even as she said it, he knew it was true. Cliff had been his best friend. Cliff would have wanted to know his twin brother.

Sophie added, "*Loneliness* isn't the right word exactly. It was more like he had a way of being alone even when he was surrounded by people. He kept everyone at arm's length."

From the sad way she said it, Clay wondered if "everyone" included her.

"So you're not our pa?" Sally asked with a downward droop to her mouth.

Clay looked away from Sophie to the little girl who'd offered him unconditional love from the first moment he'd opened his eyes. He squeezed her hand. "I'm sorry, no, I'm not."

A sudden burst of clarity in his befuddled brain made him think of something else. "I'll tell you what I am, though. I'm your uncle." He felt a wide smile spread across his face, and even as a single tear ran down the little girl's face, a shy smile bloomed on her lips.

"My uncle?" she said with wonder in her voice.

"Yeah! I'm your uncle Clay. I didn't even know I had a niece, and here I have four of them. I like the idea!"

"I do, too." Sally nodded and swiped an arm across her cheeks to dry her tears. "Are you going to stay around then?"

Clay sat up and looked from one girl to the other. His eyes paused on Laura, and he couldn't stop himself from smiling at the cheerful little girl. Then with a shake of his head that made his stomach lurch from the pain, he remembered why he'd come here to begin with. A hundred more details washed aside the joy of finding a family, when he thought he was the last. He'd known Cliff was dead. He'd heard about the lynching. He reached for his breast pocket, searching for the star the Texas Rangers had pinned on his chest when he'd accepted this one and only assignment he'd ever do for them. Not only was there no star, there was no shirt.

Vigilantes were terrorizing this corner of Texas. When Clay had heard about Cliff, he'd gone looking for justice, and he'd gotten a star. But where was it? He remembered taking it off and tucking it in his saddlebag before he'd ridden up to that campfire last night. Then he remembered how the campfire had been attacked and they'd all scattered. And he'd been pursued.

He said firmly to Sally, "You bet I'm gonna stay around. I heard about Cliff, and I came to see what happened." For now Clay didn't mention the Rangers. "I didn't even know he'd gotten married and had a family."

Clay's eyes traveled to Sophie. She was a pretty little thing. And she was even sweet-smelling now. "Is there a mule around here somewhere?"

Before anyone could answer him, Sally announced, "We're your family now, Uncle Clay. Our pa used to do all kinds of things with us girls and with Ma. Now you can do all those things."

All the things Cliff had done with Sophie. Clay looked at her. Their eyes caught and lingered for a second too long. Sophie looked away first. Clay forced himself to forget about the charged moment and turned back to Sally. "You are, for sure, my family now."

It sounded like he was staking a claim. Or making a vow. And that suited him right down to the ground.

"Let's see if we can get you up and into the house," Sophie said, rising to her feet. "We have breakfast ready."

The girls all grabbed hold, but he was steady on his feet this time. They'd delivered all the shocks while he was still sitting. He walked slowly to the house with Sally on one side, Sophie on the other, Mandy following, and with Laura and Beth running ahead.

Clay marveled again at being surrounded by so much femininity.

The gentle touches and worried looks. The soft cooing sounds of concern. He'd grown up with only his pa around. Luther and Buff most times, and a dozen others who had come and gone. He'd rarely seen a woman, and until the war, he'd never seen a child, except for a few Indian children who lived in Fort Benton when he and Pa made the long trek every spring to trade their furs for supplies. Those children had fascinated him, but the Indian women wouldn't let a curious, half-grown mountain man near their babies.

The Edwards women escorted him to the house and seated him at their table as formally as if he were visiting royalty. He was appalled. "This is where you live?" The minute the words burst out of him, he wished them back.

Sophie bristled, and all the girls frowned at him—even Laura.

"What's wrong with where we live?" Sophie asked defensively.

Clay decided to forge ahead. "It's the most pathetic house I've ever seen. It's so small." Clay rose from the table and stepped to the door to stare out. "Are we in the middle of some kind of. . .weed patch?"

Sophie appeared at his side, her hands on her hips. "This is our home. There's nothing wrong with it."

"But you can't live in this—this shack in the middle of a thicket."

Sophie crossed her arms and glared at him. "Define *can't*, Mr. McClellen. Because my girls and I have proven you can."

"And it's just one room? How do the five of you fit in here? What are you thinking, to be raising my nieces like this?" Clay looked into the fire in Sophie's eyes and wondered what was the matter with her. He'd been bending over backward to say it as nicely as he could. Of course, he'd grown up with men. They talked straight, and the closest they came to watching their mouths was when they'd refrain from saying something that might get them shot. Sophie didn't seem to appreciate his efforts at all.

"Raising *your* nieces? I've been making do pretty well raising *my* daughters for two years with no help from you or any man! What do you suggest I should have done? The banker threatened to foreclose on the ranch unless I married him. The town marshal offered to marry me, in between accusing Cliff of horse thieving. I had fifty proposals, not all of them decent, I assure you. Life in a thicket was a better idea than any of them."

"You should have taken one of them up on his offer!" The thought of Sophie with another man made his gut twist. But common sense should have made her pick the best of the lot and accept his proposal. "A woman can't live alone in the West, and you're the proof of it with this leaky house and that rickety shed!" Clay was shouting by the time he finished talking.

"If you need better accommodations, there's a path leading straight out of the thicket and into Mosqueros, about ten miles down the road. If you think you can make it in your condition, feel free to go."

He looked at the path that disappeared into the thicket. It looked like she'd settled herself into the middle of a wasteland. Then he turned and stared down into Sophie's defiant eyes. He told her the simple truth. "No, I don't want to go."

Their eyes locked again.

After a long, tense moment, Sally came and tugged on his arm. He tore his gaze away from Sophie's beautiful blue eyes.

"Well, that's settled then," Sally said. "Come and eat."

Clay looked past the sweet little girl and saw the table set with a single plate, with only biscuits and jelly for breakfast. His heart clenched as he realized this might well be all they had. Clay looked back at Sally's adoring little face, and then he turned and looked at his brother's wife. Wasn't there a Bible verse about marrying your brother's wife if your brother died? Clay looked into Sophie's pretty face and thought he had God on his side. It was his God-given duty to take care of them all.

Then he thought of a second verse about a brother dying without leaving sons. It was the job of the second brother to give sons to the wife, to carry on his brother's name. His eyes lost focus when he thought about it. He was barely aware that Sophie grabbed his arm and, with all the girls helping, eased him into a chair. His head cleared, and he was fairly certain that he'd almost passed out because of his injuries—not because he'd thought about how it was really his Christian duty to see that Sophie had another baby. Cliff still needed that son.

Clay didn't look at Sophie again. He wasn't sure he'd survive it. But he decided in that moment that, if they wanted to carry on Cliff's name, it was going to be the name Cliff was born with. McClellen. Everyone in this house was changing her name to McClellen and like it!

He pulled the plate of biscuits toward him and started spreading on jelly as he continued making plans in his head. And while he was making changes, he'd get them out of this thicket and make sure they had meat on the table. And her next child was definitely going to be a son.

With grim satisfaction, Clay decided they'd name the boy Cliff.

Five

Sophie paced around the outside of the cabin and fumed. She stopped and glared at the closed-up house and thought dark thoughts about the occupant. He didn't emerge. She started pacing again. After a long time she started to think he might have died in there. That softened her anger somewhat. True, he'd insulted her years of backbreaking effort to keep a roof over her girls' heads. True, he'd told her she should have married one of the rabble who proposed to her—and she included the banker and sheriff in that lot. True, he'd looked at her with Cliff's eyes, and she'd seen straight into his soul.

She stopped pacing and admitted that the way he made her feel when he looked at her was the real reason she was so mad at him.

Once Sophie stopped being angry, she started to worry in earnest. She was a mother, after all. Worrying was her job! He'd been in there too long. How long could it take a man to bathe? She'd left some of Cliff's clothing—rescued from the rag bag—for him to wear. How long could it take a man to dress? He was still unsteady on his feet. What if he'd fallen? He might have hit his head again. What if he'd passed out in the tub and sunk under the water? Sophie gave up her pacing and charged toward the door. She might already be too late to save him.

She was on the step when he opened the door.

"Coming to scrub my back, Sophie?" he drawled.

Sophie felt her cheeks heat up. "I was afraid you'd fallen. . .or something. You've been in there a long time."

"Trying to soak out some aches and pains." He tilted his chin slightly and gave a little one-shoulder shrug. It was a gesture so like Cliff's Sophie almost gasped out loud. He was watching her intently, but he didn't outwardly react to what must have been blatant fascination on her part.

"First things first. Where's my horse?" he asked.

Sophie and the girls, who had been waiting impatiently with her, all looked at each other.

Mandy said bluntly, "I reckon he's dead, Uncle Clay."

"Dead!" Considering all the shocks the man had endured so far today, Sophie was surprised how upset he seemed about the horse.

"You went over the creek bank," Beth reminded him. "And your horse went with you."

"We never saw any sign of a horse, Clay," Sophie said sympathetically. "It was pitch black. You were half buried in mud. I suppose your horse was down there, too. But there was no time to look. A flash flood came through the creek, and we were lucky to get out alive."

"I 'spect the fall kilt him, but iffen it didn't, I reckon the flood got him," Sally said, patting Clay on the arm.

"You girls went down into that creek, in front of a flash flood, to pull me out?" Clay asked incredulously.

Sophie hadn't been called a girl in a long time. She hadn't felt like a girl for even longer. She kind of liked it. She said in exasperation, "Well, we didn't know there was a flash flood coming when we went down!"

"You could have been killed!" Clay growled.

Sophie replied sarcastically, "I promise, if we'd have known there was the least danger, even of a stubbed toe or a broken fingernail, we'd have left you to die without a second thought."

Clay glared at her. "You need a keeper."

Sophie saw Mandy roll her eyes, and the two shared a grin.

Clay returned to the subject of his horse. "Has anyone gone down and looked? What about my saddlebags? And I had. . ." Clay stopped talking, and Sophie could see he was holding back something about what he had in those saddlebags.

Clay shook his head as if to accept the fact that he'd been wiped out by the flood. Accepting what couldn't be helped was very Western of him. It was something Cliff had never learned.

"I've got to get to a telegraph. How far is it to the nearest town?"

"Mosqueros is ten miles straight west." Mandy pointed toward the narrow trail.

Clay nodded. "I'll have to take the mule, but I'll only be gone—"

"Oh, you can't take Hector," Sally interrupted him.

"I'll bring him back." Clay's eyes slid from one to the other of them. "Don't you trust me? Do you really think I'd steal your mule?"

He sounded so hurt Sophie almost smiled. "It's not that. People would recognize Hector. He is so ornery he's almost a legend around these parts."

"So what if people recognize him?"

"Well, they'd know he was ours, and then they'd know we were here abouts," Beth explained.

Clay tilted his head again, and Sophie had that same wrenching reaction to him. She clenched her fist and held it close to her side when she realized she wanted to reach up and touch Clay's chin as he reminded her so much of her husband.

"Are you saying no one knows you live here?"

Clay spoke quietly, but Sophie heard an intensity in his voice that made her wary when she answered. "No. We were getting. . .bothered by a few of the townfolk."

"The men," Mandy said flatly.

Sophie didn't like the way Clay's eyes narrowed. She continued quickly, "So I led them to believe we'd gone to live with family."

" 'Cept we don't have any family," Beth said sadly.

"Till we got you." Sally grinned.

Clay rubbed his mouth with his hand, and Sophie thought he was trying to not say something. She forged ahead. "And if you show up with Hector they'll think we're here somewhere."

"And they might start coming around chasin' after Ma again." Sally, bouncing with energy, clung to Clay's hand.

"No one's going to bother your ma now that I'm around." Clay sounded like he was making a threat and a promise in the same breath.

"Then they'll just pester Mandy," Beth said philosophically.

"Mandy is only ten!" Clay exclaimed.

"Men!" Mandy snorted as if she'd noticed the same thing.

"There's a shortage of women 'round here," Sally said matter-of-factly. "They're thinkin' to the future."

"They won't be bothering Mandy either." Clay patted Sally on the shoulder.

"And besides," Sophie said, "and this is the important part: They might think you're Cliff, and he was supposed to be a horse thief. So you might not be safe in town."

"But everyone knows Cliff is dead!" Clay protested.

"Lots of them came and watched him be buried," Elizabeth remembered.

"Still, *we* wondered about you," Sophie reminded him. "They might, too. It was quite well known Cliff didn't have any family, especially after he died. And for a while I had nowhere to go until I remembered a 'cousin' who'd take me and the girls in."

"You better not go into Mosqueros." A furrow formed in Sally's brow. "We don't want to lose you like we lost Pa. They might just round you up and hang you to be on the safe side."

Sophie wondered if Sally could bear losing Clay. The little girl had never really gotten over Cliff's death. Sophie turned to Clay, more determined then ever to convince him to stay out of Mosqueros.

Clay snapped, "Let 'em try!"

He headed toward the back of the house without another word. Sophie exchanged anxious looks with her daughters then she hurried after him. They found him dropping a halter over Hector's head. Sophie waited for Clay to get bucked off into a thornbush. She was still waiting when he rode the disagreeable mule around the house. He headed for the gap in the thicket, and just as he rode out of sight, he stopped and turned Hector around without any effort, steering mostly with pressure from his knees.

He looked straight at Sophie for a long minute. "You know what needs to be done here, Sophie?"

Sophie most certainly did know what needed to be done. She'd been managing her life and seeing to her girls single-handedly for. . . well, honestly forever. She felt herself puff up with indignation. What did he think? Was he planning to give her instructions on what chores to do while he was gone?

She said waspishly, "Of course I know!"

"And you're willing?" Clay asked.

"Of course I'm willing. You didn't even need to ask."

Clay nodded silently for too long. "Then so be it. I'll see to it."

Sophie wondered what he'd "see" to. She opened her mouth to ask when Clay said, "Are you a God-fearing woman?"

Anything she'd been going to ask fled her mind when she pondered the question that seemed to come out of the blue. "I am, Clay. God is who has helped me through these last hard years."

Clay nodded again as he sat on Hector's back and seemed to consider all the great questions of the universe. Finally he quit nodding as if he'd worked it all out. "I'm a believer myself. I reckon it wouldn't have mattered. Taking care of you and the girls. . .well, I have it to do. But it's for the best, as far as raising the girls, that we agree on doing right by God." He nudged Hector, and the old mule obeyed Clay like the gentlest of lambs. Hector turned and Clay rode into the thicket.

He was gone before Sophie thought to call out, "What is it you have to do?"

There was no answer, but she assumed he meant something about helping with the chores later on. Sophie sniffed. She wasn't about to wait around for him.

She dusted her hands together. "Girls, let's get on with our day's work."

Sally set up a clamor about Clay leaving. Laura picked that moment to start crying her lungs out.

Beth's shoulders drooped as she headed for the house. "I'll get some dinner cooking."

Mandy bounced Laura and rubbed Sally's back and exchanged a very adult look with her mother. "Whatever he's up to, I'm planning to go along with it if it means we don't have to keep that mule scarf in the cabin no more."

Sophie shrugged and nodded. "Stay with the girls until they cheer up, Mandy. I'll go see to tidying the house."

She and the girls spent the next few hours pretending things were normal. They did their chores and ate a noon meal none of them wanted. Sophie scrubbed Clay's torn-up, muddy clothes and draped them over a bush to dry. Mandy and Beth explored downstream of the now-receded creek for over a mile, looking for any lost possessions that could be Clay's. They found nothing of his, but they did bring back a decrepit wooden pail with no handle and a tin coffee cup. Treasure.

The day wore on and Sophie was preparing their biscuits for supper when she heard a wagon come creaking into the yard. Branches from the bramble slapped back as the wagon squeezed though the thicket trail. The wagon had two horses tied on the back.

She pulled her biscuits out of the fire and ran out to see who'd come by. It was Clay with Parson Roscoe and his wife. Clay rode Hector like the old firebrand was a house pet.

She walked out to meet the parson, with the girls scrambling past her sedate walk. As she passed the unusually obedient Hector, she whispered, "Traitor!"

Speaking normally she said, "Howdy, Mrs. Roscoe. Parson."

"Get the house packed up," Clay said brusquely. "We're getting out of here."

Sophie opened her mouth and looked from Clay to the parson to Hector. None of them were any help.

"Where are we going?" Mandy, always calm and sensible, asked.

"I went to town looking for a better place for us to live. It turns out Cliff's ranch was for sale, so I bought it back. We're moving. I want to be over there before sunset."

Sally squealed and ran into the cabin. "I'll have my stuff packed in ten minutes, Uncle Clay."

Sophie was abstractly aware that she kept opening and closing her mouth, not unlike a landed catfish. She just didn't know what to say. Sally ran past her with her arms full of clothing, and Sophie realized they could indeed leave this place in about ten minutes.

"Y–you bought the ranch back?" Sophie finally managed.

Sally dumped her things in the wagon and ran back in the house. The other girls were hard on her heels.

Clay was wearing new clothes. There was no sign of Cliff's old clothing anywhere. He swung down off Hector's back and yanked the front of his new Stetson in an abbreviated tip-of-the-hat to her. "The owners had taken off a few weeks back, owing on the mortgage. No one else has shown any interest in it. I bought it."

"With what money?" Sophie asked. "You left here in borrowed clothes with no horse or saddle."

"I had my bank in Denver telegraph the one in Mosqueros confirming my draft was good." Clay headed into the cabin. Sophie followed after him. She was slowed by her girls passing her with the kitchen pots and Laura's crib. By the time she got inside, Clay was carrying the kitchen table outside. She almost got knocked back down the stairs. She stepped inside, and the girls dashed past her to grab bedding and the kitchen chairs and anything else that wasn't nailed down. Beth even thought to grab the cooling biscuits. Sophie noticed Mandy pull up the loose floorboard and take out the meager family purse.

Beth disappeared into the thicket for a minute, and when she came back, she said, "I tore down the snares so's we won't catch a rabbit and leave it to starve to death."

Clay came back in to the nearly empty little house and grabbed the milk pail with Sophie's Hector scarf in it. He pulled open the lid and dropped the pail with a gasp of shock.

He looked wildly around the room. The girls were stripping the last of their things out and running past him.

"Leave it and get out while you can," Beth yelled as she dashed past him.

Clay grabbed Sophie's arm and dragged her out of the empty cabin.

Sophie found herself plunked into the back of the wagon. The parson and his wife sat on the bench. Sally sat in front of Clay on Hector, chattering away. Clay had untied the horses from the back of the wagon and put Mandy and Elizabeth each on horseback so they could ride along beside him. Sophie held Laura.

Sophie heard Clay say to Sally, "What do you mean 'disguise'?" as they disappeared down the trail.

The steady rocking of the wagon lulled Laura to sleep almost immediately. Sophie sat quietly so the baby could sleep, even though she was fuming at being moved without being consulted.

Of course, she'd have gladly moved. She wanted to move! She couldn't wait to get out of that shack they were living in. But couldn't Clay have said something? Talked to her like she was a competent, thinking adult instead of just issuing orders?

They were thirty minutes down the trail when Sophie's jaw finally unclenched enough that she could say to Parson Roscoe, "Where did you meet up with Clay?"

The parson chuckled. "Word travels fast around a town the size of Mosqueros. I came out to see Cliff Edwards come back to life, and by then he'd been to the telegraph office, the general store, and the bank to buy his ranch back. I approached him and asked him who he was. He laughed and asked me, 'Don't you think I'm Cliff? Everyone else seems to believe he's back.' "

"I was right beside him," Mrs. Roscoe said in her peaceful voice. "I said, 'We saw Cliff Edwards buried, and although we are believers in Jesus Christ and as open to miracles as the next person, we aren't about to believe God resurrected a man after he was two years dead and buried.' "

"Clay said," Parson Roscoe continued, " 'It does seem like if God's going to resurrect someone, He'd do it right away when it'd done some good. By two years later everyone's gotten used to the idea of him being dead.' "

Mrs. Roscoe reclaimed the story, "So Irving said to him, 'Are you family?' He said, 'Twin brother. I've come to see about his death and care for his family.' "

"Then I said," the parson interjected, " 'We heard Cliff didn't have any family.' "

Mrs. Roscoe added, "Clay said, 'You heard wrong.' And since there he stood, big as life and as surely a twin brother as any man could be, we welcomed him to Mosqueros. Then he said you were all moving, which is a good thing and high time. We've worried about you something fierce out here, Sophie," Mrs. Roscoe said severely. "So we offered to help, and he said you'd be moving immediately. He said he'd bought a wagon to haul you and could use a driver."

"I see," Sophie said weakly. It wasn't that she minded moving. The thought of getting back the lovely home that she'd been forced out of made butterflies soar around in her stomach. But it was a little overwhelming to just be whisked away. Why, it bordered on kidnapping!

Then Parson Roscoe distracted her from the house. "Now you know I'm a Christian man, and if my time is up and the Lord calls me home, I expect to go praising God's name. But that doesn't mean I need to be a reckless fool. Time was, a parson's collar would protect a man of God from most everybody, but those days are gone. You and Clay will have to say your 'I do's' quick. I don't want to be on the trail after dark. Those vigilantes were out riding again last night."

"I do's?" Sophie stopped listening or caring about anything, except getting her hands around Clay McClellen's arrogant neck! There was a roaring in her ears by the time they reached the ranch house.

Clay was already dismounted and coming out of the barn. Sally skipped along beside him, holding his hand, and Beth stood in the front door of the house wielding a broom. Mandy ran from the corral to take a groggy Laura into her arms. For just a second Sophie forgot her need to beat some sense into her brother-in-law and admired the ranch she and Cliff had built.

She'd had some money when she left Philadelphia. Her father owned a large farm. He felt the need to be generous to his only child and her new husband. It had been her father's money that had made the down payment on the ranch and built the house.

Adam, one of her father's farmhands who suddenly confessed he'd always wanted to move west, was persuaded to drive the second team and stay with the Edwardses until they were established. Adam, a black man with emancipation papers, did more than help. He did everything. Cliff and Sophie wouldn't have survived without him.

Cliff had come to resent Adam. That was Cliff's way. Out of loyalty to Sophie, Adam stayed as long as he could stand Cliff's rudeness. Before he moved on, shortly after Elizabeth was born, the Edwards ranch had seen itself off to a good start.

She looked at the large one-story ranch house and remembered the adventure, excitement, and occasional disappointment of coming west as a new bride. Then she remembered her high-handed brother-in-law.

"Let's get this marriage over and done, Sophie," Clay said as he removed his Stetson to whack some trail dust off his pants. "Parson, if you don't want to climb down, you can just do the pronouncing from where you're at."

Sally giggled and whirled in a little circle without letting go of Clay's hand. The mention of marriage didn't seem to come as a surprise to her, so maybe Clay had gone so far as to mention there was going to be a wedding while he'd been riding with the girls.

"Clay!" Sophie hadn't really meant to yell, but her ears hurt just a little from the single word, so she supposed she had. The girls all froze and looked at her.

Sally's happy smile turned down at the corners. Beth quit sweeping.

Laura woke up. Mandy said, "Marriage?"

"I need to talk to you." Sophie started marching toward the house, but she didn't go in. She went around the side of the house and was almost out of sight when Clay grabbed her arm.

"We can talk later, Sophie. The parson needs to get home. Let's get this out of the way."

Sophie wrenched her arm loose and whirled to face him. "We will talk now, Clay McClellen." Sophie glanced over Clay's shoulder and saw all four of her girls watching in fascination. The parson and his wife were mighty interested, too.

"Sophie, there's nothing—"

"Not here," Sophie snapped. "In private!"

Clay narrowed his eyes. They were cold, blue, gunslinger eyes, and if she hadn't been so furious, she might have backed down and married him just to get him to quit looking at her so angrily. But she was furious, and it gave her the courage of a west Texas cougar.

"Back of the house. Now!" she roared. She jerked her arm, and he must have been agreeable to letting her talk, because she got loose, and she knew she never would have if he wasn't willing.

She marched on around the house. He was right behind her. When she thought she was out of earshot of the girls, unless she started ranting of course, she turned. "Where did you get the outlandish notion that we were getting married?"

"Outlandish notion?" Clay's brows shot up. "We talked about it. You said yes. What do you think I went to town for?"

"The parson?" Sophie screeched.

"Yes," Clay answered in a sarcastic drawl. "The parson!"

"We have not talked about getting married." Sophie jabbed Clay in the chest with her index finger. "I think I would have remembered a proposal!"

Clay grabbed her hand. He must not like being poked. Good. She'd remember that if she ever needed his attention again.

Clay got a very thoughtful look on his face. "I asked you if you knew what we had to do."

"Yes, but I can't imagine how you got, 'Yes, I'll marry you' out of that brief exchange."

Clay released her hand, lifted his Stetson, and ran his fingers through his hair, tousling it before setting his hat back on. "I asked you if you were a God-fearing woman," Clay added.

"And I am one." Sophie crossed her arms, stiffened her jaw, and waited for the man to make some sense.

"Well, we have to get married!" Clay said tersely. "So that's what I meant when I asked you if you knew what we had to do. What did you think I meant?"

"I had no idea!" Sophie could hardly remember him making the comment.

"Then why did you say you knew what we had to do?" Clay asked indignantly.

Sophie tried to think what in the world he was talking about. Clay waited as he stared at her with growing belligerence.

At last she fetched around what she could of the memory. "I guess I thought you were telling me we had the usual chores to do around the place." She snapped her fingers suddenly and said, "That's right. I said, 'Of course I know!' "

"And you said you were willing."

" 'Of course I'm willing,' " Sophie said with vicious sarcasm, "*to do the chores.* I thought you had a lot of nerve telling me that since I've been doing all the chores for two years now!"

"Why would I try and tell you to do the chores you'd been doing alone for so long? That would be stupid!" Clay bellowed. "Do I strike you as a stupid man?"

Sophie arched an eyebrow and didn't respond.

Clay's gunslinger eyes got even narrower. "We talked about having the same faith."

Sophie mulled that over. He'd asked if she was a God-fearing woman. She remembered thinking that was a question best left for a time when they could talk more. "Okay, I guess you asked me that," Sophie conceded.

"And we talked about raising the girls. I know I said something about it being best if we raise the girls in a church-going household."

"Yes, you said all of that. But I never imagined you were talking about. . ."

"It doesn't matter anyway, whether you've been asked proper or not. I guess I've heard of women who want fancy sweet talk and even rings and such, but I didn't take you for a woman who'd need that nonsense."

Sophie felt a little twinge of regret that she seemed like that kind of woman. She liked sweet talk real fine. But she wasn't the kind of woman who would ever dare ask that of one of these rough-hewn Western men. Cliff had given her those words at first, but they'd dried up almost as fast as the roses Sophie's ma had picked for a wedding bouquet. She'd missed them.

Sophie's throat closed just a little, and she tried to go back to being mad. She felt a lot more able to control Clay McClellen when she was mad than when she was near tears. "Why doesn't it matter?"

Clay shrugged. " 'Cuz we're getting married right now, whether you understood what I wanted or not."

Sophie opened her mouth to tell Clay to go try and talk a Texas sidewinder into marrying him, but her throat seemed to swell shut, and she thought for a humiliating moment that she might break down and cry. With a sudden rush of weakness, she wondered what difference it made. Why not marry him? At least she wouldn't have to live in a thicket like a mama jackrabbit anymore.

He seemed to have some misplaced desire to take the worries of the Edwards family on his own shoulders. And he was standing there with a Hectorish look of stubbornness on his face, as if it were a forgone conclusion she'd marry him. And all she was really doing was holding up the parson, who needed to get back to town before dark.

She shrugged. "All right. Let's get it over and done."

Clay curled up the corner of his mouth in a way that wasn't a smile. It almost looked like he was hurt in some way, but she couldn't imagine how. He was getting what he wanted.

He took her arm and led her back around the house. They met everybody, Parson and Mrs. Roscoe included, rushing out of the house. Sophie knew the layout of the house, and she'd bet next spring's calf crop that they'd all been standing at the kitchen window, listening to every word Clay and she had uttered. The embarrassed guilt on their faces was evidence enough.

"So what's the verdict?" the parson asked.

Sophie thought "verdict" was right. This was a life sentence. Clay looked to be a man who wouldn't die easily, unlike Cliff, so she was probably stuck with him.

Clay led her up onto the porch and said to the group waiting there, "We're getting married."

In her mind, Sophie heard a prison door slamming shut.

Six

He was free! Free from the burden that had been riding him from his earliest memory. He'd wanted his brother back as badly as he'd have wanted back one of his arms if it had been cut off. He'd spent his whole childhood bumping hard against the longing for Cliff. He'd felt the aching pain of the loss every time he laughed out loud. He'd tasted guilt every time he realized he hadn't thought about his brother for a while.

Clay held Sophie's hand, and with a feeling of triumph so strong he could almost hear angels singing, he gave up the years of loneliness. In a heartbeat the heavy weight he'd carried all his life lifted from his shoulders, replaced with a fierce desire to take care of his brother's family.

He gripped Sophie's hand. When she turned her head toward him, he smiled at her.

She scowled back.

Clay wanted to laugh out loud. He might be free, but he had his work cut out for him.

He looked around at the pretty little girls he was getting for a family and almost threw his arms around Sophie to hug her and thank her. He was a little *too afraid* of her to actually do it. Women were foreign creatures to him. He wondered why she wasn't happy. After all, she now had a man to take care of her. Wasn't that all a woman wanted? She'd actually hurt his feelings just a little bit when she'd agreed so gruffly to his proposal. The little woman should be at least as happy as he was.

The parson said, "Do you. . ." Clay didn't listen. He figured he knew what he was getting into without hearing the exact words the parson said. He just waited for a pause and said, "I do."

Then he heard Sophie say it, too. The parson pronounced some blessing Clay heard part of. He shook Clay's hand and congratulated him. He tipped his hat to Sophie, and he and Mrs. Roscoe got back in the wagon to head for town.

"I'll be in to pick up the wagon and the supplies I ordered from the general store tomorrow," Clay called out.

Parson and Mrs. Roscoe waved as they made for town to beat the sunset and the dangers inherent in the dark.

Clay turned to look at his wife. She was his. The burden of Cliff was gone. He was free!

He wanted to toss his Stetson into the air and give one of those victory yells he'd learned from all the Blackfeet who'd tried to kill him over the years. Then he had a momentary vision of Sophie fat with his child and he had another thought. He'd never in his life been to a wedding, but he'd heard of "You may kiss the bride." Was it time for that now?

Sophie looked like she might punch him if he tried. Still, he considered it.

Sally distracted him when she threw her arms around him. He ignored his tender ribs and hoisted her high in the air. He forgot about trying to coax a kiss out of his cranky new wife. Sally squealed with delight and accidentally kicked him in the stomach. Clay set her down. The other girls came up and hugged him. Even Laura in Elizabeth's arms seemed pleased.

Clay hugged them all. "I've got a family."

The girls giggled and held on tight.

"I always wanted my ma back so bad." He ruffled Sally's pretty blond hair. "And I wanted my brother back until it was an itch under my skin that I couldn't scratch. I reckon I've got something just as good as that now. Maybe better!" He mussed Beth's hair and gave Sally a kiss on top of her head. He slung his arm around Mandy and tickled Laura under her soggy chin.

The only one not having a good time was his wife. She said over the din, "I'll start getting us settled in," and headed for the ranch house.

Clay saw her go and wondered what in tarnation was the matter with her. He thought about it as he watched her walk away from him. She was a fetching little thing, with a trim waist and a beguiling smile, what little he'd seen of it. He enjoyed the view for a second, and then he dismissed her from his mind. Whatever bee was in her bonnet, she'd have to get rid of it herself. He had a ranch to run!

He headed for the barn. Sally caught up with him and clung to his hand. Clay grinned down at the little girl who wanted to be his shadow, and she smiled her heartfelt total adoration back up at him. "I'll show you around, Uncle Clay," she offered.

His niece. Clay shook his head. No, his daughter.

Never had he thought his search would come to this. He remembered when he'd started searching for Cliff in earnest. He'd fought in the war and heard rumors of another soldier that looked like him back East. Clay's time was spent along the western edge of the madness. He'd wondered if it could be his brother, and he'd tried to track down the rumors, closely questioning anyone who came to him with the tales.

Clay didn't like the East. He missed the wilderness and felt hemmed in by the crowds of people and the old hatreds and the artificial loyalties to Yankee or Confederate, just because of where a man was born. Clay had fought for freedom for the slaves. His conscience wouldn't let him stay out of it, but he couldn't believe being born south of the Mason-Dixon line made a man think it was all right to own another human being.

So he'd fought until the fighting was done, and after the war, he'd ignored his instinct to return home and headed east to search for his brother. He'd received a telegraph somewhere along on his quest that told him Pa had been killed. Luther had given him all the details he needed in a four-line telegraph, including that the killers, four of them, were dead and Pa had found a good strike and left it to Clay. Having money didn't make up for losing his pa. If anything, it made it worse, as if he'd profited from his father's death.

It had hit Clay hard to realize he was alone in the world, and finding Cliff became twice as important. He'd gone all the way to Boston. Once there it took over a month to find his mother, because it didn't occur to him that she would have gone back to her maiden name. When at last he found that out and visited her grave, he'd started searching for his brother under the name of Edwards and found out he'd gone to Texas over a decade ago.

Clay had taken the time to track down evidence of Cliff's war service, because once he headed for Texas, he didn't want to have to backtrack to the East if his brother had abandoned Texas as he'd abandoned the mountains. The men who had served with Cliff at Gettysburg knew little about him. They described him as stiff-necked and moody but smart and dedicated to the war effort. A few of them heard him speak of a west Texas ranch.

Clay had, by now, become stubborn to the point of obsession. He had gone to Texas, started in the farthest west corner of the panhandle, and worked his way east. He'd been doggedly at his search for two years when he met up with a Texas Ranger who was all heated up about a gang of vigilantes who had been terrorizing people all along the Pecos River, especially in the area north of Fort Davis.

That's when Clay had mentioned Cliff Edwards, and the ranger had told him his brother was dead. There was nothing about a wife and four children in the story.

From the obsession with finding Cliff, a new obsession grew: finding his killers. Clay, who had spent time scouting for the army in Wyoming and later in New Mexico before going to fight the war, had volunteered to work with the Texas Rangers this one time to track down Cliff's killers.

And that had led him here. Clay studied the barn and corral, proud of the sturdy construction that spoke so well of his brother. Sally skipped along beside him. The other girls were lingering around the yard, maybe a bit shyer than Sally but just as sweet.

He said to the gaggle of girls around his ankles, "The banker said there's a passle of cattle run wild in the hill country around the ranch, most of 'em ours but some of 'em maverick, so they go to whoever can catch 'em an' slap on a brand. I'm gonna ride out and see what the property looks like and find the best place to start. I'll be back at dark. Have your ma get supper." He settled his Stetson firmly on his head and went to catch up his horse.

"Can I come with you, Uncle Clay?" Sally asked, her hands clutched together as if she were begging.

Clay hadn't thought of that. He shrugged his shoulders. "I reckon there's no harm in it. You'll have to stay out a long time," he warned. "And you'll have to ride double with me. I 'spect you're a mite young to handle your own horse."

Sally grinned and promised, "I'll stay out till you're ready to come home. No matter how late that is, Uncle Clay."

Clay said, "Okay, you can come on one condition. . ."

"Anything," Sally said, clapping her hands together joyfully.

"If you come, you gotta call me 'Pa.' " Clay tried to sound stern, but a grin broke out on his face as he said it.

Sally's eyes got as bright and round as double eagle coins. For a second she looked so awestruck Clay was afraid she was going to swoon or something. Then she said fervently, "I'd be right proud to call you 'Pa,' Pa."

"Can we call you 'Pa,' too?" Beth asked.

Clay drawled, "Well, I reckon that's what I am now, your pa, so I'd say you'd better get to calling me that."

The girls all giggled and squirmed. Clay lifted Sally up off the ground and plunked her in front of him. He had a fight on his hands to wrestle her skirt and petticoat down around his Appaloosa mare's sides, and the horse didn't like it none too well. Clay knew how to handle a horse though, so after a bit of a battle of wills, Sally was settled in, and they headed out.

"You other girls want to come along on Hector? You older girls can probably make him mind."

"We'd better help Ma with the moving in," Mandy said practically.

"But I'd like to come some other time," Beth said.

"Fine." Clay wrapped his arm around Sally's stomach when she twisted around to smile at him.

"We'll have a good supper waiting for you, Pa." Mandy giggled when she called him "Pa."

Clay nodded. "Obliged, darlin'."

He turned his Appaloosa to the north, toward the rugged foothills where the high plateau country climbed into a spur of the Rockies. Plenty of places for a longhorn to hide in this terrain, but Clay had seen worse growing up in the northern Rockies. This just looked like some rolling hills to him. He rode eagerly out to explore the land that was now his home.

Sally started talking before they were out of the yard. Shocked at first, after years of riding with taciturn soldiers and trappers and cowpokes, Clay got to liking the sound of her little voice. He found he didn't have to say much to keep her talking. Whatever she said, it all boiled down to one thing: Her pa was a giant of a man who could do no wrong and whom she loved with every ounce of her heart. And now she loved her new pa just as much.

Clay was humbled and proud, and when he found evidence of a large herd of cattle coming to water at several springs, he realized he'd bought himself a fine ranch. All in all, a perfect day. Just maybe the best day of his life.

There never was a worse day landed on the shoulders of a single woman who had walked on the face of this earth!

Sophie tried to tell herself Eve had a worse day when she got herself kicked out of the Garden. And Lot's wife had to have been unhappy about being turned to salt. That was a long time ago, though. What was happening to Sophie was happening right now—and to her! She would put it up against the worst that had been handed out to anyone.

And the day showed no signs of ending. She'd been insulted for breaking her back keeping her children alive, in a country that chewed hard on regular folks and swallowed weaklings whole.

She'd been married, without really being consulted about it, to a man she didn't even know. Or so far—like!

She'd been dumped in a house with next to no food and been ordered to make supper.

Well, she'd show that man what she was made of! She made supper by taking Hector out and shooting a whitetail deer. She'd had snares set in the thicket that kept her supplied with pheasant, grouse, and rabbit. But this animal was a lot more to deal with. She knew how to skin and gut a deer, but she had no desire to do it the first night in her new home.

The deer had been the first game she found, and she'd been looking for a long while before she found it. Clay would have been her first choice of shooting targets, but he wasn't available, so she settled for the deer. Her hunting had proved difficult because, remembering the vigilantes, she had no choice but to take the girls along with her when she went. And that brought her to the worst of it. She was missing a daughter. That ornery man had kidnapped Sally!

What in the world had Clay been thinking, taking Sally with him without asking permission or at least telling Sophie.

And all the girls were calling him "Pa" now. She wanted to scold them and tell them Clay McClellen wasn't their pa and he never would be. She wanted to say they were showing disrespect to the memory of their real pa by tossing him aside so quickly. But she held back the angry words. It was Clay she wanted to punish, not her girls.

After shooting the deer, she hung it from a handy tree to bleed it and gutted it where it hung. She then slung it over Hector's shoulders, got the girls settled on Hector, and walked back to the ranch house, leading the whole bunch of them.

Then she had to find firewood. She didn't have so much as an ax, so she had to find sticks that were small enough to fit in the fireplace or were thin enough to break. That wasn't too hard; there was a nice stand of trees near the house. But it took time to get it done.

It was full dark by the time she had venison steaks roasting on a spit in the fireplace. She also was up to her elbows in a bloody deer carcass, cutting it up for jerking.

"Pa's home," Beth shrieked with pleasure.

All the girls dashed off to greet him. Sophie saw Clay set a very bedraggled but cheerful Sally on the ground and then ride to the stable, with the girls dancing in his wake.

Sophie ground her teeth together and turned back to her butchering with a vengeance.

Clay came around back with Sally on one hip and Laura on the other. Beth and Mandy were close behind. He studied her and her blood-soaked apron for a long minute. Then he said, "When's supper gonna be ready?"

Sophie didn't throw the knife at him by sheer willpower. She said through clenched teeth, "Mandy, check the steaks broiling in the fireplace. Beth, get out those biscuits we brought along."

"Good. I'm hungry." Then Clay added with a smile, "You're sure a pretty sight."

Sophie looked up, and her grip tightened menacingly on the knife. Clay didn't seem to notice. "You're sure making a mess of that buck. Leave it and I'll finish it later."

Sophie spoke through gritted teeth. "No thanks!"

Clay shrugged, as if he hadn't even noticed her outrageously sarcastic tone of voice. "Okay, if you want to do it. Come on in to supper when you're ready."

He turned and left her with two more hours of work to do on the deer! And the sun already fully set! She almost cried, which would have been ridiculous. She never cried. She was so tired and so hungry. She settled for her usual pastime when she was trying to live through the next backbreaking minute. Prayer. The usual prayer. "Give me strength, Lord. Help me, help me, help me."

Luther kicked at the fire all of a sudden and stood up in a huff. "Best be movin'," he muttered in disgust. He'd almost let himself relax before the pestering voice started in again.

"You're sure in an all-fired hurry," Buff grumbled, bolting the rest of his meal.

"Reckon," Luther said. It was the first time they'd stopped to eat all day.

Buff sighed until Luther thought the hair on his beard would part. But he didn't complain.

Luther had never intended to sleep this early anyhow. There was starlight aplenty, and the boy needed 'em.

They'd put a hundred miles behind them today, which was no small trick with a game horse and flat land. But in the mountains it was brutal, and their horses had taken the brunt. They needed the breather.

"Need horses," Buff said.

Luther just shook his head and wondered why Buff was so consarned chatty. Luther knew what was needed as well as the next man. He clucked his horse into a trot.

Seven

Clay tried to wait up for her. She finally came in so late, though, that he'd fallen asleep in his chair. She deliberately slammed the door. He started awake then studied her wet hair for a second before he asked drowsily, "Did you wash up in the creek?"

Sophie said tightly, "Yes."

"Don't go down there again without me standing watch. I saw cougar tracks today and a few wolves. And there could be bear in this country. It's not safe."

"Anything else?" she asked through clenched teeth.

Clay shook his head. He stood up and brought out the remaining steak. He set it on the table. "The girls said you didn't eat. That was stupid."

Sophie almost picked up the plate and threw it at him. She would have if she hadn't been starving. The smell of the meat she'd started smoking had been taunting her for the last hour until she'd almost chewed on it raw. If she'd have met a cougar at the creek, he might have been in more danger of being eaten than she was.

Instead of attacking Clay, Sophie focused on the incongruity between Clay holding supper for her and then calling her stupid. It was a good thing she was too tired to think, because it didn't bear thinking about. She started eating the tough, succulent venison, and she could tell Clay had been careful not to let it dry out. He silently brought her coffee and set what was left of the biscuits in front of her.

Sophie's stomach started to fill enough that she could think about something besides eating. She realized the house had been put in order. There were no more cobwebs in the ceiling corners. The windows shined brightly against the lantern light. The girls—she glanced around sharply—the girls must have all gone to bed. How had Clay managed all this? And why? Why hadn't he come out and taken over the butchering, surely a man's job, and left the house to her?

"The girls are asleep?" Sophie asked.

"Yep. I put all three of the older girls in there." He pointed to the bedroom on the northeast corner of the house.

"And I put Laura in there." He pointed to the northwest corner of the house.

"Why didn't you split them up two and two so the one room isn't so crowded?"

"Mandy and Beth said that room was always the nursery. When I tried to put Sally in there, she thought that meant I was calling her a baby, and that didn't set well," Clay said with a faint air of panic.

Sophie bit back a smile, afraid he'd take offense since he was obviously upset. She knew exactly how it had gone. The tears and the whining and the begging. "No, I don't suppose it would have."

"Are they supposed to cry so much and giggle every second when they're not crying? They never quit finding something so funny that I thought it'd break my eardrums a few times. And Laura pitched a daisy of a fit when Beth tried to give her a bath. Then Beth asked me to help, but Laura was stark naked, and I didn't think that was proper, so I said no. Then, well, maybe I said no a little. . .loud. Beth started crying." Clay ran his hands into his hair and made it stand up on end.

"Anyway, they're finally asleep, so please. . .please don't move them. If you can convince Sally to stop wailing about it, we can move them around tomorrow."

At least he'd been doing something. She'd pictured him sitting in here warming his feet by the fire while she butchered the deer.

Her belly filled as her plate emptied. She rose from the table to wash up.

"You look real tuckered. Go on to bed. The girls said you always slept in there." Clay pointed to the bedroom on the south side of the house. She had always loved the view from the window in there. She would rise each morning and look out on a sweeping green valley descending away from her and know she had a place where she belonged in the world. A place that was truly hers. Then she'd learned the hard way that nothing was ever truly hers.

She almost staggered when she took her first step. Clay steadied her. It occurred to her that he might not be so strong if he'd been working as hard as she had been today. Even so, she appreciated the strength of his grip. Without looking at him, she gathered herself and went to bed, thinking kindly of her new husband for the first time.

That wasn't strictly true. She'd thought kindly of him when she'd first found out he was Cliff's brother. She'd had several very kindly thoughts of him in fact. Then he'd married her without even really asking her permission. He'd left her to move into the house and hunt supper. He'd kidnapped Sally. And he'd left her to butcher and smoke the deer. Of course she'd told him she would, but if the man hadn't registered her sarcasm, then he wasn't making the full use of his ears.

But before all that, she'd thought kindly of him. And now she was again, just a bit. Cliff had certainly never washed a dish in his life or helped give a baby a bath. Sophie couldn't imagine a husband doing such things.

As she went into the room he called after her, "Sophie?"

She turned back. She tried to wade through her exhaustion and respond pleasantly. "Yes, Clay?" That was the first time she'd said her husband's name. She thought it fit comfortably on her tongue.

She'd married a very nice man.

Very politely he said, "Don't forget what I told you about the creek. The girls would be mighty upset if their ma got herself eaten by a cougar. You've lived on the frontier long enough to not be acting so stupid."

She'd married a troll.

She closed the door to her bedroom with a sharp *click*. She slipped her nightgown on. She was so tired she barely had the covers pulled over her before she was sound asleep. She spared one second as she nodded off to wonder where the "troll" was going to sleep.

She didn't have long to wonder.

"We'll be goin' in to services in Mosqueros this morning." Clay announced. "Parson Roscoe said the preachin' starts around nine so the country folks can have a long morning at their chores and still get there on time."

"We never go to services, Clay," Sophie said quietly.

Clay looked at his brand-spanking-new wife. He didn't give much thought to what she said. Instead he gave some thought to last night. He pulled her into his arms and planted a hearty kiss on her lips.

When he came up for air, he said, "We'll need to be on the trail in an hour." Then he kissed Sophie again, just 'cuz he wanted to. She sighed kind of sweetlike, and he enjoyed the sound while he helped her let go of his neck. When she was steady, he went out to see to the horses and Hector, with Sally tagging after him.

"Why do we have to go to church, Pa?" Sally asked.

Clay had never lived in a settled area, and although he'd stumbled on to a preacher here and there and sat through a Sunday service when he had the chance, he'd never been in any one spot long enough to have the habit of church attendance.

"I'm a believer. I've lived in the northern Rockies all my life, with my pa and the mountain men who were our friends. To my way of thinking, no one can live in the grandest cathedral on earth, the Rocky Mountains, and not know there's someone bigger than man in charge of the world."

"I'm not asking about believing in God." Sally tugged on his hand as she half walked, half skipped along beside him. "Everyone does that. I just don't know why we have to go to church."

"Well, you're wrong about everyone believing in God, Sally. When I was younger, I went through a spell when I was too big for my britches. I wrangled with my pa something fierce." Clay wondered at how comfortable he was talking to the cheerful little girl. He'd never done much talking when it was just him and pa sitting around a campfire.

Sally's eyes opened wide with fear. "You fought with your pa?"

Clay wondered why that scared her. He shrugged and went on jabbering. "There were lots of little fights when I got to thinking I was too much of a man to take orders from anybody. After my first real big blow-up with pa, I struck out on my own. That's when I learned there were folks who didn't believe in God."

"Those poor people."

Clay almost grinned. "The truth is I felt kinda sorry for them myself. Anyway, I was fourteen when I took off that first time. I was nearly six feet tall, and I'd been working a man's job since I was eight, so I didn't see anything wrong with making my own way."

"When you were fourteen?" Sally gasped.

"Yep."

"Mandy is ten; that's only four years from now."

Clay almost stumbled when he thought about his little girl going off and leaving him so soon. Then he shook his head to clear it. "Girls are different. Mandy isn't going anywhere for a long time."

"So what did you do after you left your pa?" Sally stood aside as Clay began slapping leather on his Appaloosa.

"I hunted grub and worked for a meal time to time. By the time I reached Cheyenne, I'd calmed down and went home." The truth was he'd been so homesick for Pa and the mountains, he'd signed on with a cattle drive heading into Montana and meandered home.

"I lived in unsettled places where there wasn't any church, and now that I have a chance to go worship with people, I'm looking forward to it." Clay talked with Sally as he saw to the meager chores and made note of some sagging fence posts and a couple of barn doors hanging from one hinge.

"We don't like Mosqueros much," Sally said.

"Why not?" Clay barely listened to her as he looked at the neglected ranch. It would have to wait until he got a handle on the cattle and ranch land. There were several spots he wanted to dam up on the creek before the spring rains quit, and then he had to get to the fence. He stretched his battered muscles and felt the strength of his back. He loved the life he'd gotten himself into.

Sally said, "I reckon it's 'cuz we're Yankees."

Clay suppressed a smile. He knew of the lingering hatred some people were capable of, and it sobered him to think of some of the cruelty his wife and daughters had no doubt been subjected to while Cliff was gone fighting. But everyone in town had been very friendly to him yesterday. His new family just hadn't been to town in a while.

He couldn't think of what to say to reassure her. Then he thought of those girls alternately crying and giggling at him at the same time, he already loved them. They scared him to death! So he thought he ought to head off another bout of tears. All he could think of to say was, "Don't you worry yourself about it. I'll take care of you."

Sally smiled uncertainly, and they both turned back to the chores. She was eager to do any little task for him, and although she actually slowed him down, he enjoyed being with her. When he was nearly done he said, "You better run on back to the house and get on your Sunday dress."

With wide, solemn eyes, Sally said, "But this is the only dress I have."

Clay looked at the bedraggled little dress, neatly patched but worn as thin as parchment paper. His family needed to do some shopping. "Well, go on and clean up anyway. Your ma will want to find the pretty face under all that dirt."

Sally giggled and gave him a big hug. Her soft, little arms were a wonder to him as he hoisted her up in the air to hug her tight. She ran off to the house, giggling some more. As he headed back in to gather his women, he slowed a bit as he thought of the house full of their giggling and the sudden way they had of bursting into tears. He wondered ruefully if he'd ever get used to them. Then he remembered their beautiful blue eyes and all that long, golden hair and Sally's soft, generous hugs and how they all seemed to adore him. And he remembered Sophie's warmth and hurried his step.

He was looking forward to going to town.

The thought of going to town made her sick.

Sophie thought of the evil eyes of the man who had come to her house in the thicket last night and wondered if she would run into him in Mosqueros. She thought of that arrogant sheriff and the greasy banker, and she dreaded town so much, she felt goose bumps break out on her body.

Clay hadn't even asked her if she wanted to go. The Edwards family had never attended church! Cliff hadn't cared for Parson Roscoe when they'd first moved here, Cliff being a staunch Episcopalian and Parson Roscoe coming from a Methodist persuasion. The small town she'd lived near in Pennsylvania had one church building and a circuit rider, like so many other small towns. Sophie's family had worshiped with everyone else in town, paying little heed to the denomination of the parson.

She'd tried to go to church in Mosqueros for a while, after Cliff had left for the war. But by then there'd been such hostility toward her and the girls, Sophie couldn't bear it. She'd found a firm champion in Parson Roscoe though.

They didn't announce it around town, but he and his wife had made their parsonage in South Carolina available as a stopover for the Underground Railroad, before they felt God call them to a frontier ministry. They'd been here five years before the Edwardses. But Sophie firmly believed that God had put the Roscoes in Mosqueros as a direct answer to prayers she wouldn't begin praying until many years later.

She wiped dry the last of the breakfast dishes, then with apprehension churning in her belly, she turned her attention toward preparing for church. Getting ready herself was easy. She owned one decent dress. She had it on. There were two others, but they were out of the question. She'd butchered a deer in one last night. Even though she covered it with an apron, that one was so awful she wouldn't think of wearing it out in public. And her other dress was the huge one she wore for her disguise. There was enough fabric in it to make dresses for all three older girls, providing she could get the Hector stink out of it.

She let her hair out of the braid she'd slept in, combed it smooth, then rebraided it and coiled it into a neat bun at the base of her neck. She went from one girl to the other, fixing the hair of each, although Laura didn't need much fixing with her little cap of white blond curls. Mandy had tried to braid Sally's hair. The braid was a little lopsided, and too many hairs had escaped for it to be suitable for church, so Sophie quickly tidied it, complimenting Mandy on her efforts and giving pointers at the same time. Mandy was learning. With a sigh of contentment, Sophie knew Mandy would be doing more of these little chores every day.

Sophie had put each girl's hair into a braid with nimble fingers and began tying a pink ribbon into Beth's hair.

Mandy shouted, "It's *my* turn to wear the pink ribbon!"

Beth gasped so loud it was almost a screech. She whirled around so fast she whipped Sally in the eye with her braid. "It is not your turn! It's mine!"

"My eye!" Sally squealed. She grabbed for her eye and wailed at the top of her lungs, "You hurt my eye!"

Beth ignored Sally and kept at Mandy, "You got to wear it for Christmas! That's the last time we got dressed up, and you wore the pink ribbon!"

Laura, up until now sitting on the floor contentedly watching her sisters, started crying in sympathy with Sally.

Mandy balled up her fists at her sides. "It was not Christmas! It was that night Parson Roscoe came out to visit. We got all dressed up, and Sally wore that ribbon. She's the youngest. We go oldest to youngest, so your turn must have been before that. It's my turn!"

Mandy reached for Beth's hair, and Beth slapped her hand.

"Sally, let me see your eye." Sophie added sharply, "Girls, don't fight! Mandy, it's Eliz. . ." Sally backed up, sobbing and wiping at her eye. Mandy and Beth were wrestling with each other and screaming to raise the dead. Sally knocked into Sophie, and Sophie staggered backward and would have fallen, except strong hands were there to catch her. She looked behind her as she was set back on her feet. Clay.

Mandy got her hands on the pink ribbon and, not purely coincidentally, one of Beth's braids. The screaming reached the point where it could make ears bleed.

Clay roared into the chaos, "Quiet! Every one of you girls, be—quiet—right—now!"

Dead silence fell on the room. The girls all looked at Clay, and after a few seconds of shock, Sally started crying. "Don't you love us anymore, Pa?"

Elizabeth started crying next. "I didn't mean to be so naughty!" She buried her face in her hands and wept. After a few seconds she reached back and dragged the pink ribbon out of her hair and tossed it at Mandy. "Here—" she said brokenly, "take the stupid—ugly ribbon—if you want it—so bad!"

The ribbon hit Mandy in the chest, but she didn't even try and catch it. Instead tears welled in her eyes. "I'm sorry, Pa. I didn't mean to make you stop loving us. Don't leave us. Please!" Mandy's voice cracked. With a sudden burst of grief that almost sounded like a scream, she whirled away from all of them and dashed out the door, crying.

Laura tottered toward Sophie, who was studying the drama calmly. Sophie curled up one corner of her mouth, shook her head, then she picked Laura up.

"Enough, girls," she snapped. "We're going to be late for church!"

"Don't yell at them!" Clay grabbed her arm and spun her around.

She wanted to snarl at him for grabbing at her like that, but she held her tongue when she saw the stricken look on his face, as he looked from her to each of the sobbing girls and, with complete panic, looked to the door.

"I'd better go after her! She could get hurt running around so upset." Clay hurried out the door, looking backward fearfully.

Once he got out, Sophie turned back to the girls. Beth was still sniffing a bit, but she was already tying the pink ribbon in her hair with a faintly satisfied air.

Sophie said, "Next time is Mandy's turn, and don't any of you forget it! Now Sally, it's your turn for the blue ribbon. Come over here."

Sophie had them all ready in just a few minutes. She found Clay in a near panic, searching for Mandy. Sophie told him to ready the horses. He seemed eager to obey her. Sophie rousted Mandy out of the barn hayloft, a favorite hidey-hole since she was little. She tied the yellow ribbon in Mandy's hair and plunked her on the horse. The six of them rode double on the two horses and Hector and headed for town.

Clay carried Sally in front of him. Mandy rode double with Beth in complete harmony. Sophie carried Laura like a papoose on her back.

Sophie rode beside Clay. Companionably she nodded at Beth and Mandy, riding slightly ahead on Hector's broad back. "It's certainly easier to get the girls ready for church since they got older. Going to town used to be a real struggle."

"It used to be harder than this?" Clay asked in a horrified whisper.

Sophie arched an eyebrow at him. "Well, of course. I had three girls under five years of age at one time. My goodness, it was a battle getting them all dressed and keeping them clean until we'd get to town."

Clay gave Sophie a wild-eyed look. She had no idea what he was so upset about. He shuddered slightly and spurred his horse into a trot. Sophie shrugged and increased her own speed to keep up with him. Clay treated them all like they were part sidewinder and part crystal, afraid they'd bite or break if he made a single wrong move.

Go figure men.

EIGHT

The trail to Mosqueros passed the thicket where they'd lived. Sophie looked at the familiar little path. A shiver of fear ran up her spine. She jerked back on the reins so suddenly her horse reared. So much had happened since the night she'd seen Judd, Eli, and the other man, she'd forgotten to tell Clay that the men who had killed Cliff had been chasing him. They'd called him a horse thief. They'd spoken of hangings. She wheeled her horse around to where Clay lagged behind them. He was immediately alert.

Mandy and Beth were ahead of them, but there sat Sally, enjoying the ride she was getting from her new pa. Sophie hesitated.

Clay said, "What?"

She shook her head sharply at him, just as Sally looked up from petting the horse. Sophie couldn't baldly announce, in front of her little girl, that men were looking for Clay to kill him.

Sophie immediately wiped the concern from her expression. "I was just thinking about the old place."

Clay caught her hint that what she wanted to say was best said away from the children. His eyes had that narrow, dangerous look about them, and his already cautious way of watching a trail became even more careful.

Sophie dropped back beside him. "I should tell you about life in that place sometime, Clay."

Sally piped up, "We ate roots and greens and jackrabbits. There were fish in the creek, but they were almighty hard to catch, and Ma could fetch us a deer when she had a mind to."

"Like last night?" Clay asked. "We went out riding herd, and here your ma finds food for a week."

Rather tartly Sophie replied, "Hunting with three children is quite a trick, Clay. Remind me to let you try it sometime."

Clay gave her a long, slightly horrified look, as if it hadn't occurred to him that she'd had to take the girls. Or maybe he was imagining hunting with them. "I may remind you, and I may not."

"There are other things I have to tell you. But later." Sophie held his gaze.

He tightened his grip on Sally as if to protect her. "Right after church soon enough?"

Sophie said with a brisk nod, "Just barely soon enough."

"Let's catch up to the girls a mite." Clay clucked to his horse.

Sophie stayed right beside him the rest of the trip. She tried to let go of her fear for her new husband, as well as her thirst for revenge for her old one. Every time she turned her mind away from vengeance, she thought of the enmity that was sure to face them in Mosqueros, and she tried to control her resentment.

In her opinion, her neighbors had chosen the wrong side in the war. They'd held it against her and her family when they lost, and they'd turned their backs on the Edwards family when Cliff died—when she'd needed help so badly.

None of these were emotions fit for a church service. She wasn't having much luck, but still she struggled against her anger. All over the United States, people had hard feelings against their neighbors and life needed to go on. Sophie was determined to put it behind her. While she rode along she prayed, *Help me, help me, help me.*

Adam jerked awake. He lifted his head and peered around him. There was nothing. He seemed to be lying flat out on grassland. He'd passed out after staggering along for what seemed like hours.

He fumbled for the wound on his side. The bullet had entered from the back and passed clean through. Adam wasn't surprised he'd been back-shot by that pack of cowards. He felt the dried blood, and just that little movement cut razor sharp through his side and back.

His girl needed help. "Give me the strength to take one more step, Lord. One step at a time, let me get to her."

He had nothing necessary for survival. Not food nor a weapon. Not even a fit set of clothes. But Adam figured God wouldn't give him the powerful message that Sophie needed him then not give the strength to go and help. Adam was a man of the West now. He'd learned to live with the land and let it provide for him. He pulled himself to his feet and staggered on toward Mosqueros.

"They're here, Irving. Oh, I so hoped they'd come!" Sophie heard Mrs. Roscoe's joyful pleasure when they rode up to the sagging picket fence that surrounded the little wooden church.

The small group of people milling around outside the church were staring. Sophie dismounted with grave misgivings. She tied her roan to the hitching post, alongside a dozen others, swung Laura around to her front, and pulled her out of her little leather carrier.

Clay helped Sally down, then swiftly went to lift first Mandy, then Beth off of Hector. He took Laura and had a steadying hand to spare to help Sophie alight.

Sophie took a minute to fuss over the tendrils of hair that had escaped from the girls' braids. The girls looked fine, but Sophie was delaying the moment she'd have to walk into that crowd. Clay came to stand beside her, with Laura in his strong arms.

Sophie smiled up at him. "Thank you."

Clay nodded and grinned. With his hand resting on Sally's back, he went to say hello to the parson.

"Good morning, Parson Roscoe." When Clay spoke, several people approached him.

"Clay McClellen!" the banker's voice boomed.

Sophie braced herself for trouble.

The banker extended his hand and said jovially, "Glad you could make it in to worship with us."

"Wouldn't have missed it, Royce," Clay said easily, reaching out to shake hands with the short, stocky man.

"Let me introduce the missus." Mr. Badje swept his arm sideways with a flourish.

The missus! Sophie almost choked, she was so surprised. A pretty young woman approached shyly, and Royce Badje took her hand. She clutched his hand in both of hers and hung on as if she'd caught a lifeline. Badje looked at her bowed head with adoration. Sophie knew the banker hadn't given her a thought in a long time.

"Clay McClellen, I'd like you to meet my wife, Isabelle. Isabelle, say hello to Clay." The banker gave the order and little Isabelle performed on command.

"Hello, Mr. McClellen." Isabelle nodded her head and held on to her husband even tighter.

Clay lifted his hat clean off his head and held it against his chest. "Howdy, Mrs. Badje. Have you met Sophie and my girls?"

It was as if a dam broke. Everyone flooded toward them and welcomed them genially to church. Sophie spoke to everyone, and all her girls were fussed over, especially Laura. Before long the girls were off chattering with other children, and Sophie and Clay were visiting pleasantly with the congregation.

A lady Sophie had never seen before approached her. "How do you do? I am Grace Calhoun, the new school teacher." Each word was clipped and perfectly pronounced—no Texas drawl for this young woman.

Sophie nodded her head at the extremely proper teacher. Grace

Calhoun's demeanor reminded Sophie of her more formal upbringing in Pennsylvania, and she dusted off some of her more genteel manners. "I am pleased to meet you, Grace."

"Excuse me, Mrs. McClellen, but I prefer Miss Calhoun. I feel my students must hear me referred to with respect in their homes if I am to keep order in school."

"Um. . ." Sophie felt herself blush a bit. "Of course, Miss Calhoun. As I said, I'm pleased to meet you. This will be the first school in Mosqueros, won't it?"

"No, Mrs. Badje was the teacher before she married. I mean to see things are well run. Are you intending to send the girls to school, Mrs. McClellen?"

The woman had a chilly manner. Her hands were folded primly. Her bonnet was carefully tied with a bow precisely angled under one ear. Her lips were pursed, not unlike someone who had just had a drink of vinegar. But Sophie thought behind the prissy behavior she saw truly kind eyes.

School. She'd never given it much thought. Survival had been too much work. She'd taught the girls to read with books she owned, mainly the Bible. And she'd taught them their numbers and simple arithmetic. There was so much more, though. Sophie looked sideways at Clay.

Before she could ask, Clay said, "We'll be there for sure, ma'am." Clay reached out his hand to shake Miss Calhoun's.

She flinched just a bit. "It is a lady's decision if she will shake hands with a man. It is improper of you to offer me your hand first."

Clay's hand stayed where it was for an awkward second or two, then he lowered it and rubbed it against his pant leg. "Uh, sorry, I didn't mean nothing by it."

"No, I don't imagine you did." Miss Calhoun nodded her head. "I'd best be getting inside." She turned stiffly and headed into the church. Sophie noticed Miss Calhoun went in alone and felt a stab of pity for her. She wondered if the young woman had any friends.

A flurry of friendly faces came up and greeted them. Parson Roscoe broke up the fellowship time by waving the congregation inside. Mrs. Roscoe took Sophie's arm firmly and escorted her to the front pew. Clay and the girls filed in beside her.

Sophie's head was spinning. She'd never been treated so kindly by the people of Mosqueros. It could only be due to Clay and whatever passed between him and the townsfolk when he'd done his shopping yesterday. Buoyed by the happiness of it, she faced the parson, ready to listen to the first preaching she'd heard in years.

Parson Roscoe held his big, black Bible open in one hand, lifted it to eye level, and roared, "Avenge not yourselves!"

Sophie almost jumped up out of her seat. She reached sideways without thinking what she was doing and clutched Clay's hand. She wanted to shake her head and deny the verse the parson had selected, but she held herself still. She didn't want to hear that it was wrong of her to want vengeance for Cliff. And now vengeance for Clay. She didn't want to let go of her hate for Judd and Eli and the men who rode with the J BAR M.

"Leave room for God's wrath," the parson thundered.

Sophie realized her own hand was hurting she was holding Clay's so tightly. She tried to relax her grip, only to realize she wasn't the only one holding on. Clay's hand was crushing hers.

Relentlessly the parson said what Sophie didn't want to hear, "For it is written, 'Vengeance is mine.' "

Mindful that she was sitting front and center in a very small church, she dared a quick glance at Clay.

Parson Roscoe said vehemently, " 'I will repay, saith the Lord'! "

The parson's voice faded from her hearing as she looked at her new husband. His face was flushed, and his eyes were locked on the parson. His jaw was rigid. Sophie sensed a terrible battle going on within him for self-control. She knew the words were striking home just as hard with Clay as they were with her. Clay wanted vengeance, too. Every bit as badly as she did.

But vengeance against whom? Sophie saw the anger on Clay's face, and even though she'd already had a few arguments with him, she sensed Clay was capable of anger far deeper than she'd suspected.

She'd had the impression he was a very Western man in his philosophical acceptance of bad luck—like his horse dying. And she'd noted a certain glint in his eyes when he was challenged that told her Clay could be dangerous. But this rage frightened her. Clay hated someone. Hated him or her deeply and wanted revenge. Just like Sophie did. She tightened her grip on his hand and turned back to face the parson, with stubborn dislike of the chosen topic.

Parson Roscoe had been talking for some minutes while Sophie paid attention to her new husband. Now the parson asked, "How many of you are afraid to ride the roads around Mosqueros at night?"

Sophie knew the parson himself was afraid. The self-appointed lawmen were dangerous.

"We have vigilantes working around here. Men bent on vengeance. Men who have gone too far, taking the law into their own hands."

Sophie got it. The parson wasn't talking about her and her thirst for vengeance. It was her own knowledge of the wrongness of her hatred that had made her take the parson's words personally. Yes, she knew it was wrong to hate so passionately, and she'd keep working on it. But no one, not even a loving God, would ask her to forgive the men who killed her husband. The parson was talking about the renegade lynch mob and the need to stop them. Sophie agreed completely.

"They have hurt too many people. Killed honest men. Killed guilty men who, in this country, are promised a fair trial before a judge and jury."

Sophie relaxed and her heart rose. The parson agreed with her. The parson knew that crowd of murderers needed to be hunted down and. . .

Parson Roscoe jabbed his finger straight at Sophie, then swept his hand across the entire congregation and roared, "You have to let go of your hate!" Then his voiced dropped nearly to a whisper. He said with a voice so kind it was heartbreaking, "You have to let go of your hate."

All in the church visibly leaned forward, so enthralled were they by the challenging sermon. " 'Thou shalt love the Lord thy God with all thy heart, and with all thy soul, and with all thy mind. This is the first and great commandment. And the second is like unto it: Thou shalt love thy neighbour as thyself.' To harbor hate, even against men as fearful as those who ride these hills in the night, is a sin. Do you think you harm them by sitting in your home and raging in your heart against their evil? Do you think you make the world a better place or bring a single person to believe in the Lord Jesus by gossiping about how deserving the vigilantes are of death? No! The anger only harms you!"

He pointed right at her again. "The hatred only keeps you away from God. There are only two commandments according to the scripture. Not ten. Two! If we obey those two we obey all the others. Love God. Love your neighbor. We have to find it in ourselves to love everyone."

No! Sophie didn't cry out, but everything in her rebelled against the parson's words. God could not ask her to love the men who killed her husband. He didn't ask His followers to look the other way while people were being killed.

"That doesn't mean you should be foolish. It doesn't mean that these men don't deserve prison. It doesn't mean we should let ourselves be killed while evil walks the face of the earth."

Sophie breathed a sigh of relief. He was giving his blessing, after all, to her desire for—she knew better than to call it *vengeance* now—justice. She'd call it *justice*. That was better.

"But He does call us to love. Yes, even love those who persecute us. Don't fool yourself that you can walk through life harboring hatred and still call yourself a believer in Jesus Christ. Love is what Jesus demands of us. First! Last! Always!" He looked right at her and finished his sermon in a voice full of tenderness and kindness. "First, love. Last, love. Always, always, love!"

It wasn't the ferocious demand that had begun his sermon. It was a prayer. His words washed over Sophie's restless soul and offered her, for the first time in a long time, peace.

"Dearly beloved," the parson said quietly, "avenge not yourselves.

Leave room for God's wrath. For it is written, 'Vengeance is mine; I will repay, saith the Lord.' "

The parson then led the congregation into a rousing chorus of "Rock of Ages."

"Rock of Ages cleft for me. Let me hide myself in Thee."

Her whole body trembled as she stood to sing along. Sophie heard the words of the faithful old hymn. She had spent the last two years hiding herself, literally. But had she hidden herself in God? Had she depended on Him?

The song ended, and only then did Clay release her hand. And only when he released it did Sophie realize they'd held hands tightly through the whole service. The parson swept up the aisle. Mrs. Roscoe followed.

Clay and Sophie had a second as they stood alone in the front pew of the church. "I don't think it was right," Clay said curtly, "for the parson to pick out a scripture and use it to scold me the first day I attend his church."

Sophie stumbled. Clay caught her. She looked sideways and couldn't quite stop a smile from flickering across her face.

"You think that's funny?" Clay growled.

Sophie glanced forward. In just a few steps they'd have to shake the parson's hand, so she didn't have time to say much. She tucked her hand through Clay's elbow. "I thought he was preaching it at me, not you."

Clay's eyebrows rose in astonishment. "You? What do you need revenge for?"

The girls surrounded them: Mandy with Laura, Sally holding Clay's hand, and Beth just a step behind. Sophie didn't want to get into her hatred in front of them. She said quietly, "Cliff."

Clay stopped so abruptly, Beth bumped into his back. "You reckon everyone in that church figured the parson was aiming his words at them personally?"

"If God blesses his words, I imagine they do."

Clay let a small, humorless grunt of agreement escape his lips, then he stepped forward and shook the parson's hand. "Excellent message today, Parson."

Sophie didn't think Parson Roscoe gave her a look more stern than usual. So his sermon hadn't been for her—or Clay. It was God who'd made her think that. The peace she'd felt earlier deepened and settled on Sophie's heart as she considered that. It was God who chastised her, not the parson.

She could say honestly, "I enjoyed the service, Parson."

He shook her hand and moved on to Sophie's girls. Sophie and Clay walked toward the horses.

"You wanted to tell me something on the trail?" Clay asked.

Sophie glanced over her shoulder. The girls were coming right behind. She said quickly, "I didn't tell you about the men who came to the cabin in the thicket after we pulled you out of the creek. They were hunting you. They were the same men who killed Cliff. Or at least one of them was."

"Did you. . ." Clay cut off his question when Sally came around front of them.

Sally asked, "Can I ride double with you again, Pa?"

Sophie murmured to Clay, "We'll talk later."

Clay nodded at Sophie, then turned to Sally and said, "I reckon it's Beth's turn, darlin'."

Sally pouted something fierce. But after a nice long visit with their fellow believers and a stop at the general store, whose owner was kind enough to fill their order on Sunday, the McClellen family headed home, with Beth taking her turn.

Nine

Sophie was so excited about all the food they had in the house, she almost forgot men were trying to kill her husband.

It had been so long since she'd had choices. She didn't have to try and contrive bread; she had the ingredients to allow her to choose between making rising bread, biscuits, or corn bread. She didn't have to hunt for whatever greens were growing; she had canned vegetables and fruits of every kind. Clay bought a ham and a side of bacon. He had also purchased flour, sugar, baking powder, yeast, potatoes, carrots, and onions. They'd hitched up their horses to the wagon the Roscoes had driven home and filled it with wonderful, delicious, precious food!

It took some doing for Sophie to remember how to cook with it all, but it came back to her, and they had a feast for their Sunday dinner.

Sophie told Clay she'd like to go for a short ride with him after lunch. They went alone, despite the wailing of the three older girls. It was good luck that Laura was taking a nap, or no doubt she'd have joined in with the other banshees. Sophie had to bite back a smile when she thought of the terrified look on Clay's face every time one of the girls started crying.

Before they'd ridden a hundred feet, Clay said, "We don't dare go out of sight of the ranch. We're far enough they can't hear us. Now tell me about those men who were hunting me."

Sophie told him everything. The parson's words rang in her ears, and she wondered if it wasn't a sin to pile her own list of enemies onto Clay's shoulders. She was inviting him to hate along with her.

"Judd was his name?" Clay asked. "That's all you heard? No last name?"

"Just Judd and Eli."

Clay's eyes flashed with anger.

Sophie tried not to join with him.

"And J BAR M," he said with grim satisfaction. "That should be registered. It should be a simple matter to track down the owner of that brand."

"Unless the horse was stolen, Clay," Sophie reminded him, afraid he'd act rashly.

Clay nodded. "It might have been stolen by Judd from someone from the J BAR M. Or maybe someone else stole it and the vigilantes caught up with the thieves."

"So even if we find who owns that brand, we still might not know anything," Sophie said forlornly.

Clay sighed. "It might lead to a dozen dead ends."

They rode around a small stand of trees, thin enough they didn't block the view of the house. Sophie pulled her mount to a halt and leaned forward, resting her crossed arms on the saddle horn. "Clay, what did you think about Parson Roscoe's sermon this morning?"

Clay looked at the skyline, and Sophie realized that he had been sharply alert the entire time they'd been riding, much as he had been on the ride to town this morning. It made her feel safe. Sophie tried to remember the last time she'd felt safe. They were sandwiched between the thin clump of oak trees that had sprung up by a little spring, and a vast woodland that stretched up into the rugged hills which surrounded the ranch house on two sides.

"I thought he was aiming it right at me." He gave her a sheepish grin.

Sophie smiled back. "Me, too."

"So do you think he wrote the whole sermon with the two of us in mind?" Clay teased her.

Sophie shrugged. "He could have."

Clay moved his horse. Sophie knew he was checking all around them, watching for danger.

Without ever letting his eyes rest, he said, "I guess everyone in the place might have felt like we did. It's not just the vigilantes either. I reckon every man and woman alive carries anger around and wishes for revenge for something or other."

"I have hated that man who lynched Cliff for so long my hatred is almost like an old friend." Sophie realized she was looking around, too. And it wasn't just Clay's heightened awareness that was making her do it. She had learned all the hard lessons the West had to teach.

"I don't want to give it up."

Clay nodded. "I heard that my brother was dead and all I could think of was revenge. I rode down here hunting his killers with no thought except to even the score. To pay them back for what they did to Cliff."

"I've prayed every day to stop the anger in my heart," Sophie confessed. "I've always known hatred was a sin. But to give it up seemed like a betrayal of Cliff. And those men are dangerous. How do we love them when there's a very good chance that, one of these days, they're going to come riding onto this ranch and kill you, just like they did Cliff?"

"I don't want to wait for that day either. I have been fully intending to hunt them down."

"And kill them?" Sophie asked.

Clay lapsed into silence for such a long time that Sophie had her answer. Finally he focused on her and said quietly, "I'll turn them over to the sheriff instead. That would be justice, not revenge."

Sophie raised her eyebrows, and a quirk lifted the corners of her mouth. "That might be okay. But what do we do about the hate?"

"I've been using the hate to keep me inspired," Clay said grimly. "It pushes me to never give up."

"But it's wrong," Sophie reminded him.

"It's not that I don't agree that vengeance belongs to God. I just don't see why we can't both have a turn."

"Both?" Sophie asked.

"Yeah, God and me—both." With a little grin, Clay said, "First I can have a crack at 'em, then God can punish 'em eternally in the fire."

"Clay!" Sophie interrupted. "I don't think that's quite what Parson Roscoe had in mind."

"I reckon not." Clay shook his head and looked away from Sophie to scan the woodlands and flatlands. "What the parson has in mind is to give it up to God, I s'pose. So far I'm not having any luck. I don't even want to let it go. I've never prayed, like you have, to quit hating. I've never prayed to catch up to 'em either. I figured when I got my hands on 'em, I'd kill 'em. And I guess, even without the parson's words, I knew God wouldn't want to hear a prayer like that. I think, sweetheart, that you're one step farther along the way to doing it right than I am."

He'd called her *sweetheart*. It actually made her heart feel kind of sweet. "Well, then maybe we can pray for both. We'll pray for me to quit hating and for you to want to quit hating."

"Okay. I won't go after 'em." Then Clay added playfully, "Anyway, I don't have time. I got me a wife and four daughters and a ranch to watch out for. I only got time to hate 'em part-time these days."

Sophie smiled at him, then her smile faded and she said hesitantly, "Clay."

"Huh?"

"I want us to do what God wants, but I don't want you to be hurt. Those men might not have seen you enough to know who they were chasing that night, but we can't know that for sure. They might still be looking for you."

Clay leveled his blue eyes at her. "I've lived a long time in a hard land, Sophie. I'd take a lot of killing."

He had eyes exactly like Cliff's and yet so different. They were identical, and yet she knew them apart. His eyes were the reason she'd never really believed he was Cliff, even when he was just regaining consciousness, even when he couldn't remember his name. She could take one look at the confidence in Clay's eyes and never get the two of them mixed up.

"We'd better get back to the house," Sophie said with some regret. She'd enjoyed this time with Clay. He'd actually done a little talking. In fact, this might be the first time he'd strung two sentences together. She'd like to stay and ask him questions about his life growing up in the mountains and his pa—her girls' grandfather.

Clay turned his Appaloosa toward the ranch. Just as Sophie wheeled, a wild boar burst out of the dense undergrowth in the small grove of trees about a hundred yards away from them. Sophie jerked her Winchester off her saddle and shot the boar before it could run ten feet. She dropped her rifle back into its sling, clucked to her horse, and turned back for the boar. Clay reached out and grabbed her arm.

She held up on the reins before he pulled her out of the saddle. She tugged on her arm. "I've got to bleed him."

He didn't let up his hold. If anything, it tightened. "Where did you learn to shoot like that?" he asked faintly.

Sophie took her eyes off the hog she'd brought down. "I taught myself, mostly. Adam showed me the basics." She looked at Clay, pleased with her shooting, although the boar was certainly a large target. She was surprised to see the incredulous look on Clay's face.

He kept looking from Sophie, to the boar, to her rifle.

Finally she said defensively, "What? It's a good shot. I caught him just ahead of his front leg. A clean shot through the heart. I didn't damage the hams, and there won't be powder or bone fragments in the headcheese."

Clay's grip slipped a little. "You mean you even took the time to pick a spot to hit him?"

Sophie was flustered by the question. "Well, sure."

"No woman knows how to handle a gun like that," he said flatly.

Then Sophie saw what was bothering him. She couldn't believe it. "You mean you're all ruffled because I'm good? That doesn't make sense."

"I'm not ruffled!" Clay growled. "Men don't get ruffled!"

Sophie bit back a grin. Then she remembered the deer from last night. "If it ruffles your manhood to see a woman whose aim is fast and true, then why don't you prove how tough you are by butchering that boar? You do know how to do it, don't you?"

"Of course I know how to do it." Clay narrowed those eyes at her, like he'd done time to time, and her heart sped up just a bit. He ignored the jab at his masculinity and got right to the heart of her insult.

"If you wanted me to clean that deer for you last night, you shoulda said yes when I offered to do it."

Sophie met his gaze with the coolest one she could muster. She had the feeling that many a man would back down under that look in Clay's eyes, but she had no fear of him. "I won't make that mistake again."

A flicker of surprise passed over Clay's face. Sophie wondered when the last time was that he'd been sassed.

Then he did something that took her completely by surprise. He closed the few inches between them and kissed her. He pulled back. "See that you don't."

The kiss had been over almost before it began, but it had still left Sophie's lips tingling. She had to hold herself from leaning toward him again. Then he let her arm go and turned his horse toward Sophie's catch.

Clay stopped his horse to turn and look at her. After a few seconds he said gruffly, "Get back to the house and take care of the children, woman."

Sophie laughed again. "Yes, sir!" She gave him a sharp two-fingered salute. She was afraid she'd irritated him, but not very afraid. And when she heard his deep-throated chuckle, she wasn't afraid at all.

Sophie tasted him on her lips and wondered how foolish it was to be falling in love with a man she'd only known two days. Somehow it seemed more foolish than marrying him.

Still, he was her husband. Who better to fall in love with? Then she caught herself. She thought of how much she'd loved Cliff and how much his rejection had hurt.

Of course she'd respect Clay and work hard at his side and honor him whenever possible. But love? No. She rode away, determined not to ever be such a fool again.

"What ya mean it's been sold?" Judd smashed both fists on the banker's desk so hard he shoved it back against Royce Badje's paunchy belly.

Badje stood and pulled his handkerchief out of his breast pocket to dab at his forehead.

Judd smelled the fear in the man and enjoyed it. "Who bought it?"

"R–Really, sir," Mr. Badje stammered, "b–bank transactions are c–confidential. It isn't my place to say who—"

"I want to know *who* now!" Judd reached for the massive oak desk to wrench it aside so he could get his hands on this pasty-faced city slicker. He wanted to make this man afraid of him. He wanted to crush him under his heel like the bug he was.

But Judd prided himself on his wiles. He had held back after Cliff died, so as not to draw attention to himself. He had kept his cool, played the game out his own way. Now, he had to do that again. He fought for control of his rage. Finally, he felt capable of straightening away from the desk and lowering himself into the chair, where he'd been sitting so comfortably a moment ago.

He'd been savoring the moment when he'd impress this overbearing banker with the show of cash he could produce. Instead, the banker had said dismissively that the land Judd had been working two years for belonged to someone else.

"Just give me a name," Judd said through clenched jaws. "I heard the owners had abandoned it. So I scouted it. It looked like a right nice piece of property. I might go out and see if the new owner would dicker with me."

The stout, little man puffed up, dabbed his forehead again, and with a huff of indignation, returned to his seat. "I can't give you any details. A banker has a certain position to maintain in a community. . . ."

Judd leaned forward in his seat and reached for the desk, outwardly just to balance himself while he stood, but he knew the effect he had on milquetoasts like this. He let the full weight of his fury blaze in his eyes.

Without Judd saying a word, the banker caved. "There is really no reason I shouldn't say. After all, it is common knowledge who the new owner is."

Judd settled back and smiled coldly at the banker. Judd could feel the money burning in his pocket. Thousands of dollars. The full price of the ranch. Two years' work.

"Clay McClellen. Twin brother of Cliff Edwards, the former owner. Clay bought the ranch when the Mead brothers missed their payment. He married Edwards's widow and moved out there just last Saturday." As if to make up for his unethical telling of the new owner's name, the banker added with a sniff, "It's very doubtful, with his ties to the property, Mr. McClellen will want to sell."

"Edwards's widow?" Judd's fists curled. "I heard she was long gone, living with relatives."

"How did you hear that?" Mr. Badje asked. "You're not from around here."

A killing fury made Judd want to put his hands around the banker's fat neck. After a bitter struggle, he found the self-control to say sharply, "Never mind. If it's sold, there's no point in discussing it."

He got up from his chair and left the room. He stalked out of the building, already making new plans. He'd played it too safe before. The law had been watching because the sheriff was sweet on Mrs. Edwards. But in the unsettled West, the only real law was strength. Once he owned the Edwards's place, buying the sheriff, or getting rid of him and handpicking a successor, would be his first order of business.

He strode down the street of the town he was planning to control. He was tired of waiting around. He'd worked too long and hard to get his hands on that ranch. A twin brother? Where had a twin brother come from? Judd had learned for a fact that Cliff Edwards had no family, except for his wife and a pack of worthless girl children. That had been part of what made the ranch easy pickings for him. Judd didn't ponder the twin brother's existence for long. It didn't matter where he came from; it only mattered that he was here.

Judd shrugged it off. The last brother had proved to be an easy mark, and he'd had no friends to stand up for him after his death. A twin brother would be cut from the same cloth. Judd planned to make short work of him. He stormed down the street and jumped on his mustang. He spurred the mangy critter into a gallop. The night riders weren't going to get to retire quite as soon as they'd planned.

Royce Badje straightened his string tie with all the dignity of a very big fish in a small, small pond. "Humph!" He strode out of his office and said to his teller, "I'll be out for a few minutes." He lifted his black, flat-brimmed hat off the rack by the front door and, after carefully checking that Mr. Mason wasn't about, he stormed down to Sheriff Everett's office. He found the office empty, and at the diner, he learned the sheriff was transporting a prisoner and would be gone for a day or two.

Royce Badje returned to the bank a very nervous man.

"Eeeiiyy!"

The high-pitched scream made the horse Clay was riding crow-hop to the side and rear up until Clay thought he might go over backward.

Clay hadn't been unseated by a horse since he was 15, except when he was busting broncs. He didn't wait to find out if the horse would throw itself on over. He'd known some to do it.

Clay slipped from the saddle and jumped back from the Appaloosa. The horse snorted and wheeled away from the barn. It charged toward the open field where Clay had just spent the day branding strays.

Just as Clay dropped from his horse, Laura came charging around the corner of the barn stark naked. Clay flinched when he saw the little cyclone fleeing from her mother. Sophie was hot on Laura's heels, and she scooped her up before she could get any farther. Clay whirled around and faced away from the bare-bottomed toddler. He felt his cheeks heat up, and he pulled his hat low over his face for fear he might be blushing.

Sophie had a firm grip on Laura now, and she rested the little firebrand on her hip. "She got away from me, Clay. I'm sorry. Hope you didn't get hurt when you fell off your horse." Sophie turned and went back to the house.

Clay heard her footsteps recede, along with the screaming load of wriggling girl child she was toting. Clay looked up. Four of his men were smirking in his direction.

Clay knew he needed help to run a ranch this size, and he'd needed it quickly. He had put out the word that he was hiring hands, and cowpokes started to straggle in. He hired several of them immediately. Others, who didn't measure up, he told to move along.

One of them, Eustace, a good hand but young, said, "Fell off, did'ja, boss? Them babies can be almighty scary, I reckon."

Clay amended his ideas regarding Eustace. Not just young. Young and stupid.

Two of the men turned their backs and started heading for the bunkhouse. Clay could see their shoulders quivering. It was a wise man who could laugh silently at his boss.

Eustace wasn't wise. He cracked up and started chortling until he had to hang on to the fence to keep from falling over. The other man, an oldster named Whitey, who reminded Clay somewhat of his pa, wasn't having any part of any laughter. He was trying to settle his own horse down. Whitey had ridden up Monday morning hunting work. Clay had liked what he'd seen and hired him on the spot. Whitey had worked tirelessly at Clay's side ever since.

Clay snapped, "Eustace!"

Then Clay told the young pup to pick up his pay and clear out. Eustace was laughing too hard to hear himself getting fired.

Clay planned to do it all over again, but he calmed down before Eustace stopped laughing.

"Naked babies. On a ranch!" Clay shook his head and muttered as he hunted up more work for himself to do so he could stay outside until maybe that house full of women would be asleep. He didn't do much more than round up his horse before Sally came out to lend a hand. So he wasn't going to get to escape them anyway. He was dog tired, saddle sore, and he'd had dirt for his noon meal.

Sally said something about apple pie, and after she said it, he could smell it, even if it was just his imagination. And Sally kept holding his hand with her soft fingers and looking at him with those adoring blue eyes until he wanted to see the other girls' eyes. Especially Sophie's. He gave up and went to the house.

Clay's life was better than it had ever been.

Clay's life was worse than it had ever been.

He couldn't figure out to have the better without taking the worse along with it, 'cuz they were all mixed together. And better and worse came flocking toward him all the time. He felt like he'd fallen through a hole into another world. A girlish one.

He spent the night after his fall with Sally sitting on his lap, talking about her hero of a pa. Cliff. He got a chance to referee when Mandy and Beth quarreled about whose turn it was to do the dishes. He was unfortunately handy when Laura twirled around in a circle for too long and threw up on his boots. He got drafted to hold on to slippery Laura while she was given a bath, and he thought his ears would break from the high-pitched toddler giggles. Those giggles were nothing compared to the steady stream of whining when Sophie told them to go to bed. It was a normal night.

He could have stood all of that, if it hadn't been for the crying.

It terrified him and left him feeling helpless and brutish, even if he had nothing to do with their tears. He'd tried everything he could think of to get them to stop. Yelling was the way he related to his pa if there was ever an upset. That didn't work with the girls. It only made it worse. He'd bought a little cheerfulness one night with a handful of coins, and another night he'd come up with a sack of candy that he'd picked up in town and saved for just this occasion.

Sophie was horrified when she found out about it and put a stop to the bribery.

Too bad. It had worked pretty well.

If he ran, which he did from time to time, they all thought he was going to quit loving them and leave. And there were more tears.

Once Sally had asked him between broken sobs, "Do you want us to go back to the thicket and leave you alone, Pa?"

It would have made him crazy except he also got to eat Sophie's good cooking. And he got hugged by every soft, sweet one of them when they headed off to bed. He liked the smell of Sally's hair after Sophie had washed it. He sat in the cleanest, prettiest house he'd ever lived in, full of shining surfaces and Texas wildflowers picked fresh every day. He wore clean clothes that had nary a button missing nor the littlest tear left unmended. And he was told, "I love you," ten times a day.

His pa had spoken those words to him two or three times in his life, and Clay had said them back as often, or maybe grunted an agreement. Pa loved him, and Clay figured if that ever changed, Pa would have mentioned it. He'd always figured that was enough said. Clay was surprised to know he liked hearing it more often. And he said it back to all of them. If he didn't, they'd get all teary eyed and scared.

He said it back to all of them except Sophie, who also never said it to him. He'd caught himself lately wishing she would say it.

After all, the girls loved him.

What was she waiting for?

Ten

Clay had claimed the brand C Bar for his own, by right of marriage to Cliff's widow. He'd claimed the cattle along with the brand. When he'd bought Cliff's old place, Clay had also used the healthy account in Denver, where Pa had banked gold, to buy up some surrounding property. So he'd expanded his holding considerably.

Clay rounded up over two hundred head of cattle that first week. Most of them were old, branded to the C Bar, the brand registered to Cliff.

Anything younger was branded M Slash M. No one seemed to know what had happened to the Mead brothers, who had registered that brand. Clay knew the code of the West, as it pertained to an abandoned herd: If you caught 'em, you could keep 'em. But Clay was a careful man. He knew local peace officers could be almighty prickly, and Clay didn't want to antagonize Mosqueros's sheriff.

He headed for town Saturday morning to consult with the law. Sheriff Everett was just entering his office, covered with trail dust, and looking like he'd been ridden hard and put up wet.

Clay tipped his hat to the burly man. "You look like you've been over the trail, Josiah. I'll buy you a cup of coffee, if you've got the time."

With a heavy sigh, the sheriff said, "A cup of coffee would go down mighty good right now, McClellen. I've been delivering a bandit to the territorial prison, and I haven't had a good night's sleep in a week. I'd thought to ride out and say howdy one day soon."

The sheriff went inside the jailhouse as he talked and locked his Winchester into a gun rack behind his desk. "Esther has the best coffee in town, because she has the only coffee in town. She starts out in the morning making it black as coal dust, and she keeps it boiling all the day long. We're lucky it's still fairly early. By the end of the day it gets mean enough to fight back when you try an' drink it."

"Just the way I like it." Clay's boots rang hollow, his spurs adding a sharp metallic ring, as the two men walked down the creaking board sidewalks of Mosqueros.

The sheriff pushed the diner's door open, and the smell of burnt coffee nearly took the skin off the inside of Clay's nose.

"Just coffee, Esther." A small puff of dirt rose up around the sheriff as he lowered himself onto a bench.

The dirt had a better scent than the food, to Clay's way of thinking.

Esther brought them both a cup of coffee. "I've got huckleberry pie."

"That sounds—"

"Not today, Esther," the sheriff cut Clay off. "We're in a hurry."

Esther harrumphed at them, as if it were a personal insult, and stalked away from the table.

The sheriff chuckled softly. "You'll be wanting to thank me later for saving you from Esther's huckleberry pie."

"I've never had a bad piece of pie," Clay protested.

"The woman doesn't believe in a heavy hand with the sugar."

"I'll eat a tart pie over none, any day." Clay wrapped his hands around the lightweight tin coffee cup, enjoying the warmth, even though the day was already heating up.

"And whatever berries she's using are none too ripe, undercooked, and I'll be surprised if they're even huckleberries." The sheriff shuddered. "I've yet to see a huckleberry bush out here."

"Still, now she's offended." Clay regretted that.

"I've never been able to figure out how she can leave the berries raw and burn the piecrust at the same time." The sheriff looked up from his coffee with an obviously mystified expression. "It just don't stand to reason. I once broke a tooth on her piecrust."

"It was probably a pit. A pit can get in any pie. These things happen to even the most careful cook. . . ."

"It wasn't a pit. It was a button."

"A button?"

"Off her shoe," the sheriff added darkly. "When I complained, she came and acted as close to happy as Esther ever gets, thanked me, took the button, then sat down. She pulled off an almighty bad-smellin' boot and sat beside me whilst she sewed it back on."

Clay lapsed into silence. He finally said quietly, "I'll just go ahead and thank you now."

The sheriff nodded. "Now, what did you want to see me about?"

"I've been finding strays from the Mead brothers' herd mixed in with Cliff's brand. I wondered if you have any idea how to reach them."

The sheriff took a long drink of coffee, and Clay saw him shudder all the way to his toes. "No one seems to know why they took off. I'm suspicious for a living, and the only thing that makes sense is that something happened to them."

"A lot of ways to get yourself lost in the West," Clay observed.

"I know that. And the Meads weren't neither one of 'em a ball of fire, if ya know what I mean. They weren't the hardest workers, and they weren't the smartest managers I've come across."

Clay thought of the deterioration he saw in the buildings and knew the truth of what the sheriff said.

"Still, they were getting by. Keeping their land payments up, if only by the skin of their teeth."

"You think they ran into outlaws or renegade Indians?" Clay speculated.

"I reckon it's something like that. Truth to tell, I've been assuming they're both dead almost from the first. But no bodies have turned up. They were a two-man outfit, so no cowhands were out there with them to come and report them missing. We only decided they'd taken off when Royce Badje reported their payment didn't come into the bank.

They could've been gone a month before we noticed 'em missing."

"Do they have any family?" Clay sipped at the vile excuse for coffee in front of him. "Those cattle I'm rounding up should go to their heirs."

Sheriff Everett swallowed the last of his coffee and chewed on the dregs thoughtfully before he said, "How many head?"

Clay fished something solid out of his cup and wiped it on his pants. He didn't look close. He didn't want to know what it was. "Forty-five last count. We're not done shagging 'em out of the hills."

Clay watched Sheriff Everett swish his cup around to liquefy the solid black goo separating at the bottom, then take a healthy swig while holding his breath. "They had a sight more'n that. Maybe a couple hundred head. They were so scattered when I went out to look around, I couldn't be sure if any had been stolen or not, but it sounds like they have been."

"To some people one hundred and fifty head of cattle are worth killing for." Clay strained the coffee grounds out with his teeth.

The sheriff nodded. "I talked to the Meads time and again since they bought the place two years ago. Neither of 'em mentioned any family. Just keep track of how many you find."

"I'll fatten 'em up a bit and cut out the older stuff. When I market the herd, I'll be mindful of what should be the Meads'."

Clay watched the sheriff signal to Esther for more coffee.

"I'm impressed, Josiah. I didn't know if you were man enough for another cup."

The sheriff narrowed his eyes at Clay. "Watch it, McClellen, or I'll order you a piece of pie."

Clay started laughing, and he and the sheriff were still chuckling when Esther poured their coffee. Then Sheriff Everett introduced Clay to Esther and proceeded to sweet-talk her out of her mad.

The three of them talked awhile longer, as other citizens of Mosqueros came in and met Clay. With everything settled, Clay invited the sheriff to drop in after church for Sunday dinner. Then he headed home.

"Where is that man?" Sophie muttered as she combed the few snarls out of Laura's white curls.

Sally stood at the window, staring out. Suddenly she whirled around. "He's coming. He's got the wagon hitched up."

"Oh, good. We can all go to church together then." Sophie smiled at her tidy little family.

"Is Parson Roscoe gonna yell at us again?" Beth's eyes got as wide as saucers.

"That's his job, honey." Sophie brushed the wisps of hair off Beth's forehead. "He's trying to point out the error of our ways."

Beth stared at the floor for a long second. "I reckon he can't do a fearful thing like that if he's speaking softly."

Mandy buttoned up the back of Sally's dress. "Still, we get in trouble when we yell too much. Why is it okay for him?"

Sophie didn't have an answer for that, so she was glad Clay chose that moment to come inside. He glanced at them all standing, ready and waiting. Sophie saw him heave a sigh of relief. She couldn't imagine what he was relieved about, unless he thought they wouldn't be ready on time.

"Let's hit the trail."

The girls ran past him for the wagon, in a swirl of calico and braids.

Sally called out, "I get the front seat between Ma and Pa!"

"You don't get to sit up there! We need to take turns, and since I'm the oldest. . ." Mandy's voice faded as the girls raced away.

Sophie heard Clay sigh again, so deeply she thought it stirred a breeze in the room.

"What's the matter?"

"They're fighting again."

Sophie cocked her head a bit to listen to the squabbling that distance had nearly erased. "You call that little spat fighting?"

"What do you call it?" he asked impatiently.

Sophie shrugged. "There isn't room for any of the girls on that seat, and they all know it, so they're just making noise. I didn't pay it any mind." She walked up to him and patted him on the arm. "That's just how little girls are. You'll get used to it soon enough."

Clay nodded silently for a while, then turned to go to the wagon. As he walked out Sophie heard him mutter, "I'll get used to it or go deaf. In the end, I reckon that's the same thing."

Sophie smiled all the way to town.

This Sunday wasn't such a shock for Sophie. She was prepared to be greeted politely, and she wasn't disappointed. She leaned over to Clay as he guided the wagon toward the church. "How did you get all these people to like us so quickly? They've never been anything but awful to me."

"The war is fading from people's minds." Clay pushed his hat back on his head with one gloved thumb and looked at her. "The country is healing. It's time for them to forgive and forget. They'd've been kind, even if I hadn't come, if you'd've given 'em a chance."

"Except for them all trying to marry me, of course."

"Well, that was another lil' thing that got in the way of you living peaceably around here." Clay smiled down at her.

She couldn't quite help smiling back. "I guess marrying you solved that."

Clay pulled back on the reins to halt the horses. "Indeed it did, Sophie darlin'. Indeed it did."

They mingled with the other worshiping citizens of Mosqueros.

Miss Calhoun came up and said a prim, "Good morning."

Sophie smiled and returned the greeting, careful not to forget to call her "Miss Calhoun." She studied the young woman. Miss Calhoun was a first-year teacher, most likely still in her teens, but she carried herself as if she had a steel rod in place of a spine—a steel rod so long it tilted her neck up. Either that or Miss Calhoun kept her nose in the air on purpose.

Sophie put aside her misgivings about the young woman's acutely "proper" behavior. There was kindness in Miss Calhoun's eyes, and Sophie had heard good things about how the school was run.

"I have my appointment book with me today, Mrs. McClellen. I'd like to schedule a time when I can come out and see you."

Sophie, mindful of all her manners, said, "We would love to have you join us for Sunday dinner."

Miss Calhoun industriously consulted the small, black book in her hand. "Today isn't convenient, but next Sunday would work nicely."

Sophie noticed a fine trembling in Miss Calhoun's hand as she poised her pencil over the blank spot in her carefully kept book. It struck Sophie that a lot of Miss Calhoun's fussiness could really be a cover for shyness. It warmed her toward the teacher.

Sophie rested her hand on Miss Calhoun's arm. "Are you from around here, Miss Calhoun?"

Miss Calhoun seemed startled by the question. Sophie noticed a faint tint of pink darken Miss Calhoun's cheeks. She immediately regretted asking such a personal question.

Sophie didn't wait for Miss Calhoun to answer. "Next Sunday will be fine. You can ride out to the ranch with us after church, and we'll see you have an escort back to town. It's no time for a young lady to ride the trails alone."

Miss Calhoun seemed to gather her composure during Sophie's little speech. "That sounds excellent. It's very thoughtful of you to provide me with an escort. Not everyone around here thinks of things like that."

Sophie had a moment to wonder if Miss Calhoun had ever put herself in danger to visit her young charges. She seemed like the type of woman who would do what she saw as her duty, regardless of how difficult that might be.

Sophie wanted to warn Miss Calhoun to be careful, but the parson chose that moment to shoo them inside. They settled in the same pew as last week, alongside Mrs. Roscoe. Only this week Mandy was on Clay's left, Beth was on Sophie's right, Laura was on Sophie's lap, and

Sally insisted on squishing in between them. They were all scared to death.

When the parson stepped up to the pulpit, Beth grasped Sophie's hand until Sophie thought she heard her knuckles creak. Sophie had to be very careful not to smile.

The parson opened his mouth. Sophie saw her big girls lean forward as if bracing themselves against the force of the words. Parson Roscoe spoke so softly, the whole congregation, as one, leaned forward to catch what he said. "An expert in the law said to Jesus. . ."

Beth fell forward off the pew and banged her head on the wooden panel in front of them.

Sophie reached and pulled her back up.

Beth rubbed her head. "He snuck that soft voice in when I was ready for him to go to yellin'."

Without a pause, the parson went on preaching in a near whisper. "Which is the greatest commandment? Jesus replied: 'Love the Lord thy God with all thy heart, and with all thy soul, and with all thy mind, and with all thy strength: this is the first commandment. And the second is like, namely this, Thou shalt love thy neighbour as thyself. There is none other commandment greater than these.' "

The parson solemnly closed the big, black Bible in front of him and lifted it up into the air. "This whole book of God's Word is full of the call to love. And the darkest parts of the Bible deal with the failure of people to love. You don't need anything else, brothers and sisters. You don't need a parson preaching fire and brimstone at you. You don't need a parson at all, or this church, or. . ." The parson's voice dropped to a rasping whisper, "Or forgiveness."

After another extended silence, broken only by the sound of the breathing of his mesmerized followers, he said, "If only we would love God and love each other completely."

The parson spoke a bit louder, but Sophie noticed Beth's hand was no longer gripping hers, and all the children were listening closely to the words.

Sophie thought of how violently she had hated the men who had come for Cliff and chased after Clay. She was guilty. She needed God's forgiveness. Even as she listened and prayed, she could feel the rebellion in her heart. The anger wouldn't go away easily. She knew it was Satan battling for control of her life. She turned from the anger with all the meager strength a human can muster and begged for forgiveness. Begged for an end to her need for vengeance. Begged, *Help me, help me, help me.*

She left the church feeling more at peace than she had in years. They milled around for a bit outside, saying good-bye to the other church members. Sophie barely registered that all her girls but the baby had run off to play with a group of very noisy little boys Sophie had never seen before.

Clay stood at her side, holding Laura, and introduced her to Daniel Reeves. "Daniel just bought the mountain valley to the north of us, Sophie. He's got himself a houseful of boys to match our girls."

"Hello, Mr. Reeves," Sophie said.

Daniel reached out with more enthusiasm than Sophie was prepared for. Hesitantly she offered her own hand, and Daniel's huge mitt swallowed her hand whole. He pumped her arm up and down.

"It's Daniel, ma'am." He almost shouted his greeting. "Don't 'spect I'll be thinkin' to answer to any other name. I'm one up on y'all, ma'am. Got me five strappin' boys, I do. Every one of 'em a chip off the old block!"

Sophie had to control a desire to recoil from the man's loud voice as she tried to remember her manners. "Is your wife here, Mr. Reeves?"

"Daniel. Daniel it is, ma'am. Nope, no wife. Died birthin' the last of my boys, she did. Five sons in five years."

Sophie didn't want to imagine what the poor woman had gone through bearing that many children so fast. Everyone in the West knew childbirth was dangerous, and most men were thoughtful enough to spare their wives.

Daniel mentioned his wife's death with such negligence that Sophie felt a surge of anger. Then, annoyed, she looked closer at the callous brute and saw a shadow settle in his eyes.

"Sad when it happened. Almighty sad. The kind of thing that makes a man believe in God or wash his hands of Him altogether. Well, I'm here, so I guess that tells the story."

Sophie watched Daniel Reeves slap Clay on the back and turn to shout a greeting at someone else.

She said faintly to Clay, "Do we have to have a baby every year until we have a boy?"

Clay's laughter pulled Sophie out of her strange mixture of sympathy and annoyance with Daniel Reeves.

"Daniel's story isn't as bad as it sounds."

Sophie said emphatically, "I suppose that's true since *nothing* could be as bad as that sounds."

"He had one set of twins, and then five years later the poor woman gave birth to a set of triplets."

Sophie gasped. "You're right. It's not as bad as it sounds; it's worse!"

Clay grinned. "You can't blame the twins and triplets on Daniel though."

"Triplets! I've heard of such a thing, but I've never known any."

"Well, take notice when they come by. They're as alike as two peas—or I guess I should say three peas—in a pod. They're five now, and the older boys are ten. They look like older versions of the triplets. They're all full of mischief, from what I've seen."

Sophie stared across the expanse of stubbly weeds that grew around the church. She watched a crowd of children, her own included, run and scream and laugh. There was no problem picking out the Reeves boys. They all had shocks of snow white hair that hung shaggy, well past their shirt collars. Then, after the startling resemblance, was the fact that they were the loudest, the most reckless, and by far the dirtiest and most ragged children in the group.

Clay laughed again. "I bet they'll keep Miss Calhoun's hands full if he sends them to school."

Sophie only shook her head. "Thankfully, I'm not their teacher."

As Sophie had that unkind thought, she remembered the sermon and immediately felt guilty. She wasn't going to think unloving thoughts. She was a new woman. From now on she was going to let all the happiness of her heart flow over everyone.

"Clay McClellen, I can't believe you invited that man over to our home for Sunday dinner!"

Sophie was looking at him like she was a wolf ready to fight the pack for fresh meat.

Clay froze, just in the house from waving Josiah off. He purely hated being scolded. It wasn't like when a man started taking after him. He'd just slug the guy till he shut up, and that would solve everything.

Clay didn't know much about women, but his gut told him that wouldn't work worth spit with Sophie. Sophie was a soft little thing, and he liked holding her close at night, so he didn't want her mad.

But mad she was, and he took it to heart, especially when the three older girls, Beth carrying Laura, gave their ma a fearful look and dashed into their bedroom.

"What's the matter with the sheriff? He's a good man."

"Good man?" She turned back to her dishes. Clay hoped the plates survived her temper. He hoped he did.

"He's a low-down scoundrel! He accused Cliff of being a horse thief, refused to chase after the posse that hung him, and asked me to marry him, all in the same breath!"

A woman could sure get upset over the least little thing.

"Now, darlin', don't get all fussed about that."

"Fussed! About a man calling Cliff a horse thief," Sophie stormed. "I will never stand by and listen to talk like that!"

Clay carefully reached for his hat, hoping Sophie wouldn't notice he was planning to run for it. She was fuming at him with her back mostly turned, only peering over her shoulder once in a while to scorch him with a furious look.

Clay tried to placate her. "After all, the man had a job to do, Sophie darlin', and what man wouldn't want you to marry him?" There, a little flattery. Wasn't that what women wanted?

In case it wasn't, because more often than not he guessed wrong, he slid the hat off the peg and hid it a mite behind his back. He got a firm grip on the doorknob. "And he's been right nice about the herd. He told me I could round the cattle up and sell them. And if the Meads show up, I have to turn the money over, but I can take out cash to pay for feed and time and the like."

He inched the door open, lifting, mindful of the squeaky hinges if he didn't. "And since the Meads seemed to have quit the country, it figures the animals are mine until someone tells me different."

Sophie whirled around, but Clay was too fast for her. He swung the door shut and was all the way across the yard at a fast walk—only a coward would actually run from a woman—before he heard the cabin door open. He ducked around the corner of the barn.

He caught up a horse and rode out to check a few more cattle, careful to keep the barn between him and the cabin until he'd covered a lot of ground.

Sophie went back to wiping the dishes with a fine fury riding her, when suddenly she remembered the parson's words. She almost dropped the plate. "Oh, Lord, help me."

"What's the matter, Ma?" Beth came in from outside and settled in the rocking chair to soothe Laura into a nap.

"I made a promise to myself this morning. And I've already broken it." Sophie frowned down at the churned-up dishwater.

"Ma, you've told us never to break a promise. And you promised you'd never break one," Sally said fearfully from the doorway.

Sophie was almost sorry she'd spoken out loud. But she was also determined to be honest. "My promise was to try and be loving to everyone, just like the parson said. I don't think I was very nice to the sheriff, and I'm sure I wasn't nice to Pa."

"I couldn't tell you were mean to Sheriff Everett." Mandy brought up the rear. The most practical of the bunch, the girl usually let time pass when tempers flared. "I didn't even think of such a thing until you started hollering at Pa."

"In my heart, I wasn't a bit nice to the sheriff. And I'm pretty sure God counts what's in your heart just as much as how you act."

"That don't seem fair." Sally took the washcloth from Sophie's idle hand and wiped the cleared but still messy table off. "You oughta get some credit for controlling yourself."

Sophie fervently hoped she did.

Beth, half asleep herself from the rocking with Laura, murmured, "Well, I reckon that's what Jesus died for. So you could be forgiven for things like this."

Sophie looked at her very wise daughter and thought of what Jesus had said about having a childlike faith. She immediately felt better. "You're right, Beth. I need to ask God to forgive me, and then I'm going to tell Clay I'm sorry and I'm going to start over. Even if I have to start over ten times a day, for the rest of my life, I'm going to keep at it. If Jesus died for us, we'd better be smart enough to accept the sacrifice He made."

Sally went to the window. Absently she said, "Might as well."

Sophie imagined she was looking for Clay to tag along after him. Sally loved him so much. All the girls did. And he'd done so much for them in the brief time since he'd come hunting Cliff. Sophie definitely didn't want Clay to be upset with her.

Mandy took the towel out of Sophie's idle hands. "I'll finish the dishes. You'd best get on with it."

Sophie smiled at her girls and left the room. She knelt humbly by her bed and prayed for a new attitude toward life. A new ability to love. She began, "Oh, dear Lord, help me. . . ."

Luther groaned and tossed out the last swallows of his coffee. His muscles ached, and his backside was saddle sore, and he hadn't had a good night's sleep since that woman had started hounding him.

Buff didn't say a word. He got up and started saddling the horses. He didn't need to ask; he knew what was eating Luther.

"The boy has got himself tied up with a naggin' woman."

"Is there any other kind?" Buff asked.

Luther shrugged. "Don't rightly know nothin' about the strange little critters."

They made tracks down the trail for Texas.

Adam pulled at the last of the disgusting, unripened juniper berries as quickly as he could and swallowed them. He'd gotten through the day without opening up his bullet wound. If he could drink a lot of water, maybe get lucky with a rabbit snare or find a creek with some fish, and get a good night's sleep, then he could regain enough strength to start pushing hard for Mosqueros tomorrow. But all of that was driven out of his mind the instant he heard her. His Sophie. Calling to God for help, and God giving the great honor of sending that message on to Adam.

Adam knelt by the spring that gushed out around the roots of the evergreen shrub and drank his fill. Then he got to his feet, careful not to put any stress on the skin around his wound. He started toward Sophie. He didn't need a good meal and a long sleep. He only had to find the strength for each step. God would have to provide that.

Eleven

I love owning a ranch." Clay leaned forward to rest his forearms on the saddle horn.

Whitey sat his horse alongside Clay's as they watched the newest batch of a dozen mavericks gambol down the hill to join the herd. "I've been with enough operations to know which ones are well run. You've picked up most of the ways of ranching along the trail, and it's already starting to show."

Clay sighed with pure contentment. Having Whitey's respect meant a lot to him. There was nothing about cattle and ranch land the old codger didn't know. "I've been wondering though, this ranch—there's a kind of weird quality to it. Maybe it's just the Mead brothers' working over what my brother did and nothing matches, but it seems like more than that."

"I know what you mean." Whitey studied the ranch laid out below them. "This ranch was selected by a knowin' man. This has to be one of the few really good stretches of lush grazing on this plateau. Your brother really had an eye for land when he picked it."

Clay pointed to the house, barn, and corral so far below. "And they're laid out so the northern winter wind is blocked but the summer breeze comes through. And the buildings are well built, sturdy, and nice to the eye. And the springs have been dammed in exactly the best spots and spread out to water more acres. Still, there's something. . ."

Clay's respect for his brother grew daily. But under that respect was a tinge of jealousy. All the girls spoke of their father as if he was the nicest, strongest, smartest man who ever lived. It was demonstrated to him almost daily that he would never take his brother's place. That might be why he noticed every little flaw he found around the place.

"I don't think it's the Meads who did the shoddy patchwork or who added the lean-to on the barn," Whitey said as he stared down at the ranch yard. "They only came here two years ago, and the poor work looks older than that. And I see a different hand in some of the newer repairs."

Clay had had the same thought himself. "Did someone live here between Cliff and the Meads?"

Whitey shrugged. "I'm new around these parts. I didn't even know the Mead brothers."

"It doesn't matter." Clay smiled. "It's just that it's mine, and I want to know everything about it. I'll need to fix the place up."

Whitey grunted his agreement. "First things first, though. Gotta get those cattle rounded up and branded."

Clay sat a few minutes longer and stared at his home. He saw Sally dash out of the house so far below and run to the barn. Clay couldn't hold back a smile. Yes, he loved everything about owning a ranch.

By the end of two weeks of ranching, he had some steady cowpokes on the place. He knew these men. He didn't know them personally, but he knew their type. They were men of few words. Men who worked from sunrise to sundown. Men who knew the job and didn't need to be given orders but who knew how to take orders.

He'd grown up around men just like this, and he felt comfortable with them. He had to fight the inclination to stay out on the range with the men till all hours, so he wouldn't have to go into the house and get giggled at, or worse yet *cried on*.

Then he'd get lonely for his girls and the sweet kisses he'd sometimes steal from Sophie, and he'd find himself practically running for the house. He loved his nieces—daughters, he corrected himself. He'd sort of expected to do that. But he hadn't expected Sophie.

A quiet woman most of the time, she worked hard, was a stern disciplinarian with the girls, but quick with a laugh and ready with a comforting word. She was always turning her hand to something he would have thought was man's work.

He shook his head. "Time to quit thinking and start working."

He and Whitey rode out to hunt strays. He stayed out until the sun was setting.

As he unsaddled his horse, he looked between the uncomplicated friendship of the men in the bunkhouse and the "nuthouse" he couldn't resist. He couldn't decide where to go. While he considered what kind of coward that made him, Clay loitered around the corral, trying to work up the gumption to go into the house. Pounding came from the back of the barn, and he walked around to see what was going on.

Sophie knelt, holding a sagging board in place on the shabby little lean-to tacked on to the otherwise tightly constructed barn. Clay intended to tear the little room off and start from scratch. Now here Sophie was patching it, and it sparked his temper. She treated him like he didn't take care of her.

"What are you doing?"

Sophie jumped at his harsh tone and whacked her thumb. "Ow!" She grabbed her finger and looked at it for a minute, then stuffed the tip into her mouth and glared at him.

Clay forgot his temper and chuckled at the sight.

"There is nothing funny about me smashing myself with a hammer!" she growled around her thumb.

"You look like Laura sucking her thumb. It's cute." Clay smiled at his wife. Her hair was bedraggled. She had on her stained work dress. She was wearing boots five sizes too big for her, and she was wildly irritated. He thought about how pretty she was and wondered if he could tease a kiss out of her.

"Cute?" Sophie withdrew her thumb, scowled, and bent over to go back to work on the board.

Clay remembered why he'd hollered at her to begin with. His

amusement faded. "I'll do that. You wouldn't have hurt your thumb if you'd been doing the work God intends for a woman to do. Get back in the house!"

He strode over to where she crouched beside the board and jerked it out of her hands. At the same time he noticed that she was half finished, and the job was well done. It reminded him of. . .

Sophie yanked the board back. Distracted, he lost his balance and fell over on top of her. They tumbled to the ground.

A bullet ripped a hole in the barn just over their heads.

Clay grabbed Sophie, kicked the new boards—and a couple of old ones—out of the lean-to, and literally threw her through the hole. Gunfire exploded all around them, and Clay rolled well into the barn. Keeping low, he dragged Sophie toward a stall. Splinters of wood shredded the barn under the hail of bullets.

Sophie got her feet under her.

"Stay down," Clay roared.

Sophie cried out and fell flat on her back. Clay looked at her, and from the way she was squirming around to get behind the stall, he figured she was all right. The pounding gunfire eased up. Return fire erupted from the bunkhouse. That turned his attention from surviving to finding out what was going on. He edged himself around the corner of the stall and scrambled to the back wall of the barn.

He heard the barn door slam and turned to face an assault. All he saw was Sophie gone. Outside! Maybe right into the teeth of more rifles! Running scared, the fool woman. She should have trusted him to do repairs around the ranch, and she should have trusted him to protect her.

The girls trusted her to protect them.

They might come outside when they heard the commotion. They knew right where Sophie was working, and they might come running straight for her. But no, her girls wouldn't come. They'd know just what to do. Just as they'd know she'd come.

She dashed for the house, grateful that the barn was in a direct line between where she was heading and where the bullets were flying. She did the little quickstep that avoided the traps on the porch and slammed her way into the house. Mandy tossed her a loaded rifle. Then Mandy pulled the shotgun off the rack and commenced loading it.

"Where are the others?" Sophie dropped to her belly, double-checked the load, and skittered along on her elbows to the front window. Mandy didn't need to answer. Sophie knew where they were. Her girls were Texans after all.

Still, Mandy responded, "The crawl space under the house. Beth and I went down with 'em right off. I watched from the crack under the porch, and when I saw you coming, I came up and started loading."

"Good girl. Did you pull out the support boards on both sides?"

"Yep." Mandy crawled close and laid another rifle next to Sophie. "First thing after the little 'uns were safe. The front and back porches will collapse if anyone tries to step on 'em. I haven't closed the front window shutters yet."

Sophie listened and heard that the gunfire was still focused on the barn. She hoped Clay was all right. Cautiously, she inched up to the glass windows and pulled the heavy, wooden shutters closed.

"I got the ones in the back and on the sides. There was no gunfire from that direction." Mandy jacked a shell into the shotgun and then loaded the second barrel. Matter-of-factly she added, "I knew you wouldn't want me going close to the front. Although the gunfire seems to be aimed at the far side'a the barn."

Sophie took the shotgun when Mandy was finished with it and added it to their arsenal. She looked out the narrow slit in the shutters, just wide enough for a gun barrel, ready now to pinpoint the exact location of the assault. She heard shots from the little grove of trees that the boar had come charging out of and studied the situation in her mind. She was listening to at least five different guns booming from up there. She heard return fire from the barn, which meant Clay was faring well, and there was plenty of noise from the bunkhouse.

Sophie waited with bated breath, never taking her eyes off the landscape. She glanced over her shoulder and saw Mandy looking out the gun portal of one side window. Then Mandy crossed the room in a crouching run and looked out the other side.

As Mandy lowered herself to the floor, she looked sideways at Sophie, and a furrow appeared on her very young brow. "You're bleeding, Ma."

Sophie saw that the left sleeve of her dress was soaked in blood. She reached for the little hole that marked the highest point of the bleeding—about halfway between her elbow and her shoulder—and tore the hole a bit wider. She studied it for a long second. "It's just a scratch. He must have clipped me in the barn. Humph. This dress had another year left in it. Now it's ruined."

She went ahead and tore the sleeve all the way off and fashioned a bandage around her freely bleeding arm. Mandy came over and helped her tie it tight, then went back to checking both windows.

Beth popped her head up through the trap door Mandy had covered with a rug. "Need any help, Ma? Sally's got Laura safe. I could go out through the tunnel to the cave and scout around."

Sophie knew Elizabeth could move as quick and quiet as an Indian, when she chose. It made Sophie's stomach lurch to think of Beth out in those dangerous woods, but if it had come to life and death, Sophie would have sent her.

Help me, Lord. Help me, help me, help me.

The gunfire from the grove fell silent. Sporadic shooting continued a few more minutes from the bunkhouse and barn, then quit. Beth wouldn't have to go. *Thank You, Lord.*

"It seems to be over," Sophie said. "Replace those braces in the porch so we don't catch one of our own menfolk in our trap."

Beth grinned and ducked out of sight. Her head reappeared a second later. "Your arm's bleedin', Ma. Are you okay?"

Sophie waved the concern away. "Just nicked me. I didn't even notice it till I had things secure in here."

"Good. I'll have a look at it later." Beth vanished back into the floor, and the rug dropped neatly in place.

Sophie heard the sound of running horses from a distance and knew that whoever was shooting at them was riding off. Men came pouring out of the bunkhouse and fired a few shots at the retreating gunmen, but the riders never showed themselves, leaving the grove and riding into the heavy woods.

Clay came charging out of the barn. "Whitey, get some men and make sure they keep moving! Don't try and run 'em down, though. They're pure coyote to shoot from cover thatta way, and they might do it again. Just lag back, and see what you can learn from readin' their tracks."

Sophie opened the front door. She heard the posts that supported the crosscut boards in the front porch being wedged back into place and noticed that Whitey, as well as the rest of the cowhands, had headed for the corral before Clay had begun giving orders.

Clay looked at the house furiously, and his eyes zeroed in on her arm. Sophie sighed. She knew what was coming. It was going to be just like repairing the barn. Apparently staying alive wasn't woman's work either.

Judd sat his horse and worked the action of his carbine. The sound eased his fury a bit.

So they'd missed today. There was always tomorrow. He'd ridden up to scout the McClellen place, thinkin' to go charging in and drop a necktie on McClellen, like he had Edwards. This time Judd would step right in and buy the land.

He'd have to deal with Clay's wife, too. Judd hadn't thought of it at first, but now he remembered that Sophie Edwards had seen the men that took her first husband. Judd had worried about it at the time, because she'd raised such a ruckus. But then he heard she'd quit the country, and he'd forgotten all about her. There were others who had seen him, in the early days of his night riding, before he'd gotten smart and started seeing to it that there weren't any witnesses.

It didn't sit well with him to kill a beautiful woman, but Judd knew it had to be done. McClellen first, then the woman. It needed to look like an accident when he did her in. Or maybe he could stage something that looked like an Indian attack. There hadn't been any in these parts for a while, but there could always be just one more.

One way or another, Sophie Edwards McClellen had to die.

He'd come today thinking to take care of McClellen. He'd figured the hands wouldn't be much trouble. They'd all be drifters who wouldn't measure up any better than Cliff Edwards had. Since Edwards had been a weakling, it followed that his twin brother was one, too. And the next step in reasoning told him a man wouldn't want cowpokes around him that showed him up. But McClellen had hired himself a salty bunch. And plenty of 'em, all armed.

Studying the layout, Judd had seen a chance to take McClellen out from cover.

With a quirk of humor, Judd thought of the look on Harley's face when he'd been ordered to back-shoot McClellen. Harley hadn't like it one bit. Judd had enjoyed making his saddle partner do as he was told.

And then that no-account Harley had missed! McClellen must be a lucky one to have stumbled forward at the exact moment Harley had fired. The missed shot gave McClellen the warning he needed. He'd taken cover until Judd had called off the attack.

Judd rode off in a fine fury, but his calculating mind told him anything he wanted this bad wouldn't come easy. He'd regroup and pick his time more carefully.

He pulled Harley aside as they strung out over the rugged trail that led over the bluff behind the McClellen ranch. "Harley, I need someone watching this place."

"I'll do it." Harley studied his back trail.

"No, I need you with me. Pick whoever's best at ghostin' around. I want to know McClellen's routine. I want to catch him when he doesn't have his guard dogs so close to hand."

Harley nodded. "Percy is the best, and Jesse's good. There are a couple of others who'll do."

"Get 'em started," Judd ordered.

The two of them moved out. Judd couldn't remember the last time they'd had to hightail it. It was a bad omen. Harley fell in behind him, and they picked up the pace to leave the C BAR far behind.

"Sophie," Clay growled as he strode toward her. "You are the most ridiculous. . ."

Her husband was a man of few words. This wouldn't last long. But he surprised her. He kept up his lecturing the whole time he bandaged her arm.

Beth edged up next to him. "Let me do it, Pa. I've done a sight of doctorin' alongside Ma."

"I'll do it," Clay grumped at the little girl.

Beth's eyes got round and filled with tears.

Clay hunched his shoulders like he was taking a beating. "Now don't start in crying. I have some experience with this from the war, and I want to see to it."

The tears spilled onto Beth's face. "I'm sorry, Pa."

Clay sighed deeply, but Sophie noticed he didn't run, which was his usual approach to the girls' tears. He turned back to the wound on Sophie's arm and started fooling with it. Sophie wished for Beth's gentle touch, but she didn't tell him that.

"Get some rags and tear them up for a bandage, Beth honey," Sophie said quietly, wanting to include her daughter.

Clay was still fuming over the wound and scolding her to beat all.

Sophie interrupted his tirade as soon as Beth was out of earshot.

"So who wants you dead, Clay McClellen?"

Clay stopped fumbling. They stared at each other for a long moment. Sophie found herself caught in the worry she saw in his eyes. Kind eyes. True, he was being as grouchy as a grizzly bear with a sore tooth, but she could see it was because he cared about her. Something warm inside of Sophie heated up past warm, and she rested her hand on his where he touched her arm.

With a swift glance at the girls, he whispered, "I don't think he was after me, Sophie. It would take them awhile to get set up in that grove. Why did they pick that spot? It's mostly blocked off from the rest of the yard by the barn. I think they were after you."

Clay's hand came up and caressed her cheek. Suddenly he looked dismayed. "I'm sorry." He pulled his hand away and looked around for the wet cloth Beth had brought when she was preparing to clean the wound.

"Sorry about what?" Sophie asked, not wanting him to look away.

"I got blood on your face." He touched her cheek with the cool cloth, so gently that Sophie forgot the sting in her arm and the bullets that might have caught one of her girls.

"I'm so sorry, Sophie. I should have been more watchful. They should never have gotten so close to the place." Clay looked from her cheek where he caressed her with the cloth to her eyes. His eyes flickered to her lips and then to her arm, and he seemed to gather himself. Suddenly brisk, he washed her face, then went back to his ham-handed doctoring. Sophie didn't mind his rough skill anymore.

"Who do you. . ." Sophie's voice was husky—not her normal voice at all. It seemed to sharpen Clay's attention on her. She cleared her throat. "Who do you think it was?"

"I don't know." Clay tied off the rough bandage. "But it appears someone. . ."

"I counted five different guns."

"There were at least five of them. And it appears they want one, or both of us, dead."

Clay and Sophie exchanged long, solemn looks. Their silence was broken by the giggling and chattering of the girls in the background.

"Well." Sophie's jaw tightened. "I'd say that *someone* is going to be disappointed."

Clay nodded in firm agreement.

Sophie hoped he'd say something complimentary right then. Something along the lines of, "It takes quite a woman to pick out five different gunmen in all that excitement." Or maybe, "I'm right proud of you for running in to protect the girls and having the house all closed up and safe." Or maybe even, "That was quite a carpentry job you did on the barn, before I kicked it in."

As usual, he failed her.

"What kind of blamed fool notion got into your head, to go running out of the barn while there were bullets flying. There I had you all tucked away safe, and instead of staying put, like anyone would who had half a brain, you had to go haring off. . ."

It went on the rest of the day. He even woke up a few times in the night. At first he'd hold her tight and close and long and touch her as if he were desperate to make sure she was alive and well.

Then he'd start in on his scolding again.

Adam chafed at the slow pace. He had no money, and no one would be inclined to trust a black man enough to loan him a horse, so he didn't ask.

The world was full of food to anyone who would just open his eyes. He unraveled enough thread from his tattered shirt to rig a snare. He caught grouse or rabbit most nights. He fished. There wasn't much growing yet in the early spring, but he found a few wild strawberries and a steady supply of greens.

He wouldn't have minded living like this forever, if it hadn't been for the voice. He refused to think about his murdered friends. He was afraid the hate would overcome his need to get to Sophie. He kept his mind always on her.

His back still hurt like fire. The gunshot dragged on his strength, but he didn't let up on himself. One night, he made himself a soft bed of pine needles under a loblolly and had the best night's sleep he'd had since he'd been heading for Sophie.

He awoke with a jerk. He froze, trying to think what had disturbed him. Maybe he'd heard Sophie again. He stared straight up, and looking through the limbs brought memories. Branches. Nooses. Swinging bodies. His friends had been lynched. Adam had been presumed among the dead, and he'd walked away. Guilt wracked him. He should have gone after the killers! He should have hunted them and killed every man jack of them!

Adam swallowed the hatred and remembered why he'd walked away. Sophie. He reached for his side and felt the tender bullet hole. He swore that when he had done whatever Sophie needed doing, he'd find those men and make them pay.

He lay flat on his back and stared up at the sky through the pine boughs. He had to get to her. He didn't know why, and he didn't care. He wasn't a superstitious man, and he wasn't given to notions. Sophie needed help. God had placed it in his heart.

He hoisted himself to his hands and knees and started to crawl out from under branches that sagged so low to the ground he had to lift them to get past. Just as he reached for one, he heard in the distance the sound that had awakened him. Hoofbeats.

He held himself as still as a wild hare and listened to silent men, riding fast in the direction he was headed. He slowly, carefully, moved his head, aware that any motion on his part could attract their attention. He saw stirruped feet, he heard creaking saddle leather, but faces were blocked from his line of sight. He didn't see anything that he could recognize. Then the last few riders went by.

One of them wore Dinky's boots.

They were ridiculous black boots, overloaded with glittering silver trim. Dinky had them special made with money from his first cattle sale. He'd laughed and talked about how he hadn't owned a single pair of shoes until he'd joined up with the Union army. He'd picked cotton and tended horses barefoot until he was twenty-five years old. The man who owned him thought shoes were above the station of a slave.

Dinky loved those boots. Adam had scoffed at him and told him his boots would spook the herd, but Dinky, always happy, always finding joy in life, only took those boots off when he slept. Adam looked closely at the last few riders. He saw William's rifle. It was a .50 caliber Sharps. William, handy with a knife, had carved scroll work in the wooden butt.

He saw a rawhide rope that had old Moses's fine braiding about it, and a single pearl-handled pistol that also belonged to the elderly man, who had been the steady one of the foursome.

Then Adam saw his own blanket rolled up behind another saddle. It could have been another blanket, nothing special about it. But the bloodstains settled it in Adam's mind. Couldn't this lynching party even count? They'd stolen the outfits from four men, but they'd only hanged three.

Adam's fury built until it was all he could do to stop himself from leaping from cover and begin killing. He'd grab the last one, take his rifle, and empty it into the lot of them, grabbing another rifle from a fallen man when his was empty.

But he held himself frozen. He'd die with a plan like that. But it would feel good every last second of his life.

Then he thought of dying that way, in a killing rage, and finally that gave him the strength to hold his hiding place. God had blinded their eyes to the obvious. Maybe he'd survived for some reason of God's. Maybe he'd done something right to earn him a few more years here on this earth. More likely, he was alive because Sophie needed him.

Adam let the men go. What other choice did he have? But he counted twenty of them, and he risked his life to see a few faces. Then he noticed the brand. . . .

J BAR M.

TWELVE

Luther rode steadily into the night, with Buff galloping relentlessly by his side. They could make Texas before they slept, if they kept up their pace. But the closer Texas got, the bigger it loomed.

A distant pinpoint of light had them both pulling up.

"Coffee'd taste almighty good 'bout now, Buff. Whataya say?"

Buff grunted, and they headed slowly for the light. The fire was miles away. They knew from reading signs, they were riding into the camp of a herd being pushed up the trail rather than into a bunch of outlaws.

They weren't afraid of being shot by no-accounts now. They were afraid of being shot by law-abiding men.

Before they got within shooting range, Luther hollered out, "Hello, the camp!"

A voice out of the darkness called, "Ride in easy."

They heard the clicks of a dozen rifles being cocked.

Buff and Luther knew how to approach a cow camp, and the drovers knew how to hold their fire until it was needed. Within minutes, the two were settled in with coffee, biscuits, and beans. The fire crackled, and the scent of boiled coffee and mesquite wood soothed Luther's edgy nerves. He hoped it was working on everyone here. The *clink* of the coffeepot on the tin cups melded with the soft lowing of a cow out on the range and made Luther feel right at home.

Every cowhand in the group had left his bedroll and joined the newcomers at the fire. A cowboy was always hungry for news and a different voice than the few he heard all day every day for weeks and months on end. And cowboys were a friendly lot. But Luther knew, the cowpokes came to the fire mostly to help with the shooting if there was trouble.

"Huntin' work?" the trail boss asked. "We can always use a few more men."

"Headin' to Texas," Buff replied.

"Looking for a friend of ours," Luther added. "Anyone know of a young feller by the name of Clay McClellen?"

One of the drovers said, "I served with a Clay McClellen during the war. We were with Grant up to Shiloh. Then I got stuck in the siege of Vicksburg and lost track of the major. I remember he was always huntin' news of his brother."

"Cliff," Buff said.

Luther nodded. "His twin brother. He hadn't seen him since they were kids."

"That's right," the young cowboy said. "There was talk of some soldier in the East that looked just like Major McClellen. He was tryin' to track him down."

"My last job was scouting for the Texas Rangers. I heard of a Clay McClellen workin' with the Rangers over some trouble with vigilantes in west Texas," an old-timer said. "There's been real bad doin's along the Pecos. Lotta men hung. Good men along with the bad. Heard McClellen hired on to help out."

"Why would Clay quit searchin' for his brother to take a job with the law?" Luther knew Clay wasn't the type of man to get sidetracked. So if the trail boss had it right, and there weren't two Clay McClellens, working for the Rangers must have something to do with Cliff.

"Maybe he just needed to make some money along the trail," one cowboy said reasonably.

Luther exchanged a quick glance with Buff. Clay didn't need money, not with all the gold his pa had left him.

"Whereabouts in west Texas?" Luther asked.

The old-timer said, "Vigilante trouble is all over the panhandle and up north almost to Indian territory. The place I heard the name Clay McClellen mentioned was in connection with a little cow town name of Mosqueros."

Luther drank the last of his boiling hot, inkblack coffee in a single swallow and wiped his hand across his mouth. "Mosqueros," he said with some satisfaction. He stood up and headed for his horse.

"You oughta stay in camp for the night," one man offered. "You'd be safer in a crowd, and it's already mighty late."

Luther changed his saddle from one of his horses to another they'd picked up along the trail, while Buff did the same. *We might as well ride,* Luther thought. *We're getting too close to bother with sleep.*

"Whereabouts is Mosqueros?" Luther wasn't a man who had traveled much in his life. He'd come from the East, like everyone else who was in the West, except the Indians. But he'd headed straight up into the peaks of the Rockies like he was kin to the mountain goats. And he'd stayed.

Still, he was a man who'd sat at a lot of campfires, and like all Western men, he listened to talk of the world away from his mountain home. He tucked away information about trails he never figured to trek and rivers he had no notion of ever crossing. He knew a sight about Texas, even though he'd never laid a foot in it.

"If you're pushing hard," the trail boss said, "you can be there in four or five days. This herd is out of Lubbock, three days' ride straight south of here. Mosqueros is another day south."

Luther said, "We'll find it."

"Obliged," Buff called over his shoulder.

"Five days," Luther muttered to himself.

"You got something powerful ridin' you, Luther."

As powerful as the voice of God. "Let's make it in three," Luther said as he kicked his horse into a ground-eating lope.

Clay was on razor's edge, trying to track down the men who had taken a shot at him and Sophie. All the men were working double time, scouting the hills and standing the night watch. Clay had taken the shift before dawn, so he was tired. As he settled into his chair after the noon meal, he sighed with contentment. Good food. Clean house. Pretty wife. Sweet daughters. He was a lucky man.

"Sally, you give me back my underclothes," Beth screamed.

Sally came running out of her bedroom, with Elizabeth hot on her heels. Beth dove at Sally. Sally dodged out of her reach and darted behind Clay.

"They're prettier than mine," Sally shrieked. "They've got lace on the tummy and mine don't. It's not fair!"

Beth circled Clay's chair.

A bloodcurdling scream behind his back made Clay jump out of his chair and whirl around just as Beth caught Sally and began pulling up her skirt to take the underclothes back by force. Sally slapped at her sister. Both girls were emitting such high-pitched squeals, Clay thought his ears would bleed. He wanted to shout at them, but he knew they'd cry. He wanted to run out to the bunkhouse, but he knew they'd cry.

Suddenly, something snapped inside him. All his tightly held self-control around the soft-hearted, little monsters blew away in a blaze of anger. "I—want—quiet!"

Sally and Elizabeth froze. Their eyes widened.

"Quiet! Quiet! Quiet!" Out of the corner of his eye, Clay saw Mandy stiffen with fear. Laura, in Mandy's arms, shoved her fingers in her mouth as if to make herself be quiet. Sophie looked from Clay to the girls fearfully, as if he might start shooting any minute.

It was all too much. He looked back at Sally and Beth. Their eyes were already filling with tears. He stomped his foot in the perfect picture of a man putting his foot down. "You stop that crying right now," he stormed. "There are going to be some changes around here."

"Pa," Sally quavered, "don't you. . ."

"Don't you dare ask me if I love you," Clay roared. "I don't go lovin' and stopping lovin' any time I feel like it. All this means is, I can get purely perturbed with someone I love, and you all might as well know that now!"

A tear spilled down Beth's cheek. She nodded as if she were frightened not to agree with him. That just made him madder.

"Stop that cryin', both of you. I'm not putting up with any more of this screaming and fighting."

"But, Pa," Beth said, "we weren't. . ."

He jabbed his finger at her. "Don't interrupt me, young lady."

Beth clamped her mouth shut and shook her head solemnly as if she would never, ever, even under threat of death, interrupt him again.

"There is a right and fittin' way for folks to get along, and you girls aren't doin' it to suit me." Clay crossed his arms and got his fury under control. He pointed at Mandy and said sternly to Beth and Sally, "Get on the other side of the room with Mandy so I can talk to all of you."

The girls hurried to obey. They lined up beside Mandy, who was holding the squirming toddler. Sophie went to stand beside them. "Get over here by me, Sophie. This is for the children, and what I say goes for both of us."

Sophie arched an eyebrow at him, but she walked over and turned to face the girls.

Clay said, "Rule number one: There will be *no more crying*! No more! None! Never!"

"But, Pa, what about my. . ." Beth began.

"I'm not finished yet!" Clay snapped.

Sophie murmured, "A little child can't always. . ."

Clay turned to her. "I said no more, and I meant it. I can't stand the sound of womenfolk crying, and I want it stopped."

Sophie crossed her arms and started tapping her foot. Clay could see she didn't like minding him. Well, that came as no surprise.

She remained silent, so he forged ahead. "Rule number two: There will be no more taking things that don't belong to you, without permission!"

Beth turned to Sally and wrinkled her nose at her little sister.

"Rule number three: No more screaming!"

"Rule number four—"

"What about Laura. . ." Mandy interjected.

Clay's concentration was broken. He was kind of coming up with these rules on the fly, thinking up what would make his home a peaceful one, so he hadn't rightly decided what to say next anyway. "What about her?"

Mandy asked, "Can Laura cry? 'Cuz sometimes. . .well, she's pretty little, and she can't always. . ."

"Laura can cry," Clay decided. "Until she's three. Then that's the end of it."

"Until she's three?" Sophie shook her head and stared at Clay as if he'd lost his mind. After an extended silence, she said, "Why three?"

Clay stared at her while he thought about it. Finally, he said, "She's a baby till she's three."

He turned back to the girls. "Rule number—"

"What if we get hurt?" Sally said. "If I stub my toe or get a bee sting. What if—"

"If you're hurt, you can cry of course. . . ." Clay waved his hand at the interrupting question. "Now, let me get on with setting the rules. Rule number—"

"Why is getting a stubbed toe okay to cry over but not getting my feelings hurt?" Beth interrupted.

Clay plunked his fists on his hips. "Feelings aren't like getting hurt. Feelings—"

"Yes, they are," Mandy insisted. "Sometimes my heart hurts worse'n a hundred bee stings. Sometimes—"

"No crying over hurt feelings," Clay snapped. "Look, if it's a problem, then how about if you don't cry when you get hurt either. If you get hurt you just. . .I don't know. . .say 'ouch' or something."

Sophie said dryly, " 'Ouch'—or something?"

Clay pressed on. "You need to learn to control yourselves. If you're ever in a gunfight or get cornered by a grizzly or some such, you need to be thinking. Having feelings at a time like that can—"

"Now, Clay. . ." Sophie rested her hand on his arm, and that distracted him some from setting his house in order. In the mountains he had never been touched by women. He never quite got his fill of it now.

Sophie shook her head doubtfully. "The chances of the girls ever getting in a gunfight are—"

"That's not the point." Clay completely forgot about rule number four, which was easy because he hadn't made it up yet, although he was pretty sure there ought to be a rule against all the high-pitched giggling, and naked babies, and Sophie saying he'd been bucked off his horse while the men could hear her, and. . .

"Well, of course it's the point." Sophie smiled, distracting him some more. "Why teach the girls how to react in a gunfight if they're never going to be in a gunfight?"

"It's not about being in a gunfight." Clay patted her poor, little female hand and explained as he would to a rather slow-witted child, "It's about keeping your head in a crisis. There are lots of times they might be in a tight spot, when they need to be thinking. . . ."

"I don't want to shoot anybody," Beth said firmly. "You can't make me shoot someone, if'n I don't want to. Can he, Ma?"

Elizabeth sounded so afraid toward the end of her question that Clay was afraid she was going to break rule number one.

"I'm not going to try and make you shoot someone, Beth," Clay said in exasperation. "Don't be stupid."

"Clay!" Sophie jerked on his arm.

Clay turned to her. "What did I do now?"

"I don't want you to ever call one of the girls stupid again," Sophie commanded.

"Well, what if they are stupid? Am I just supposed to pretend to not notice?" Clay asked.

"Clay, I mean it."

"But I've called you stupid a whole bunch of times, when you've done some lame-brained thing, and you never minded."

"Clay McClellen!" She made just saying his name sound like a threat.

"Well, you didn't."

"Yes, I did!"

Silence descended on the room.

"You did?"

"Of course I did. No one wants to be called stupid—or lame-brained for that matter. It's a cruel thing to say."

"No, it's not. Not if it's the truth. It's just how to teach people to use their heads before they get themselves in trouble." Clay tried to remember how this had all started. Then he thought of his rules. He couldn't even remember them anymore, except for the crying.

"It's hurtful." Sophie lifted her skirts indignantly and walked over to stand beside the girls. "And we don't like it."

And Clay didn't like the fact that she wasn't touching him anymore. Clay looked from one of them to the next. They all had the same stormy look in their blue eyes. It panged something in his heart to see them all standing together, against him. Then Clay remembered he was in the right in this matter, and he was the head of this house. He jammed his fists against his hips. "Well, I don't like it when you all get to screaming and crying and fighting!"

They squared off against each other. Five against one. Clay figured he could take them, but it might be a close thing. And his ears would never survive.

Sophie crossed her arms. "We might agree to try and stop the crying and screaming, if you'd agree to quit calling us insulting names."

"When you do something stupid, it's not an insult to point it out. It's just the truth. And I'm not making a deal!" He jabbed his finger at the lot of them. "I'm making the rules, and you're obeying them."

"That not how it's going to be," Sophie said through clenched teeth. "You can't run a home that way. A family has to work together, everyone taking charge of what they do best. Everyone pitching in wherever they can. Your brother let me make a lot of decisions around this—"

"I'm not my brother!" Clay roared. He was tired of hearing about what a fine, brave, wise man Cliff was. He knew he'd never measure up, but that didn't mean he wasn't pulling his weight. That didn't mean Sophie had to take up the slack for him.

The girls got weepy-eyed again. In that instant, Clay was fed up. He didn't know anything about raising girls, but people were people, and the West was thc West, and everybody needed to know the same things to get along.

"That's it." Clay strode to the front door, snatched his hat off its peg, and turned back to them. "Mandy, come with me. I'm going to teach you girls to behave proper."

"Behave proper? What does that mean?" Mandy asked fearfully. "Are you going to give me a whipping? I didn't do anything. It was Beth and Sally who were fighting. Give them a whipping."

"I'm not going to give you a whipping," Clay said in disgust. "Have I ever raised a hand to one of you girls?"

He almost heaved a sigh of relief when they all shook their heads. At least they agreed with him on that.

Beth wrung her hands. "But we haven't known you all that long."

Clay almost started in hollering again, but instead he said, with a strict fatherly tone that he decided he liked, "I'm going to teach you how to rope a steer. I'm going to teach you to drive a nail and hitch up the team to the wagon and work a running iron."

"Clay, there's something you should know," Sophie said. "Cliff hasn't just been gone two years. He was in the war before that. The girls and I have really been doing for ourselves—"

"Out, Mandy." Clay'd finally figured out what the whole problem was. They'd been coddled. They'd been in an all-female household for too long. All the screaming, all the fighting, all the crying—it would all end if he did what he should have been doing from the very beginning.

He'd make boys out of 'em!

"Mandy will spend the afternoon with me, Beth will have tomorrow afternoon, then Sally the next. We'll do that for as long as it takes to teach you girls the proper behavior for life in the West." Clay pointed to the door.

Mandy looked uncertainly at Sophie. Sophie shrugged at her and, after a few seconds, gestured toward Clay and the outdoors.

"Okay. Life in the West. I can do that." Mandy's expression changed, and Clay wasn't sure what she was thinking. If he hadn't known better, he'd say she almost looked sly there for a second. He must have imagined it. She gave Clay a sad, rather wide-eyed look and batted her lashes a couple of times. "I mean, remember I'm only ten, now, Pa. Go easy on me."

Clay, thrilled he was winning a fight for a change, rested a hand on her shoulder. "Don't you worry now, lil' darlin'. I'll make sure you're safe while you get the hang of things."

He paused at the door and looked back at Sophie. "If you don't like me calling you stupid, you gotta tell me. How am I supposed to know otherwise?"

He left the cabin.

"How could anyone not know it is hurtful to call someone else stupid?" Sophie asked in amazement. "Is it possible the man is really that. . ."

Sally supplied uncertainly, "Stupid?" Then Sally asked, "Why didn't you tell Pa that Mandy's been roping cattle since she was six? Why didn't you tell him we all know how to do most of those things?"

Sophie said smugly, "I did try and tell him."

Beth chided, "You didn't try very hard."

"And why didn't Mandy tell him?" Sally wanted to know. "Why did she act all sad and scared?"

Sophie grinned a little. "She probably wants to let him think he's teaching her things. It might hurt his feelings if he found out you girls can all handle yourselves as well as he can."

"So we're all supposed to act like he's teaching us stuff we already know?" Beth asked.

Sophie shrugged, "I suppose we'll have to." With some venom she added, "It's either that or tell the poor man he's stupid!"

Royce Badje set his coffee cup down with a bang. "I've been looking for you all week, Josiah. You can't go off and leave this town unprotected when there're men like that around." Royce thought about that thug who'd come to his office and shuddered.

"Nothing happened while I was away, Royce. Even the vigilantes don't come into town."

"Don't tell me nothing happened. I don't have to put up with that kind of business."

Sheriff Everett went over it one more time. "It's not a crime to kick up a fuss, Royce. The man didn't do anything wrong."

"He threatened me," Royce said indignantly.

"None of what he said—and I only know what you told me—sounded like a threat." He waved at Esther, and she came over with the coffeepot.

"It wasn't what he said." Royce fidgeted with his collar and felt the sweat break out on his forehead again. "It was the way he said it. Surely there is something you can do before he hurts someone. I'm telling you, Josiah, he is a dangerous man!"

"I told you I'd keep an eye out and I'd have a talk with him if he showed himself again. You didn't even get his name. You didn't see his brand. I've only got a description. Chances are, when he heard the place was sold, he moved on, hunting rangeland somewhere's else."

"Whozat, Royce?" Esther asked.

Esther stood beside them, her dress and apron none too clean, her body whipcord thin. As far as Royce was concerned, griminess and thinness were powerful bad things in a woman who made her living cooking. She was also the town's biggest busybody, and Royce was impatient with himself for talking in front of her. He probably sounded like a coward.

"Just some roughneck, come into the bank trying to buy the Edwards's place," Royce said. "After McClellen'd already bought it. The man threatened me, and I want the sheriff to pick him up!"

"Royce." Sheriff Everett sounded tired. "I told you. . ."

"Great big man?" Esther cut in. "Near six and a half feet tall, and weighs three hundred pounds if he weighs an ounce? Dark hair, beat-up black Stetson? A man who needs a bath and a shave even more than most of the stinkin' men in this town?"

Royce nodded with enthusiasm.

"Carrying two tied-down Colts?" Esther went on. "One of 'em with fancy carving in the wooden handle? Kinda man that makes people clear the sidewalk when he's comin' at 'em?"

"That's him," Royce said. "I particularly remember that gun. The stock was handcrafted. A beautiful piece."

Sheriff Everett glared at Esther. "I been askin' around town for two days about such a man. How come you didn't know I was huntin' him?"

Esther finished filling their cups. "I've been gone. I left on the Saturday stage to ride over to Brogado to visit my sister. I know the man you're talking about. In fact I saw him the day he came storming out of the bank."

"It was the middle of the afternoon, Monday," Royce prompted her.

"That musta been him." Esther went across the room, filled a tin cup with coffee for herself, and brought it back.

Royce thought she looked like she was settling in for a good gossip. He barely held on to his patience. "Did he come in?"

"To the diner? Nope." Esther sniffed as if any man not eating her cooking was immediately suspicious.

Sheriff Everett asked, "Do you know anything about him?"

"Heard he caused a ruckus in the Paradise a coupla weeks ago. Upset 'cuz the whiskey 'tweren't no good. Knocked Leo out cold. One of his men broke Rufus's nose."

"Why didn't someone send for me?" Sheriff Everett asked with a scowl.

"It was over before it started. Leo came around. Rufus quit bleedin'. The man who caused it all was gone." Esther shrugged. "Everybody knows the Paradise can get rough. What were you gonna do?"

Josiah didn't answer.

Royce knew Esther was right. Josiah would have done nothing. "And you're sure it was the same man who came out of the bank?"

"I'm sure." Esther slurped her coffee. "Ain't much goes on in Mosqueros I don't know about."

"Well, if someone would have called me," Sheriff Everett said, "we might know enough about him to track him down and find out what's got him all worked up about the Edwards's place. As it is, I'm stuck just keeping an eye out in case he comes back to town."

"Well," Esther drawled, "you know a bit more about him than that."

"No, I don't," the sheriff barked.

"You know his name."

"No, I don't."

"You will after I tell it to you," Esther said with a smirk.

"You know this hombre's name?" The sheriff rose partway out of his chair.

"I reckon I do. He made a big enough fuss about it to Leo."

Royce waited. Seconds ticked by while Esther sipped her coffee. The woman dearly loved to be the center of attention. He nearly squirmed with impatience. Finally, he snapped, "If you know his name maybe you'd like to share the information!"

Esther stiffened, but Sheriff Everett reached across the table and pressed her weathered hand. "It'll really help me out, Esther. If he hit Rufus and Leo and threatened Royce, you'd be doing a service to this whole town by telling us. Why, I reckon you'd be a true hero."

Esther turned away from Royce. "Well, of course I'm a-gonna tell ya, Sheriff. There just 'tweren't no call for Royce to speak to me thatta way."

Royce could almost see the old hen's ruffled feathers lay down, and he bit his tongue to keep from saying something that would make her ruffle up again.

At last, apparently satisfied she'd tortured him sufficiently, Esther said, "His name is Judd Mason."

"Judd Mason," the sheriff said thoughtfully. "Not a name I've ever heard before."

"Maybe he's wanted." Royce rubbed his hands together gleefully. They could lock this thug up and he'd be safe. "You oughta check the name against the WANTED posters."

"I know my job, Royce." The sheriff drained his coffee cup and chewed the dregs. "I'll do that, and I'll send a telegraph, with his name and description, to the Texas Rangers."

"We'd best warn the McClellens about him," Royce added.

"Don't forget to mention the brand on his horse." Esther picked up Josiah's cup and stood from the table.

"You saw the brand?" Josiah leaned toward Esther.

"What was it?" Royce could hear the cell door slamming already. "A brand's a lot harder to change than a man's name."

Esther gave him another snooty look, and Royce thought he'd pushed her too hard—again.

Finally, she deigned to answer, "J BAR M."

Thirteen

Adam had learned the hard way to never expect anything but trouble. As he came within a day's walk of the ranch, he faded back into the high-up country, scouting around to see why Sophie would need help bad enough that God would come, personally, to so lowly a creature as Adam Grant.

As Adam ghosted around in the woods surrounding the ranch, he began to take stock of the situation. He saw Sophie and she seemed fine. He also counted four little girls and couldn't stop himself from smiling at all the little tykes.

But he saw no sign of Cliff. Instead, another man came and went from the house as if he lived in it. Had Edwards abandoned her? Adam had always expected the man to cut and run back to the safety of the East. But he'd always expected Edwards would take Sophie with him when he went. No man was such a fool that he would have a woman like Sophie for his own and give her up. More likely Edwards was dead. The West could kill a man in a hundred ways, and—if a person was stupid—it could kill in a thousand. Despite his sharp clothes, classy education, and polished manners, Adam had pegged Edwards as stupid from the minute he'd come riding up to the Avery farm in Pennsylvania.

Adam's fear of what would become of Sophie was why he'd come West with them. Nothing in the two-plus years he'd been with the family, before Edwards drove him off, had changed his mind.

Adam wasn't close enough to see the new man's face, but he knew from the way he moved, the competent way he sat a horse, and the way he held the attention of his cowhands, that it couldn't be that worthless Cliff Edwards.

While he wondered about Edwards and worried about the voice saying, "Help me," what really had Adam upset were the tracks. Men were coming and going in the rough country above the ranch. The men were good in the woods—quiet, leaving few signs. Adam hadn't managed to spot one in person yet, but he started to recognize four different men, usually out in pairs, usually leaving during the nighttime and only scouting during the day.

Sometimes they'd follow the hands, but mainly they seemed to be keeping an eye on Sophie's man and the ranch house. Sophie's new man was savvy in the woods himself, and Adam had his hands full keeping from being discovered. He wasn't ready to come out in the open yet.

Before he could go down to say hello, he had to know why Sophie was being watched.

Sophie knew exactly why she was being watched.

They were coming—coming for Clay.

Well, she wouldn't have it! She was tired of breaking in new husbands. She was keeping this one!

Sophie hadn't survived in a confounded bramble bush for two years by being careless. She knew her property. She knew how to track, and she could read signs like the written word.

Clay rode out to check his herd every day, always scolding her to "leave man's work to men." Sophie waited until his dust settled, and she and the remaining girls that hadn't been taken off by Clay to learn how to be boys got to work.

"Ma, I finally landed a rope on a yearling yesterday," Mandy announced, as she shinnied up to the highest rafter in the barn to settle a basket of rocks on a board.

"Mandy, you didn't!" Sophie stopped prying up the floorboard she'd spent all day yesterday laying in front of the barn door.

"Pa sure threw hisself a fit when he saw you'd put a wood floor across the barn door, Ma." Sally had quit pouting because Elizabeth had gotten to go with Clay just as Sophie expected. Now that Clay was gone, there was no reason to fuss about it, because she knew Sophie wouldn't change her mind regardless of the ruckus.

"Pa and I talked about it again, Sally. I told him it'd keep down the mud, and he came around to my way of thinking once he saw I'd already done the work. His main complaint was that the barn was his territory and he didn't want me dirtying my hands with such hard labor."

Mandy giggled.

"I think that's right nice of him to want to spare you hard work, Ma." Sally said in stout defense of her beloved father.

"Kinda dumb," Mandy pointed out. "Since you haul buckets of water from the creek a dozen times a day and chop wood for the fireplace and work over the fire for hours and hunt food and clean it. . ."

"I'm not supposed to hunt anymore," Sophie reminded her.

"That's right. I remember. Pa said it was man's work, 'ceptin' he never brings in food so what are we supposed to cook?"

"I don't think he's keeping track." Sophie set the three center boards aside and began digging. "He's waiting for me to tell him I'm running low on something, then he'll go and fetch us a deer. But he's powerful busy these days, and I hate to bother him. Besides, I like to hunt as much as the next person. I hate to give it up. His heart's in the right place. He means to help."

"So now you don't just have to hunt food, you've got to do it on the sly." Mandy shook her head in disgust.

Sophie laughed. "Hunting is a sneakin' business anyway, little girl. It's no bother. And if I hadn't been hunting, I'd have never found out we're being watched. We laid traps during the years your pa was gone to war. Then we had them in the thicket. But I might not have thought to rig anything up in the barn, what with so many men around."

"You'd've thought of it." Mandy attached the braided hemp rope to the basket handle and threaded it through the notch she'd drilled in the nearest rafter. Then, she carefully eased her way out on the board twenty feet above the ground until she could reach the barn wall. She hooked the rope around a little notch left there from years back.

Sophie laughed again as she dug down to make a man trap out of the entrance to her barn. "I reckon that's so."

Mandy dropped the long rope off her shoulder until it fell to within four feet of the barn floor. Sally caught it and, careful not to upset the basket, tucked it behind the door frame so no one could pull it by accident. Mandy nimbly clambered down the barn wall and dropped to the floor.

"Anyway," Sally reminded her mother, "you'd've found out about it 'cuz Pa told you he'd seen tracks."

"True, true enough." Sophie nodded. "This pa is a fine tracker."

They worked companionably together in silence. Laura slept peacefully on a pile of straw in the corner of the barn. The hole got about shoulder deep and Sophie stopped. A man just had to fall far enough for the sharpened, wooden spikes she was going to plant in the bottom to have some poking power.

"Are you gonna tell Pa about the traps, Ma?" Sally wondered.

"I think I'd better." Sophie laid her hands on the ground and vaulted out of the hole. "I'd hate to catch him by accident."

"You know he'll have a fit," Mandy warned. "He'll figure it for men's work."

Sophie nodded and shrugged, then went to the floorboards she'd split and sanded smooth. "Still, I'd better tell him. So you roped a yearling? Already? Do you think that's wise?"

"I'd been missing for a week. It was driving me crazy!"

"Still, it took you months to learn it the first time," Sophie reminded her as she took the chisel to the floorboards. "We don't want to hurt his feelings."

"It's all right. I acted all excited and told him what a good teacher he was. I made sure to miss three or four times, and then make one again. I did that most of the day. But toward the end I started getting right dependable." Mandy snagged a lariat hanging on the wall and whirled it around her head for a few seconds before she sent it sailing toward a post on one of the stalls. It settled perfectly in place. Mandy snapped the noose to pull it off the post, coiled it again, and lassoed the post, again and again.

"It's nice of him to work with you, but you have to go slow or he'll catch on. I just wish you could get on with learning a little faster so you could actually start helping the man."

"Oh, he's not going to let me help once I learn." Mandy replaced the lariat and started whittling on one of the spikes her mother was going to plant.

Sophie straightened from the boards she was cutting halfway through. She stood too suddenly and for a moment the barn spun around. She stepped quickly to the side of the barn and leaned, one arm out straight, until her head cleared. "What do you mean? Why would he teach you then not let you help?"

"It's men's work." Mandy looked up from her whittling and grinned at her mother.

Sophie shook her head and turned one corner of her mouth up in disgust. "Then why, may I ask, is he teaching you?"

Mandy giggled as she dropped her sharpened stick and started on a new one.

"Ah, Ma, don't let him get you all stirred up." Sally tugged on the hemp rope she was braiding. "He means well. He wants us to know just in case we ever have need of the skill, but he also keeps promising to take care of all of us forever. And that's right thoughtful of him."

"It is thoughtful." Sophie slid back into her hole and imbedded Mandy's sticks so they pointed straight up. "But how does that man think we lived without him for two years?"

"It was really more like seven years, Ma. 'Cuz Pa—I mean our first pa, you know—not the one we've got now."

Sophie said snappishly, "I'm not likely to forget the man I was married to for nine years!"

Mandy hastened to point out. "I was just trying to be clear on which pa I was talking about."

"You make it sound like there've been a dozen of them." Sophie jabbed the spike hard into the ground.

"Sorry." Mandy went on sharpening. "Anyway, my point was, our first pa wasn't around much, what with the war and all. We've been on our own almost from the first. And here we are, alive and well. How does he think we managed it?"

"I don't reckon men are supposed to think," Sally said philosophically, as the pile of hemp rope grew at her feet. "That's why God gave 'em big muscles."

Mandy tilted her head sideways for a second. "Makes as much sense as anything else."

Sophie nodded. "Men do the lifting and women do the thinking. That sounds fair. I suppose God could have planned it that way." She added, "That's enough spikes for now."

Sophie set the last one in place as Mandy laid aside her bowie knife. Sophie hopped out again.

With the girls' help, Sophie braced the boards that covered the hole much the same way they'd done to the front porch. These were sturdy enough a man could ride a horse across them, but if Sophie tripped the braces, they'd collapse.

They had a dozen other snares and booby traps set up around the perimeter of the property, not to mention a collection of clubs and sharpened sticks tossed in unexpected places so there was always a weapon close at hand.

Nope, no one was getting this husband. Sophie had become purely fond of him.

Sophie began filling buckets with dirt so there'd be no evidence of digging. "You know, I've done a fair amount of lifting to get the traps all in place, so Sally's theory about muscles isn't perfectly sound."

Mandy nodded. Sally shrugged. Laura stirred in her sleep. Sophie thought that "fond" didn't really describe how she felt about her new husband. It was a whole lot more than fond—even if he did have weird notions.

"Where do womenfolk get all their weird notions?" Clay shook his head at Beth's inept efforts saddling his Appaloosa. Why would the little mite think a horse would want to hear all five verses of "Bringing in the Sheaves"? All the girls were proving difficult to teach.

Mandy couldn't seem to twirl a rope for more than a few seconds before it would drop on her head and get her so tangled she had practically tied herself up. Her eyes had gotten all teary a couple of times, and Clay had been forced to remind her about rule number one. She'd finally gotten the hand of landing a lasso on a bored, little calf who wasn't even moving.

Sally was a trooper. She was picking things up fairly well, although she still had a long way to go, and sometimes her chatter about how brave and strong Cliff was grated on Clay's patience.

And today he had Beth. He knew she could catch up a horse. He'd seen her do it with Hector. But she was the almighty slowest little thing he'd ever imagined. She kept getting distracted by petting the horse's nose and talking about how soft the "'paloose's" fur felt. She also had a tendency to giggle at things that weren't funny in the least, and that made the horse nervous. It made Clay nervous, too. They never got anything done.

And Sophie—well, Sophie had the weirdest notions of all. Clay had decided that it wasn't too late to teach Sophie a few things. So he'd started taking her out—never going far, of course, because of the girls, and setting her to practice man things. He'd needed to tell her about the men watching the ranch yard and give her orders about being cautious, both for herself and the girls.

He'd told her he didn't expect much from someone as old as she was, citing the adage, "You can't teach an old dog new tricks," but she might as well try.

She took a notion to get huffy when he mentioned her age, and all the things he taught her came a little faster. He'd have to remember a few little jabs about her being old seemed to spur her on. That might come in handy.

She was a good shot—better than good, he reminded himself, as he thought about the day she'd brought down that wild boar. And she knew how to slap leather on a horse, although to Clay's way of thinking, she spent too much time talking to the horse, too.

She started talking once about laying snares and booby traps for night riders. Clay did his best not to laugh at her, but he couldn't stop himself. He told her to quit worrying her pretty little head about man things. She worked harder than ever after that, mainly because she wasn't speaking to him at all.

But the most unusual reaction she'd had so far was when he brought the material home for her to make pants for the girls. He'd brought some other material, too, because the girls needed a spare Sunday dress, but the brown broadcloth was his favorite purchase.

Mandy hugged the bolt of flowery blue to her chest, and Beth and Sally had started a tug-of-war over a bolt of pink nonsense the lady in the general store had told him was just the thing.

"I remember once Pa brought us four different colors of cloth for dresses." Mandy nudged Beth. "Remember? He got us ribbons to match and said Ma was to make us each a matching dress, 'cept in different colors?"

Beth nodded and with a hard wrench got the fabric away from Sally. In the tussle Beth dropped the cloth, and Laura crawled over and sat down on top of it.

Clay felt his jaw tighten until it likened to break under the strain. Of course Cliff had gotten them more. Of course there'd been four pretty colors and ribbons to match. Clay felt his temper rising. He remembered he'd made a rule about the girls taking things away from each other, but the cloth didn't belong to anyone yet, and the girls weren't screaming or crying, although they were too close for comfort. And Clay didn't want to be cranky right now. Not while they were all thinking about how much better their other pa was than him.

Laura started chewing on the material. Sally turned her attention to the bolt Mandy was holding. Beth was scolding Laura, who started to cry. Clay longed for the day Laura was three. They all ignored the brown. Clay told Sophie about his plans for the broadcloth while he was trying to think up a rule to cover this kind of racket.

"There is no way on earth I am putting my little girls in men's clothing." Sophie harrumphed. "It isn't proper! You can teach them all the manly skills you want, but it's my job to teach them to be ladies, and that means dressing as God intended!"

"Now Sophie, don't go getting all persnickety on me," Clay said. "I don't know where in the Bible it says anything against pants on a woman, so we're okay with God on this one."

Sophie stirred her soup as if her life depended on it. "We are *not* okay with—"

"We're living way out here where no one but the coyotes and the cattle see any of us."

"And the cowhands," Sophie reminded him.

Clay refused to be distracted. "No one's gonna care if the girls wear a pair of pants. It's not safe for them to ride sidesaddle. It's just a plumb fool idea. They're riding astride, and their skirts are flying all over and. . ."

Sophie wheeled away from the stove and stormed right up into his face with a steaming, heavy metal ladle. Clay almost took a step back before he found his backbone.

"You have to be mindful of their skirts, Clay." She waved the ladle under his nose. "They're out there with the hands, and I won't have their skirts flying about!"

Clay caught the ladle and relieved her of it so he could keep bossing her around without any danger to himself. He tossed it onto the table with a loud clatter and stepped up until her nose was practically pressed against his shirt. She looked up at him. The angry glint in her eye told him she wasn't going to back down. Since it was up to a man to do all the thinking for a family, especially one that had as many females as this one, Clay examined his idea for flaws. There were none.

He bent over Sophie until his nose almost pressed against hers. "Either you sew up a pair of pants for each of these girls and do it right quick, or I'll take 'em into town and buy 'em a pair right in the general store, in front of everybody!"

Sophie's eyes flashed so much fire, Clay wouldn't have been surprised if his hair was set ablaze. He held her gaze even at the risk of his charred skin. Something feral crossed Sophie's expression, and Clay got ready to catch a fist if she threw one.

Before she could attack, Mandy piped up, "Remember the schoolmarm with that split skirt she wears sometimes, Ma?"

Sophie broke the deadlock of their clashing eyes and looked at her eldest daughter.

Clay grinned. "I remember that skirt. I saw her ride by me just today in town. Why, Mrs. McClellen,"—he chucked Sophie under the chin so she'd look back at him—"are you going to stand there and tell me that Miss Grace Calhoun, Mosqueros's one and only school teacher, isn't a proper lady? Why she's the most stiff-necked, starchy female I've ever met. If she wears one of those whatchamacallem skirts, right in the middle of town mind you, I reckon my girls can, too."

Sophie jerked her chin out of Clay's grasp, looked at Mandy, then planted her fists on her hips and turned to her husband with a much more serene expression. "Yes, I hadn't thought of Miss Calhoun's riding skirt. When you showed up with brown broadcloth, I just naturally thought you were expecting men's pants for the girls, like you wear."

That's exactly what Clay had been expecting, and he hadn't once thought of Miss Calhoun until Mandy mentioned it, but since he was winning the fight, he decided to let Sophie think whatever she wanted.

Mandy, from behind them, said, "Pa brought us yellow calico, remember? It was mine first, but we all wore it as we grew into it."

Clay wanted to snap at Mandy, which he knew wasn't fair. It wasn't her fault her first pa had been so much nicer than her second pa. He focused his temper where it would do some good—at his stubborn wife. "Next time I give an order, Sophie, I expect it to be obeyed. We're not having a debate every time I decide the way of things. That's not how a marriage works!"

"How do you know how a marriage works?" Sophie asked tartly.

"I just do. The man's in charge, just like God intended. And that it *does* say in the Bible." Clay tried to hold on to his mad. It stung a little that Mandy had needed to jump in and convince Sophie to make the pants. But he was getting his way, and he could always go back to town for more cloth and a bunch of stupid ribbon, so he started to cheer up some.

"You've never been married before," Sophie pointed out. "I know a far sight more about marriage than you do."

"Yes, I know. My perfect brother." Suddenly it was easy to be mad again. He was sick of hearing about Saint Cliff. "Cliff, the world's bravest man. Cliff, the nicest pa who ever lived. Cliff, the best cattleman. Cliff, the world's best—"

"Who in the world ever told you Cliff was the world's best cattleman?" Sophie asked incredulously. "The man barely knew the horns from the hooves, and he didn't know how to dodge either one."

"He didn't know. . ." Clay stopped, dumbfounded. "But. . .he built this place. All these buildings. . .that herd. . .the old C BAR animals are healthier than. . ."

"Adam built the buildings," Sophie said. "For that matter, Adam picked out our cattle, bought our horses, and hired our hands."

"But what did Cliff do?" Clay couldn't get his mind around what Sophie was telling him. He'd never heard a one of these women say a word against Cliff.

"Well, he built that rickety lean-to on the barn," Sophie said.

It all clicked into place when she said that. He'd thought something looked familiar about the patching job she was doing. There were signs of it all over the ranch. Buildings and corrals that were well built and laid out intelligently. Ramshackle little add-ons that were almost universally falling down. Tidy little patch jobs that were holding the shoddy lean-tos and fence rows together. Adam did the building. Cliff did the adding. Sophie did the patching.

Clay suddenly quit worrying about his girls wearing pants and focused all his attention on his wife. His wife who had never had much to say about his brother. Of course, he'd never asked her about him. His wife who went around doing men's work without asking for help.

She wasn't doing it because she thought Clay was a lesser man than Cliff.

She was doing it because she thought Clay was *exactly* like Cliff!

Clay's heart lightened until he wanted to launch into a chorus or two of "Bringing in the Sheaves" all on his own.

"Girls, I gotta talk to your ma for a minute. You stay in the house." He grabbed Sophie's hand and dragged her outside, striding toward the barn until he was almost carrying her.

"Tell me!" he ordered as he pulled her around the corner of the barn.

Sophie's eyebrows arched with confusion. "Tell you what?"

"Tell me about my brother. Tell me what kind of husband he was."

"Oh, Clay," Sophie said apologetically, "I don't want to say anything against Cliff. I didn't mean to be unkind."

Clay wanted to hear every unkind thing she had to say, which caused him a second of sadness. He shouldn't want to hear ill of his brother. Even without her saying a word, she was saying a lot to admit that talking about Cliff would be unkind. Clay lifted Sophie by her waist until she was pulled hard against him and kissed the daylights out of her. He wasn't sure just when her arms went around his neck, but sure enough, they were there. He reluctantly pulled her away. "Tell me."

"Clay,"—Sophie rested her hands on his chest—"your brother was a good man. He truly was. I cared about him, and I tried to help him the best I could."

"Help him? What does that mean?" Clay was hoping to hear that Cliff got bucked off his horse every time a naked baby went screaming past him. He didn't expect Sophie's voice to be so warm when she said Cliff's name.

Well, he'd asked for it. He braced himself as he prepared to listen to Sophie sing the praises of his brother.

Fourteen

Well, he'd asked for it. She braced herself as she prepared to tell Clay unflattering things about his brother.

"Do you remember me telling you, when I was saying Cliff was an only child, that I didn't think Cliff lied about it?"

"I guess," Clay said. "It sounds kind of familiar. A lot of that first day is a blur. You said something about Pa keeping the memories alive for me, and maybe Ma didn't do that for Cliff."

Sophie leaned against the barn and rested her hand on Clay's strong arm. "I believe that, Clay. I don't think he remembered you consciously, but I think he missed you all his life. Cliff was a sad man in so many ways. It was like he was always lonely, even when he was surrounded by his family. He was moody and critical, and he wasn't. . .well, I wouldn't have minded so much for myself. I'm an adult woman, and I don't need a lot of emotional nonsense."

Clay said quietly, "Maybe you needed a little of it."

Sophie smiled up at him and shrugged. "Maybe. Maybe I did. But I know the girls needed him to love them. You've noticed how they're always asking you if you've quit loving them?"

Clay nodded. "How could they think I'd just quit loving them?"

"Cliff trained them to think that way. Cliff had a way of punishing you for—I wish I could say for being disobedient or bad—but the truth was, he'd do it just because the mood struck him. If there'd been any rhyme or reason to it, we could have learned what his wishes were and tried to please him, but his temper had only to do with his own feelings. We never knew when he was going to have a black mood come over him. Sometimes, he'd go days without talking to any of us."

"I can't imagine the girls letting him get away with that. They climb all over me. They never stop chattering and giggling and crying. How could anyone avoid talking to them?" Clay almost sounded envious.

Sophie had to bite back a grin. "Cliff managed it."

"It sounds like my brother wasn't a very nice man," Clay said.

"There were bad times before the war, but he was a complicated man, just like any person is. Mostly, he was all right. He could be a charmer when he wanted to be. He sure convinced me to marry him quick enough. And I'll always believe he really wanted me, not just my pa's money. But after the war, it was like he left all the softer parts of himself on the battlefield. I think it was you he was missing. It was like he didn't want anyone to be close to him. Maybe he'd learned that loving was a risk. It hurt too much."

"And what about the buildings and the herd?"

Sophie reached down to her side and patted the sturdy barn. "Adam built the barn and the ranch house with his own hands, selected the site, laid out the corrals, and handpicked good stock."

"Didn't Cliff do anything?"

Sophie said sheepishly, "He bought Hector."

Clay's eyebrows disappeared into his hairline. "What about Adam? Who is he? You've mentioned his name before."

"Adam came with me from my father's farm. He was an emancipated Negro who had worked as a hired man for my pa all my life. He heard Cliff was taking me to Texas, and after twenty years on the same farm, all of a sudden Adam announced this yearning he'd always had to go west. I never asked, but I think he saw Cliff's weaknesses better than my folks or I did, and he knew I was going to need help."

"So then, why'd Adam abandon you?"

"Cliff drove him off. Cliff was a difficult man to work for. He alienated most of the townsfolk, even before he went and fought for the Union. Fighting for the North was the last straw."

"I fought for the Union. No one's braced me with it."

"Maybe it was just Cliff. He didn't get on with people."

"Does that include you, Sophie?"

"I loved your brother, Clay," Sophie said quietly. "I loved him as much as he would let me. I won't have the girls remembering him unkindly."

"That's why you've never complained about him. That's why you do so much of what I think should be man's work. You've always covered for him."

"I guess you could put it that way. I just saw it as helping." With a deep sigh, she continued, "A few months after Adam left, my pa and ma died, leaving me a nice bit of money from the sale of their farm. Adam had always urged us to stay out of debt, but Cliff wanted to expand. He bought a lot of land and increased the herd. He even mortgaged our ranch and the cattle, so he could buy all he wanted." Sophie shaded her eyes and looked at the wooded hills above the house. "He bought all those bluffs to the west."

"But that's mostly wasteland." Clay looked at the rugged timberland.

"And he bought Herefords. He was always wanting red cattle for some reason." Sophie shook her head.

"Herefords aren't fit for west Texas. You need longhorns to survive in this dry country."

"They're expensive, too. Then he went off to fight, and I held everything together with a couple of old hands and the girls."

Sophie wondered if Clay would get the hint that they were all seasoned ranchers. Now wasn't the time to drive that point home. "Then Cliff came back, more distant and sullen than ever. He was here long enough to get his long-dreamed-of son coming along the way."

"That'd be Laura?" Clay said with a quick grin.

"Cliff would have been furious. He always was when a girl-child was born."

Clay's smile vanished. "Cliff was a fool."

"I think he was trying to replace you, Clay. Without even knowing it, he was longing for another little boy that had been lost to him. He never got his son—at least one that lived."

When Cliff gave her an astonished look that obviously asked what she meant, she told him of the son she had lost as an infant. As she finished, Sophie's voice dropped to a whisper, "And he never quit punishing me and the girls for the loss of his son."

Clay rested one arm across her shoulders, then, when she leaned into him, he pulled her close and hugged her tight. "I'm sorry, darlin'."

Sophie pulled back a bit. Clay was so close and so warm, it made her head swim. She leaned forward and rested her forehead on his chest. "I don't want you to feel sorry for me, Clay. I meant it when I said I loved Cliff. It was just that, caring about him like I did always made me sad that I couldn't find a way to make him happy. He's the one we should feel sorry for."

Clay lifted her chin. "Okay, I think I can manage to feel sorry for a man too foolish to know how lucky he was to have a house full of pretty girls all wanting nothing but to love him. And Sophie darlin'. . ."

Sophie's head swam a little more, and she hung on to Clay tight. "What?"

"You can fill that house to the rafters with all the baby girls you want, now that you're married to me. And I promise to be nothing but grateful."

The thought made Sophie dizzier yet, and her knees collapsed. Clay caught her and hoisted her into his arms. She saw the fear on his face and wondered what she looked like. She felt like all the color had drained from her face, and her eyelids wanted to fall closed.

"Sophie, what's the matter?"

In that very instant Sophie knew. Of course she knew. She was no young girl still in pinafores, after all. She'd felt this way before. Exactly five times. She said with quiet awe, "I think we might get to filling that house sooner than you think."

It took him a minute. Sophie almost smiled as she waited for him to add up all the information she'd given him.

"A baby?"

Sophie tucked her head under his strong chin. She took one arm down from where it was wrapped around Clay's neck and laid her hand on her belly. "The only time I've ever come close to fainting in my life was when I was expecting. It's the first I've thought of it, but now I can think of some other symptoms." She looked into Clay's shining eyes. "Yes, there's definitely a baby on the way. *Our* baby."

Clay swung her a bit in his strong arms and grinned until she thought his face would split in two. "You know they're all ours, Sophie darlin', but I can't help but be tickled to be adding to our brood."

The smile left his face—replaced by worry. "You can't go around riding or working outside if you might faint dead away. You've got to settle down now. You stay in the house and make sure and not overdo. You need to rest!"

Clay hoisted her a little higher against his chest and started walking toward the house so fast he was practically running. "Mandy is a right handy cook, and if she's not up to it, Whitey can make enough grub at the bunkhouse for all of us. I don't want you leaning over the fireplace. You might get dizzy and fall face first into. . ."

Clay's voice faded away, and he looked horrified. He hugged her so tight she almost squeaked, but Sophie was enjoying his concern too much to beg him to let her go for so little a thing as breathing.

"And no more riding horseback."

"Clay, I'm perfectly capable of. . ."

"If you fainted on the back of a horse, you might break your neck. You might get trampled. We'll hitch up the team for church and errands in town." Clay stopped so suddenly he almost skidded. He whirled around to head for the barn.

Sophie's head started spinning again, but it was the wild ride Clay was giving her at fault, not a baby. "We don't have to hitch up the team right this minute. We don't have church or any errands right now."

Clay lurched to a halt and stared at the barn uncertainly. "We've got to tell the doctor you're expecting so he's ready when it's time to deliver the baby." He began striding rapidly toward the barn. He looked down at Sophie as if he were carrying some dangerous wild animal in his arms. "Maybe the doc should stay out here with us when your time is close."

Sophie patted Clay's chest. "Hush now, we don't need to go to town. I've never needed a doctor. Having a baby is the most natural thing in the world. I lived in a thicket and delivered Laura with no one around."

"No one?" Clay stopped his headlong dash for the barn. His grip loosened on her, and Sophie grabbed hold for fear he might drop her.

"The girls were there, but they slept through it, thankfully. I didn't want them to see a baby born. It wouldn't be proper. Anyway, the thicket wasn't so bad. For mercy's sake, Clay, I had Mandy along a creek on the trail west. I was alone. Our wagon had broken an axle, and Adam had gone off to the nearest town, which was forty miles away, to get a new one. Cliff didn't want to see a baby born, so he went off hunting until it was over."

That didn't seem to reassure him at all. This time he did drop her. She was ready though. She had a firm hold of his neck, so she landed on her feet. She wondered for a minute if he was going to faint. She suppressed a grin.

Her desire to smile faded as she remembered the rest of the story. "Then Cliff came back. When he saw it was a girl, he wouldn't speak to me for three days. Then Adam came back. He did everything he could think of for me, but it was all over. There was nothing for him to do. He repaired the wagon, and we continued on the trail for Texas."

Clay's pupils dilated. His cheeks flushed with anger. "If my brother were here, I'd beat him to within an inch of his life!"

"At the time, I'd have held him down for you."

"Well, it's not gonna be like that this time. There'll be a doctor, and there'll be no creek, nor a thicket!" Clay seemed to gather his wits about him. "And you're not gonna do anything that might hurt you or the baby."

He seemed happiest when he was issuing orders, so Sophie let him. His eyes suddenly got serious—serious to the point of frantic. He grabbed both her arms and almost beseeched her, "You're going to sit in that house and rock in a rocking chair and rest!"

"Clay, we don't own a rocking chair."

"I'll build you one." He slid his hands down her arms until he was gripping her hands tightly. "Please, tell me you'll stop working outside. I've only got two more days until we move the herd up closer to the ranch. If you'll give me two more days, three at the most, I promise I'll get to the work you've been doing."

He was squeezing her hands hard enough that she was losing feeling in her fingers. She wanted to make him happy. She really did. That's why she risked being honest. Anyway, it was high time she told him about the traps she'd set, before he caught himself in one. "The only thing is I've got a few booby traps to rig. I've hauled tree trunks off to the side of the trails up in the hills. They almost have enough rocks piled behind them to be ready. I need to find a few more rocks and get them in place and rig a trip wire and. . ."

"Booby traps? What are you talking about?" Clay shook his head, and Sophie got the impression he was trying to jiggle his brains around so they'd work a little better.

"I told you about the booby traps I was going to set. I just need a little more time. . . ."

"And I told you to forget it!" Clay commanded. "I'll see to the protection of this family, Sophie McClellen. You insult me every time you do it yourself. Now I don't want you hauling any trees." Clay's tone grew increasingly horrified, "Especially in your condition."

Sophie didn't think he'd heard her right. She'd already hauled the trees. And most of the rocks. She'd let Hector do the heavy lifting of course. She was determined to try and explain again. The man really needed to know where the booby traps were for his own good.

He swung her back up into his arms as if that was the only way he was going to let her move from now on. His strong arms around her distracted her from pressing the point. He bounced her just a bit as he headed for the house humming to himself. Sophie wasn't sure, but she thought she recognized "Bringing in the Sheaves."

As he hoisted her up the steps, he said, "I can't wait to tell the girls."

Sophie warned darkly, "There's only two possible ways they'll react."

Clay's forehead furrowed with concern. "What are those?"

"They'll either laugh or cry. Maybe both."

"It'll be laugh," Clay said with a firm nod of his head. "They wouldn't dare break rule number one."

They cried all over him.

And with three of them on his lap at once, Clay couldn't escape. Sophie said they were crying because they were happy. Clay thought that was just a plain waste of salt and water. He reminded them that they had promised to only cry if they were stung by a bee or the like, but they cried anyway.

He went straight to work building a rocking chair, and Sophie was sitting in it by the end of the day. After some worry on his part, Clay decided it was okay for Sophie to hold Laura on her lap as long as she didn't stand up holding her. Sophie kept smiling a sweet, mysterious smile that made his palms sweat, even while he couldn't take his eyes off of her.

That look also made him want to run for the bunkhouse and the men, people he understood. But he couldn't leave her for fear she'd quit resting and hurt the baby or pick up one of the crying girls. So he kept watch of his contrary wife and took charge of the overflowing tears. He held his girls, and even though he ended up with a soaked shirtfront, it was the sweetest night of his life.

"It's all set, boss." Percy rubbed the grizzle on his chin and groaned as he sat down at the fire. Eli handed him a cup of coffee.

Judd slapped the cup out of Eli's hand, and the boiling liquid splattered over Eli's pants and shirt. Eli danced away screaming, tearing at his clothes.

"Tell me whatcha found out," Judd demanded. "You can rest later."

Percy clenched his jaw and Judd waited, almost hoping for a fight. He was keyed up from the long hours of idle waiting. He'd called off the vigilante raids for the time. He didn't want to leave the area, and he didn't want to risk being recognized, leaving him and a band of restless outlaws cooling their heels in a rough camp.

The whiskey had run dry. The coffee was low. The cards were all marked, and some of the dumber ones had gambled all their earnings away and were pushing for another strike. Judd had enjoyed beating a few of them senseless when they pushed him too hard, but he couldn't do it often. Some of the men had taken off and hadn't come back. He'd started this with twenty hardened men. Most of them had been with him for two years. Since they'd started stalking McClellen, he was down to a dozen.

It wasn't just the restlessness or the fighting that had made the men take off. It was when they'd found out Judd intended to kill Sophie McClellen. There were men who would kill their own father for a chaw of tobacco. Men who would sell out their best friend for the cash on a WANTED poster. Men who would back-shoot a preacher for the contents of a collection plate. But they wouldn't touch a woman.

Women were too rare in the West. It was in many a man's nature to protect a woman, and nothing anyone would say or do could make him go against his nature.

Eli wasn't such a man and neither was Harley. Judd had worried about that because Harley was a quiet man who kept to himself a lot. But Judd had mentioned Sophie McClellen being able to put them all in a hangman's noose, and Harley had stayed put and listened in on the planning.

Now the first part of the planning was done. Percy was back with his report, and Judd would be hanged if he'd wait while the man had a cup of coffee to hear what he'd learned.

"He's got two men standing watch all night in such a way they can see down on the house. McClellen always takes the last shift before sunup. I've figured a way to sneak up on him and catch him flat-footed." Percy wiped the coffee away that had spilled on him.

"Why sneak up on him?" Judd asked brusquely. "Why not go in guns a'blazin'?"

Percy shook his head. "We need to do it quiet iffen we can, 'cuz the hands'll come a'boiling up that hill if there's any sign of trouble. Since we took those potshots at McClellen t'other day, the whole place is on a hair trigger."

Judd noticed Harley move restlessly when Percy mentioned the way they'd tried to dry gulch McClellen.

Jesse, one of the men who'd come from scouting with Percy, added, "There's army men among the hands and only a few that'd be called green. Even the green ones are game."

"We can't all go," Percy said. "Just a small group. Any more and we'd make too much noise."

"That whole bunch is mighty salty," Harley said. "They'll come up fightin' sure as anything."

Judd grunted. He gazed into the campfire and thought about that land. It was his. He'd claimed it in his belly a long time ago, and he didn't intend to give it up now. "Get some rest, Percy. I want you and Jesse and two others to go tomorrow night. We're gonna have this finished. I'm sick of waiting."

"I'll go along, boss," Harley said quietly.

"You're staying here." The closer they got to their goal and the tougher the McClellen outfit shaped up, the more Judd wanted Harley's quick gun and cool head at his back. "I don't want to risk being seen myself and that goes for you, too, Harley. We sit this one out. But I promise you'll be in on it when we get rid of Mrs. McClellen. I'm gonna enjoy shutting that woman's mouth for good."

Judd felt the restlessness of the men. He shouldn't have reminded them of what was in store for Sophie McClellen. No one left the campfire though, so they accepted it.

"Can I have some coffee now, boss?" Percy asked.

Judd almost sneered, but he controlled himself. By the time he was done training these men, they'd ask his permission before they so much as scratched an itch. "Yeah, have your coffee then get some rest. Tomorrow's the beginning of taking back what's mine."

Fifteen

Sophie was an honest woman. She prided herself on it.

Of course pride was a sin. And didn't the Bible say a sin was a sin? No difference between 'em? So telling a few lies kept her pride in check and therefore kept her humble.

Sophie found she couldn't quite let her mind make peace with that bit of foolishness. So she tried harder.

While lying was one sin, pride and the lack of humility were two. So she was ahead. She rolled a rock toward the pile and decided she was on to something.

Then she caught herself. Was a lack of humility the same as pride? Sophie shrugged and lifted the rock in place. If it was, her sins were a tie. Six and one, half a dozen of the other. Or rather, one of one and one of the other since she wasn't committing six sins after all. Why make things worse than they already were?

So since one sin was what she didn't want to do, and the other sin was what she *did* want to do, she decided to just do as she wanted.

Anyway, she didn't really consider finishing up her traps as lying. Yes, Clay had ordered her not to do it, but he'd gotten distracted by the girls' excitement over the baby before he managed to wring a "Yes, my lord and master" out of her. And since she'd fully intended to refuse to make a promise, it wasn't her fault the man issued his orders then got sidetracked.

She would have told him, straight into his teeth, that she was going to go ahead and finish what she started, but she didn't bother. Silence was just her way of trying to keep her husband happy. She sighed deeply as she heaved another rock onto the stack without disturbing Laura, who was strapped to her back. It seemed like she'd spent her whole life trying to keep one husband or another happy.

Great! Now *she* was making it sound like she'd had a dozen of them.

"It's not that I don't think he'll get to it, girls," she explained carefully because the girls knew how Clay felt—in fact he'd given them a stern talking-to about taking the load off of Sophie's shoulders until after the baby came—and more and more they were taking his side in things.

"It's that I feel pushed to hurry. I can't forget the men shooting at us. Those tracks prove they're nearby, and it's riding me to have everything in place. I've been sitting in the house all week waiting for your pa to get done with the cattle, but it's driving me crazy. I just can't sit in the house stitching away on trousers of all things—for myself and you girls—while the whole family is in danger."

"I like wearing trousers." Sally tugged at the full-legged riding skirt. "I think all of Pa's ideas are good 'uns."

Sophie wasn't about to admit it, but she liked wearing pants herself. She looked down at the brown broadcloth that she'd cut wide enough to look like a skirt. She marveled at how much easier it made everything. "We'll just fill this one last trap with rocks and then we'll leave it go. I promise I won't sneak around anymore after today."

Beth snorted as she hefted a rock onto the travois they'd rigged on Hector. "You shouldn't oughta be out here, Ma. I've checked, and there's none of them varmints standing watch right now, but what if one comes while we're in the middle of things?"

"Hector will give us a warning of trouble." Sophie glanced at the stubborn old mule doubtfully while she rolled another rock in place. She dusted her hands together in satisfaction. "I'd say we only need one more load after this one and we'll be done."

"It's not just the varmints watching us. I don't think you should be carrying such heavy loads." Sally laid her smaller rock on top of the teetering pile. "Those rocks you're hefting weigh almost as much as I do, and you'd never think of carrying me around."

"Well, now, Sally honey, if these rocks would sprout a pair of legs like you have, I promise I'd make 'em walk."

Elizabeth—the animal lover, the nurse, the little girl who wanted to take care of the whole world—said, "The point is you might get hurt. Or you might hurt the baby. I never thought about lifting heavy loads being dangerous, but Pa says it is."

"Beth, your pa doesn't know the first thing about babies. He's just worried about me, which is real nice of him, and so he's trying to take care of me. But he's just guessing about me not lifting things."

"It makes sense to me, Ma," Beth insisted.

"Don't you remember what it was like when Laura was on the way?" Sophie balanced her rock on the load and decided this one was full enough.

"I remember we moved into the thicket." Beth threw the straps over Hector's head. She chirruped to get him moving to where the fallen log was resting against a brace.

"Do you remember I carried everything I could out of this house and sneaked down through the thicket on foot to stash it in the shack we moved into? I took two or three trips a night, carrying everything—even the tables and chairs—on my back because the shortcut trail we had to take was too steep for Hector. I did that for most of a month. All while doing the chores around the ranch every day and hunting and cooking for you girls. I worked ten times as hard as I am now, all with Laura getting big in my belly." Sophie walked along behind Hector, carefully concealing the travois tracks.

"I know." Beth shook her head. "You did it, and you and Laura survived it. But that doesn't mean you weren't plumb lucky. Now we got Pa here to take care of us, and I say we oughta let him. There's still plenty for us to do."

They reached the braced tree trunk and started piling the rocks behind it. Sally attached the hemp rope to the brace and ran it down the hillside. She covered it with dirt and dead leaves as she went.

Sophie looked at the booby trap with satisfaction. "We've got time for one more load before dark. Then, I'm going to scout higher up the trail and check the spots those men have been watching from, while you girls go down and get the evening meal started. I'll be back before Pa, but if he shows up, we can honestly say you girls cooked supper and I went for a walk. All honest. All just to suit him."

Beth rolled her eyes at Sophie, and Sophie knew her little girl was growing up.

They loaded rocks one last time, dragged them across the steep, treacherous face of the bluff, and unloaded them. Sophie transferred Laura to Beth's back, pulled the shotgun out of the saddle boot, and sent the girls home riding Hector.

As they walked away, Sophie heard Sally say, "It sure is a shame about men having all those muscles."

Beth was dusting out the tracks Hector left behind. She looked up from the ground. "Why's that?"

Sally's shoulders slumped, " 'Cuz we could sure stand to have some help thinking around this place."

"Ain't that the truth," Beth replied gloomily.

Sophie decided she was going to have to quit including the girls in her sneaking. She was teaching them all the wrong lessons. Since she had to keep them with her all the time, she supposed what it amounted to was she was going to have to quit sneaking altogether and rest the way Clay kept telling her to.

Rest. She had heard that word out of Clay's mouth so many times she was hearing it in her sleep. In fact, she was quite certain that she'd been awakened last night to the sound of Clay's voice whispering into her hair, "Rest, rest, rest," like some kind of chant. She hoped she'd dreamed it. Otherwise, her husband was getting weird.

It went against the grain, but Sophie knew she had to start minding him better, for the girls' sake. And she'd do it, just as soon as all this mess with the night riders was settled. As always, when she thought of all her shortcomings as a wife and mother, all she could do was think, *Help me, help me, help me.*

As surely as he knew his name and his face and his God, Adam knew it was time.

"Buff?" Luther jumped to his feet, in front of the hat full of fire in their tiny, concealed camp.

"Huh?" Buff swigged at his coffee.

"Put out the fire. We gotta ride."

Buff didn't even ask why.

"I've been watchin' you fer days, McClellen, an' now we're to the end of it." Percy sidled from the base of one tree to the next. He knew just what trail McClellen always followed. He knew just what time of day to strike. Judd had told them to wait till just before dawn, but Percy was hankering for a whiskey and maybe a kind word from one of the saloon girls. If he could finish this now, he'd have the whole evening ahead with nothing to do. He might not even tell Judd he'd done things his own way, Judd being extra cranky these days.

McClellen always rode down to his evening meal a little after the other hands. He was easier pickings right now than when he'd be standing watch in the night.

Percy hunkered down just uphill of where McClellen always appeared, pulled his Arkansas Toothpick out of the knife sheath slung down his back, and checked the razor-sharp edge. Percy could nail a fly, dead center, from twenty feet.

He could kill McClellen quick and quiet, just like he'd been told. The other three men were lying back, waiting for the morning hours. Percy told 'em to sit tight whilst he did some scouting.

Percy had to stifle a chuckle when he thought of how he'd go awalkin' into camp, calm as you please, and say, "Let's go to town, boys. I've done in McClellen, and we've got nothing to do all night but celebrate!"

He settled in, quiet as a waiting sidewinder.

Clay enjoyed the ache of his tired muscles. He'd pushed hard today, but he'd gotten the last of the cattle rounded up. He was going to spend tomorrow branding the last of them, and then the next day he'd move them down to the lower range.

After that, he planned to spend every hour he could squeeze out of a day seeing to the chores his little wife wanted done around the place.

He grinned when he imagined how it would be when Sophie started getting round with his baby. Something caught hard right around his heart when he pictured another little girl-child to add to his brood of pretty daughters.

Then he thought of a roughhousing little boy to torment the girls and tag along after his pa, and he liked the thought of that, too. Clay didn't figure he could lose.

He began drifting down off the high bluffs toward the ranch house. As he rode along lost in thought, he thanked God for all he'd found when he went hunting for his brother. He thought of all the ways a man could mess up raising his children. The thought scared him almost as much as crying girls did.

He didn't make a sound as he prayed, *Help me be a good father to these young 'uns, Lord. Help me.*

Sophie eased her way up the hill. The bluff was so steep, it was slow going. She moved silently and slowly over a particularly slippery spot, careful not to set any little stones rolling and make a noise. She got to a level stretch and stood upright for the first time in a while.

The whole world spun around. She was only vaguely aware of falling forward into a mesquite bush as everything went black.

Percy froze when he heard brush rustle. It didn't come from where he expected to see McClellen. If someone else was around, he might not get his killin' done till breakfast.

A second passed and then another. The rustling stopped after that one slight sound, and Percy began to ease back from his spot. The sound he'd heard was fabric on brush. It wasn't a deer. He knew the woods better than that.

He shifted without making a sound, sliding from hiding place to hiding place. Sweat broke out on his forehead. Someone was out there. Someone was stalking him just like he'd been stalking McClellen. He decided waiting till morning suited him after all.

He began to rise from his crouched position when he saw McClellen emerge from the trees. Percy had moved farther than he intended, but McClellen sat there on his horse, not looking left nor right. As ripe for plucking as a sleeping goose. Percy pulled his Toothpick out of the sheath hanging in the center of his back, stopped breathing to steady himself, and let fly.

Out of the corner of his eye, Clay saw movement in the bushes. He straightened his legs to raise himself up higher. A blow hit him hard in the shoulder, and even more than the white hot pain, an instinct for survival sent him crashing to the ground on the downhill side of his horse. Facedown on the ground, he fumbled for his six-shooter, but his right arm wasn't working. A quick glance told him there was a knife lodged in his shoulder. He reached across with his left hand, but before he could grab his gun, cold steel pressed up against the back of his neck.

"Don't move, McClellen. Don't even twitch."

Clay heard the sharp *click* of the gun's hammer being pulled back. He recognized it for a rifle, and he knew he was going to die. He braced himself to fight, knowing he didn't want to die like this, flat on his belly with a gun at his back. He had to reach across the entire length of his body to grapple for the gun. He knew he was going to lose.

"It's you who doesn't want to twitch, old man." Sophie jacked a shell into the chamber of her rifle.

The pressure eased on Clay's neck, and with a single lightning move, he turned and grabbed the outlaw's gun.

Clay stood up, holding the gunman's weapon in his left hand. Sophie stood directly behind the man who'd been fixing to shoot him in the back. Her own weapon jabbed into his dirty neck.

"Clay, you're bleeding." In a voice so sharp it could peel the hide off a grizzly bear, Sophie snapped, "Back away from my husband right now."

Worried as she was, Clay watched his wife keep her senses enough to stay out of reach of the man who'd attacked him as she circled to his side.

Before she could get to him, Clay reached up and pulled the knife out of his arm.

Sophie gasped. "Be careful."

The pain of pulling the knife out almost buckled his knees, but he ignored it. There were more important things to do.

"It wasn't deep. It just caught the skin." Clay looked at the knife that had hit him. It was razor sharp and thin as a nail. "This is nice. I reckon I've always wanted a knife like this."

The man stood in front of them, looking side to side like a wild animal hunting a bolt-hole.

"You're not going anywhere old man"—Clay aimed his gun straight at the outlaw's black heart—"except into Mosqueros to talk to the sheriff."

"We don't think that's such a good idea, Major." A second man came out of the brush. A third and fourth were just a few paces behind him. All three of them had rifles. All the rifles were pointed at Clay.

"Percy, we were getting right worried about you." One of the men stepped in front of the others.

"Right nice to see you and the boys, Jesse." A sneer twisted Percy's face. "Talking to the sheriff is a bad idea. We didn't come for naught but you McClellen, but we'da needed to see to your wife by and by. So it might as well be now."

"Yep." Jesse glanced at Sophie but looked right back at Clay, as if Sophie wasn't part of this standoff. "She's seen us now for sure. We can't let the little lady walk away."

"You may not be the ones walking away," Sophie said.

Clay realized that they hadn't been watching her, and now she had that nasty old shotgun raised and pointed straight at them. Clay felt a surge of pride in his feisty little wife. Then, in the next second, he felt sick. There was no way he and Sophie were going to get through this without getting bloody—either getting shot themselves or shooting someone else. He'd been to war. He knew what it cost a man to kill. He didn't want to do it again, and he didn't want Sophie to live with killing on her conscience. But they had to fight, or these prowling wolves would kill both of them and Clay's unborn child. Then they might turn their murderous eyes on his girls.

"She's got a shotgun, Jesse." Percy watched Sophie now.

All four men went rigid. Clay knew every one of them had seen the damage a shotgun could do at close range.

Percy stood between the three men and the McClellens. "There's two of them and four of us. And that little lady doesn't have the guts to pull the trigger on that cannon she's aholdin'."

The other men turned their attention back to Clay, which is how he wanted it. He thought with grim amusement that Percy was standing in a direct line of fire between all of them. Clay looked straight at Percy. "Whoever else dies here today, you're gonna be the first to go."

Clay didn't mean it. He had no intention of wasting a shot on an unarmed man. But Percy seemed to be giving orders, so if he backed down, they might all think twice. That was the only way everyone could come out of this alive.

"Four agin' two, and one of 'em a gutless, little female," Percy said with a cackling laugh. "I'd say that makes you purely outgunned, McClellen."

"Guess again, you low-down polecat," Adam roared from out of the trees. Adam raised his gun and took aim at the unarmed man closest to his Sophie. Fury such as he'd never known cut through his soul.

He gripped William's gun until the carved stock cut into his hands. He'd spotted horses and this rifle on a sling on the saddle. He knew he'd found the cowards who had killed his friend.

He'd taken the gun and slipped through the woods in time to listen to that murderous scum threaten his own sweet Sophie. Adam squeezed slowly on the trigger. *Revenge.* The time was now. It stood to reason that if the one man was with the lynching party, then they all were. From his vantage point, he could open up on them and take them all.

Vicious satisfaction burned low in his gut. His finger tightened. His finger trembled on the trigger. He had killed in the war. It was a horrible knowledge to carry around inside a man—the fact that he'd taken another life. Then in his mind's eye he saw William and Moses and Dinky. Swinging. Lifeless. Someone had to pay for them. These men would go on killing until someone stopped them. He aimed at the unarmed man's black heart, then he looked at Sophie.

She stood there, so fearless. His Sophie had always been tougher than any woman should need to be. Adam's devotion to her offset some of his rage when he thought of his girl witnessing the destruction Adam wanted to rain down on these brutal men.

And he thought of her call for help. The call God had allowed him to hear. Would God speak like that to a man only to bring him to this place of murder? Because killing the unarmed man would be murder. There was no other word for it.

Adam's anger still battled for supremacy, but there was Sophie. And there was God.

With a sudden jerk of his hand, Adam eased off the trigger. He'd still have his revenge. There would be other chances. But for now he would try and end this standoff without bloodshed.

His unexpected voice froze the group. "With me there's three of us. That makes us even, 'cuz you got a man without a gun. And I've got an angle on all of you. Every man jack of you is gonna die where he stands if you don't drop your weapons." Adam couldn't keep the cold amusement out of his voice when he added, "And don't you ever think Sophie don't have what it takes to pull that trigger."

Clay saw Sophie's head come up. She never took her eyes off the men who had attacked them. Her shotgun never wavered. But Clay knew from the gleam in her eyes that she recognized the voice.

He looked back at the men who had waylaid them and saw they still weren't sure. They weren't ready to back down yet.

"Make it five to three," another voice growled from the opposite side of the clearing from the first voice.

"Luther, is that you?" Clay asked in disbelief.

"It's me, boy." There was a sharp *crack* of a rifle shell being levered into a chamber. "Let me see some hands in the air. I hain'ta askin' twice."

"Buff?" Clay's heart lifted. "Buff, you, too?"

"It's me, boy."

"We had a hankerin' to see you, so we drifted down Texas way." Luther sounded closer, and the brush rustled under his approach. "Looks like we picked ourselves a good time."

It was too much for the outlaws. Guns dropped to the ground. Clay shoved Percy toward the three men and frisked all of them for hidden guns and knives. He found a few.

A middle-aged black man, wearing only a pair of tattered trousers, stepped out of the woods. Sophie lay her shotgun aside and turned toward him. "Adam? Adam, I can't believe it's you!"

Sophie took a couple of running steps, then stopped. She turned unsteadily away from Adam. "Clay?" She sounded bewildered.

"Sophie, what in tarnation are you doing way up here all alone? I told you to stay at the house and rest." Clay saw Buff and Luther come straggling out of some brush. Clay tipped his head at the men they'd caught. "Watch 'em."

"Clay, could we talk about. . .about. . ." Her voice dwindled to nothing.

He strode toward his disobedient little wife. "Talk about what, Sophie?"

She went pale as a ghost. "Help me."

Clay caught her before she hit the ground. Adam was one step farther away, but he was at Sophie's side immediately.

Luther, busy hog-tying Percy, said to Buff, "That's her. That's whose been a-callin' me all this while."

"Figured." Buff finished off one man, bound hand and foot, and started another.

Clay turned to look over his shoulder, when Percy hollered, "Hey, not so tight!"

Luther leaned over him and growled, "Now's not the time to complain, you yellow-bellied, back-shooting, would-be lady killer."

Percy quit whimpering in the face of Luther's venom and sank against the ground.

Clay knew Buff and Luther had things in hand, so he lowered Sophie gently to the forest floor. He brushed her disheveled hair back off of her forehead. Adam knelt across from him, studying Sophie.

Her eyes fluttered open before either of them could speak. "Did I faint again?"

The fear that had burned Clay when she collapsed turned into a feeling he was way more comfortable with—rage. He roared, "Again? Again! When did you faint before? And what are you doing up here?"

"Now don't go. . ." Adam looked at Clay for the first time. "I—I—" He gathered himself. "Mr. Edwards, sir. I thought you were someone else. That is. . .I'm glad to see you. I hope I haven't overstepped myself by coming home thisaway. I know you said I wasn't to come back and make a nuisance of myself with Sophie. I'll just be movin' on through. Please don't take me being here out on Sophie or the young 'uns, sir."

Sophie rubbed her face. "This isn't Mr. Edwards, Adam. This is my new husband."

Adam looked doubtfully at Sophie. He patted her softly on the head and spoke as if she were a little child, and not a particularly bright child at that. "Why, sure it's Mr. Edwards. I can see that plain as day."

Sophie sat up, and Clay pushed her right back down on her back. The fact that she let him told Clay just how bad she was feeling.

"This isn't Cliff," Sophie said to Adam. "Cliff died a couple of years ago. This is Clay."

"You reckon this is why God's been tellin' me and Buff to come see you, Clay?" Luther had a sling on his rifle. He hung it across his back while he worked on tying up their captives. "Just to wrangle with these hombres?"

Clay looked over his shoulder. "God told you to come here?"

Luther nodded.

"Iffen this is what God wanted us to do, can we go back now?" Buff asked Luther.

"Not sure. Better keep listenin' fer a while."

"Yer hearin' voices in yer head," Percy jeered. "That makes ya crazy."

Jesse laughed, then grunted.

Clay looked around to see what caused the grunt, but all he saw was Buff busily binding him.

"Shut his mouth whilst you're at it, Buff," Luther said.

Buff pulled Jesse's neckerchief up and tucked it in.

"Adam, what happened to you?" Sophie asked.

Clay turned back at the alarm in Sophie's voice. She was reaching for Adam, and that's when Clay saw Adam had been shot—not too long ago.

Adam caught her hand and stopped her from touching his wound. "I'm fine, Sophie girl. And just so you know, God's been nagging at me, too. Something fierce. I've heard you purt near every time you've called out."

"Called out?" Sophie shook her head. "What did I call out?"

"Help me," Luther and Adam said at exactly the same second.

Clay looked at Sophie, and they both said, "God?"

Luther and Adam stared at each other for a long moment.

"The last time, it was Clay. Heard it plain as day, and we were miles off." Luther pushed his furred cap back on his bushy, shoulder-length head of hair and sniffed. "Guess God let me hear both of 'em whilst Adam only heard one."

Adam shrugged, stopped looking at Luther, and turned back to Sophie. Clay had a little dig of annoyance at the adoring way Sophie looked at Adam. She'd come close to looking at him like that a few times.

"About Cliff, Sophie, I don't know why you fell down just now, maybe from the upset or something. But I can see that Cliff is here beside you."

"No, you don't understand, Adam. Cliff died."

Adam looked worried and started inspecting Sophie's head for bumps.

"I married Clay just a short time ago." Sophie patted Adam's work-scarred hands.

"It's not such a short a time!" Clay caught Sophie's hands so she'd quit fawning over Adam. "I've had time to buy a ranch and corral a herd. Time to find out I'm a hand at running a ranch. Time to start a baby growing in you."

"A baby?" Adam smiled, but then his smile faded. "I'm right sure it'll be a boy this time, Mr. Edwards. It's just bound to be."

Clay started to tell Adam again that he wasn't Cliff, but then he remembered what he'd started to ask Sophie. "What are you doing up here? I told you to stay in the house. You could have been shot! If Adam, Buff, and Luther hadn't come along, you could have been killed."

Clay was so furious that he wanted to throttle her, except killing her would have to wait till later. Right now he was too busy keeping her alive.

"A young 'un, eh?" Luther sounded proud, like he'd arranged it himself. "Congrats, boy."

Buff chuckled, and Clay glared at them over his shoulder. "We don't have time to talk about the baby right now."

He stood with Sophie cradled in his arms. "Buff, Luther, you got 'em under control?"

There was no answer, which Clay deserved. If Buff and Luther were having trouble, they would have mentioned it. It gave him a jolt to realize just how chatty he'd gotten in the last few weeks, living with a house full of women. He looked over his shoulder and saw that they'd not only bound and gagged the varmints, they'd hunted up their horses. Luther grunted from the effort of hoisting Jesse facedown across a saddle.

"Let's go down to the house," Clay said to Adam.

"Yes, sir, Mr. Edwards, sir."

"I'm not Cliff. Sophie isn't lying to you."

"Why, I know as sure as I'm standing here that Sophie would never lie, Mr. Edwards." Adam followed Clay to his horse, as if he wanted to be handy to catch Sophie when Clay dropped her. "But I'm thinking she might be a bit overset from all this commotion, and it mixed up her thinking. Don't be mad at her for forgetting you. There's no call to be angry with her. I'm sure everything will come back to her real soon."

Clay hung on to his patience. This was the second time Adam had referred to Cliff's temper and that Cliff aimed that temper at his wife and children often enough that Adam was trying to placate him.

"I'll explain everything to you once we get home." Clay's Appaloosa stood with its reins dangling. Clay shifted Sophie around so he could catch the horse. "For right now we need to get my disobedient, little wife home so she can *rest*."

Sixteen

Sophie needed to get home all right. But she had no intention of resting or doing anything else Clay told her to do.

And she didn't like him calling her *disobedient* either!

Before she could tell him so, Clay asked, "Where'd you tie up Hector?"

Sophie got very busy straightening her riding skirt. Clay leaned down so he was in her line of vision. "Do you mean to tell me you climbed all this way on foot? You're miles from the cabin!" Clay looked like he wanted to explode.

Sophie sighed and braced herself.

Instead of hollering at her, he shook his head with disgust and set her up on his Appaloosa. He was very gentle, considering his clenched jaw and the bright red color of his face.

She would have explained to him that she couldn't rightly go to bed when she had company, but Clay turned his attention to getting Adam a ride.

"I'll be glad to walk down this ol' hill, Mr. Edwards," Adam said.

Clay swung up behind Sophie and pulled her onto his lap. He growled at Adam, "Call me Clay."

Adam took a worried look at Sophie, where she lay in her husband's arms. "Clay it is."

Sophie saw that Buff and Luther had led four horses out of the woods after they'd tied up the outlaws. Clay's two friends had full beards and were dressed in fur and leather. They looked like every mountain man Sophie had ever heard tell of. They'd been throwing a man over each horse, until they noticed Adam was on foot.

Buff unceremoniously tossed Jesse and Percy on the same blue roan and jerked his thumb at the sorrel. "Ride this 'un."

Adam took a couple of steps toward the now unoccupied horse then stopped. "Let's toss 'em both on the sorrel, and I'll ride the roan."

"What difference does it make which horse you ride, Adam?" Sophie asked.

"The difference is the roan is mine." Adam strode toward his horse.

For the first time, in the fading light of evening, Sophie got a look at Adam from behind. "What happened to your back?"

Adam grabbed both men by the scruff of the neck, dragged them off the horse, and let them fall to the ground with a little more force than was necessary. He didn't answer Sophie's question. He just led the sorrel over beside the men.

Adam didn't ask for help. Sophie couldn't remember him ever asking for help. But Sophie could see that Adam was taxing the limits of his strength. Clay's friends stepped in and loaded the men before Adam could get to them.

Adam went back to the roan, and the horse whickered softly at him, clearly greeting an old friend. Adam petted the horse's neck. "Missed ya, Blue."

Then Adam turned to look between Clay and his two friends. "There's a C-shaped scar under this horse's belly, and there's a ROCKING M brand on the other side of her. . .the side I haven't seen yet. She's my horse. That brand is registered to me."

None of the men bothered to check out the scar on the horse's belly, but Sophie could see the ROCKING M from where she was sitting. She could also see the look in Adam's eyes. Cold—bitter cold—and furious.

Adam had endured Cliff's constant criticism until the ranch was well started. Then, when he knew Sophie and the girls had a solid roof over their heads and land and cattle to support them, Adam had left because Cliff had taken his sullen dislike of Adam out on Sophie and the girls. Adam, who was so politely confused over Clay looking like Cliff, was a man of patience and kindness and wisdom. The cold in his eyes didn't go with any of it.

Buff tugged on the edges of his deerskin coat. "Stolen?"

"Stolen by the men who lynched my three partners, shot me in the back, and laid a whip on me for the first time in my life."

Sophie gasped.

"Not too many black men could make that claim. But I could." Adam ran his hand over the gunshot in his side. "Till I ran afoul of this gang."

Clay's arms tightened around Sophie, or she might've jumped off the horse and gone to Adam right then. Clay whispered to her, "Leave it for now."

Adam swung up on the roan's back. "This blanket strapped on the back of this saddle is mine, and the Winchester I carried out of the woods with me belonged to my partner, William. He carved it. I just took it off the sorrel's saddle a few minutes ago."

"Reckon that makes it yours." Luther slipped a foot into his stirrup.

"These four ain't all the men. Four alone could never have taken us. There were at least twenty." Adam gave the prisoners a contemptuous glare. "Back-shootin' cowards, every one of 'em!"

"There were around twenty men in the posse that came after Cliff." Sophie twisted in Clay's strong arms to keep her eye on Adam. The look in his eyes frightened her.

Luther settled on his horse. "Four down, sixteen to go. We'd best hang around for a spell, Buff."

Buff grunted.

Adam turned to Sophie. The icy rage faded from his eyes as he looked between her and Clay. She saw concern plain on his face. She had to hold back a smile.

"Clay is Cliff's twin." Sophie patted her husband on the shoulder as if that would somehow convince Adam. "He came hunting news of his brother and stayed on to help me when he found out his brother was dead."

"Cliff never had no family, Sophie girl." Adam spoke soothingly as someone who was facing a lunatic with an ax might. "You 'member how he talked about it, what with wanting a son so all-fired bad?"

Clay tensed behind her, but Sophie didn't think much about what Adam said. Cliff's wish for a son had been a lament made long and loud with no care for who might hear. She patted Clay's arm to get him to relax and continued trying to persuade Adam. "Cliff and Clay were separated when they were very young. Cliff didn't know he had a brother."

Adam studied Clay for a long moment. "When I came into the area a few days ago, I scouted the lay of the land. I saw you from a distance. I took you to be other than Mr. Edwards by the way you sat a horse and worked the ranch, and I never got close enough to see different. Then, up close, I decided I'd been mistaken, and Mr. Edwards had just picked up Texas ways at last. But I was right all along. You're not him."

Sophie heard a snort from Adam that sounded. . .satisfied. She didn't want to think about that, so she thought of her husband. He'd been stabbed. She couldn't believe she'd forgotten.

"Let me look at your arm, Clay."

"Twenty men in a lynch mob chasing after him, and Clay has to stop to get a scratch looked at." Luther tugged on his reins and the saddle creaked as he pointed his horse down the mountain. "This might be more fun than the Rockies after all."

Buff chuckled and mounted up.

"With twenty men on our trail?" Adam asked shortly.

There was a second of silence. "Not twenty anymore," Buff said.

Adam looked at the prisoners hanging across their horses. "Sixteen."

"Sixteen to four," Luther said. "That's only four apiece."

"Fair fight then." Adam nodded.

Sophie was tearing at the blood-soaked slit in Clay's sleeve. Clay pulled her away from it and started his horse moving ahead of the others. "I'll keep."

"Clay, don't you think we should bandage it?" Sophie tried to squirm around to see the arm Clay was using to support her back. He'd lifted her on the horse and swung on himself, never showing a bit of pain.

Luther started to laugh.

Clay glared over his shoulder, and the laugh turned into a coughing fit. Then Clay squeezed her so tight it got her attention—and cut off her air. "Hush, woman."

Sophie didn't know what to make of Clay's tone. It was very dictatorial for being so quiet. She hadn't heard him talk like that much lately, not since he'd more or less ordered her to marry him. She considered that his friends might be an undue influence on him. Still, they'd saved her life. She'd have to make allowances.

"We should at least get the bleeding stopped."

It was Buff's turn to cough, and even Adam cleared his throat for a bit too long.

"Sophie McClellen," Clay said so grimly, it got her undivided attention.

"Yes, Clay?" She was surprised she had such an obedient tone at her disposal.

"If you can't keep your mouth shut, what's say we talk about what you were doing up here when I told you to stay in the house and rest!" He'd started out whispering, but by the time he was done, he'd built to a roar.

Sophie looked around to see how Adam and Clay's friends were taking this. Clay had moved out first, so the others were strung out behind them. Clay's broad shoulders blocked her view.

She sat up abruptly, ready to put him in his place. He had no right to speak to her—to humiliate her—like this in front of his friends and Adam. And she wasn't about to lie placidly in his arms while he berated her. Clay didn't let her go, and they had a very brief tussle that she was doomed to lose from the first instant.

Finally she subsided against his chest, exhausted and slightly dizzy from the effort. She had no intention of letting him talk to her like that, and she had no intention of going down to the house to rest. And she would have made that clear to this tyrant she'd married if she could just keep her heavy eyelids from dropping closed.

"Can we please talk about this later?" She didn't mean to be pathetic. She had no respect for the tricks she'd seen women use against men. Her girls cried, but she wasn't prone to it herself. And she didn't bat her eyelashes or pout or nag. But she saw the anger leave Clay's expression, replaced with worry.

"Are you all right? You're not going to pass out again, are you?" His brow furrowed as he studied her face.

That's when Sophie decided a few women's wiles might just be the very thing. "I'm dizzy again. You were right, Clay. I need rest. I should never have gone out so far. I'm sorry I disobeyed you." She looked up at him, and without really meaning to, she was sure she felt her eyelashes bat something fierce. It didn't take much effort to make tears well up in her eyes. All she had to do was think of Clay's wounded arm.

"Please don't shout at me anymore." Sophie buried her head in Clay's chest and hugged him tight around the middle.

Clay's arms closed around her. "I'm sorry I yelled. Just please don't take such chances again. I'm glad you were there this time." He tapped on her chin, and she raised her head to look at him. "You saved my life today, Sophie. Maybe Adam and Luther and Buff woulda come in time, but it woulda been a close thing. So I'm glad you were there. But thinking you might be shot by those men. . ." His arms tightened around her. "Sophie, I—I don't think I could stand it if something happened to you. I want you to quit trying to do so much. Just tell me what you need, and I'll do it for you. I want you to take care of yourself. Please promise me."

Sophie didn't have to fake any tears. They were just there. She reached up and kissed him. She was fully aware that, while she might fail to tell him the exact, whole, absolute, entire truth on occasion, giving a promise was something else again. She wasn't a woman to break her word. Even knowing that, she didn't hesitate to give it. "I promise, Clay. I'll only do what chores you say I can do. I know you'll take care of me."

Clay looked down at her. He was so worried, so kind. Sophie was ashamed of the sneaking she'd been doing. She was going to have to tell the girls she'd been wrong and see that they didn't learn any bad lessons from their ma. She was going to turn over a new leaf.

She turned her face up, looked at him squarely, and repeated firmly, "I'm going to do as you ask. I promise."

She was going to give the sweet man the wife he deserved.

Clay was going to give his wife the spanking she deserved.

He pulled her close up against his chest so she couldn't see his expression. He was pretty sure that what she'd see was disgust. He was disgusted with himself for tricking the poor, foolish, little female into promising to mind him by using such wily methods as sweet talk and gentle touches.

He was finally figuring it out. Women weren't really that much trouble to manage. They needed to be handled like a fractious horse for the most part. A firm hand mixed with patience, careful training, and a pat now and then.

He'd almost gotten the girls trained to the ways of ranch life. He was very satisfied with their progress working the herd. They'd been hopeless at first, but these last few days all three older girls had begun dropping their loops over running steers. They were coming along faster than he had dared hope.

Now he was starting to make some progress with their headstrong mother. At that moment, he was really glad Sophie was pulled up close because Clay couldn't keep the smile off his face.

As they wound down the steep mountain path, the sun began to drop behind the trees. The night birds sang their songs, and the soft *clop* of the horses' hooves lulled his mule-headed wife into relaxing. He glanced down and saw that avoiding her sharp gaze wasn't necessary. She'd fallen asleep. She was resting just like he'd ordered.

His smiled widened until he almost chuckled out loud as he looked down at her. Her eyelashes brushed across a faint bloom on cheeks he thought were too pale. Her pink lips were slightly pursed until he was tempted to kiss them.

In sleep she was perfect innocence, perfect peace, perfect obedience. He suspected it wouldn't last. But now he knew the trick. Now, today, finally, he'd learned how to handle her—his wife, the green-broke filly.

Clay didn't wake her when he carried her into the house. The girls gave him anxious looks, but he held his finger to his lips and walked on into their bedroom, tiptoeing so his spurs didn't jingle her awake. He lay her down and walked back out.

"We've got three extra men for supper, girls. But we won't be ready to eat for a while. We've got business in Mosqueros."

"Is there something wrong with Ma?" Beth wrung her hands and looked at the bedroom door. "You didn't—I mean, were you upset to find her up there?"

"If you mean did I give your ma's backside such a tanning when I found her on that mountainside that now she's fainted dead away, the answer's no." Clay pulled his leather gloves from behind his belt buckle. "She was just tired and she fell asleep on the ride home."

"Who were the men you brought back draped over the saddles?" Sally peeked out the window.

Mandy and Beth ran to the window and stared out.

Clay wondered why womenfolk had to talk over every little detail of what went on. "Those men tried to waylay me on the trail. The other men who road in with us helped us sort things out. Two of them are old friends of mine, and the other one is Adam. I know your ma has talked about him."

"Ma always spoke kindly of Adam." Sally turned back to Clay.

"That's him? The one with the black skin?"

"That's him." Clay tugged his gloves on.

"Was the sheriff up there with you, too, Pa?" Beth asked.

"No, the sheriff wasn't there." Clay needed to get moving to take the prisoners to town. He didn't have time for chitchat. He struggled to speak calmly because he knew the girls were prone to tears, even with the new house rules. "We'll see him when we take those men into the jailhouse."

"We might be hard-pushed to find food for all of them," Mandy said.

"You'll figure something out." Clay headed for the door.

"Do we need to feed the prisoners, too?" Beth glanced at the pot on the stove.

Clay turned back. "No, of course you don't have to feed them. We'll be leaving them in town."

Sally stared curiously out the window. "What about the sheriff and the banker?"

"What about 'em?" Clay tried to follow their winding female thinking.

"Do we have to feed 'em?" Sally asked.

"Well why on earth would you have to feed them?"

"There's more'n just them. That one's a deputy, and the other's. . .I don't know. We'd best get to peeling taters." Beth turned tiredly from the window.

"You don't have to feed that many people. Just the three I told you about. The others aren't here."

"Yeah, they are, Pa. The sheriff and his deputy and Banker Badje. And a coupla other men." Mandy pointed out the window.

Clay went quickly to the window and saw what had prompted the girls' questions. Sheriff Everett was in the ranch yard, holding one of the dry-gulcher's heads up while he studied his face.

"Why didn't you tell me the sheriff was here?"

"I thought we just did." Beth set the potato aside.

Clay clapped his hat back on his head. "I want your ma to rest, so keep the noise down."

He strode across the yard to greet the newcomers, who were talking with Buff, Luther, and Adam. His ranch hands had started straggling out of the bunkhouse as they finished eating, interested in what was going on.

The sheriff turned as Clay walked up to him. "They told me what went on up on the mountaintop."

"Only a Texan would call that anthill a mountain." Luther shook his head in disgust.

Buff grunted.

The sheriff ignored them both. "These rangers came to town in answer to a telegraph I sent about another matter."

Clay recognized one of the rangers. "Howdy, Tom, I've been meaning to get in touch with you but I haven't had a chance. I've been keeping my eyes open, but I haven't had anything to tell."

Texas Ranger Tom Jackson reached out his hand. "Looks like you been busy." He introduced the other ranger as Walt Mitchell.

"Busy don't begin to describe it." Clay shook both men's hands. "Do any of you recognize these men?"

"I think I've got posters on a couple of 'em." The sheriff studied the men. "I'll take 'em into town and lock 'em up."

Clay jerked his thumb at Percy. "That one threw a knife at me from cover when I was riding down the trail." Clay glanced down at his blood-soaked sleeve. "He was trying to kill me plain and simple. And since he had a gun on him whilst he used his knife, I've got to figure he wanted to kill me quiet."

The rangers' sharp eyes went to the wound on Clay's arm. Clay realized how much it hurt. He didn't have time to fool with it now.

"I was aiming at a grouse," Percy snarled from his awkward position over the saddle.

The whole group turned toward him. He'd pushed the gag out of his mouth, and now it rested between his upper lip and his nose.

"When you messed up my throw, I got mad for a minute," Percy growled. "I wouldn'ta done nothin' to you."

"I reckon he used his knife so they could sneak on down to the house. They said right out loud they were after Sophie, too." Adam crossed his arms and stared with cold eyes at Percy. "I heard it clear as day."

"Percy was the one doing the knife throwing," the man hanging over the horse next to Percy said around his loosened gag. "We didn't know he'd tried to kill someone. We just came along and tried to help out our saddle partner."

"Shut up, Jesse." Percy awkwardly elbowed Jesse. "You're in this just as deep as I am."

"We were there, too, Sheriff." Luther stepped up beside Adam. "It was as cold-blooded as it gets."

"Heard it." Buff nodded in agreement.

"His friends here backed him up all the way, even with Sophie. . ." Clay's voice failed him for a moment as he thought of Sophie, standing in the middle of these cutthroats. He tried again. "Even with Sophie right in the middle of it."

"Ain't too many men low-down enough to kill a woman," Adam said fiercely.

"They were planning to kill her even before I came down that trail," Clay went on. "They said they were planning to see to her sooner or later, so it might as well be now. They said those very words to me before my friends here bought into the fight."

"He"—Luther pointed toward Jesse—"said, 'She's seen us now. We can't let her walk away.' "

The sheriff looked at the men standing around Clay, and they all nodded.

Mr. Badje broke into the conversation. "None of these men was the one who wanted to buy McClellen's land."

"What do you mean buy my land?" Clay raised his eyebrows in surprise. "My land's not for sale."

"I reckon they know that, Clay." Sheriff Everett jerked his head at the outlaws. "Why else would they think they needed to kill you?"

Clay pulled his hat off his head and whacked at his pants. His nostrils filled with the honest scent of sweat and trail dust—a smell he worked hard for and was proud of—while men sneaked around in the woods plotting his death to take what they couldn't earn. "You're saying you're out here about some other man who wants to buy my land?"

"He came into my bank saying he heard the Mead spread was for sale." Badje's arms swung out from his sides. The banker's black suit was wrinkled and dirty, completely out of place with the Western dress of the other men, and in utter contrast to the rough hides and leather clothing of Buff and Luther. "When I told him it had been sold, he went crazy. I thought he was going to attack me, he was so mad."

"He tore up the Paradise about a week ago, too," the sheriff added. "Big man by the name of Judd Mason."

"Judd?" the feminine voice from the house behind them turned them all around in their tracks.

Clay groaned aloud and plunked his hat back on his head. His little filly had taken the bit in her teeth again.

SEVENTEEN

Sophie strode toward the crowd of men. With the sheriff's group and the cowhands and the prisoners, it had grown to the size of a town meeting. She wasn't sure it was safe to take her eyes off her cranky husband, but she had to. What Royce Badje had just said was too important.

"Royce, did I just hear you say his name was Judd?"

"Sophie, I told you to stay in the house and rest." Clay tugged the brim of his hat down until Sophie couldn't see his eyes. "I don't want you out here listening to talk of a man who went crazy mad and tore up saloons. It ain't fittin'."

Sophie didn't even glance his way. She said to the sheriff, "A man called Judd was chasing after Clay on the night I met him. I recognized Judd as the same man who killed Cliff two years ago. This man after our land must be the same man."

"More'n likely." The sheriff's eyes sharpened with interest. "Describe him."

"He was a big man, like Royce said. Rode a horse with a J BAR M brand."

"J BAR M," Adam exploded. "The men who stole my cattle and killed my partners had horses with J BAR M brands."

Sophie again saw the fury in her old friend. She could see it ran deep, and it scared her. She knew the look of vengeance. She'd seen it in Clay. Who was she kidding? She'd seen it in herself.

She didn't want Adam to be eaten alive with the thirst for revenge. Silently, in her heart, she said, *Help me.*

Luther turned and looked at her funny. He said rather tiredly, "What now?"

Sophie covered her mouth with her hand as if she could keep her prayers more private by the action. She looked sideways at Adam to see if he was still being directly connected to her prayers. He didn't seem to have heard her, and while that was normal, it worried her. She was afraid his hate was overwhelming the part of him that was open to God.

With a short shake of her head, she remembered why she'd come out here. She threaded her way through the crowd of men to Clay's side and pulled scissors out of her apron pocket. "Hold still while I bandage this."

Clay pulled away from the hand she'd latched on his blood-soaked sleeve. "Confound it woman, it's stopped bleeding now. It'll wait till later."

Sophie turned to the sheriff. "Josiah, would you mind arresting my husband until I can mind this wound?"

"Let her see to it, Clay." Josiah ambled over. "You know better'n to ignore an injury like that for long."

Clay growled under his breath, but he stood still for Sophie's nursing.

"These men we have right now are part of a lynch mob," Luther interjected. "They killed three men, and they had Adam's horse and his partner's gun."

Dead silence descended on the group. While Sophie tried to gently clean and bind Clay's arm, she was adding up all the information just as she could see everyone else was.

Luther walked over to stand beside her. He didn't speak, but she knew he wanted an explanation for her latest prayer.

Finally, into the silence, Ranger Jackson spoke. "It's gotta be the same gang who's done all of it."

Ranger Mitchell added, "It's the vigilantes that have been roaming these hills for years. We've been looking for them, and it looks like we just swept up a big ol' handful of 'em. That means if Mason is the boss, he's got to be close around here."

"If Mason is interested in the ranch today, he might have killed Cliff all that time ago so he could have it." Clay ignored Sophie prodding at his wound.

"And now he sends men to kill you so he can get it," Royce Badje said.

"Kinda makes you wonder what became of the Mead brothers." Sheriff Everett narrowed his eyes at the bound men.

"It surely does," Ranger Mitchell said.

"It never made sense, them running off and leaving their spread." Badje pulled a white handkerchief out of his back pocket and mopped at beads of sweat that streaked his face in the late summer afternoon.

"The wound isn't deep." Sophie fastened a quick bandage in place. "It just caught the outside edge of your shoulder."

Clay reached over to pat her hand where it lay resting high on his arm. He said softly, so only she could hear, "I know, darlin'. Thanks."

Sophie smiled, and Clay looked like he might say more, maybe say something else nice. For a change. Jackson chose that moment to turn on the men tied over the horses.

With soft menace, Jackson said, "We need to know where you boys have been hiding out."

Percy grunted. "Forget it. We ain't tellin' you nothin'."

"They'll tell us," Mitchell said. "They'll tell us and like it."

"Separate 'em." Ranger Jackson started forward. "I don't want 'em knowing what their friends are saying. We'll see who talks first."

"Ain't none of us got nothin' to say to any of you." Percy struggled with his bonds until he tipped himself off the horse's back. Nobody rushed to break his fall, but Ranger Mitchell did walk over and stuff Percy's gag back in his mouth.

The sorrel pranced sideways, and Mitchell crouched down beside Percy. "The way I see it, a whole lotta things got *almost* done up on that mountain today. When we all start talking to the judge, some of you may have been innocent bystanders backing up a saddle partner, and some of you may be guilty of planning cold-blooded murder."

Ranger Jackson pulled Jesse off the sorrel and let him slump to the ground. "Just 'cuz one of you is riding a stolen horse, another is carrying a stolen rifle, and maybe a third throws a knife at a man from cover and tells a woman he's planning to kill her doesn't mean you all have to hang for it."

"I wasn't even with 'em till a few days ago," Jesse shouted. "I didn't know about no lynching."

Jackson slapped the gag back in Jesse's mouth. "Mitchell, take the one on the buckskin into the barn." Jackson gestured at the gathered ranch hands. "A few of you men go along."

Whitey nodded and took hold of the buckskin's reins.

"Sheriff Everett, I'll let you talk to Jesse. He seems eager to tell you how innocent he is. Go behind the bunkhouse. And take your deputies. We want Jesse here to know for sure he hasn't got the slightest hope of escape."

"C'mon boys," Everett said. "It's always fun to try and see how tough a man is who'll threaten a woman."

Jackson caught the bridle on a mouse gray mustang. It pulled against the firm grip. The metal hasps on the reins clinked as the horse whoofed out a fearful snort. "I'm taking this one behind the house. That way they can't hear what the others say and concoct some kind of story together."

Ranger Mitchell rubbed his chin. "Maybe they should be farther apart, Tom. Whatta ya say? They'll be able to hear if anyone starts screaming or crying or begging for mercy."

All four prisoners turned to look at Mitchell, fear evident on their faces.

Jackson said, "I think that'll only encourage the others—"

"—the ones who ain't screaming yet—" Mitchell put in.

"—to start talking sooner," Jackson finished.

Sophie started rolling up the portion of the bandage she hadn't used. She could tell this was a routine the two rangers had done many times before. But the prisoners didn't seem to think they were being conned. They looked eager to be led a safe distance away so they could start telling all they knew.

Ranger Jackson looked at Percy. "I think I'll let Adam here question you, Percy. He seems to have a powerful mad on him about you, and I don't think it'd be wrong to give him a chance to work that off. Clay can talk to you, too. Maybe it'll make that stab wound in his arm feel a little better. And there's no way you're walking away from any of this, so making you talk isn't necessary." Jackson's words could have left bite marks.

Sophie looked at the furious satisfaction on Adam's face and thought, *Help me.*

A heavy hand rested on her shoulder. She looked at Luther. For all his grizzle and trail dust, she saw kind, understanding eyes.

"We won't let Adam do nothin' what carries hard on his conscience, ma'am," Luther assured her.

Ranger Mitchell started leading the buckskin away. He slipped the gag off the man, and although she couldn't make out the words, Sophie could hear the prisoner talking fast to the ranger.

"Adam is a good man," Sophie said to Luther. "One of the best men I've ever known. But he's so angry. I can see the hunger in him for revenge."

She and Luther watched the sheriff lead another horse toward the bunkhouse.

"I know, and I'm right honored that I'm the one who hears your worries and can step in to help. But he's not the only one here that's wanting vengeance. I see it in Clay."

Sophie's eyes darted to her husband. His attention was squarely on Percy. Clay, Adam, and the remaining hired men had moved away from where Sophie stood with Luther. They surrounded Percy where he lay sprawled, faceup, in the dirt.

She saw the anger Clay had banked down. These were men who ha(a hand in his brother's death. They had tried to kill him and threatene(to kill her. He had it under better control than Adam did, but yes, Cla was very angry.

Ranger Jackson pulled a vicious-looking knife out of his boot anc slashed the rope binding Jesse's feet and hoisted him up. He shoved him away from the group.

"It's not just them neither, ma'am. I see it in you, too."

Startled, Sophie looked back at Luther. Their eyes held. After she got over the surprise, she realized there was truth in what he said—a lot of truth. She'd like very much to do some damage to these evil men. "I might feel anger, but I wouldn't do anything to hurt them."

"I know, ma'am, but hatred can burn a hole clear through a person's gut without her ever lifting a hand. Buff and me are here to make sure nothing happens. But it's a man's business, and it might be ugly before it's over. I think it's best if you go on back to the house."

"No. If I'm here they'll control themselves better."

"Or they may shame themselves deeper," Luther said. "It's a poor thing for a man to shame himself in front of a woman he loves."

Sophie looked away from Luther and stared at the ground. She knew he was right. She didn't want to go. She was eager for some revenge of her own. She wanted to see these men get hurt. She wanted to hurt them herself. She whispered aloud, "Help me."

"He is helping you, gal. But you gotta let Him."

Suddenly Sophie felt something give inside her, and she relaxed and smiled at Luther. "I'll go. I trust you to see that nothing's done to that scoundrel that'll hurt these two men of mine."

"I won't fail ya, ma'am." Luther tipped his hat, and Sophie turned and walked back to the house.

When Sophie left, Clay heaved a sigh of relief. At the same time, he couldn't believe it. The woman had a knack for knowing what he wanted her to do and then doing just the opposite. And right now he wanted her out of the way. Bad.

So it stood to reason she'd stick like a burr to a horse's tail.

He couldn't sort out all his fury. His shoulder ached like fire, and he should beat Percy's face in for that alone. But this man had been party to killing his brother. Clay knew it just from watching the trapped look on Percy's face.

Still, the thing that kept pushing every other thought out of his head was the way they'd threatened Sophie. That's what made him clench his fists. That's what called out to his blood and made it boil.

Reacting to the growing fury, Clay leaned forward to put his hands on Percy. Before he could reach him, Adam had the man by his shirtfront. He hauled Percy to his feet and shook him like a cat shakes a rat to its death.

Two of Clay's hired hands stepped forward and caught hold of Percy's arms. Adam let go of the vermin's shirt and pulled back a powerful fist. Luther moved quickly for an old mountain man. He was suddenly beside Adam. He had the strength of the mountains he'd lived in, too. He caught the flying fist, and with a loud *whack* of flesh against flesh, Luther stopped Adam cold. Then he spun Adam around to face him. Rage flared in Adam's eyes, and Clay wondered if Adam would strike Luther.

Clay saw Adam fight for control and knew it didn't come easy to him. Adam's chest heaved, and he jerked at the hand Luther had imprisoned in his massive grip.

Clay watched Adam's black skin shine with sweat. Muscles bulged on his back and arms as Adam tried to free his hand. He looked to be over forty. His tightly curled hair was salted with gray, and his face had the weathered crow's-feet of a man who had lived all his life in the sun. But his body, bare to the waist, had the corded muscles of a man who worked long, brutal hours wrangling cattle. His expression was shot through with rage.

With all his strength and the added power of his fury, Adam

struggled against Luther. Luther was no taller than Adam, but he was twice as broad and it was all solid muscle earned carving out survival in the northern Rockies.

Adam struggled. Luther held fast. An unstoppable force. An immovable object. Something had to give.

On his best day, Adam would have had trouble besting Luther, and today wasn't close to being Adam's best day. Clay could see the lines around Adam's eyes deepened with pain and fatigue. The bullet hole, low on his right side, still oozed a clear liquid. Clay thought of the ugly stripes on Adam's back. They were a mass of scabs and puckering scars.

"Seems to me," Luther said, "before you beat information out of a man, you oughta at least ask him some questions."

Adam pulled back his other fist, his eyes fastened coldly on Luther.

"Think, man." Luther shook Adam's fist, still clenched in his massive hand. "You don't want to hit me."

Adam jerked his hand away from Luther. "You weren't there. They came onto us in our sleep. Dinky was standing guard, and they backshot him."

Adam's chest heaved and his eyes blazed with hate. "The shot woke me up, and I saw him fall forward and try to get to his feet. By the time I'd thrown my blanket off, they were all around us. Twenty of 'em. They had whips and clubs. They didn't just hang my friends,"—Adam ran his hands through his coiled hair—"they beat 'em halfway to death first."

"I heard 'em laughing and gloating about how much money our herd would bring. I crawled away into the bushes like a worthless coward. I must have passed out, because when I woke up it was over." Adam added with bitter self-contempt, "I slept through my friends' hangings."

"And why didn't they come after you?" Luther asked quietly.

Adam shrugged. "Reckon they forgot about me in the confusion. Lost count."

Luther prodded him. "This gang has ridden these hills for two years.

No one's had so much as a hint about who they are, and that's mainly because they've never left a witness. And you're telling me they couldn't count to four?"

Adam ignored the question. "I came around and lay there, hiding, and watched my friends twist in the wind, already dead. The men who attacked us were gone. I could see they'd picked over the camp, stolen our supplies. I should have gone after them. I should have given an accounting of myself, even if it meant I died fighting."

"And why didn't you?" Clay had to know.

Clay could see Adam was so completely lost in his memories of the attack that he had to make a huge effort to think past it.

Finally Adam said, "Sophie called me."

Clay shook his head a little, hoping Adam's words would make sense. "She called you?"

"I heard her voice, clear as day."

Luther nodded. "She said, 'Help me.'"

Adam nodded. "My back was ripped open from their whips and they'd shot me. But I heard her, and I knew she needed help. I turned away, left my friends swinging. Didn't even cut 'em down and bury 'em. I started walking to Mosqueros."

"That's what happened to us," Luther said.

"You're telling me that you heard Sophie's voice asking for help, both of you, hundreds of miles from here?" Clay asked. "Hundreds of miles apart from each other?"

Luther nodded.

"Clear as if she were standing by my shoulder," Adam said.

"It was her voice," Luther added. "But I knew it was about you. I knew you needed help, boy."

"How can that be?" Clay wondered.

Adam's head and shoulders drooped as he whispered, "It was God saying I was the answer to Sophie's prayer."

"God let us hear it," Luther said. "And do you think the answer to Sophie's prayers is to beat the tar out of this man?"

Anger sparked in Adam's eyes as he looked from Luther to Percy. "Why not? God is a God of justice."

A hungry satisfaction roared through Clay as he heard Adam's words. Yes, a God of justice. Except, God was more than that. The miracle of what God had done seeped into the roiling hate in his heart and began to settle him. Reluctantly, Clay said into the moment of silence, "But this isn't justice, it's vengeance. And vengeance belongs to God."

"So are you saying we're supposed to let them go?" Adam whirled around to confront Clay. "Let them do as much damage as they want and wait for God to settle for them in the next life?"

"No." Clay didn't want to give up his revenge. "This country has a system of justice. These men have to face the law and its penalties. It's not up to us to hand out punishment for their crimes."

Even as he said it, Clay knew it wasn't what he wanted to do. He sighed. "Leave room for God's wrath. 'Vengeance is mine; I will repay, saith the Lord.' "

"If either of you killed this scum just to make yourselves feel better," Luther said, "that doesn't leave much room for God's wrath, now, does it?"

"It would speed him on his way to God's wrath." Adam crossed his arms.

Clay knew Adam didn't want to give up this chance to hurt the men who had taken so much from him.

At that moment, Ranger Mitchell came out of the barn. He yelled, "I've got the gang's hideout."

Ranger Jackson emerged seconds later from behind the house. "And I've learned most of what they've got planned."

Clay looked down at Percy's fearful expression. "It won't speed him up much. The territorial judge in this part of Texas is almighty fond of hangings."

"Yeah, they should swing from a tree, just like he done my friends."

"Just like they did my brother." Clay looked at Adam.

Clay could see that Adam's thirst for revenge could latch on to the vision of Percy in a noose. It wasn't a victory for God. Adam's hate was still in control.

Adam leaned over Percy. "And without me dirtyin' my hands on you one bit. I think you've just earned yourself the noose you've been handin' out to others for the last few years. Then you'll get a chance to meet your Maker and find out what kind of vengeance God has in store for you."

Adam straightened and looked sideways at Clay. "I think that's somethin' I can live with."

"Yeah, so can I." Clay turned to Luther. "Thanks."

Luther grunted. "I should hope you thank me. That's more words'n I've strung end to end in my life."

"He's gotten plumb talkative since your missus started speaking to him," Buff said drearily. "It wears on my ears."

EIGHTEEN

Ma, they're starting to clear out." Sally hung on one window ledge. Mandy was stationed at the other. Beth peeked out the door.

"I told you girls to get away from the windows." Sophie darted over to stand beside Sally. She'd avoided looking out the window, mostly. And she'd tried to keep the girls away. She remembered Luther's words about a man shaming himself in front of the woman he loved and knew that they were true.

Except for the part about love.

Why did Luther think Clay loved her? The very thought made something warm grow in her heart.

Although she was a might too sneaky to be considered truly respectful, and that husband of hers was given to grunting or yelling instead of speaking normally, Sophie thought she and Clay got on nicely enough. But love? She'd been in love with Cliff, and it had hurt. She had adored him, and he'd repaid her with coldness and criticism. No. Love was a very bad idea.

"The sheriff is loading that one on the ground onto his horse." Sally leaned until her nose smudged the window.

"Who were the other men, Ma?" Mandy asked. "The two tall ones."

"They're Texas Rangers," Sophie said.

Mandy quit spying for a second to give Sophie a startled look. "What are Texas Rangers doing here?"

"They're on the trail of the gang who shot at us the other day. The heriff and the rangers are hoping to find the rest of them. Then this vill finally be over."

"I want things to go back to how they used to be when I was young," ight-year-old Beth said, "when we only had to be afraid of cyclones and rattlesnakes."

Ten-year-old Mandy nodded. "Those were the good old days."

Sophie was tempted to smile, except she really wanted things back ike the "good old days" herself.

The remaining men stood around for a bit longer.

"Are they talking?" Sally asked.

"I reckon." Beth swung the door open just a crack wider.

"Why do you only *reckon* they're talking?" Sophie eased the door back closed a little, not wanting Beth to get them caught.

"Because you never see their lips move," Sally observed.

Sophie looked closer. They were communicating somehow. There were lots of shrugging shoulders and the occasional nod, but there was certainly no animated discussion going on.

"It's no wonder Indians can talk with drumbeats and smoke signals." Sophie's eyes narrowed as she watched closely for signs of conversation. "From a man's point of view, it must be possible to be quite eloquent."

"The cowhands are heading for the bunkhouse," Sally reported unnecessarily, since they were all watching with rapt attention.

"You know, girls, I'll bet if we were all men, Sally wouldn't have just said out loud what she said."

"I didn't mean to do anything wrong, Ma." Sally looked away from the window, worried.

"No, you didn't do anything wrong." Sophie rested her hand on Sally's silky, blond head. "That's not my point. I think, instead of saying anything, she'd have just watched silently, knowing we were all seeing the same thing."

There was a prolonged moment of silence.

"Or maybe she'd have grunted." Mandy broke into a fit of giggles.

"Or pointed." Beth closed the door and started laughing.

"And the rest of us. . ." Sally couldn't speak as she started laughing with her sisters.

All the girls started giggling until they could hardly stand up. Sophie couldn't help joining in. Finally, she finished Sally's thought. "The rest of us would have scratched ourselves and nodded while we glared at the one who had grunted, wondering why he'd gotten so all-fired chatty."

They were all laughing like maniacs when the men walked in. Clay and the other men stared silently, which sent all the girls into further fits of laughter.

Clay sighed as if he carried the weight of the world on his shoulders. Sophie saw Clay look over his shoulder at Adam, who simply shook his head. Buff shrugged. Luther harrumphed.

The girls all thought it was hilarious.

Sophie managed to get ahold of herself enough to dry the tears from her eyes with her apron. "I've got coffee."

The men all nodded. Buff scratched the back of his neck. The girls fled into their bedroom, giggling.

The men sat at the table as Sophie poured. They drank in silence. An occasional high-pitched giggle would escape from the bedroom, and the men would flinch or look over at the door as if it were dangerous. As the silence lengthened, Sophie lost whatever spark of amusement had taken hold of her, and she started to get mad. Before she could say something she'd regret, she decided to give them a chance by starting with the obvious. "Introduce me to your friends again, Clay."

Clay said, "Luther 'n Buff."

Each man nodded when his name was spoken. Sophie looked at Luther. "You're the one who said I was calling you, isn't that right?"

"Yes," Luther wrapped both hands around his tin cup. Sophie remembered cold nights in the thicket when she'd saved every ounce of heat by warming her hands that way. Out of habit she still did it, even in the Texas summer heat, just like Luther.

Sophie stifled a request for more details. She turned to Adam, who sat at her table, battered and shirtless, but with his head up and his spine straight. He used to talk to her some. "It's wonderful to see you again, Adam. I hope you're planning to stay with us."

"Long as I'm needed." Adam took a long pull on his coffee.

Despite his short answer, Sophie's heart lifted to think of having Adam with them again. "What happened with the sheriff, and what did those men tell you? Are you going to be able to track down Judd Mason? I want to know all about it, Clay, while I patch up your knife wound better."

Clay sighed so deeply it seemed to come clear from his toes. As if it violated the Code of the West, he reluctantly said, "All right."

Sophie took him at his word and went to find her doctoring supplies. She carried them over, set them on the table, and began undoing the quick bandage she'd put on Clay's arm. "This wound is going to need stitches. And when I'm done with Clay, I want to look at your wounds, Adam."

Adam shook his head. "No need, Sophie girl. I could have used your touch a few weeks ago, but I'm fine now."

"You'll sit still while I check you over," Sophie informed him. "Then I'll get a meal on the table."

"You've been through more today than I have," Clay said. "You sit while you work on my arm, or I won't let you touch it."

"Clay, I don't need to. . ."

Luther was already dragging a chair over to the table and moving his out of the way so Sophie could sit.

Sophie decided this wasn't a fight she was going to win, so she sat.

Clay caught her hand as she reached for his arm and held it tight. "And the girls can get a meal on, or we'll go eat in the bunkhouse. I want you to rest."

"Clay, I don't need to rest." Sophie dabbed at his oozing wound. "There is nothing in the. . ." Sophie realized her fingers were going numb as Clay squeezed tighter and tighter. "The girls can do it. They have a stew already done, so they just need to mix up biscuits and set the table."

She was talking fast at the end. Clay released her. Sophie sighed with relief and had to control the urge to rub her hand. She arched one eyebrow at her husband.

"Good girl," he said, like she was a well-behaved horse.

"Well, I'm not too tired to listen." She pulled her needle out of its cotton wrapping and threaded it. "Now I want to hear why there were rangers out there, and what's going to happen to Judd Mason?" She pointed the needle right at her husband's nose. "And I want to hear it right now."

Clay smiled again.

Luther eased himself back in his chair. "Reckon it's a yarn I don't mind spinnin'." Luther relaxed as if he was in front of a campfire after a long day riding the range. "I woke up in the night, three weeks ago—"

"Four weeks," Buff cut in.

Luther frowned, then shrugged and continued, "To the sound of a woman saying, 'Help me.' I knew it wasn't the boy," Luther said, nodding at Clay.

"I'm father of five these days, Luth. Knock off calling me 'boy.' "

Luther grunted what might have been half a laugh. "But I knew it had something to do with him."

"We headed out." Buff slid his heavy coat off his shoulders.

The men unwound their tale, with Adam adding some and Clay filling in what had been going on at the ranch while they traveled. Sophie stitched up Clay's arm then scooted her chair around so she could stay seated while she cleaned Adam's wounds.

A warm corner of Sophie's heart, always filled by her love for God, began to expand and grow until she wanted to laugh and cry at the same time. "God heard me. He's really listening."

Clay rubbed her shoulders while she sat with her back to him, tending Adam's wounds. "He always is."

"I always pray, 'Help me,' " she said quietly.

Together, Adam and Luther said, "We know."

"And He really did. He helped me." Sophie quit talking before she broke rule number one. She pulled her faintly trembling hands away from Adam's back before she hurt him. Clay's comforting, calloused hands stilled on her back, steadying her so she could finish with Adam.

She at last felt able to look at the three men who were sitting with Clay and her. "Thank you. You saved us."

Buff grunted.

Luther ducked his head. " 'Tweren't nothin', ma'am."

"Didn't have no choice, Sophie girl," Adam said. "A man's got God in his head, there's not much choice a'tall."

"Thank you." Then Sophie turned to Clay. "I'm really tired. The girls can get dinner on. I think I'm going to go rest."

Clay smiled his approval at her, and she wondered again at Luther's assurance that Clay loved her. It was bound to lead to hurt, but she found that she really liked the idea, especially since she was very much afraid she loved him, too.

Her eyelids almost fell closed before she found the strength to stand up and leave the room. She lay down on the bed fully clothed, planning to rest long enough to make her husband happy, then get up and help get a meal on. As she drifted off she realized it wasn't just Luther, Buff, and Adam who had been sent to her. It was Clay, too. She held sleep at bay as she thanked God.

The wonder of the words *help me* threaded through her mind, and tears pricked at her eyes. She shook her head to prevent such nonsense, but all that did was send the tears over the edge of her lower lids. She heard chairs slide around a bit in the other room, and the door to her bedroom opened.

Clay came in and sat on the bed beside her. "Adam and Luther said something was wrong."

Sophie couldn't hold back a smile even though the tears didn't quit flowing. Clay rubbed a rough thumb across one cheek. His touch was so gentle that Sophie felt as if she were made of the finest crystal. "Please don't cry, Sophie darlin'. You know I can't stand cryin'."

His sweetness and concern made the tears flow faster.

"When you cry I feel like some kind of a monster who has hurt you or scared you half to death or. . ."

Sophie lunged forward, wrapped her arms around his neck, and kissed him hard to get him to quit talking crazy. She pulled back and smiled at his stunned expression. Softly enough to ensure privacy in the crowded house, she said, "A woman doesn't always cry when she's sad or hurt, Clay. I was lying here thinking that God gave me a miracle when he sent Adam, Luther, and Buff to me."

"He did, didn't He? A true miracle."

Sophie nodded and swiped at her tears. "And He gave me a miracle when He sent you."

Clay looked confused. "It's the other way around, near as I can tell. You saved my life. You pulled me out of that creek and patched me up. You're the only one in this room who's a miracle."

Sophie kissed him again, then tucked her head under his chin and hugged him. Clay held her so tight it hurt, and it was the best hurt in the world.

At last she pulled back far enough to see him. "We are just going to have to disagree about who the miracle is."

Clay smiled and brushed the hair off her soggy face. "I reckon that's a disagreement I can live with." He offered her a handkerchief.

Sophie turned away a bit and blew her nose and clenched the handkerchief tight. "I keep thinking about how you came here and how much better my life is because of it. Then I thought about God doing a pure, real live miracle just for me, and I was so honored and humbled, it made me cry."

"Kinda like when the girls cried over the baby?"

"Just like that," Sophie said, relieved he understood.

"Waste of water and salt," Clay grumbled.

Sophie smiled and kissed him again, and only the men in the next room, who might be listening, and a twinge of old fear kept her from telling him she had fallen in love with him.

"Try an' get some rest, darlin'." Clay pressed her back against her illow.

Sophie nodded. Clay stood and took a couple of steps toward the oor. He paused and looked back at her, and then he awkwardly came ack, leaned over, and kissed her on the forehead, then the cheek, then er lips.

He brushed her hair back again. "You and the girls, and this life I've ot myself into, will always be a miracle to me, Sophie."

As if he'd embarrassed himself, he straightened away from her and urried from the room.

Sophie lay there awhile and did a little more crying, but she was ery careful not to think *help me*, not wanting to overtax the Lord's upply of miracles or Luther's and Adam's supply of patience. She urled onto her side and hugged Clay's baby in her arms and let her yes drift shut, thinking she'd just rest for a second, to please Clay. The ext thing she knew, Clay was pulling her into his arms, and she woke n the pitch-black room. She was just awake enough to say, "I need to nake biscuits."

Clay snuggled her up close. "You just rest."

She thought how odd it was that he was so fixated on her need to est. She had to explain to him how tough she was and how hard she ad always worked. Really, her husband didn't know her at all. And he'd tell him so, as soon as she finished her little nap.

'Percy never came back," Harley said. "Something's gone wrong."

Judd threw back his blanket and started pulling his boots on.

Harley said sharply, "We're breaking camp!"

Eight of the ten men left were asleep. Harley's voice woke them as f it were a rifle shot. The two men on watch came charging into the camp. A quick glance at the heavy-lidded eyes told Judd they'd both een asleep. Judd didn't waste his lead on them.

"If they're caught, they might tell where we're hid out," Harley said.

Judd looked around the campsite. "If they'd have done for McClellen they'd have come back into the camp hootin' and hollerin'. You're right. We break camp."

Harley was already saddling his horse. Judd noticed he wasn't particularly interested in what the rest of them did or if Judd agreed with him. Harley had lived longer than most men in his profession, and Judd trusted his instincts.

Harley said, "Let's head into the Santiagos for a few days then figure what to do next."

"What if you're wrong?" one of the men asked. "What if Percy comes back? He won't be able to find us."

"The three best trackers we have went with him. They'll find us." Judd hoped they wouldn't, since he was sure they'd have a posse with them when they came back—*if* they came back. He knew what kind of a man Percy was. A low-down, cowardly coyote who'd sell his own mother to save his skin.

"We'll drop back and come up with a new plan to get that ranch," Judd said. "We killed Edwards; we can kill his twin brother."

"We've been watching long enough to know McClellen's nothing like his tenderfoot brother." Harley spurred his horse and didn't look to see if anyone in the gang was with him.

Judd fell in behind him. As he pushed his horse into a gallop, he realized he was running. This was the second time McClellen had made them run. The defeat tasted like ashes in his mouth.

Nineteen

The ranch settled into a routine with the capture of the four outlaws. Every cowhand did his work as usual, but all kept their guns close at hand and stayed on razor's edge. As a week slowly passed, Sophie began to hope the rest of the gang had hightailed it.

Parson Roscoe picked this Sunday to yell at them again. Sophie thought the man was on to something, changing the tone of his sermons from week to week. She certainly listened to every word he said. But why wouldn't she? He'd obviously heard how Sophie had lied by omission to her husband, and he'd written the sermon just to scold her.

She thought it was rather rude of him to pick on her, especially since she'd been trying to be more loving and a more obedient wife. But she had only decided about being a better wife after the run-in with the outlaws, so maybe the parson already had his sermon written, based on the way she used to act. Besides, it was a full month into her marriage, which was kind of late to begin behaving herself, so she figured she deserved it.

She probably also deserved to have Sally and Mandy clinging to her, one on each side, and Laura sleeping dead away on her lap. The seemingly boneless little girl seemed to gain weight with each passing moment.

"How is it that Satan has so filled your heart that you have lied to the Holy Spirit?"

Sophie didn't like to think Satan had filled her heart. She would have sunk further into her seat if she could have—she was practically slouched out of sight as it was.

"You didn't really tell a lie," a quiet voice whispered. Sophie suspected it was the voice of Satan himself, tempting her to justify her disobedience to her husband. Mentally, she told him to get away from her.

I've already decided to change, she thought. *You aren't going to convince me to keep sneaking around.*

Sophie snapped her attention back to the parson when he thundered, "Later Ananias's wife came in to the assembly and repeated the lie she and her husband had agreed on."

That's when Sophie realized the parson was reading a Bible verse, and it wasn't her heart that Satan had filled but the heart of Ananias. *Whew!*

"Peter said to Sapphira, 'How could you agree to test the Spirit of the Lord? Look, the feet of the men who buried your husband are at the door, and they will carry you out also.' " Parson Roscoe's voice kept gaining strength.

Sally and Mandy squirmed closer. Sophie, ever the mother, glanced down the row at Beth and saw that she was now sitting on Clay's lap with her face buried in his chest. Sophie wondered if the McClellen clan shouldn't start sitting nearer the back.

" 'At that moment Sapphira fell down at Peter's feet and *died.*' " The walls of the church nearly vibrated as the parson roared out the last word. Parson Roscoe stopped to take a deep breath and mop the sweat off his brow.

Sophie wondered if Sapphira wasn't Hebrew for Sophie. It was close enough to sting. *I'm done with lies, Lord,* Sophie prayed in her heart. *I am. I'm going to love everyone and be honest right down to the ground. You gave me a miracle, and I won't give back anything but my very best. Now could You please make the parson quit yelling at me?*

God had given her a miracle all right. But He didn't give her another one now. About halfway through the sermon—which stretched on so long Sophie began to wonder if there weren't more liars in the building than ıst her, since God should have told the parson that she got his point right ff—Sally relaxed her death grip on Sophie's arm. Sophie looked down to ee her little girl fast asleep. Sophie looked sideways at Clay, who caught he glance and smiled. He reached across Sally and lifted the, by now, wo-hundred-pound Laura out of Sophie's arms and settled her beside the linging Beth. Then, with a deft move that should have required a third and, he shifted Sally's slumbering form so it rested on his arm, instead f Sophie.

Sophie whispered, "Your arm."

Clay mouthed back, "I'm okay."

Sophie wanted to protest, but having the weight lifted off of her vas too heavenly. She sighed aloud in relief and Clay smiled at her.

The parson began to wind down shortly after that. "Ananias and apphira died because God looked into their hearts and knew that here was no repentance and no love. There was time for both of them o change their minds and tell the truth. There is time for all of us, right ıow, to accept the love of God, repent of our sins, commit our lives to esus Christ, and accept His salvation."

The parson lifted his Bible, draped open over one hand. "It's the ternal theme. It's love. There are no lies when there is love. Can any of ou imagine a more complete waste of time than lying to God?"

Several people in the congregation shook their heads, and Sophie ound her head moving along.

"He already knows." The parson lowered the Bible and leaned orward. "He knows the truth in everyone's heart. Save your energy for omething that has a chance of success."

Sophie reached her hand over the top of Sally's nodding head and ested it on Clay's strong, wounded arm. She didn't say anything, since hey were in the front row after all. But she smiled at him and made promise to herself that she'd tell Clay all about her booby traps and idden weapons this very day. Why, she'd tell him on the trip home vithout another moment's delay. No more lies. None ever. Sophie felt a ightness come over her heart, and she knew it was the right thing to do.

With a quick prayer for forgiveness and a promise to God that sh was going to start a new life this second, much as she'd promised la week, Sophie turned back to the parson and sang along to "Amazin Grace."

Just as the song ended, a loud *crash* sounded from the back of th church. It woke Sally and had both Beth and Mandy turning aroun in their seats.

"Is everyone all right back there?" the parson asked with a worrie frown.

When he talked like that, Sophie couldn't resist looking behind he even though it was bad manners to turn around in church. She though the noise came from the farthest back pew, which was teeming wit toe-headed little boys—the Reeves family.

"Did something get broken?" Parson Roscoe peered toward th noise.

One of the five-year-old triplets poked his head out from wher he was crouched behind the pew. He said, in a tone that screamed of guilty conscience, "No, sir."

As the raggedly dressed, dirty-faced, little boy stood up, no on could fail to see the wooden rack in his hand that was only moment ago nailed on to the end of his pew to hold the hymnal.

"Mark, you little liar." One of his older brothers elbowed th little boy.

Everyone in the church started to chuckle.

The parson walked down the center aisle and extended his hand t the little boy. "Don't worry about the book rack. It can be fixed."

Daniel Reeves stood up and took the piece of lumber out of hi son's hand before the parson could reach it. "I'll repair it, Parson. A Reeves fixes what he breaks."

"I'll bet that keeps him busy," Clay murmured.

Sophie tried not to start laughing again. She was a bit surprise to see Adam standing against the back wall of the church. He hadn' ridden in with them. Luther and Buff were on either side of him, all o them standing, although there were a few seats left. She saw Eustace and Whitey standing off to the side a little, and several others of the McClellen hands were about the room. It struck her that they were doing more than attending church—they were standing guard. It sent a chill down her spine to realize that, even in this holy place, they all needed to be on guard.

As she turned back to the front of the church to await the closing prayer, her eyes swept the cheerful congregation. She was relieved to see that the people seemed to be unconcerned about a child doing a bit of damage. Then she noticed Miss Calhoun.

Miss Calhoun sat rigidly facing forward. Sophie had the impression she'd never turned around. This was a woman who minded her manners. A look of such profound disapproval was etched on her face that Sophie wondered if it might be frozen in place.

Sophie shook her head as she considered what kind of teacher Miss Calhoun must be if she couldn't accept high spirits and a few mishaps from active little boys. Or maybe there was something more going on. Maybe the Reeveses had begun coming to school this week and proved to be too much for her to handle.

Well, Sophie imagined she'd find out today. Miss Calhoun was coming to eat with them after church. Even after the craziness of this week and the outlaws, Sophie hadn't forgotten that, and she had a wild turkey she'd snared early yesterday roasting, waiting for their return.

Sophie sighed when she thought of the meal ahead. She had to tell Clay to build them a bigger table and a few more chairs. As soon as she thought it, she cheered up. She would never have considered asking Cliff to take on such a project. And Sophie also knew it was significant that her first thought hadn't been to ask Adam to build it.

Yes, she was going to let her husband handle nearly everything that could even begin to be considered man's work from now on. And she was going to obey him, be honest with him, and most of all love him with all her heart.

"You are the sneakin'est, most disobedient wife in the whole state of Texas!" Clay snatched his hat off his head and whacked his leg with it. Sophie suspected what he really wanted to whack was her backside.

The horses pulling the wagon jumped a bit at the sudden motion behind them and picked up their speed.

Sophie looked over her shoulder at Miss Calhoun, who was riding her own horse. She was trailing along behind them far enough to avoid the dust, so she didn't hear Clay growling.

"Now, Clay, I know you're angry. But remember that I've already promised not to do anything like this again."

"Rocks! You were hauling rocks!" Clay clobbered his leg a few more times.

"I told her not to, Pa," Sally piped up from the wagon box.

Sophie glared over her shoulder at the little tattletale, and Sally subsided into a sitting position on the floor of the wagon.

Sophie just barely heard her daughter mutter, "Well, I did."

"I deserve any yelling you want to give me." She stared straight forward, fully intending to accept any criticism Clay handed her way.

Clay wedged his hat roughly back on his head. "I fully intend to. When I think what could have happened to you on that hillside hauling rocks, I want to—"

"Just know before you start with your lecture," Sophie interrupted him, "that I'm used to doing for myself. I've been on my own completely for two years, and what with the war and all, I spent most of my married life fending for myself."

"I realize that." Clay clucked to the horses to keep up their speed. "But things are going to—"

"So it's been a hard-learned lesson not to just do whatever needs doing." Sophie gave her chin a firm nod.

Laura, still asleep, began to whimper on Sophie's knee.

"I'll take her, Ma, so Pa can finish up telling you how stupid you are, without being interrupted." Mandy poked her head between Sophie and Clay, scooped Laura up in her arms, and went back to sitting.

Sophie straightened her skirt. "Yes, go ahead, Clay."

"Now, Mandy, I'm not going to tell your ma she's stupid. She don't like that, and I'd never do something she said she don't like."

"It doesn't matter." Sophie figured she deserved whatever Clay dished out. "You can call me stupid if you want to. As of today I'm going to learn a new way. If I want something done, I'm going to tell you."

"I don't think you're stupid, Sophie." Clay seemed to be sidetracked from his lecture, and Sophie really wished he'd get on with it.

"Sure you do," Sophie reminded him. "You called me stupid for going out at night when there might be cougars to eat me, and you called me stupid—"

"I only called you stupid because I know you're *not* stupid."

Sophie was unable to think of a sensible response to that, so she fell silent.

Her girls weren't speechless. "You called us stupid, too," Beth said. "Does that mean you don't think we're stupid, neither?"

"Of course I don't think you girls are stupid. I know you're a right smart bunch of children," Clay reassured her.

"So if you call us stupid when you think we're smart," Mandy asked hesitantly, "does that mean when you say you love us you really hate us?"

Clay pulled his hat off his head and started whacking his leg again. Sophie knew there wasn't a speck of dust left on his hat or his pants. She was also curious about how Clay would answer.

"If I really thought you were stupid, I'd expect you to do stupid things. But when I know you're smart and you do stupid things, then I think I've got reason to complain. Do you understand that?"

"I guess that makes sense," Sophie said. "You expect better from us. But the word *stupid* is so hurtful. . . ."

"Not if you're smart it isn't," Clay protested. "It's like if I called you ugly, when you're so pretty. You'd know I didn't mean—"

"Did Pa just call you ugly, Ma?" Sally asked from behind them. She stuck her head between them with a worried frown on her face.

Clay plunked his hat back on his head and ran one gloved hand over his face, as if he could scrub hard enough to wash the whole trip home from church out of his mind.

"No, Sally, in fact I think he just called me pretty."

"But that's not what I heard," Sally interrupted.

"And he didn't answer about hating us," Beth added with a break in her voice.

Mandy said quietly, "That's mean, Pa."

Laura bounced on Mandy's lap and said, "Mama ugwee."

"Quiet!" Clay roared.

Sophie was afraid that even the trailing Miss Calhoun could hear that one.

"I think you're all as smart as any girls I've ever known," Clay shouted. "Of course I've never known any girls, but. . .well, just never you mind that. I never heard tell of girls who could be so smart. Don't ever say I hate you. It's just a plain dirty lie to say such a thing." Clay turned to glare at the girls over his shoulder with an expression that was as unloving as any Sophie had ever seen. In a strange way, that made her believe him.

"I told you all I love you, and if that ever changes I'll let you know. So unless I've said different, I love you and that's that." Clay turned back to the horses in a huff.

"And I think you're all beautiful. Your Ma is the prettiest lady in church, in Mosqueros, in Texas, and maybe in the whole world. She's prettier than any I've seen before, and you all look just like her, so you're pretty, too. Now, could we just ride quiet the rest of the way home?" He shook the reins as if he wanted the ride to be over.

Sophie thought of her work-roughened hands and her scattered hair and her plain dresses. "You really think I'm pretty?"

Clay looked away from the horses. His expression made her wonder what he'd heard in her voice. "I think I'm the luckiest man alive to have such a pretty little wife as you, Sophie. You have to know how beautiful you are."

If Sophie had ever thought about her looks, it had been a long time ago as a dreamy-headed teenager. She hadn't given it much notice since.

She looked into Clay's warm eyes for a long time, wishing she could be alone with him for just a few minutes. She'd tell him she loved him, and she'd reassure him one more time that she'd never lie to him again. Which reminded her, "Um, Clay, I don't think you ever finished lecturing me about the booby traps."

Clay sighed. "Are you going to quit setting your traps now?"

Sophie nodded.

"And leave the outdoor repairs to me?"

"I promise."

"And trust me to protect this family?"

"I will, Clay. I already do," Sophie said fervently.

"Then I reckon the lecture's over." Clay turned back to the horses and clucked at them again.

Sophie felt like Clay had been cheated out of his scolding. She deserved it after all. But she couldn't quite bring herself to urge him to yell at her.

As the ranch came in sight, Sophie's mind turned to the dinner ahead and the fussy Miss Calhoun. Sally poked her head between them again and turned to Clay.

He looked down at her. "What?"

Sally said with wide-eyed innocence, "I think you're pretty too, Pa."

Clay seemed taken aback for a moment, then he smiled down at Sally and chucked her under the chin with his gloved fist. "Well, thank you darlin'. I reckon that's about the sweetest thing anyone's ever said to me."

Sally grinned and pulled her head back. The last few yards of the trip were completed with Clay chuckling softly while he guided the horses.

Clay helped Miss Calhoun down off her horse just as Adam, Luther, Buff, and the others came riding into the ranch from different directions. They'd ridden out of church ahead of the McClellen wagon and disappeared to scout the trail for danger.

Sophie thought of the huge bird she had roasting. "Clay, we have plenty of turkey. Ask the men if they want to eat with us."

"That's a right nice idea." Clay went and talked to them out of Sophie's hearing. She wondered if they were talking about more than the invitation. She was a mite annoyed to be kept in the dark. But remembering her promise to herself and God, she minded Clay's obvious wish to confer privately with the men and turned her attention to Miss Calhoun.

"Did you enjoy your ride out here, Miss Calhoun? We could have made room for you in the wagon."

"I need to take my horse out when I can." Miss Calhoun neatly removed her black gloves, tugging gently on one finger at a time. "He stands idle in the stable too much of the time."

Her gloves tucked neatly away, she followed Sophie and the girls into the house. "Let me help get the meal." Miss Calhoun carried a satchel with her, and she produced a large white apron from it.

Miss Calhoun proved to be more approachable when she was working side-by-side with Sophie and the girls. Sophie was pleased when the young woman produced a carefully wrapped loaf of bread from the satchel to add to the meal.

When Sophie called out to the men that the food was ready, they all came trooping in the front door.

"There's a stew warming in the bunkhouse, too." Whitey pulled his hat off his head and twisted it in his hands. "We'll only have a bite of your turkey, ma'am. Thank you for inviting us."

Each of the men had a kind word of thanks to say as they filed through. Sophie became alarmed as she sliced away at the ever-shrinking turkey and filled the plates the men brought from the bunkhouse. The big bird lasted though, and after the last of the men went outside, she began filling plates for the women. She noticed Clay went outside with the men, and Sophie felt betrayed—and a little jealous. Then the very proper Miss Calhoun sat down, and Sophie began to think of her daughters' table manners.

They didn't have any.

Miss Calhoun sat at the McClellen's undersized table with all the dignity of a queen. She ate so neatly and cut her turkey so precisely, every move Sophie made seemed clumsy by comparison. Sophie spent the whole meal correcting the girls' manners, and from the surprised looks they gave her, she knew they'd never heard a lot of this stuff before.

"How long have you been in Mosqueros, Miss Calhoun?" Sophie asked. "Is this your first year?"

Miss Calhoun chewed thoroughly and swallowed. "I started with a winter term. I took over when the last teacher married Mr. Badje."

Sophie remembered the banker's very young wife and nodded. "How do you like it?"

Miss Calhoun lay her fork down daintily and folded her hands in her lap. "There were far fewer students for the winter term. The school is growing."

Sophie noticed Miss Calhoun didn't answer her question. "More people are moving into the area." Sophie then thought of all the men who had proposed to her two years ago. "There weren't many women here when we first settled. I know the Reeveses are newcomers." The minute Sophie mentioned the Reeveses, she regretted it. She remembered the tense expression on Miss Calhoun's face in church. She was reminded of it because that exact look reappeared.

Miss Calhoun made an effort to answer; then with a sudden fumbling movement that was at odds with her usual manner, she dragged a handkerchief out of her sleeve and pressed it to her lips. At first Sophie thought the young woman was trying to physically hold words inside herself that she thought were better left unsaid. Then she saw that Miss Calhoun was crying. There was no sobbing, but a tear ran down Miss Calhoun's cheek, and she took an occasional broken breath.

The whole table fell silent. Sophie saw the girls all stare wide-eyed at the sight of the very proper teacher losing her composure. Sophie finally got past her surprise and jumped up from the table. She wrapped her arms around Miss Calhoun's trembling shoulders. "What is it, Grace? Did something happen? Are the boys too much trouble at school?"

Miss Calhoun didn't correct Sophie's use of her name, which told Sophie just how upset she was. Miss Calhoun shook her head slightly, then shrugged, then nodded. At last the trembling subsided. Sophie thought Miss Calhoun cried more neatly than anyone she'd ever seen.

"I'm going to be fired," Miss Calhoun whispered.

Sophie gasped. She'd heard only good things about how the school was run. "Daniel Reeves doesn't like the way you handle his children?"

Miss Calhoun shook her head. "It isn't him. It's that since those boys have come, everything is in chaos. I don't seem to be able to make them behave. And now the other boys are beginning to imitate their unruliness, and the girls are being neglected. It's been pandemonium for two solid weeks. The school board made a surprise inspection on Friday."

Miss Calhoun's voice faltered. "They found everything in an uproar, and even though the children settled down once they knew the men were from the board, it was too late. I'm sure I won't be asked back after this term. And I don't have anywhere else to go." Miss Calhoun's voice broke again, and Sophie heard real fear under the tears.

"It's taking every cent I have to live," Miss Calhoun sobbed. "I have no savings and no family to go back to."

"I'm sure the board understands that it's not your fault. Anyone would have trouble making those children behave. A new teacher will be in the same situation."

"I think they're looking for a man. That's probably for the best."

Miss Calhoun made a supreme effort and made a tidy swipe of the handkerchief over her cheeks. "I'm sorry." She squared her shoulders. "I shouldn't have made such a spectacle of myself." She shook her head as if she couldn't get over the shock of crying in public. Then she moved her shoulders restlessly, and Sophie realized Miss Calhoun wanted her to move away.

Sophie obliged and sat back down at the table. Miss Calhoun turned back to her meal.

"You are not going to be fired, Miss Calhoun," Sophie said. "One unruly family shouldn't be able to drive out a good teacher. We will figure something out, and we just might start with a visit to Daniel Reeves to insist he take his sons in hand."

Miss Calhoun looked terrified. "Oh, please don't do that."

Sophie reached out to pat Miss Calhoun's hand, but Miss Calhoun jerked away. She pushed her chair back from the table. "It was wrong of me to bother you with my little problems. I've just got to try harder to manage my classroom. This is my problem, and I'll solve it myself."

She stood. "Thank you for the meal. I hope the girls can make it to school for the fall term. For who–whoever is the teacher." Miss Calhoun's voice broke. "I need to get back." She turned and ran out of the ranch house.

"Wait, Grace." Sophie dashed for the front door in time to see Miss Calhoun untie her horse and swing herself up on his back.

"We thought you'd spend the afternoon with us, Miss Calhoun," Sophie called out to her.

Grace was already guiding her horse away. She called over her shoulder, "Thank you again."

Sophie heard Clay call out from the side of the house where he sat eating with the other men, "Miss Calhoun, someone needs to ride back with you."

Miss Calhoun was far enough away she didn't hear him—or she pretended she didn't. Sophie suspected it was the latter.

"Luke, Andy, ride with her. Eustace, Miguel, Rio, get ahead of her and check the trail around her. Hurry." Clay came around the house.

There must have been horses already saddled, because there wer[e] men riding out within seconds. Only then did Sophie breathe a sigh o[f] relief.

"Why'd she leave so fast?" Clay walked up to stand beside Sophie.

"It must have been something I said," Sophie said weakly.

Clay shook his head. "Why am I not surprised?"

Sophie thought of the promises she'd made to God the last tw[o] weeks that prevented her from replying scathingly to Clay's observation. "Clay, you are a lucky man."

Twenty

He agreed when she told him he was a lucky man, but something about the tone of her voice warned him. "What do you mean by that?" He didn't find out because Sophie had stormed back into the house.

He shrugged and returned to the men lounging in the shade on the east side of the ranch house telling tall tales.

"It don't suit me none, Clay, to sit back and let the sheriff handle this." Whitey pulled out his bowie knife and began whittling on a whip handle he was making from cedar branch. "I say we find out where the rest of the gang is holed up and root 'em out. Let's get this over an' done."

"It's not just the sheriff, Whitey." Clay pushed his plate aside and sat on the edge of the porch. He stared at the ground between his splayed knees. "The rangers are working on it, too. They're good men. They know we're here if needed, and if we go off hunting on our own, we may get in their way. Our job is to protect this ranch and the women. I don't want to spread ourselves thin and leave this place unguarded."

Whitey nodded. The smell of cedar cut the smell of Texas dust kicked up by the departed horse.

"A few of us could go." Adam sat up straight on the porch steps a few feet down from Clay. His every moved reminded Clay of the wicked cuts on his back. "We'd leave plenty of men back here."

"Reckon I could scout back up in the hills." Luther smoothed his full, black beard in a motion Clay could remember from his earliest childhood. "I saw what direction those varmints come from."

Clay knew how good Luther and Buff were on a trail. "Waiting pits me against my own instincts. It doesn't suit me to sit by and wait while someone else takes care of a threat to my family. But I've got other instincts telling me to stay close to Sophie and the girls."

"It's a fearful thing to hear a man talkin' 'bout killin' a woman the way those polecats were." Buff shook his head.

"It was the cold-bloodedest thing I'd ever heard," Clay agreed. "And we know those men we caught weren't ramrodding this operation."

He looked from one man to the next. Every one of them got his meaning. If those men came for Sophie once, they would come again. Sure, they'd been after Clay, too, but a man learned to look out for himself. A woman was defenseless.

"I still owe those men," Adam said. "And I mean to pay 'em back every penny."

Clay heard the depth of rage in Adam's simple announcement. He looked sideways at the gaunt, scarred man and felt the echo of his own anger. Adam had lost friends. Clay had lost a brother.

"Right now we've got to concentrate on the living, Adam," Clay said. "We make sure no one else is hurt before we start taking old sins outta their hides."

Clay saw Adam tamp down hard on his anger. Adam rubbed absently at the bullet wound on his side. "I reckon it don't matter when."

Clay felt the same way.

"Hating can eat away at a man." Luther shifted his weight to get more comfortable. His boots scraped across the porch. "It can warp a man until his family don't recognize him."

Clay jerked one shoulder in a guilty shrug. "I'm working on it."

"I wonder if hatin's what turned Judd Mason into the monster he is?" Luther asked.

"I know the hunger I got in me to hurt him, hurt him bad, and all those he rides with is a powerful sin." Clay clenched his hands between his spread knees.

The men sat silently and slowly they relaxed to contemplate hate and revenge and the whereabouts of a dangerous man. All but Adam.

After a long while Adam said, "It's a powerful sin all right." Quietly he added, "It won't be my first."

With Adam, Luther, and Buff working alongside the other men, Clay expected the cattle to all be brought in closer to the ranch house by the end of the day Monday, with plenty of men left for guard duty.

Sophie had tried to get Adam to spend the day being nursed and coddled, but he wouldn't spare himself any of the hard labor. Clay marveled at Adam's knowledge of the ranch and his ideas for its development. It was plain to see that Adam loved this place as if it were his own.

Clay laid the last brand on a stray and told the men he was riding up to the house for a spell.

Sheriff Everett came riding into the ranch later on that afternoon. He rode straight into the barn where Clay was hanging up his C BAR branding iron. The man was exhausted and carried more trail dust on his clothes than Clay.

"Howdy, Josiah. You look like you've had a hard day of it."

"I've spent more time in the saddle than out of it since Saturday. The men we locked up all told the same story, and we rode straight out to the vigilante camp. They'd hightailed it."

"As long as those men are running loose, Sophie is in danger. You heard what they said about her knowing too much." Clay took off his hat, and with a dejected pass of his arm, he wiped a coating of sweat off his forehead. He'd worked up a sweat branding, but this wasn't hard-work sweat. This was fear.

The sheriff swung down off his buckskin, and Clay walked alongside as the sheriff led his horse to the watering trough.

"That was before we caught these men, though." Everett's plodding feet sounded almost as loudly as his horse's hooves. "Now that we have 'em, Mason has a lot longer list of people who can identify him. There's no point anymore in comin' after one little woman. And there's no way he can buy this ranch now, so there's no reason to go after you. My gut tells me they've started running and they won't stop. I think they've quit the country. The rangers are still on their trail."

They reached the water trough, and Clay stopped and crossed his arms. "It doesn't set right with me to stand aside while someone else takes care of my problems."

The sheriff hung his hat on the horse's saddle horn and dunked his head in the water with a rough splash at the same time his horse was drinking. Everett scrubbed at his face, then came up dripping wet and brushed both hands over his streaming hair until it was pushed straight back. The water soaked his shirt, but the sheriff sighed with pure pleasure. "You've more than made yourself clear. I know you're holding back because the rangers and I asked you to."

"That's not the only reason I'm holding back," Clay said.

The sheriff asked, "Why else?"

Clay ignored him. He wasn't about to get into a debate about the hate that ate inside him and how he was trying to battle the surge of pleasure he got when he thought of smashing Mason's face with his bare hands. "I'm not about to relax my guard just because your instincts tell you Mason is on the run."

The sheriff shrugged, plunked his hat back on his head, and threw his reins over the buckskin's neck. "No man ever relaxes much in the West. It just ain't a country that inspires relaxation."

Clay had to admit that was true.

The sheriff mounted his horse. "We're not giving up, Clay. I just thought it'd be neighborly to tell you what's going on with the investigation."

" 'Preciate it, Josiah. While you're investigating, you might remember that if Judd Mason killed Cliff two years ago and waited till now to kill the Meads, then he's a planning man. He's not a man who's gonna give up easy."

The sheriff looked unhappy with that obvious bit of truth. "Nothin' worse than a patient outlaw."

"Good luck." Clay tugged on the brim of his hat.

"I wish I didn't need it so bad." Everett rode out of the yard.

Clay had been planning to go to the house, but he didn't want to go in there and have Sophie start nagging him for details of what the sheriff had said. He was mad enough to tell her everything and not soften his words, even in front of the girls. Instead he spent another hour working around the ranch. By the time he was done with the grueling work, he'd settled down.

Clay didn't like the fact that Mason had disappeared. They'd have to remain on guard. But the hard work of rounding up strays was over. He and the men would have more time to do just that.

It was time to start proving to his new wife that he was the best husband a woman ever had. Way better than Cliff. He thought she already believed that, but he wanted to make sure.

Smiling for the first time all day, he came in to supper, slung an arm around Sophie's waist, and gave her a loud smack on the lips. "The cattle are settled in the summer pasture. Tomorrow I start working around the place, repairing and adding here and there. The men will be able to help, too. I hope you didn't do all the man's work yourself, Sophie darlin'. You did leave something for me, didn't you?"

"Clay, you're filthy." Sophie slapped at Clay's chest, but he could tell by her grin that she was pleased with his attention.

"It's hard work and honest dirt, darlin'. Let me share a little with you." Clay pulled her closer, but she jumped back, grabbed a ladle off the stove, and waved it threateningly at him, failing to suppress a smile.

The girls started giggling, and maybe for the first time, Clay didn't mind it at all.

"Have you had a chance to inspect the traps I built, Clay? I don't want you or any of the men to stumble on them and set them off by accident."

"I haven't gotten to your little surprises, darlin'. I'll add it to my list of things to do tomorrow." Clay turned away from his wife to wash his face in the basin full of warm water she always had waiting for him. He sighed as he scrubbed his face and hands. He thought of the sheriff dipping his head into the cold tank. Many's the time he'd done that himself, but he hadn't considered it today, even though he was as dirty as the sheriff. He'd purely gotten a taste for warm water in a clean basin.

He marveled at the hundred ways a woman made a man's life better. He dried his face on a towel. "If I'd've only known how nice havin' a wife was, I'd've gotten married when I was twelve years old."

"Well, I would have been ten at the time." Sophie poked him smartly with the ladle. "You wouldn't have married me."

Clay grinned and lunged at her. She didn't have a chance to get her ladle up. He hoisted her in his arms and swung her around in a circle. "Well, I'm glad I waited then."

He set her down and held her steady until he was sure she wasn't dizzy, then he turned on the girls, growled at them, and charged.

They squealed and ran, but they didn't run out of the room. They just dashed around in circles, colliding with each other. Clay snagged Mandy first, and while he held her and tickled her with his whiskery face, Laura toddled up and latched on to his leg. Being careful not to shake her loose while he dragged her around after the others almost made it a fair fight.

He grabbed Beth when she danced too close, then, with his hands full, Sally jumped on his back. By the time they were done, Clay was flat on the kitchen floor, buried under three sets of petticoats and one soggy diaper.

He remembered his first impression when he'd regained consciousness in that awful shed, that he'd died and he was surrounded by angels. He hadn't been far from wrong.

Judd Mason pulled up on his black mustang, then wrenched the reins to turn the horse around. "We're not shaking 'em. Whoever's on our trail is a bloodhound."

Eli rode up beside Judd. "It's rangers, Mr. Mason. I worked up close enough to see their stars with my spyglass. They're still a few hours behind us, but they're reading the trail like it was the written word."

Rangers! Judd had been smart enough in his life to fight shy of Texas Rangers. They were the toughest, most relentless lawmen the West had to offer.

"It's time to cut our losses, Judd." Harley reined in his horse to look back in the direction of the men hounding them. "The only way to leave a ranger behind is to leave Texas behind and not come back."

"I've heard of 'em following someone clean across the country, chasin' after 'em," one of the gang said gloomily.

"We're not quittin'," Judd roared. "I'm not leaving this country without making McClellen sorry he ever tangled with me. And I'm not leaving that woman behind to live on a ranch that she stole clean out from under my feet."

Harley rode up until his horse pressed against Judd's mustang. "Let's ride off a ways and talk this out, Judd," he said under his breath. "There's a few things the men don't need to know."

Judd wanted to refuse, but he wondered just what Harley knew that he didn't want to talk about. With a terse nod of his head, Judd wheeled the mustang around, and the two of them rode off a fair piece.

Judd jerked on his horse's reins viciously and turned to Harley. "This is far enough. Say your piece and let's get back."

"What's this really about, Mason?" Harley asked calmly. "You know there's no way you can take that land now. You're a known outlaw in these parts."

"That ain't news, Harley," Judd sneered.

"Then why hang around? You've got a lot of money in your saddle bags. You've got your whole share and the share of every member of this gang who has lit out. There's nothing for us here 'cept a bullet or a noose."

"I'm not leaving without paying McClellen back for taking my land." The mustang reared up, fighting Judd's hard hand. "I avenge a wrong done to me."

"Judd, no wrong has been done to you. *You* killed Edwards. *You* killed the Meads. *You* plotted the murder of McClellen and his wife. You've handed out all the wrong in this mess. You don't need to get revenge against McClellen. That's just your pride talking, and pride won't stop a bullet."

Judd turned red in the face and his mule-headedness kicked in full bore. He shouted over his shoulder, "Men!"

The rest of the vigilantes rode into the clearing.

"Harley wants to cut and run."

Eli rode his horse up beside Judd, showing his loyalty. One by one the men, most of them showing far less assurance than Eli, rode to Judd's side, spreading out, mindful of Harley's quick hand with a gun, until they'd formed a circle around Harley.

Judd knew Harley Shafter was nobody's fool. He wasn't about to challenge the whole gang. Harley kept his hands held loosely on his saddle horn. Judd knew it was so no one could make the mistake of thinking Harley was going for his gun.

"I see you all don't share my view." Harley watched them with cool eyes.

Seven tough men sat silently, waiting for a wrong move from Harley.

Harley kept his voice calm and his eyes flat. "If you're all still in, I'm in."

The moment strung itself out, until abruptly Judd relaxed. "I'm glad to hear you're still with us, Harley." His voice was ice cold when he spoke.

He turned to Eli, who'd been gone most of the last two days. "Did you take the horses and hide them out where I said?"

"They're waitin', boss"—Eli nodded—"right up top of Sawyer Canyon."

"Okay, then it's time for a little plan I have in mind that should settle things between me and the McClellens. Then"—he looked square at Harley—"*after* I've done for the McClellens, we'll leave this lousy country and go find us some ranch land."

Harley fell into line with Judd leading and Eli bringing up the rear.

"Ma, isn't that one of the sheriff's deputies?" Beth came in from sweeping the front porch.

Sophie hurried to the door in time to see a man come charging into the ranch yard. "Yes, I recognize him from last Saturday."

There was an urgency about the way the man rode that sent Sophie to the edge of the porch. The man ignored her. He galloped on past the house toward a pair of men herding the cattle. The deputy talked to the men, then rode off into a valley where Sophie knew there were more cattle.

"What do you reckon he wants, Ma?" Mandy tugged on Sophie's skirt.

Sophie heard the fear in her daughter's voice and regretted all the girls had been through. "I guess he just wants to talk to the men, not us." Sophie hoped Mandy wouldn't notice she hadn't answered her question.

Sophie looked around the corral and barn. There'd been someone close-up all day, working on repairs she'd been itching to get at ever since they'd moved back. Having someone else do things for her was a luxury.

"I don't see any of the men who've been guarding the house." Sally came out and went down the porch steps, looking all around.

It struck Sophie as odd. Clay had been in and out of the house a dozen times. She'd made extra coffee because Luther, Buff, and Adam had stopped in to talk more than once. She'd also offered it to the hands and had a few takers, although they had their own pot brewing in the bunkhouse.

She'd even had Clay bring in several grouse for supper when she hadn't thought to put hunting on her list. She hadn't needed to leave the house all day, and at Clay's insistence, she'd taken a nap after the midday meal, with Laura nestled at her side.

Sophie and the girls kept watching the direction the deputy had gone. After several tense moments, Clay came galloping back toward the ranch house with the deputy at his side. He swung down off his horse and strode toward the cabin.

"What is it, Clay?" Sophie expected the worst. All four girls edged up beside her to hear whatever Clay had to say.

"The sheriff has Mason cornered in the rocks a few miles south of here. The posse he has with him saw the whole gang ride into a box canyon."

"That's got to be Sawyer Canyon. It's the only dead-end canyon in that direction."

Clay nodded. "Sawyer Canyon. That's the name Deputy MacNeal used. They chased them in there last night. The sheriff has the only way out blocked, but Mason and his men are undercover. The sheriff isn't going to risk any lives staging some kind of assault. He's planning to wait them out. He wants me to send as many hands as I can spare to spell his men."

Sophie heaved a sigh of relief and hurled herself into Clay's arms. "It's over then. Finally. All but this last showdown."

Clay held her tight. "Yes, it sounds like it's finally over."

Sophie squeezed her husband tight for a long second, then released him and stepped back. "Of course we need to send help. There—there won't be any shooting will there?"

"The sheriff hopes to take the gang without anyone getting hurt," Clay said soberly. "But Mason is facing a noose."

"He won't come out with his hands up." Sophie tried to steady her nerves.

Clay pulled his leather gloves off his hands and tucked them behind his belt buckle. He brushed Sophie's hair back with one hand. "We won't be reckless. We won't trust him for a minute."

"Do you have to go?" As soon as she said it she was ashamed. She covered her mouth quickly with one hand, wishing she could call back the words.

"Sophie, I can't ask my men to go do something I'm not willing to do."

"I know," Sophie whispered. "I know. If you could, you wouldn't be the man you are."

Clay nodded. "I'm leaving six men behind to guard the ranch. That should be plenty. We'll stay at the canyon for a while, then when the sheriff's posse is rested, we'll come back to eat and sleep. It may be awhile. We don't know what supplies Mason has. He could stay holed up for a long time."

"Like a siege," Sophie said.

Clay caressed her face again. "And like a siege, there'll be a lot of waiting but not much fighting."

Sophie leaned into his hand. "Just promise me you'll be careful."

Clay grinned at her. "I wouldn't be able to go if you hadn't said that."

The girls had lined up beside her, and now in a rush, they all said, "Good-bye, Pa. Be careful."

He gave them each a quick kiss on the forehead. "I will."

He turned just as Adam came out of the barn, leading two horses. Clay walked to the horse and swung himself up. Adam mounted his roan at the same time. Clay waved and Adam tugged the brim of his hat and they rode away, the deputy leading.

A group of the hands, including Luther, came riding around from the corral and fell into a line behind Clay.

Sophie didn't see Whitey in amongst them, but then she didn't see much through her tears. She had a sudden flash of the memory of Cliff riding off to war. It had been the saddest day of her life. He'd come back, but he'd been changed, his youthful charm forever wiped away by the brutality of war.

This was nothing by comparison. Still, Clay's retreating back brought a wash of tears to her eyes, and she sent him along with a prayer for God to protect him. She prayed it fervently and remembered how Luther and Adam had been tuned in to her prayers. "Yes, Lord," she murmured "help him."

She saw Luther look back over his shoulder and tip his hat to her. She smiled. She pushed back the tears and waved cheerfully. Luther shook his head like he thought she was getting to be a plumb nuisance.

"Nuisance or not, I'm not about to quit praying, Luther."

He was too far away to hear her, but somehow she thought he'd gotten the message.

Whitey and Buff came around the corner of the cabin just then. Sophie looked at the two of them. They'd been forged in different fires. Buff in the bitter cold mountains, Whitey in the heat and dust of a hundred Texas cattle ranches. But they had been burned down to the same hard iron. Sophie was glad they were here, and at the same time she wished they were with Clay, watching his back.

"I'm posting Andy, Luke, Rio, and Miguel in the hills as lookouts," Whitey called out to her. "They'll all have a clear view of the ranch, and they can be down in a five minutes. Buff and me'll stay up close. It sounds like they've got all of Mason's men treed, but no one really knows how many were riding with him. There could be others skulking about. There are plenty of us to keep watch but not 'nough to do much else. The boss said to tell you we'll need a meal, ma'am. Iffen you don't mind feeding us."

"Of course I don't mind," Sophie hastened to assure him.

Whitey gave a satisfied jerk of his head. "We'll eat in shifts."

Sophie said, "Supper will be ready for the first shift in half an hour."

"Obliged, ma'am." Whitey headed back to the bunkhouse.

Buff lagged behind and turned to Sophie when Whitey disappeared around the cabin. "Prepare for the worst an' you've got a right to hope for the best. That's what we're doing here, Miz McClellen."

Sophie smiled at Buff. It was the longest speech she'd ever heard ıim give. "I'll do the same, Mr. Buff."

Buff ducked his head. "Ah, Miz McClellen, it's just Buff. There ıin't no mister about it."

"It's just Sophie, Buff. You're my husband's good friend, and I'd be ɔleased if you called me that."

"Ain't likely I'll ever call you much'a nothin'." Buff jerked one ;houlder.

Sophie smiled. "Well, just in case you do. . ."

Buff nodded and almost managed a smile, but Sophie thought his face seemed close to cracking. He stopped the smile, grunted at her, then turned and followed Whitey.

TWENTY-ONE

Clay rode away, trying to make peace with leaving Sophie and the girls. He wanted to stay and watch after them himself, but he also had a powerful urge to help the sheriff clean up the mess that surrounded the McClellen/Edwards ranch.

The group rode to Sawyer Canyon at an easy lope that spared the horses, while making good time. As they drew nearer, Clay's tension increased. It didn't help that he rode alongside Adam. The black man wound tighter and tighter until Clay half expected the man to explode. He urged his horse closer to Adam's. "We're not going into this looking for revenge."

"I know that." Adam's jaw was so tense it barely moved when he spoke.

The summer breeze sifted the dust being kicked up by the riders ahead of them. "Ever since you heard they had Mason cornered, you've had the look of a man ready to go charging in, guns blazing, to get that payback you've been wanting."

Adam looked at Clay.

Clay was stunned by the cold fury in his eyes.

"I didn't come out here looking to mess up the sheriff's standoff," Adam said. "I know how this is going to go down."

"And you can live with that?" Clay drew in a long breath, as he silently asked himself the same question. The smell of the Texas dirt and the working horses steadied his temper. "You can sit and wait until

Mason gives himself up?"

"I haven't led the easiest life, Clay. I was a free black man living in the South before slavery ended." Adam gave a humorless laugh. "To protect a young girl I love as if she were my own daughter, I put up with a man who used me to survive and hated me for it."

"My brother?"

Adam didn't answer. Clay wondered how much Sophie had whitewashed Cliff's true nature out of kindness.

"I fought for the North," Adam went on as if Clay hadn't interrupted. "Many's the time I stood and fought with men who gave me less respect than they gave their horses. I rode the borders of Indian territory, rounding up longhorn cattle that were three and four generations wild and as mean as any grizzly bear you've ever heard tell of."

Adam subsided for a moment, then he added, with an icy rage that was more frightening for being spoken quietly, "I watched my friends die at the hands of thieving cowards. And I walked barefoot three hundred miles with my back lashed open and a bullet wound in my side. So don't ask me if I can live with watching a man being hanged when I want him to die by my own hand."

Adam inhaled deeply. "I've found out I can live with purt' near anything. I know what I want is wrong. I'm a man who walked halfway across an almighty big state because God let me hear a woman's prayers. I know right and wrong. I know the hate burning in me is sin."

"And yet," Clay said, "I can see the fight inside you to control your desire for vengeance."

"Yeah, I ain't doing a very good job of covering it up."

"I have my own need to hurt these men." Clay tightened his grip on the reins, and his horse whickered in protest. He forced his hand to relax. "They killed my brother and threatened my wife."

Luther rode up between them at the moment, and even though he'd been lagging toward the back of the line of riders, Clay could see at a glance that Luther knew exactly what they'd been talking about.

"Leave room for God's wrath." Luther settled into the loping pace of his horse. With his wild beard and long hair, his coarse clothing and easy riding style, Luther looked for all the world like he and his horse were a single living creature.

"What's that mean?" Adam looked sharply at him.

Clay already knew. He'd had it preached to him just a couple of weeks back.

Luther edged his horse in between Clay's Appaloosa and Adam's roan. "I think Mason's got a lot to answer for when he meets his Maker. Nothing you can do to him will begin to match that."

"But it would make me feel so much better." Clay knew that wasn't true even as he said it.

"Leave room for God's wrath." Luther dropped back.

"He's right." Clay tipped the brim of his hat back on his head with one gloved thumb.

"I know." Adam looked over his shoulder at Luther. "I'm getting purely sick of that man."

Clay nodded, and they fell silent.

The sheriff had a man waiting to bring them to the position he had fortified.

"Smart man, the sheriff." Luther swung down off his spirited bay. "Not a good idea to be riding up to a nervous, trigger-happy posse."

They were directed to safe positions, well hidden by the jumble of rocks at the mouth of the canyon, and they waited.

It didn't take long before the wait was driving him crazy, which wasn't like him. Normally, Clay was a patient man.

"I am a patient woman." Sophie crossed her arms and tapped her toe. "I am, and no one had better make me wait agreeing with me!"

Mandy said quickly, "We know you're patient, Ma."

The other girls nodded, except Laura who had fallen asleep.

"What is keeping those men?" Sophie charged over to the door and rasped the handle for the tenth time, if she hadn't lost count.

"Ma, you know Buff and Whitey want us to stay inside." Beth dashed .p beside her and laid her little hand over Sophie's on the doorknob.

Sophie held on to the knob as if it were a lifeline. At last, through ure force of will, she let it go. "Well, why aren't they in here by now? 've still got men to feed, and I can't get the dishes cleaned up until hey eat. Besides, it is time for you all to be in bed, but when they come rooping through here, they'll make too much noise."

Mandy came across the room. "We'll go on to bed, Ma. It's only wo more of 'em left to eat. Just warn 'em to be quiet. If we do wake up, t'll be okay. I just hate to leave you to clean up alone."

Sophie noticed her daughters were acting more grown-up than she vas. "I guess you might as well. Maybe I misunderstood. Or maybe he men didn't want to take the time to come all the way in for supper. Maybe they ate on the trail somehow."

"I'm sure it's something like that." Sally, with Laura snoozing in her ırms, walked over with a maternal rock to pat Sophie's arm.

When Sally reassured her so maturely, something snapped in Sophie. All of a sudden the fear that had been tangled up inside her for weeks nerged into one lightning bolt of terror. She knew that terror didn't come strictly from adding up all that had her worried. That fear was a warning—straight from God. She wasn't about to second-guess the message she was receiving.

She turned sharply to the girls. "No, it isn't something like that."

'Adam, come back," Clay hissed. He had been so focused on the entrance to the canyon that he hadn't been watching the men around him. Why would he? They weren't the threat.

Adam waved one hand behind him as if to swat Clay away like a pesky fly. Adam was a hundred feet away from all of them, using every ounce of cover the terrain provided.

Ranger Mitchell sidled up to Clay, pitching his voice low so the sound wouldn't carry, "Where is he going?"

Clay said in disbelief, "I noticed him just now."

Jackson grabbed his hat off his head and slammed it on the ground where he lay on his belly beside Clay. "We have this set up so no one gets hurt. I don't want a grandstanding fool looking to put notches in his gun, charging those men."

Clay shook his head and wiped sweat off his brow. They'd been lucky the canyon opened on the east. The sheer bluffs gave the posse some much-needed shade as the sun lowered in the sky, but the day was hot and still, and keeping down to avoid a bullet warmed a man.

Clay said, "Adam's not after a reputation, he's after revenge. He's had it in him to even the score with this gang for weeks."

"I know his story, and I've seen his scars," the ranger said. "I talked to him when you first got here. He said he was content to wait."

"I had a talk with him myself. I didn't like what I was seeing in his eyes." Clay lay, watching Adam slink like a shadow between slight depressions and whisper-thin sagebrush. Adam wore a white shirt, stained brown from being soaked with sweat, as he crawled on the ground. His body was nearly invisible against the coarse dirt. "But he convinced me he had himself under control."

The two of them watched, expecting a gunshot to ring out any second and leave Adam, with his meager protection, bleeding and dying in the Texas sunset. Adam continued forward as silent as a breeze, as fluid as trickling water. As mad as sin.

"He's good, isn't he?" Clay blinked and Adam seemed to vanish. Even his black hair was coated now in the dust that came as a partner with the dry Texas heat. Then Adam moved and Clay could see him again.

"Very good," Tom Jackson replied with grudging respect.

Clay became aware of the dozen other men who had formed an impenetrable wall along the front of the canyon. All of them watching. All of them silently rooting for Adam to get through the canyon opening alive. All of them fearing the worst.

Adam reached the mouth of Sawyer Canyon and ducked behind the first good cover he'd had.

Clay breathed a sigh of relief and looked across several other men to see Luther shaking his head. Luther looked away from Adam and caught Clay's eye. The two of them shared a moment of regret. They knew what drove Adam to do this desperate thing. It would be bad for Adam if he managed to kill the lot of them. He'd carry this act of hatred like a burning stone in his soul for the rest of his life.

"He's in," Jackson whispered.

Clay looked back at the canyon. Adam had disappeared like a wisp of smoke on the air. They waited. Clay smelled the sweat of a dozen men strung tight as piano wire. He heard someone breathe raggedly, and it reminded him he'd been holding his own breath for a while. The canyon wasn't a large one. The good place to cut a man down was right at the mouth. After that, a man had a fighting chance. The silence drew out long. Clay suddenly pushed himself to his knees. "He got through. I'm going to see if I can."

Jackson shoved Clay sideways. Only the *crack* of a gun being triggered stopped Clay from shoving back. He looked down the barrel of Jackson's Winchester. "I'm not risking another man on such a reckless attack. Don't even think about it."

Clay didn't think the ranger would shoot him, but the heat of the day and the tension of the moment were taking their toll on everyone. He didn't make any more sudden moves.

"They're gone!" Adam came running out of the canyon, no longer making the least attempt to hide himself.

"They can't be gone." Sheriff Everett jumped to his feet, leaving cover behind in a way that proved he believed Adam, even though he denied it. "This is the only way out."

Adam stormed toward the group of men then passed straight through the line, heading for the horses.

After one frozen moment, Clay started after him.

"They're gone," Adam shouted without looking back or slowing down, "but their horses are still there!"

"They climbed out?" Clay walked faster.

Adam jerked his head in agreement. "It looks like they've been gone for hours. I thought there was something too neat about this."

Adam called back to Sheriff Everett, "They set you all up. They led you to this spot so they could tie up your whole posse while they made a clean getaway."

"Whitey would have told me if his plans changed. The men were coming in to do more than eat. They needed to check in with Whitey and Buff." Sophie was the mother again. Not a fidgeting worrier who needed small children to keep her calm. "Girls, something's happened to those men. Get into the crawl space. Now!"

The girls didn't hesitate. Beth threw back the rug and pulled up the trap door. Sally dropped into the dark hole in the floor, carrying Laura. Mandy went into the hidey-hole next.

"I'll make sure the rug lies flat," Sophie said.

"Ma, I think you oughta come down." Beth looked at the front door, her face pale but determined.

"I need to keep watch, Beth. You know how we do this."

Beth hesitated again, and Sophie didn't hurry her. Sophie respected all her girls' instincts.

"I don't know why, Ma, but I've got a feeling you need to clear out of the house. If you come with us, we can work our way out to the cave and scout the men who are supposed to be standing watch. We'll know if there's any real trouble."

Sophie was torn.

"We can leave Mandy, Sally, and Laura here underground," Beth added. "They can run the porch traps. If one of our men comes, they can let 'im know where we are."

Sophie and her girls had faced a lot of danger in the years they lived one in this house. And they'd always handled it with Sophie remaining bove, guarding the house. She hesitated. It set wrong with her to leave er home undefended, but the look on Beth's face held her fast.

"Something inside me tells me that this is a good time to be afraid, Ia. Something is telling you that, too. We all need to go, Ma. Now!"

Sophie went. She left the lanterns burning to provide a little light or the underground room and to make the house looked lived-in. She rabbed the rifle and shotgun hanging on nails above the front door nen followed Beth into the hole. She closed the trap door over her ead. As the door swung shut, closing the five of them into the cramped arkness, she prayed, "Lord, help me, help me, help me."

uther was beside Clay and Adam, and all at once he froze in his tracks. Adam stopped so suddenly he almost fell over.

Clay looked at both of them. "I heard her."

Luther was running. Adam sprinted ahead of him. Clay, adrenaline oursing through his very bones, tore the reins loose from the branch.

"Where are you going in such an all-fired hurry?" Sheriff Everett ollered. "We don't even know what direction they headed."

"They're at McClellen's," Luther shouted as he spurred his horse.

"How do you know?" Everett said.

The rangers were already swinging up on their horses, responding o the urgent riding of the three men.

"We heard Sophie call for help," Adam shouted over his shoulder s he kicked his horse into a canter.

Clay's only thought was to get to Sophie and the girls before it was oo late. He was a mile down the trail at a full gallop before he looked ack. The whole posse, regardless of the nonsense of Adam's words, ad fallen in line behind him, all bent on one thing: Get to the ranch. Save Clay's family.

Sophie couldn't help being a little disgruntled. It looked like she wa going to have to save her girls herself.

As usual.

What was the point of men anyway? She looked at her four preciou daughters and thought of the child growing inside her. She loved he children fiercely and was glad she had them, so she begrudgingl decided men had their purpose.

"I'm going out the tunnel to the cave entrance," Beth said. "It's righ above one of the best lookouts on the ranch. If they've got someon watching us, he'll be there."

"I'm going with you." Sophie started crawling toward the tunnel. I was low and dark. They would be on their hands and knees the whol way. "If we find trouble, the both of us will need to get in position t spring the traps."

Sophie left the shotgun leaning against the dirt wall of the crampe little crawl space. The only thing that kept the little cellar from bein pitch-black was light coming through tiny slits between the floorboard overhead. The musty dirt smelled like safety. "Mandy, take the brace out of the porch. Sally, keep Laura asleep if you possibly can. Her cryin could alert someone that you're down here. If she wakes up and start crying, get down the tunnel about halfway. No one can hear her there."

Mandy was already working on the front porch. Sally sat back an cradled Laura in her arms.

The ranch house was built just a few dozen feet in front of the firs rocky crags that grew into bluffs to the west of the McClellen ranch Sophie had dug a tunnel in the years after Cliff had gone to war, wel braced with timbers she'd cut herself, burrowing herself a little escap route. Those hadn't been particularly dangerous years, although ther had been a few incidences of Indian trouble and the inevitable small-time rustling.

Sophie hadn't felt safe, and she wasn't a woman to sit by and hope for the best when there was something she could do. She'd dug her way to the cave, which had a series of caverns she could follow all the way to the top of the bluffs.

Sophie and Beth crawled through the tunnel. Sophie felt the weight of the mountain crushing down on her in the stygian darkness. They emerged in the cave and could see again, even with dusk darkening into night.

They stuck together until they reached the highest point in the underground cave system. Beth looked at Sophie, and Sophie gestured for her to go check for a lookout.

Elizabeth, at eight years, had a gift for the woods that she had honed in the thicket, sneaking up on deer because she loved to study animals. Sophie didn't like sending her daughter into danger, but Sophie knew her children's strengths. She knew Beth could do this better than she could.

Beth slipped away silently, and Sophie didn't have long to wait for her return. Beth held a finger up to her lips and led Sophie back down into the tunnel out of earshot.

"I found him right outside the cave entrance," she whispered. "He's not one of our men. He's got Rio hog-tied, lying on the ground unconscious."

Sophie's stomach did a sickening twist. Up until now she'd just been following a small voice in her head that said there was danger, but she'd had no solid proof.

Now she had it. That man could be no one but a member of Mason's gang. Adam had said there were twenty of them. They'd caught four. Clay had mentioned that several of the gang had run off. The sheriff had seen eight men go into Sawyer Canyon. Eight men.

"If Rio's tied, he's alive." Sophie made sure Beth didn't hear one ounce of fear. "If we can get him loose and he's not hurt too bad, he'll be a help."

"I wish Pa were here." Beth looked toward the cave entrance.

How had these men gotten out of that box canyon? And what had happened to the posse who had them cornered? Sophie thought, *Just once, I wish he were here, too.* Then she stiffened her backbone. "If you want to help, you'd best do some praying, Beth."

"What should I pray, Ma?"

"I haven't prayed much of anything for years," Sophie said grimly, "except, 'Help me.'"

There it was again—Sophie's sweet voice. The first time it had been laced with desperation. This time she sounded resigned and very tired. A thrill of fear cut straight to Clay's heart. He looked behind him. Luther and Adam had gotten the message, too.

In an odd way, hearing her prayer made Clay feel better. He hadn't given it much thought, but it had occurred to him that Luther and Adam had been hearing her prayers when he should have been the one God was calling to go help Sophie. Of course, up till now, he'd been on the spot, not in need of being called by a miracle since he was within shouting distance.

They had five miles to go, but it was five rugged miles, some of it up and down instead of across. They'd be an hour or more getting home. If he pushed his horse to the limit and the horse fell and broke a leg, he might not get there at all. He pushed his horse to the limit anyway. The Appaloosa was so game, Clay wondered if he hadn't heard Sophie calling, too.

Twenty-Two

"I reckon asking God for help is about all most of it boils down to anyway." Beth squared her shoulders and started for the opening.

Sophie nodded and patted Beth on the arm.

"Then why does the parson have to go on so long on Sunday morning with his praying?" Beth asked.

"Well, we need to say thank You, too." Sophie pulled her riding skirt close against her legs to keep the fabric from rustling. "And usually when you get to counting up, we've got way more to thank God for than to ask Him for, so it can take awhile."

Beth seemed skeptical. "It's not that I mind saying, 'Help me' and 'Thank You'; it's that I mind the parson saying it so slow for so long."

Sophie didn't have anything much to say to that, so she changed the subject. "Let's get down to saving this ranch."

Beth got in position just outside the cave entrance behind the lookout.

Sophie moved through the tunnel to a lower level and slipped out to hide behind some rocks. The rocks were in a tall, jumbled pile. When she was setting her traps, Sophie had moved the pile around a bit so there was a small opening she could see through without being seen. Carefully surveying the area for others in the gang before each movement, Sophie crept up behind the rocks. She watched the man, who was only about twenty feet away from her, most of it straight up. Sophie lifted a small rock and pulled a folded oilskin paper out from under it. She unfolded the paper and took out the prettiest hanky she'd ever owned. She touched the delicate thing, all white linen and tatted lace, then she picked up a few tiny rocks and a little damp earth and slapped it into the middle of the handkerchief to weigh it down. Then she waited for Elizabeth.

Sophie couldn't hear what Beth did, but Sophie knew her little girl. She wouldn't make too much noise, nor too little. The man turned away from watching.

Sophie deftly rose from her hiding place and tossed the weighted handkerchief onto a spot about a dozen feet off the trail, in plain sight of the outlaw. She ducked back out of sight.

When the man turned around from studying the land behind him, he went back to his careful watch. It took him ten minutes to spot the hankie, and Sophie was about to explode from frustration by the time he saw it.

The man straightened. Sophie was close enough to see his eyes sharpen. Sophie had to give him credit. He was a good lookout. He didn't go down to look at the handkerchief right away. He waited, made sure there was no one around, and then started sidling down the steep trail.

He walked over to the handkerchief, and as he bent to pick it up, Sophie heard him mumble, "Was this lying here before?"

Sophie yanked the rope that released the net the man was standing on. With a startled yell, the man was jerked thirty feet in the air as the sapling sprung up straight. Just as Sophie had planned, the man ended up dangling very close to the steepest drop-off. Before he could make a second sound, Sophie stepped out from the clearing and brandished her hunting knife near the hemp rope that stretched from the ground to the tree. "If you yell again, I'll cut the rope and you won't quit falling until you've rolled all the way to the ranch house.

The man looked frantically at the knife, then he looked at the jagged rocks that covered the hillside for half a mile, mostly straight down, and didn't make a peep.

Sophie ducked back behind the rock and called out softly, "I'm waiting for your friends back here. Don't make me regret letting you live."

Sophie sat quietly behind the rock for a few minutes until she started to believe the man was actually going to remain silent. Then she soundlessly slipped back into the cave and ran up to meet Beth. Beth had Rio untied, but although breathing steadily, he was out cold. He had a good-sized welt on his forehead.

Sophie said, "We're not going to get much help from him."

Beth shook her head. "Let's drag him into the cave so no one bothers him."

It took a lot of tugging to move the burly Mexican. Sophie paused to rest several times, mindful of the unborn baby she was supposed to be coddling. They got him hidden, then they headed through the honeycomb of caves for the next most likely lookout.

"I hear someone coming in the back," Mandy hissed at Sally.

Sally lay Laura down. "The braces?"

"All out," Mandy answered. Both girls fell silent. Mandy gripped on the pigging string in her hand and two more in her mouth and waited. She'd played this game so many times with her ma that she knew exactly what to do. The only thing was, she'd never actually had to do it before. This time, it looked like it was really going to happen.

She moved to the back of the house and peeked through a hidden slit. It definitely wasn't one of the McClellen men. It was a dirty-looking man with no good on his mind, judging from the rifle in his hands. The man stepped up onto the back porch, and it collapsed under him. His head cracked with a solid *thud* on the crossbar Ma had rigged for just this reason. It left the man stunned as it was meant to.

Mandy dove at the man. She whipped the leather around his hands behind his back, then took another pigging string out of her teeth and whipped his feet together. She'd hog-tied a two-year-old steer many times, and this man didn't wiggle a bit more than that. She had him tied up tight and gagged before the dust had settled from the fall. She tossed his rifle to Sally, who caught it deftly and set it aside. Mandy dragged the man away from the hole in the porch floor with quick, practiced moves, while Sally reset the porch boards. The trap was ready again.

"I wonder how Ma and Beth are doing?" Sally asked calmly.

Mandy didn't like the way the man was staring at her, all meanlike, so she put a blindfold over his eyes from the supply of pigging strings, ropes, and neckerchiefs Ma had stored down here for just such an occasion. The man struggled as she covered his eyes, but she had him bound tighter than a year-old calf at branding time. Then she turned to her little sister.

"Ma planned this trap and it worked. No reason the others shouldn't."

"I sure wish Pa would get here." Sally settled herself to watch through the slits in the front porch steps.

Mandy checked the load in the rifle, snapped it back shut, and laid it well out of reach of the outlaw. "Me, too." She went to her lookout in the rear of the crawl space. "Someone needs to get here and save us."

"I think there's someone coming from the front." Sally backed out of the way to let Mandy through.

"Got it." Mandy caught up the pigging strings and clamped them with her teeth.

The second man Sophie and Beth snared didn't yell, because he cracked his head smartly on the trunk of the tree when he got snapped into the air and hung unconscious in the net Mandy had woven from hemp.

They freed Andy, another ranch hand, but although his eyes flickered open once, he was in no shape to help them. He had a nasty gash on his head, and when he tried to talk, he mumbled something Sophie couldn't understand. Sophie took the time to stop the bleeding and bandage him; then she and Beth left him lying in another cave to recover.

A quick but thorough check of the mountainside didn't turn up any more outlaws. "If the sheriff was right about there being eight men, six of them might be down there right now with the other girls. We'd better get down there and help."

"Ma, look!" Elizabeth pointed to the cabin, which they could see from their vantage point. Sophie looked just in time to see a man fall through the front porch floor. In seconds, Sally was visible covering the porch back up. She wouldn't have done that if the man had given them trouble.

Sophie looked around the ranch yard to see if anyone had noticed one of their own disappearing. No one else was in sight.

"All right. That takes care of three of them. Five left." Sophie studied the terrain all around them. Frustrated, she muttered to herself, "Where are they?"

Beth was silent, also looking the land over. Finally she pressed her hand to Sophie's. "Right above us, off to the left."

Sophie turned and saw two riders. "They'll be passing right in front of one of our rock slides."

The two of them silently ducked back into the cave and ran.

Clay saw the final turn in the trail that would give way to a view of the ranch. The trail widened and flattened out. Adam and Luther caught up to him and galloped with him, three abreast.

Luther said, "No shooting."

"We'd've heard gunshots all the way to Sawyer Canyon, Clay." Adam raced his roan, bent close to its neck until he was talking into its mane. "I haven't heard a one."

"I haven't heard Sophie calling for help again either." Clay couldn't decide if that was good or bad.

They kept pushing and just rounded the corner of the trail that put them within a long uphill mile of the ranch, when they heard a thundering *crash* in the hills behind the cabin.

"What's that?" Clay sat up straight on his Appaloosa, but he didn't slacken his pace.

Luther stared at the distant hills behind the ranch house even as they charged on. "It sounds like an avalanche."

"It's a booby trap being sprung." Adam laughed over the thunder of hooves. "It's something I taught Sophie to do years ago."

"She told me about those," Clay remembered.

Luther's voice echoed with satisfaction. "That means she's alive." Luther's furred hat blew off his head, revealing a shining bald scalp. Clay glanced quickly behind him and saw the hat spook the sheriff's horse, where Josiah rode just a few lengths back.

"And she's made it through the caves into the hills," Adam said with pride. "She's got room to move in the hills. My Sophie-girl is an almighty fine woodsman. She'll be okay."

"It's one woman and four little girls facing down a gang of desperate men." The wind whipped Clay's words away as he growled, "Forgive me if I keep on worrying."

Mandy noticed Laura's eyes flickering open seconds before the little girl sat up.

"Where Mama?" Laura rubbed her eyes and stretched her chubby little arms up to ruffle her blond curls.

"Great, now we have to chase after her b'sides catching all these low-down varmints." Sally scrambled on her hands and knees over to Laura.

Mandy put a blindfold on the other outlaw. This one had knocked himself senseless when he fell through the porch, but she didn't like to think of his beady eyes on her should he happen to wake up. "I declare, the work just never ends around a Texas ranch."

Laura whimpered a little, confused by the murky crawl space. Sally lifted her into her lap. "I'd better get her up the tunnel afore she gives us away."

At that moment they heard rumbling on the mountain. Mandy's

heart lifted and she looked over at Sally. The two girls beamed at each other in the murky cellar.

Mandy gave her chin a satisfied jerk. "It sounds like Ma and Beth are all right."

Sally patted Laura's back. "Maybe, when I take Laura to the tunnel, I'll meet 'em coming back down. It's got to be Beth's turn to baby-sit by now."

Mandy checked the outlaws for hidden weapons. "You know you're in charge of baby-sitting during attacks, Sally."

Sally turned to Laura. "Why don't you grow up so you can help us fight off bad guys?"

Laura quit whimpering and stuck her thumb in her mouth.

"She'll most likely get to do most of the work with the new one Ma's having," Mandy said brightly, "now that we're working as ranch hands for Pa."

"Yeah." Sally joggled a burp out of Laura and gave her a disgusted look. "But what are the chances of us getting attacked again? Texas is getting purely peaceable these last few years."

"As long as she's quiet, why don't you stay here with me?" Mandy asked. "It's a lot quicker getting the porches put back together with your help. And with you watching out the back while I watch out the front, no one can get past us."

"Sure." She glanced at her now-contented baby sister. "I think Laura's okay for now. I'll stay as long as I can."

Sally scooted over to the lookout spot. Laura kicked her feet, seemed to decide she had all the dirt off one thumb, and switched to the other. Then she sat on Sally's lap, staring curiously at the two men who were in the crawl space with them.

Sophie quickly examined the two men their avalanche had felled. "Neither of them is dead."

"Are you sure?" Her bloodthirsty daughter sounded disappointed.

"Beth, we don't want to kill anybody." Sophie plopped her hand on her hips and turned to her daughter. "The Bible says, 'Thou shal not kill.' "

Beth tightened the cords on the motionless man's arms then go busy on his legs. "Surely even the Ten Commandments have except ions, Ma."

Sophie thought about it, even though they really needed to ge moving before someone came to check out the noise. "That may be true but to be on the safe side, we'd best not be killing anybody if we car possibly avoid it."

"Fair enough." Beth straightened from her work and watched the trail for trouble.

Sophie winced as she bound a leg she was sorely afraid had beer broken by a falling tree trunk. "Let's get down to the ranch and see i there's any of this vermin to clear out around there."

"Should we go back by the cave and see how the girls are doing ir the cellar?" Beth asked.

"I think I see someone holed up in the barn." Sophie studied the yard below.

"The barn?" Beth perked right up. "We can do some real damage to someone in the barn."

"Beth," Sophie said sternly, "quit enjoying yourself."

"Yes, Ma." Beth forced her face into a frown.

They worked their way down the hillside, avoiding the trail and keeping cover around them at all times. Sophie stopped several times to inspect the land in all directions. She saw definite activity in the barn, but she couldn't figure out why anyone would be holed up in there. Did they think they were hiding?

"They're waiting to ambush anyone who rides into the yard," Beth said abruptly.

The minute she said it, Sophie saw a group of men round the far end of the trail. She recognized Clay riding in the lead of at least a dozen men. "By the way they're riding, I can tell they've figured out we're in danger."

Beth grabbed Sophie's arm. "He'll come charging in to save us and ride right into gunfire."

"Maybe those men expected him and that's the whole reason they're in there."

Elizabeth whispered, "I like havin' a pa, and he's been a right good 'un. I don't want to have to hunt up another."

"Then let's go try and keep this one alive." Careful to remain out of sight, Sophie led the way toward the barn.

"That sounded like an avalanche." Judd looked away from the window.

"Why would there be an avalanche?" Harley asked. "I don't like it."

Judd sneered. "I swear you're getting so's you worry just like a woman these days, Harley."

"Worrying has kept me alive this long," Harley said.

Judd ignored him.

Harley asked, "You're sure Eli got into the house?"

"I'm sure. I saw him run in." The truth was he'd been looking out the other side of the barn at the exact instant Eli had run into the house. His view of the front door had been blocked. But he'd seen Eli head for the house and now he was gone. There'd been no resistance. Where else could he be but inside? He didn't bother Harley with the pesky details.

"It don't set right, Judd, turning Eli loose on that woman and her children."

Judd looked at his partner with disgust. Harley was going soft on him. Harley had scouted the place for hours after they'd lured the posse then left 'em there guarding Sawyer Canyon like a pack of headless chickens. "McClellen's wife is uncommon beautiful, and she had four of the prettiest little girls to ever roam the hills of Texas."

"I don't like to think about Eli in there with those defenseless females."

Judd didn't like anyone questioning him, and Harley knew it. Judd glared at him, but Harley didn't look like he cared much what Judd thought.

Judd would have taken Harley on—he had it to do—but right now he was preoccupied with spying. "Sid's in there with him. That might keep Eli under control."

"You wanted Eli in there," Harley said with cool contempt. "You know how he treats a woman."

Judd took a second to check the two horses they'd brought into the barn with them. They were ready to ride when it was time to hit the trail. The mustang tried to bite Judd's hand, and Judd clubbed the horse hard on the head.

"Eli could have been the lookout," Harley added. "You're hoping he kills the McClellen woman so you won't have to."

"You're supposed to be keeping watch, Harley." Judd went back to his watch. He didn't look down the trail. Instead he scowled at Harley. "Don't think about what might be happening in there. Have you seen any of our men on the bluff?"

"No, but I wouldn't expect to. Do you think all the McClellen hands are dead?" Harley asked. "How much poison did you put in their coffee?"

"I put enough in to bring down a herd of buffalo. They're dead."

"You gave 'em a lot, but did they drink it?" Harley worked the action on his rifle.

"We saw the two in the bunkhouse laid out flat," Judd growled.

"They looked dead to me, too. Now we've sunk to poison. I'm a gunslinger, Judd, and proud of it. My fights used to be fair ones—they were against horse thieves. Then, at least, they were against men. We were ruthless, but we had a code. We had some honor, Judd. But where is the honor in poison? Where is the honor in turning a coyote like Eli loose on a defenseless woman and children?"

Judd looked at Harley. He didn't like the cold scorn he saw in Harley's eyes. They'd been together a long time, and what Harley said was true. They'd been hard, brutal men. Judd reveled in that. But they'd been strong. They'd taken what they wanted face-to-face, with the power of their fists and guns. It had all gone wrong along the way. And now they'd sunk to this. They were sneaks, killing women and children and poisoning honest men. Judd refused to think about it.

"As far as that avalanche goes," Harley said, "I'm not a man who believes in coincidence."

Harley quit talking. The time for talking was past. He'd never killed a woman before. He'd never even stood by while someone else did. More than that, he'd never so much as raised his hand to a child. In fact, the few times in his life he'd even seen children, he'd been fascinated by them and found pure pleasure in watching the little tikes.

He wasn't a back-shooter either. That one day, when Judd had sprung it on him that he wanted Harley to dry-gulch McClellen, he'd done it—taken his shot. But he'd had a chance to think it over since then.

Harley crouched here in this barn and knew shame.

He watched the house and thought of those little girls and the vengeful man behind him and he wanted out. He wanted out of this mess and out of this life. But how did a man turn his footsteps back from a path he'd been treading so long?

That's when Harley heard a voice. A voice he hadn't heard for years. A voice that whispered to him things his long-dead mama had told him about while she held him in her lap. About Jesus. About love. About God having a plan for his life.

Harley eased himself away from the door and forgot about keeping watch. He let all his life spin through his mind. All the little steps that, one by one, had led him to this place and this act of pure, unforgivable evil.

And that's when he remembered something else his mama had said. Forgiveness. A man was bound to do wrong because that's just the way humans were. But there was forgiveness for those who trusted in Jesus Christ. Harley reached out for it and felt years of death and hatred melt away from his heart.

Then he saw Mason tense. "Posse coming up the road," Judd called out to the man who had just changed sides. "McClellen's in the lead. He's still a ways off."

Judd lifted his gun to aim at the lead rider. Harley lifted his gun and aimed it at Judd and hesitated, torn now between his desire to save all these innocent people and his own complete unwillingness to take another human life—even a life so despicable as Judd Mason's.

A soft rustling of cloth caught his attention by a little door near a corner of the barn. Harley didn't turn to look. He knew that sound. It was soft material and lots of it. A woman.

Mason turned to the sound and with a sudden roar of rage he leapt to his feet and yelled, "I'll get that meddlesome woman myself!"

Harley turned to see her dart back outside.

Judd ran for the back door then suddenly he veered away from it. "She's not getting away from me!" Mason shouted. "You and the men in the house will have to hold off the posse!"

Mason didn't notice Harley's gun. He whirled and jumped on the back of the fiery little mustang. The horse reared and fought. Mason kicked it viciously. He didn't go toward the back door. He headed for the wider door next to it. Harley heard a soft noise that sounded fearful, and he looked straight up over the smaller door. There was a little girl. Harley was so amazed it took him a second to realize the child was holding a rope. Harley's eyes followed the rope and saw it was fastened to a basket of rocks.

If Judd went out that rear door after Sophie, he was going to get peppered with rocks. The little girl looked down from where she was perched above him, like a hovering angel. He saw the terror cross her face when she realized she'd been seen. Harley shook his head and pointed his gun at Judd, still fighting the horse.

The little girl stared at him with unconcealed relief, then—she smiled at him. Harley was in awe. The heartfelt smile of a brave little girl fighting for the people she loved was a gift as sweet as the loving words of his mother.

God rested His hand on Harley's shoulder as surely as if He stood beside him in that barn. It was the finest moment of Harley Shafter's life.

Mason spurred his horse and suddenly the feisty, little mustang went wild. After months of abuse, or maybe inspired by its Creator, it reared until it looked to be going over backward. Then, with a squeal of rage, the horse twisted its body and landed stiff-legged on the floor. It arched its back and, with an impossible gyration, hurled Judd to the ground. He landed, almost as if the horse had aimed, right underneath the little girl and her basket.

The ground caved in under Judd. Harley heard Mason scream in pain. A basket of rocks rained down on Mason's head, and Mason was still.

Mrs. McClellen poked her head in the door and glanced up into the rafters. Harley looked up and saw the little girl grinning at her mama. Harley stood slowly and drew both women's attention. Mrs. McClellen looked at him fearfully, and he quickly tossed his gun aside. "Don't shoot, ma'am," he said to the unarmed woman. "I give up."

Clay and the posse came charging into the yard just as Harley marched out of the barn with his hands in the air.

Twenty-Three

"He just surrendered?" Clay asked in disbelief for the tenth time.

"He had a gun," Sophie repeated. "He didn't so much as threaten us."

"Just tossed his gun away and raised his arms? Harley Shafter?" Clay shook his head.

"If that's his name, Clay. I don't know the man!"

"Just like that? Did he think you or Beth were armed?" Clay shuddered when he thought about his little girl perched in those rafters under the rifle of a man as dangerous as Shafter. He was a known gunman and as tough as a hobnail boot.

Sophie set a cup of coffee in front of Clay, then got more cups out for the other men who had crowded into her kitchen. They were leaning against walls and sitting on the floor. All four girls had gone into one bedroom, just to make space in the cabin for everyone.

A very embarrassed Rio was leaning in the open doorway. Buff and Whitey had been knocked cold in the bunkhouse by whatever had been added to their coffee. Only the fact that they had eaten with Sophie and mostly drank the coffee she made had saved their lives. They were still too ashamed of themselves to talk. Of course, when had either one of them ever talked anyway?

Andy had the same rough bandage on his head Sophie had put on in the cave. He wouldn't let Sophie doctor him. He seemed to think he deserved to get an infection and die for letting himself be drugged and then knocked senseless.

The wounded outlaws had been hauled away. It had been a real chore to get the two out of the trees. Sophie had answered the ranger's questions with all the men listening. Now, except for the questions Clay couldn't seem to quit asking, none of them had much to say to her at all.

In other words, everything was back to normal.

Sophie had run out of coffee cups, and Eustace had fetched all there were in the bunkhouse. And except for the silence and general air of humiliation amongst the men, it had become a party.

"What do you men want for supper?" Sophie asked into the silence.

"I can't believe you put spikes in the bottom of that pit." Clay nursed his coffee and shook his head. "That was a plumb mean thing to do."

"Sorry." Sophie served the third pot of coffee she'd made in the last hour.

"No, you're not. You're just trying to buck me up."

"I taught her about those traps, mostly," Adam put in. "But she came up with a few tricks of her own."

"Living in a thicket gives a woman time to use her imagination."

Adam nodded.

"And how many more of these traps are there?" Clay crossed his arms and scowled. "Mightn't they be dangerous?"

Sophie noticed Clay conveniently forgot that she had tried to show him the traps on a couple of occasions. He'd smiled at her "little surprises" and put her off.

"I made them so you had to trip them. No one can stumble into one. Why, you and the men have been walking over the pit under the side door of the barn all week."

Clay sat up straight and glared at her.

Sophie patted Clay on the chest as she passed him with the coffeepot. "I'm sorry."

She wasn't, but she hoped Clay appreciated that she tried to sound sincere.

The rangers came riding into the yard. They and the deputies had taken all eight of Mason's men into town. Sheriff Everett's jailhouse was fairly bulging at the seams. Most of the men were wanted for holdups and murders all across the West. There would be enough reward money to add another valley to the ranch if they had a mind to.

Ranger Jackson strode into the house. "I want you to tell me again just what Harley Shafter did when you went into the barn."

Sophie crossed her arms and glared at him. "I've told you ten times already!"

Jackson said, "No, you've told me twice."

"You've told *me* ten times," Clay said. "But the ranger's been gone for eight of them."

Sophie sighed and repeated her story. Jackson listened, absorbing every word of it. Finally he said, "Shafter has been talking. He's confessed to everything and spared himself none of the guilt. Every member of that gang will be found guilty because of what he's said. And we found a lot of money on Mason. We'll be able to return money to the heirs of most of the men who have been killed."

"Why's he telling everything?" Clay asked. "Usually a gunman like that is mighty closed-mouthed."

"He said he heard God talking to him in that barn. He said he was ready to turn on Mason and protect the posse when it came into the yard."

"It don't sound to me like he's taking responsibility for much if he's trying to say he was on our side," Eustace said with contempt.

"No, it's not like that. He's not trying to get out of any charges. In fact, he's saying he deserves a noose, and he'll take it. He just smiles when we try and break his story. Says he knows he deserves God's wrath, but he's made his peace and he's ready."

"Leave room for God's wrath." Adam looked across the room at Luther. "Just like you said."

Luther nodded.

"I believe him." Sophie, done with her inquisition for now, began slicing up a hunk of venison she'd put on the baking rack. "The look on his face when he surrendered was almost. . ." Sophie shrugged. "I know it sounds strange, but it was the impression I got at the time. It was almost. . .holy."

Sophie filled her fourth pot of water to make more coffee. Suddenly her knees wobbled a little, and she had to grab for the edge of the water barrel to steady herself.

Clay was beside her in a split second, lifting her off her feet. "No more questions. Sophie needs to rest."

Adam chuckled. "She's as sturdy as a Texas cottonwood, Clay, but if you want to try and slow her down, I wish you luck."

One by one the men left the cabin. Luther said as he went out, "Reckon me and Buff'll hang around Texas for a spell. It's too far to ride iffen she calls me again."

Buff grunted. As he shuffled out of the room, he said, "Sorry I failed ya, Miz McClellen."

"That's okay." Sophie blushed so prettily, Clay couldn't believe she was the same little wildcat who'd captured a gang of cutthroats.

Buff shook his head.

"Me, too, ma'am." Whitey stared at the floor as if afraid it might disappear under his feet. Andy and Rio apologized, too, on their way out. They'd each done it a dozen times apiece already.

Clay smiled as he watched the dejected group go. They were Texans. They'd bounce back.

The last one to leave was Adam. He came up to Sophie, undeterred by the stern look of *get out* on Clay's face. "Mason kept saying, when they were yanking that wooden stake out of his leg, that he'd get even with you, Sophie, if it took him the rest of his life."

"His life may not be that long." Clay tightened his grip on his wife.

"It sounded like he wanted revenge for something. But I never did anything to him." Sophie's brow wrinkled in confusion.

"It got me to thinking about the revenge I've been hungerin' for ever since my partners died. In the end, I stood by and let the law take its own course."

Clay snorted. "You went charging into Sawyer Canyon alone. I don't call that letting the law take its course."

"I know," Adam said with a sheepish shrug. "I had a real bad moment there when lettin' Mason hide out from us was more than I could bear. I admit that."

With the men gone except for Adam, the girls came out of the bedroom and sat at the table. Clay watched his family, all pretty and sweet smelling. They were soft as baby calves and tough as full-grown longhorns. He loved them.

"It's a good thing you did," Sophie said. "It brought you back to the ranch."

"Yeah, none of these outlaws would have gotten out of here alive if we'd left them to my girls for much longer," Clay said dryly.

Sophie and the girls grinned. Clay hugged his armful of a wife then set her on a chair at the table.

"Anyway, I realized that the difference between my need for revenge and Mason's is the difference between God and Satan. It's as simple as that. Mason insisted on delivering his wrath on those he was angry with, and in the end he was just a pure tool of the devil. No matter how angry I got, I could never have crossed that line and committed cold-blooded murder in an act of revenge. God has made me strong enough not to do that."

"He's made us all strong enough, Adam." Sophie reached her hand across the table to pat Adam's rugged hand. "In the end we all did the right thing."

Beth crossed her arms and tapped her toe rapidly on the wooden floor. "I think Sally and Mandy enjoyed taking those men prisoner a little too much."

"I did not! I purely hated having to catch those bad men." Sally grabbed Beth's long braid and gave it a hefty yank.

Beth screamed and backed up, pulling her hair all the more. She slammed into Mandy.

Mandy pushed her hard. "Be careful! And we did not enjoy ourselves! Not hardly none at all!"

Sally gave Beth's hair another tug, and Beth started screaming at the top of her lungs. Laura began crying in the midst of the chaos.

Sally shrieked. "And the next time we're attacked, you have to babysit. It's your turn."

"We don't take turn on attacks. Ma says—" Beth jerked her hair free, fell backward, and staggered into Clay, who threw his arms wide to keep from falling over and smacked Adam across the face.

Adam ran.

Sally and Mandy attacked Beth as a team.

Clay roared, "You girls settle down!"

The girls completely ignored his yelling, so he yelled louder. Sophie went to his side. "Aren't you pleased?"

Clay decided his wife had lost her mind.

"Can't you see the girls have decided you won't quit loving them just because you're mad?"

Clay hollered over the tumult, "And that's a good thing?"

"Sure it is." Sophie scooped Laura up as she toddled past, shrieking. "Now, if you'll excuse me." She thrust Laura into his arms. "I'm going to lie down and rest."

Clay didn't know whether to laugh or cry. She retreated to her bedroom and closed the door as calmly as if the screaming and yelling were a lullaby to her.

Clay faced his raging daughters and had a bright idea. He charged.

The screams turned to giggles as he was buried under petticoats, while his pretty wife obeyed him in the next room. Life didn't get any better.

Epilogue

Clifton Lazarus McClellen was born early on a bitter winter morning. All the girls slept through it, and Clay probably would have, too. Sophie was determined not to make the doctor ride clear and away out to the ranch in the cold for such a simple thing as bringing a baby.

Except there came a time during her laboring that Sophie quit trying to be brave and quiet and decided all men should die. And since Clay was handy, she might as well start with him. She was too busy to actually do him any damage before he could get out of her reach, though.

Clay panicked as she knew he would, what with him being a man and all. He started to get dressed to go for the doctor. Sophie was in the midst of a tearful appeal to not kill himself going out in the dangerous weather—ironic when a moment ago she'd really wanted him dead—when Cliff made his appearance.

His twin brother, Clayton Jarrod, was born five minutes later, while Clay was trying to wrap Clifton in a blanket Sophie had ready and, at the same time, frantically ordering Sophie to stop being in pain now, since the baby was already here.

When the whirlwind had passed and another blanket had been found, Clay finally calmed down enough to say with immense satisfaction, "We really narrowed the gap between girls and boys in this family."

"I thought you said you wanted another girl," Sophie challenged him, still not very happy with the man who had caused her a very uncomfortable night.

"I lied," Clay announced with an unrepentant smile. "I wanted a son like the very dickens. I didn't know how much until this very second."

Sophie looked at the arms full of babies Clay held and smiled. "I didn't know how much I wanted a boy either."

"If you keep having them at this rate, we'll be tied by next Christmas."

Back to wanting to kill him, Sophie said, "Just for that, you're getting up in the night to change their diapers."

"What's a diaper?"

Sophie slumped back on the bed and started to cry. Clay sat down beside her. "Sophie, what about rule number one?"

Both boys chose that moment to start howling their heads off.

They wriggled and cried, and Sophie couldn't take her eyes off of them—until she noticed that Clay's expression had turned from insufferable pride to pure unadulterated horror.

"I didn't think boys would cry!"

Sophie forgot all about breaking rule number one because she wanted to laugh. "I'm going to enjoy watching you learn to be a pa to infants."

Clay looked up from the babies and leaned over to kiss her soundly on the lips. "I'll be great at it, just like I've learned to be a great pa to the girls."

Sophie laid her hand on Clay's cheek. "We've been through so much together this last year, Clay. I've learned as much as you have."

Clay nodded and looked back at his sons. "We're going to teach the boys to be good men. To work hard. To respect a woman's strength."

Sophie turned the edge of the blanket back on the baby closest to her. "You've never gotten over me protecting the ranch all by myself."

"Why should I get over it? I learned what a special woman I married. And I learned to trust God in everything."

"Except birthing these babies," Sophie teased him. "You wanted the doctor for them."

Clay ran his rough finger over one tiny fist, looking first from one son then to the other.

Sophie wanted to start crying again from the sweetness of it. She couldn't hold back what was in her heart. "I love you, Clay." She knew she shouldn't say it. Clay wasn't a man who wanted to talk about such nonsense.

He said very calmly, "I love you, too, Sophie."

Sophie straightened away from him. "Since when?"

Clay looked away from the babies. "Well, since always, I reckon."

"But you've never said such a thing. Why didn't you tell me?" Sophie took one of the babies from him to punish him for being such an insensitive clout.

Clay stroked the soft cheek of the baby he had left, not appearing punished at all. She nudged him sharply with her elbow. "Well?"

His eyes never moved. "Well, what?"

"Why haven't you ever told me you love me?"

"Of course I love you." Clay shook his head, still staring. "How could I not love someone as sweet and pretty as you? It'd only be news if I didn't love you, I'd think."

Sophie tried to remind herself of the lessons they'd learned about revenge, and the wildly fluctuating moods she was prone to after a baby was born. And she still almost throttled him. He was saved by the babies between them.

Sophie remembered how much he'd learned to talk in the last year and how completely he'd been surrounded by men all his life, and she decided to let him live. "It gives me a nice feeling inside to hear it said now and again."

As if he didn't know the danger he'd been in, Clay said, "Okay. How often?"

Sophie sighed deeply then decided this might be her only chance. "At least once a day is nice—at bedtime. And then throw it in out of the blue once in a while besides."

Clay nodded, rocking the baby in his arms to quiet it. Sophie thought he was getting very good at being a pa already.

He said, "Once a day and then some. That'll be fine."

Sophie shook her head. "You're hopeless."

He didn't appear to hear what she said. He was lucky she was a Christian woman—a Christian woman with her hands full. They sat together and watched their babies until the sun came up.

Then the girls came in and broke rule number one all over again.

About the Author

Mary Connealy is an author, journalist, and teacher. She is a graduate of Wayne State College with a degree in Mass Communication. She finds great joy in writing. Her hope is that her work is worthy of that God-given gift of joy.

She lives on a Nebraska farm with her husband, Ivan and has four mostly grown daughters, Joslyn, Wendy, Shelly (and her husband Aaron), and Katy.

If you hunt hard enough, you can find Mary on the Internet like a middle-aged, female "Where's Waldo" at www.myspace.com/petticoatranch or www.maryconnealy.com. Mary is a GED Instructor by day and an author by night. And to keep it straight in her head whether she's teaching or writing, she likes to wear a little crown and a Wonder Woman cape while she types.